A PLUME BOOK

THE BURN PALACE

STEPHEN DOBYNS is the author of more than thirty novels and poetry collections. He teaches writing at Warren Wilson College and lives in New England.

Praise for *The Burn Palace*

"I've read some very good novels this year, but this one is the best of the best. In a real sense, I didn't read it at all, after the first five pages; I entered the small-town world Stephen Dobyns creates with such affection, horror, and fidelity. I can imagine Nathaniel Hawthorne, Sherwood Anderson, and—yes—Grace Metalious rising to their feet in that special Writing Room of the Dead and giving Dobyns a standing ovation. Dobyns has always been good, but this book is authentically great. . . . This one is the full meal, by turns terrifying, sweet, and crazily funny. . . . It is, simply put, the embodiment of why we read stories, and why the novel will always be a better bang for the entertainment buck than movies or TV. Great story, great prose. Musical prose. You can't ask for more than this book gives. I loved it." —Stephen King

"With nods to Nathaniel Hawthorne and Stephen King, two other writers who know something about terrorizing small New England towns, Dobyns has created a riveting work of the imagination."

—*San Antonio Express-News*

"A terrifying supernatural thriller, and a sly horror comedy . . . A tour de force genre buster." —*Publishers Weekly* (starred review)

"A hard-hitting literary mystery-thriller . . . An engrossing story with a satisfying spine-chilling mystery." —*Winnipeg Free Press*

"Dobyns isn't above scaring the reader silly with surprise twists and turns. . . . Nicely done—and you may never look at doctors the same way again." —*Kirkus Reviews*

"[*The Burn Palace*] punches and thrusts and bangs its shoulders hard against the confines of the genre in ways as entertaining as any new work of fiction you'll read this winter. However, the best part of the book isn't the range of characters or the style . . . it's the unfolding of a complex plot that moves all of the characters about in such fashion as to produce that frisson of American despair and horror."

—*The Boston Globe*

"An unsettling mix of sharply observed small-town New England life and a supernatural abduction-and-murder spree . . . An interplay of black-comedy touches, nuanced small-town portraits, and stomach-churning violence." —*The Philadelphia Inquirer*

"In the space of a few days, a newborn disappears from the local hospital, and a corn snake is left in its place; a stranger arrives in town and is gruesomely murdered; and marauding packs of coyotes start attacking civilians. . . . [*The Burn Palace*] is an exquisitely unexpected, delightfully believable exploration of what normal looks like when it goes through the (evil) looking glass." —Oprah.com

"A huge, seamless tapestry of narrative . . . You can't wait to turn the page to see what happens next, to what might be hiding right around the next corner, or living quietly in that sleepy house next door to yours."

—*Shelf Awareness*

"Dobyns peoples this literary chiller with a fully rounded cast of memorable characters. . . . Expertly paced and smoothly written, this should appeal to both thriller and horror fans." —*Booklist*

"Mysterious and engaging." —*New York Journal of Books*

"An intricate who-done-it with richly drawn characters, a superb sense of place, and just enough otherworldly action to tantalize."

—*Library Journal*

"A story that rocks along without a word wasted . . . Dobyns writes a straight thriller, but his mastery of language puts the reader into empty streets swirling with bits of paper and dead leaves, makes us feel at one moment hurried along and at the next expansive and thoughtful. . . . Read slowly (if you can!) to enjoy his craftsmanship."

—*The Charlotte Observer*

"What starts off as a paranormal thriller turns into a dissection of small-town life when violence rears its head. . . . *The Burn Palace* starts out like a run-of-the-mill Halloween-season slasher script, but then morphs into a police procedural. That in turn is a device for Dobyns to conduct a semi-comedic dissection of small-town life and how unexpected violence both challenges and infatuates." —*Los Angeles Times*

"[*The Burn Palace*] is Stephen King–ish in the way it mixes Sherwood Anderson–type description with thriller plotlines. In other words, the virtue of *The Burn Palace* is that it is a good thriller."

—*The Asheville Citizen-Times*

"*The Burn Palace* is a blast . . . one of those great, big, old-fashioned doorstoppers. . . . It is highly recommended." —*Bookgasm*

"All of the characters are so well drawn that they seem like familiar people from your own hometown." —*Read Me Deadly*

ALSO BY STEPHEN DOBYNS

POETRY

Winter's Journey

Mystery, So Long

The Porcupine's Kisses

Pallbearers Envying the One Who Rides

Common Carnage

Velocities: New and Selected Poems, 1966–1992

Body Traffic

Cemetery Nights

Black Dog, Red Dog

The Balthus Poems

Heat Death

Griffon

Concurring Beasts

NONFICTION

Next Word, Better Word: The Craft of Writing Poetry

Best Words, Best Order

STORIES

Eating Naked

NOVELS

Boy in the Water

Saratoga Strongbox

The Church of Dead Girls

Saratoga Fleshpot

Saratoga Trifecta

Saratoga Backtalk

The Wrestler's Cruel Study

Saratoga Haunting

After Shocks/Near Escapes

Saratoga Hexameter

The House on Alexandrine

Saratoga Bestiary

The Two Deaths of Senora Puccini

A Boat off the Coast

Saratoga Snapper

Cold Dog Soup

Saratoga Headhunter

Dancer with One Leg

Saratoga Swimmer

Saratoga Longshot

A Man of Little Evils

THE BURN PALACE

STEPHEN DOBYNS

A PLUME BOOK

PLUME
Published by the Penguin Group
Penguin Group (USA) LLC
375 Hudson Street
New York, New York 10014

USA | Canada | UK | Ireland | Australia | New Zealand | India | South Africa | China
penguin.com
A Penguin Random House Company

First published in the United States of America by Blue Rider Press, a member of Penguin Group (USA) Inc., 2013
First Plume Printing 2014

THE LIBRARY OF CONGRESS HAS CATALOGED THE BLUE RIDER PRESS EDITION AS FOLLOWS:
Dobyns, Stephen, date.
The burn palace / Stephen Dobyns.
p. cm.
Includes index.
ISBN 978-0-399-16087-5 (hc.)
ISBN 978-0-14-218044-0 (pbk.)
I. Title.
PS3554.O2B87 2013 2012028038
813'.54—dc23

Printed in the United States of America
10 9 8 7 6 5 4 3 2 1

Original hardcover design by Michelle McMillian

For Phyllis Westberg
with love and
gratitude

THE BURN PALACE

ONE

NURSE SPANDEX WAS LATE, and as she broke into a run her rubber-soled clogs went *squeak-squeak* on the floor of the hallway leading to labor and delivery. It was two-thirty on a Thursday morning, and if Tabby Roberts—Tabitha, she called her to her face, because she'd never liked the head nurse—ever learned she had left those two babies alone, she'd be royally screwed, which made her laugh because that was why she was late, she had been getting royally screwed back in 217, where that poor colored woman had died in the afternoon. That's where Dr. Balfour had pushed her, and that's where she'd gone—to a bed stripped of sheets and pads—because she'd worked hard to get Dr. Balfour motivated and once she got him unzipping his fly, she wasn't going to complain where he took her; she'd let him screw her in the toilet if that's what he wanted, like Dr. Stone last March, but then Dr. Stone took a job at Providence Hospital and so nothing had come of it except a few teary phone calls with her doing the crying, but it didn't do any good because Dr. Stone had stayed where he was.

Nurse Spandex was a full-bodied woman in her mid-thirties, but don't call her fat, "full-bodied" was how she described herself, big-boned, and her scrubs had spandex at the waist and a spandex-and-polyester V-necked top with a pattern of pink and purple flowers. They weren't loose like most girls' scrubs, because she'd had her mother fix them a little on the new Singer she had bought her online for Christmas two years ago, so her scrubs went further in showing off her figure, which was why some girls called her Nurse Spandex, which Alice Alessio (her real name) didn't like.

The rooms in maternity she hurried past were mostly empty. Only two were occupied with mothers, because October was a slow period and it was still a week till the full moon, which always motivated things and created a fuss. Tonight only two tater-tots were in the nursery, so she didn't see why Dr. Balfour couldn't have used one of these rooms instead of one in cardiology. But he had said cardiology was where he had to be, because he was the chief resident and didn't want to get in hot water, which he should have thought about earlier. Anyway, she was the one who'd get in trouble if Tabby Roberts, the bitch, ever heard she'd been getting laid in cardiology. She'd lose her job.

The ceiling lights hummed and an elevator dinged; there were distant bubbling noises and buzzing noises, a few moans, a few night mumbles, and an announcement for Dr. Schmitt to come to the ER—linking them all together was the *squeak-squeak* of Nurse Spandex's white clogs as she ran toward the nursery. One of the lights had gone out, so she'd have to call maintenance, which always meant calling half a dozen times before they'd do anything, down there smoking weed and listening to rap music, most likely. So the nursery was dim, as if the two babies needed the quiet darkness, which they didn't, because sleeping was what babies did second best, right after slurping at their mommies' boobs.

There were eight cribs, bassinets with Plexiglas sides and stainless-steel cabinets beneath, and in Nurse Spandex's four years in labor and delivery they had been full to capacity only once and that'd been during tourist season, with out-of-towners dropping their tater-tots far from home instead of in Hartford or Springfield. During the year five babies was the most they had had together, because this was a small fifty-bed hospital in a small town and most girls were on the pill, the sluts, and Nurse Spandex—who went to Mass every Sunday, or pretty near—thought if she'd really got knocked up in cardiology, then Dr. Balfour was in for a surprise. He'd be putty in her hands, is what she told herself; but then she saw something was wrong, and she stopped as if she'd hit a wall. It wasn't the Petrocelli kid, he was fine, all wrapped up like an Indian papoose. It was the other baby, the Summers baby, he'd gotten unwrapped somehow, and his little yellow blanket with the ducks and chickens and rabbits had gotten on top of him and he was kicking and squirming, because he must be smothering, maybe even dying, and he was kicking to get free.

Nurse Spandex didn't have the chance to tell herself she'd never seen anything so strange before, because now she reached the side of the crib and snatched away the blanket, but it wasn't the Summers baby at all, it wasn't even a baby. It was a snake, a huge snake with red and yellow stripes, but she hardly saw its colors as it rose up toward her, seemed to want to grab her and squeeze her and have its way with her, which made her fall back, knock aside an empty crib, and then another as she screamed a high, awful noise she'd never made before, like it was somebody else's scream, somebody else's mouth, but she kept screaming as the snake twisted and writhed; kept screaming like she meant to shatter glass, as thudding, squeaking footsteps came running down the hall; kept screaming as other nurses and orderlies and doctors and even patients came rushing into the nursery; kept screaming until someone grabbed her arm and slapped her good.

• • •

Now, like an airborne camera, we move back from the hospital, which is called Morgan Memorial here in the town of Brewster, Rhode Island. The sky is mostly clear, and the three-quarter moon lets us see the town under a milky light. A stiff wind out of the northwest energizes the few clouds, tugs the fall leaves and sends them swirling. Windows rattle, and bits of paper and dead leaves swirl down the streets. Already the temperature has dropped to freezing, and those folks who haven't covered their tomatoes are going to lose them. But isn't that often a relief? With the garden gone, except for the Swiss chard and winter squash, it's just one less thing to take care of.

Rising above the hospital's lumpy roof with its compressors, heating and cooling units, its elevator, we see the hospital's two wings and outbuildings and parking lots, its two-story office building with labs and doctors' offices. An ambulance sits idling near the emergency entrance, its heater turned up and two men snoozing in the front seats. The driver, Seymour Hodges, turns restlessly. Soon he'll call out, shouted warnings to ephemera, at which point his tech, Jimmy Mooney, who has heard all this before and hasn't an ounce of patience left, will strike him sharply across the chest and shout: "Cut the shit, Seymour!" Then, with grunts and protests, Seymour Hodges will settle back into silence.

In the moonlight, the shadows of the maples planted along the driveway to replace the dying elms swing back and forth across the body of the ambulance like predatory cobwebs, while the blowing leaves are like fluttering bats, and dark forms skitter past like goblins, or this is how it seems to Jimmy Mooney, for whom Halloween remains a significant holiday. These ghostly maples line Cottage Street, on which the hospital is situated, not quite at the edge of town, but what was the edge of town seventy years ago.

Rising higher, we see the town spread out along Water Street—technically, Route 1A—forming a bulge on the five miles of road between Route 1 and Hannaquit at the beach, like an anaconda with a pig in its belly. Even higher we see the shadow of Block Island five miles offshore, while to the south there's the tip of Montauk on Long Island. To the north shine the lights of Providence, but to the northwest toward West Kingston and Hope Valley are great blocks of darkness—Burlingame State Park, Great Swamp, Trustom Pond National Wildlife Refuge, the Narragansett Indian reservation, Watchaug Pond, and others. You could walk through Burlingame or Great Swamp for miles and never see a soul—that is, if you didn't sink into the muck, until nothing was left but one hand waving good-bye.

On the north side of the swamp, past the railroad tracks, an obelisk commemorates the Great Swamp Fight of December 19, 1675, at the start of King Philip's War. More than one thousand Narragansetts were killed, mostly women, children, and old people, burned to death in their wigwams—two hundred Colonial troops were also killed—but this finished off the Indians as a power in New England. Most of those captured were sent to Jamaica as slaves, to cut sugarcane.

A few summer camps are scattered around Worden Pond, and for decades counselors have terrified the kids with late-night tales of how the screams of the Indians can still be heard deep in the woods, how boys are lured into the swamp by flickering lights, and how three Boy Scouts wandered off and were never seen again. And sometimes the tales mention a wolf darting among the trees with a severed hand in its mouth, a boy's hand. Pure silliness, of course.

A bunch of small roads wind back and forth around the edges of Great Swamp, with half coming to a dead end at the railway tracks and then resuming on the other side. At two-thirty in the morning, the houses scattered along those roads are dark, though most have outside lights to scare away predators, both the two-footed and four-footed variety. But just because the house lights are out doesn't mean everybody's asleep. Take that farm backed up against the western side of the swamp. Barton Wilcox and his wife, Bernice—everyone calls her Bernie—have thirty merino sheep, as well as a bunch of other animals—geese, chickens, cats, and a couple of Bouviers. In the sixties, Bernie and Barton lived on a commune in Big Sur, but after five years they moved back to Rhode Island, where they were from. Bernie went into nursing, while Barton went to graduate school in English. Then twenty years ago Barton's parents died in a car accident, and he inherited enough money to quit his teaching job and buy the farm. Bernie now works part-time at Morgan Memorial. Otherwise, they're weavers, using the wool from their own sheep, and organic farmers. Barton is sixty-four, but he still has a ponytail, gray now and bald on top, while Bernie favors the colorful peasant skirts she makes herself. Bernie's a few years younger than her husband, tall and heavyset, more muscular than fat. She and Barton sell eggs and produce, while in spring they sell Easter lambs to the Greeks.

With them lives their granddaughter Antigone, who's ten. No telling where her mother is—maybe Big Sur, maybe Berkeley or Boulder, Madison or Ann Arbor. She calls herself a free spirit; her parents call her irresponsible. Sometimes Bernie thinks if they had named her Joan, instead of Blossom, she might be more levelheaded, capable of being a parent, not just a mother. During the summer months, Blossom sells T-shirts, candles, incense, counterculture buttons, hash pipes, rolling papers, bongs, and such stuff at outdoor rock concerts—still a groupie at thirty-three, calling herself a new-age traveler. So Barton and Bernie have had Antigone in their charge almost since she was born, which they find a delight and a blessing, so it's hard to be critical about the details of her birth. No telling who the father was. Blossom claims not to know, and maybe that's the truth, but the girl's high cheekbones and black hair suggest some Hispanic or Native American blood. She's tall for her age and as thin as a tenpenny nail. She also has long, thin fingers and can work the loom almost as well as her grandparents. In her fifth-grade class, in Brewster, she's called Tig, which is all right, and several boys call her the Tigster, which is not all right, but she doesn't get angry or call them names; she just doesn't look at them or talk to them, ever, so it's as if they don't exist.

It's Antigone who's awake at this hour, and she's listening to the yapping of the coyotes on the far side of the stone wall circling the five-acre pasture. Occasionally the yapping is punctuated by the single bark of one of the hundred-pound Bouviers, either Gray or Rags, dogs she's known, it seems, for her entire life and that used to pull her on her wagon around the farm when she was smaller. As long as the dogs patrol the walls, no coyote will cross over. Just how many coyotes are out there is what Tig is wondering. Barton has said he recently saw a pack of about ten out on the road at daybreak, and she thinks that's about how many she hears right now, yapping as if they're discussing the sheep, how good they taste and what to do about it. Such thoughts normally wouldn't keep her from sleep, but now Barton's laid up after knee replacement surgery and she's sure the coyotes know this, because just this evening she saw two of them streaking across the pasture with Gray in pursuit. The coyotes know Barton is laid up, they know the dogs are getting old, and as Tig listens to the yapping beyond the stone wall she thinks that's what has the coyotes so excited. Yapping like that, it's like plans being made.

Actually, the town of Brewster began as Brewster Corners, a post house on the Boston Post Road between Stonington and Providence, built in the 1730s by Wrestling Brewster, great-grandson of Elder William

Brewster, the preacher who came over on the *Mayflower.* Wrestling Brewster was descended from Elder Brewster's son of the same name, who'd been kicked out of the Massachusetts Bay Colony in 1640 for criticizing the clergy. Pugnacity, perhaps, was an inevitable part of his nature. When Wrestling Brewster opened the post house, Hannaquit was a tiny fishing village seized from the Narragansetts during King Philip's War. Soon a few houses were built near the post house and blacksmith shop, and then a dry-goods purveyor and church.

At the beginning of the nineteenth century there began a drift toward the sea. More houses were built, and Brewster Corners became simply Brewster, where it stayed, overshadowed by Wakefield to the north and Westerly to the south. Then, in 1907, in a burst of ambition, Brewster absorbed the beach town of Hannaquit, while keeping a toehold on the Post Road, now Route 1. From then until 1950, Brewster grew by fits and starts, what with the fishing and farming—mostly potato fields—as well as the quarry, a knitting mill, and a small cannery on the river. By mid-century it had a more or less permanent population of seven thousand, a number that doubles after Memorial Day with the summer people. As the town enters the twenty-first century, only one scallop boat remains to compete with the small fleet from Stonington; the potato farms have become turf farms; the quarry that supplied the granite blocks from which the downtown was built produces only crushed stone; the knitting mill—vacant for fifty years—is at the edge of collapse; and the cannery has been ripped down, forgotten by almost everyone except old Mrs. Loy at Ocean Breezes, a home for the elderly on Oak Street, because she lost two fingers at the cannery more than eighty years ago and she'll wave her mutilated hand at the aides and squawk, "See this hand? The fish bit back," till everyone is sick to death of her.

We can see Ocean Breezes four blocks east of the hospital as we rise above the town: a nineteenth-century inn and boardinghouse that was tucked, stretched, expanded, and renovated into a residence for seniors, as it's called today. Most of the lights are out, though twenty elderly insomniacs stare up at their ceilings in wonder or dismay at where they find themselves. That happens when their numbers lessen. Eighty-year-old Florence Pritchard passed on early in the evening, and it made the others morbidly alert, or at least those for whom alertness remains an option.

Margaret Hanna is on duty, but it's hard to know if she's awake or asleep as she nods over her computer's Facebook page on the first floor. Dozing, she relives a summer moment at the beach when, partly covered by a towel, she slipped a hand into Marty McGuire's shorts. Then, awake again, she tells herself she must check on Herman Flynn, former owner of Flynn's Furnishings, who might not last the night, poor man. Then it's back again to Marty's shorts.

Not much activity at two-thirty in the morning. The twenty-four-hour Citgo station is open, but Shirley O'Rourke is asleep at the cash register. At police headquarters the dispatch officer, Joey Manzetti, nods over his console. But even in daylight Brewster tends to be sleepy, at least during the months when the summerhouses are shut up. Some of the locals commute to jobs in Providence, some to Wakefield, some to the university in Kingston. These days quite a few, relatively speaking, work at home, staying in touch with their jobs by computer. And there are a few small factories. Crenner Millwork Corp. makes high-quality windows, doors, and cabinets, which they ship all over New England and New York. Jack Crenner employs fifty people in good times. Mercurio Inc. makes acoustical materials and also has a contracting side. Duke Power Inc. builds, rebuilds, and repairs electric motors—dynamic balancing, vibration analysis, laser shaft alignment, that sort of thing, as well as having a twenty-four-hour emergency service.

Herb Fiore's on call tonight, but at the moment he's asleep on a cot in the back room. Donner's metal fabricators for furnaces and air-conditioning units; Jersey Jackets & Caps specializing in sportswear; Mitchell's plastic extruders and high-pressure laminates. There's even a small factory for hot tubs, saunas, and spas. Yes, you'll find quite a few companies in Brewster, although nothing actually thrives.

Everything downtown is shut tight. The two restaurants stop serving at nine—ten o'clock on the weekends. CVS/pharmacy closes at ten. The bars close at midnight. The only living soul is Ronnie McBride, curled up asleep in the doorway of Crandall Investments, which happens at least five times a week ever since his wife died of cancer two years ago. Often one of the patrolmen wakes him around three-thirty when he drives by on his rounds, and tonight it would be Harry Pasquale, but tonight Harry will be busy elsewhere.

Ever since the larger stores shut up shop—McGafferty's Department Store, Mills Men's Shop, and the rest—downtown Brewster has been in a steady decline, as the chains situate themselves in strip malls along Route 1. About every six months a new store starts up, but it usually closes in under a year. Two consignment shops, two beauty parlors, a tanning salon, an art gallery, a coffee shop called the Brewster Brew, a jewelers, the *Brewster Times & Advertiser*, Betty's Breakfast, a karate school—I forget what kind—and a fluctuating number of gift and souvenir shops, the library, Rudy's Pizza, and that about does it. Four churches and, oh, yes, four bars, a bowling alley, and the Brewster Inn, which is a forty-unit motel with half the units closed until May 1. Until five years ago it was called the Brewster Motel, but then the owner, Melody Baker, decided she could raise prices ten percent by changing the name to the Brewster Inn. Now she wants to change it to the Brewster Arms. The downside of a name change is she'll have to slather the trim with a fresh coat of white paint, which it sorely needs. A fresh bed of geraniums wouldn't hurt, either.

Tonight she has three guests, though two of the efficiencies are booked through the month. In fact, one of her guests arrived thirty minutes ago, having driven down from Boston. His name's Ernest Hartmann—he dislikes being called Ernie—and he's an insurance investigator, though right now, as he told his office, he's on vacation. In truth, he almost never takes a vacation, which was a contributing factor to his divorce six years ago. But in Boston he recently questioned a fellow who had unsuccessfully torched his own boutique as a way of coping with a small mountain of bad debt. When confronted, the fellow told Hartmann about some folks in Brewster—kidnappers or cultists or neopagans, it was hard to make sense of it, but it was something the fellow's brother knew about, and the fellow thought if Hartmann was interested, and he should be, he might then agree with the state fire marshal that the fire was accidental. Yesterday he'd given Hartmann a brass coin with a five-pointed star within a circle on one side and a goat standing on its hind legs on the other, as well as some marks like letters, though Hartmann was sure they weren't from any Western language. But Hartmann felt if he could turn this tip into a profit he might get that transfer to LA, where his two kids, twin nine-year-old girls, lived with his ex-wife. However questionable his current quest might be, it would be worth it if it let him spend more time with his daughters.

Even so, Hartmann had about decided not to make the trip, but on Wednesday evening he ran into Tommy Meadows, a state health investigator, who told Hartmann he also had a question about Brewster, and if Hartmann could look into a few nooks and crannies, he, Tommy Meadows, would make it worth his while. So Hartmann had agreed. Still, he wouldn't be surprised if it ended up as a wild-goose chase. As it was, he had only started at midnight and nearly turned around three times on the drive down.

Hartmann put his bag up on the table next to the TV. He is a pudgy man in his late thirties, and he likes to wear a Hawaiian shirt under a blue blazer. What he has a lot of is hair, a thick dark brown mop that he combs back over his head and that gives him another two inches of height, and today it looks as it did when he was sixteen. He's been lucky in the hair area, as he likes to tell himself.

Hartmann took out his shaving kit and pajamas, then took out a photo of the twins, a pair of pretty blondes who, even in the photograph, looked like they had trouble standing still. Once into puberty they'd be holy terrors, and Hartmann believed if he weren't living nearby, he could end up as a grandfather by the age of forty-five. Most nights before his wife left, he'd check on them two or three times just for the pleasure of seeing their blond hair tousled on their pillows. These days he was lucky if he got a chance to telephone, luckier still if they answered. No, he had to get to the West Coast, and whatever these cultists or kooks were doing, as long as it was illegal and moderately sensational, it might present him with a ticket to LA.

Reaching again into his bag, Hartmann took out clean underwear and socks for tomorrow, as well as a black nine-millimeter semiautomatic that made a slight clunk as he set it on the night table next to the photograph. It was a thirteen-shot Browning Hi-Power that had belonged to his father, who had died before his daughters were born. Hartmann had fired it only on a practice range, though he'd been lugging it around for fifteen years. He never even needed to show it, but he always thought it might be useful, though he often left it at home. He wasn't sure why he'd brought it tonight. Just hasty packing, most likely.

Nothing was pretty about the pistol, a solid mass of chipped and scratched black metal, with black plastic grips. It was functional and matter-of-fact, more like a bouncer than a dancer. Glancing at it, Hartmann decided he didn't want it next to his daughters' photograph, so he moved it to the night table on the other side of the bed. After all, the pistol didn't come from a world that Hartmann wished the twins to have any part of.

If you think Hartmann is basically decent you're right, and it could lead him down paths that others might have avoided. He did too many favors and good turns for people who didn't deserve it. Looking at the twins' photo as he pulled up the blankets and prepared to cut the light, he felt himself choking up. They were so goddamn cute!

Most likely you've visited a town like Brewster. The town isn't poor, thanks to the taxes paid by summer people. The schools are good and the new police station on Water Street seems bigger and brighter than necessary, since the cops do little more than keep an eye on the closed-up summerhouses, nab drunk drivers on Route 1, and break up occasional domestic violence. At times one of the bars—Tony's, in particular—offers a good fight on the weekend. What else? A funeral home is situated in an old mansion on Water Street. There's the usual handful of doctors, lawyers, and dentists, and then the hospital, which is small but thriving. Oh, yes, downtown, on the top three floors of the four-story Metcalf Building—Brewster's tallest building—The You Within You, a holistic health alternative, has set up shop in the former showrooms of Bates Home Furniture. Along with yoga classes—Kundalini, Vinyasa, Svaroopa, and Heated Baptiste Power Yoga—are classes in tai chi and meditation, classes in chanting, gong meditation, crystal ball meditation, even belly dancing. Or you might visit the various practitioners in Reiki, reflexology, polarity therapy, magnetic therapy, massage, and so on. Placebo U, it's called by Dr. Balfour at the hospital. You-You, it's called by everyone else. As an alternative health co-op, it has a warren of large and small rooms where various teachers, adepts, gurus, savants, masseurs, masseuses, and specialists in the aerobic and anaerobic, as well as yoga, can rent space, while all the day and half the night the old showrooms reverberate with people jumping, hopping, stretching, and striking martial attitudes. There's lots of talk about energy flow, or qi, lots of words like moxibustion, Kampo, bagua, and Zang Fu organs. This isn't to poke fun. You-You is Brewster's biggest business and soon it means to open a store to sell lotions, potions, and pills, a whole catalog of items to wear, eat, sniff, or rub on your body.

Two-thirds of the people in Brewster were born here, went to school here, work here, and will most likely die here—lifers, you might call them. They're not entirely sick to death of one another, but they know one another's secrets, or imagine they do, and turn gossip into a fine art. If you overheard two of them in the Stop & Shop, it might sound like this. Shopper 1: "Sonny's on a tear again." Shopper 2: "Tammy in Warwick?" Shopper 1: "Baby's got a virus." Shopper 2: "Can you blame him, I mean considering?" Shopper 1: "Pop says the same thing over his eggs." Shopper 2: "You can cry wolf on remission only just so often." Shopper 1: "Knocked down his own mailbox."

Fill in the blanks, you'd have a novel; keep it short and it's a play by Beckett.

As for the remaining third, some are retired, some work, some commute, some fish, some just like the water, some hide out, some are trying a geographical cure, some are busy discovering themselves—much of which is also true of the lifers. Most might strike you as regular people, just plain folks, but hookers and rent boys regularly drive down from Providence. One of the hookers says, "When I was a kid, I'd go up and down streets like these and wonder what went on in the houses. Since I've been a working girl, I've found out."

Brewster has half a dozen AA groups. Al-Anon, Narcotics Anonymous, Overeaters Anonymous—all have stories. A Gamblers Anonymous group started up after Foxwoods opened. The casino is a thirty-minute drive, and some people in town work there. You look at the social effects within fifty miles of a big casino, the jump in the number of thefts, divorces, suicides, traffic accidents, bankruptcies, you name it. In AA, you see a lot of cooks; in GA, you get a lot of lawyers; in NA, you get doctors and nurses. Each occupation has its own form of self-medicating. R. James Huntington was a lawyer in Brewster who attended Saturday-night GA meetings in the basement of St. John's. He kicked the habit, but it didn't help. One September night he walked outside and before going ten feet he took a pistol and blew his brains out. Father Pete had to hose down the stained-glass window on the north side of the nave before Sunday Mass and he still missed some sticky bits. Huntington had drained three of his clients' trust funds. He had kicked the habit but was a million bucks in debt.

These twelve-step meetings can give a taste of what goes on in these "hibernating" New England towns. Sister Chastisement, a dominatrix from Narragansett with a clientele in Brewster, spends two hours with her physical therapist working on her carpal tunnel after a busy night in Brewster. And she won't even look at a client unless he's college educated.

But at two-thirty in the morning even Sister Chastisement has gone home to bed. Cats are on the prowl, as well as coyotes and a few fishers. Owls wait among the branches, and some nights you'll hear a rabbit scream. As we rise above the town, we see street after street of darkened houses. The big Victorians on Oak, Spruce, and Water streets, the smaller houses around where the mill used to stand; then, as we move toward the edges of town, we find ranch houses and Cape Cods. Despite the hour, through some windows you'll see a flickering TV and, this is strange, someone reading a book by the fireplace. In a town of seven thousand, half are sexually active. So either singly or in pairs, even a threesome, a few are still at it. The couples tend to have schedules, but for single folks, like Nurse Spandex, it's catch-as-catch-can. As for other late-night diversions—crossword puzzles, card games, jigsaw puzzles, board games, computer solitaire—maybe fifty insomniacs are still busy. Look through the kitchen window of that split-level on Mason Street. Ginger and Howard Phelps are playing their five-thousandth game of gin rummy. Ginger has won 2,600 games to Howard's 2,400, but Howard thinks he's catching up. Mugs of warm milk with honey and slices of Ginger's pecan-cranberry bread—some nights it can take them three hours to get to sleep.

A few are still up because they work late. Larry Rodman got back to his small white clapboard house on Millman Street ten minutes ago, and right now he's taking cold pizza out of the fridge. Larry's forty-five and weighs the same as he did when he graduated from Brewster High: 150 pounds. He could eat pizza with double oil and double cheese all day and never gain a pound. He's lucky that way. He lives in his parents' house, which he inherited. His father died in 2000, his mother in 2005, and now the house belongs to Larry, though he had to buy out his older brother and sister, who live in southern California. No way were they going to move back to the "weather from hell."

As the pizza heats up—in the oven, not the microwave—Larry takes three stoneware cookie jars down from the shelf and sets them on the kitchen table. Then he digs a ring out of his pocket and holds it up to the light: a woman's ring, fourteen-carat gold. That means the middle jar. The one on the left is for eighteen-carat, and the one on the right is for twelve-carat. Anything under twelve-carat, he ignores. Before he puts them back, he gives each jar a shake, taking pleasure in their heft. A fourth jar for engagement rings is still on the shelf. None of those tonight. But these jars and the jewelry they contain, they're one of the perks of working at the Burn Palace.

For others, what keeps them up is what a friend used to call "the four a.m. oh-my-Gods." There's Vicki Lefebvre chewing her knuckle at her living room window in a white colonial on Market Street. Nina, her sixteen-year-old, has been gone two nights. She had called earlier to say she was staying with a friend from school, but then the friend herself had called looking for her. A few times recently Nina had been gone all night or come back at three or four. But this is the first time she's been gone two nights. Vicki's ex-husband lives in Groton, and Vicki is tempted to call him, get him out of bed to share the pain, though she knows she'd only get his voicemail, just as she only gets her daughter's voicemail. Where Nina goes on these nights is a mystery, except she comes home with mud on her shoes, and once with burrs stuck to the sleeve of her wool coat. When Vicki asks where she's been, Nina says "nowhere" or "a friend's house" or "it's none of your business." And when Vicki says, "Everything you do is my business," Nina says, "Whatever." This would be a worry in any case, but five days ago Vicki saw Nina with three others in the Brewster Brew, and these others, a man and two women, were in their twenties and thirties. One was positively gray-haired. They were laughing as if they'd known one another all their lives, Nina included. They weren't teachers; Vicki didn't know who they were. When she asked her daughter, Nina had said, "Nobody. They weren't anybody." So Vicki stands at the window, chewing her knuckle, and watches the branches blow back and forth. She knows she has to do something, but if she tries to ground Nina, Nina will only laugh. Then what will she do?

Surely fear is the oldest emotion. Not love, not pride, not greed. The emotion urging you to run is older than the one telling you to embrace.

Take screams, for example: screams of excitement, happiness, sex, laughter, success, terror. When Nurse Spandex screamed in the hospital nursery, those jarred from sleep didn't wonder, "Hmm, what kind of scream *is* that?" They knew. And their bodies responded before their minds. We say their blood turned cold, but words can't do justice to the terror that woke people from sleep. Jamie Shepherd, lying in bed with two broken legs, wanted to jump up and run; Mabel Flynn, ninety-seven years old and nearly flatlined, felt a surge of adrenaline that would send her crawling down the hall if she weren't hooked to a dozen machines.

As when a stone is dropped in a pond, the ripples activated by those screams spread outward—the terror of those jerked awake in the nearest rooms, terror down the hall, terror upstairs and downstairs. Then, more slowly through the sleeping town, telephones began to ring: first the police, then the hospital chain of command: nurses, nurse supervisors, doctors, department heads, chief of staff, chief of medical affairs, right up to the hospital administrator. From volunteers to members of the board of trustees, telephones jangled, buzzed, or chirped in the night. All had friends, and many felt a need to call them, and soon reporters were called, teachers, psychologists, social workers, and busybodies. Then it moved past Brewster, to the larger world, as people learned a baby had been stolen from the hospital and replaced with a snake.

So there's a difference between who is awake before two-thirty and who is awake after. But of those awake before two-thirty, let's look at Carl Krause. Do you see the craftsman bungalow on the corner of Newport and Hope, the one with gray shingles? Do you see those two small lighted windows in the gable above the front porch? That's where Carl is after a fight with his wife, Harriet; that is, he raged and she stood back. But instead of being asleep, he's lying on his bed fully dressed; he's even got his boots on. He's a big man, with unruly black hair, and he needs a shave. Years ago the whole bedroom was done over in knotty pine paneling by Harriet's first husband, and Carl's lying very still, staring at the knotholes. He's trying to catch them move; he knows they're doing it. When he turns his head, he can see them shift from the corner of his eye. They don't move a lot, only enough to be a worry. And they change their shapes. Those two above his head that look like two eyes in the top half of a face, Carl saw them blink. He saw their eyebrows move. Do you believe eyes are the windows to the soul? These souls are dark and nasty. Carl knows they don't mean him any good. Sure, you could say any knothole looks like an eye, but can you say the knotholes have faces and heads, even ears? And they're not necessarily human faces, not even animal faces, or not animals Carl has seen. Maybe reptiles or snakes. And some of the eyes look like dead people's eyes. Even when they move, they look like dead people's eyes.

You might think Carl's been drinking, he's dry as a stone in Death Valley. Not that drinking hasn't been a problem, just like anger's now a problem, which is a reason why he's upstairs and not downstairs. Harriet's downstairs and his step-brats are downstairs and the dog and cat are downstairs, and he's upstairs by himself, sober and calm. His only problem is knotholes, the sly ones creeping across the ceiling, gathering news, making plans. And who do they tell his secrets to, that's what he wants to know, who does he have to watch out for? So Carl isn't moving even a little finger; he's making like a dead guy just to trick them, like he's lying in his coffin, staring up like a corpse might stare up. But lying like that takes effort. It's hard work and he starts to sweat and the pressure starts to build. He can feel it, like something in his gut trying to break free. Pretty soon it's going to blow and then people better watch out.

TWO

WOODY POTTER'S PHONE on his night table began ringing at two-fifty-three a.m., and his cell phone joined in two seconds later, so even before he was technically awake he knew it was something big, and he reached out blindly with a mixture of anticipation and dread. Hoping to shut off the sound before it disturbed Susie, he made a grab but knocked his cell to the floor, sending it skittering under the bed, and then he remembered that Susie wasn't lying next to him and might never again lie next to him. But by then he had the phone to his ear and was on his belly, trying to grab the other, and urgent voices, blessedly, put his female problems on the back burner.

Hank Alvarez, the trooper on duty at the Alton Barracks was on the cell; Brewster acting police chief Fred Bonaldo was on the house phone. Woody knew it was a mistake to listen to both with a phone to each ear, an atonal duet about snakes, missing babies, escalating hysteria, and the crime scene unit being on its way. He wanted to tell them he was wandering in a sleep-deprived dead zone, a fog of unknowing. Instead he said he was leaving for the hospital immediately, which, really, was all they wanted to hear.

Woody swung his feet onto the floor and then sat with his elbows on his knees, his chin in his hands. Although he had gone to bed before eleven, he'd tossed and turned for an hour. Ajax, his golden retriever, padded over in the dark and licked his toes. Worse than whatever horror show was on display at Morgan Memorial was the vacancy on the other side of the queen-size bed, a vacancy matched by an increasing vacancy within him, a hole so big his entire life seemed in danger of tumbling into it and he wanted to lie down and put his head under the pillow. Then he shook himself, grabbed his jeans and boots, and four minutes later he was hurrying out the back door to his Tundra as Ajax and Tufito, the cat, stared at him from the top of the kitchen stairs as if saying, "What-zup, what-zup?"

Woody Potter was one of five state police area detectives assigned to Washington County, and he knew what lay ahead was something Fred Bonaldo felt he couldn't handle alone. Brewster had thirty full-time police officers, with another fifteen part-timers who worked May 1 to October 1. If acting chief Bonaldo needed more assistance, he would call the troopers; or if, say, he needed a SWAT team, he might instead call Westerly or South Kingstown, since Bonaldo would probably yell for a SWAT team if a toddler threw a snowball at a cruiser. *But aren't I being unfair?* thought Woody. And wasn't this something Susie's been complaining about? His negativity? The question mark floated above him like a striper might consider a fishhook as he drove the dark roads toward Brewster. Then he said "Fuck it!" so loudly he jumped, as if the voice belonged to someone squatting in the narrow seat behind him.

He was thirty-nine and, he'd thought, on the cusp of his second marriage. No kids. A year after graduating from Tolman High School in Pawtucket, he'd joined the army in time for the first Iraq War: six months of stultifying boredom and several moments of terror. Next came four years at the University of Rhode Island, a degree in political science, a minor in criminology and criminal justice, the continuation of a heavy drinking problem, and Cheryl, his wife. A year later, he entered Roger Williams law school. He lasted nine months, got his drinking under control as his marriage went careening out of control. This, he used to think, was Cheryl's problem. "You're no fun anymore," she'd said. She liked to party and he was sick of partying. Now he thought the problem had been likely his. He was short-tempered and silent if things bothered him. In any case, they divorced. Cheryl was in Oregon, and they'd probably never see each other again.

Even before the divorce had been finalized, Woody had entered the State Police Training Academy in Foster for a twenty-six-week program, with the first twenty-one weeks living at the academy five days a week. It was like basic training—worse in some ways, better in others, since he got to go home Friday nights. Now he had been a trooper for eleven years. What had happened since graduation from the academy and where he was this morning was, on one hand, the soothing exactness of trooper discipline, and, on the other, a series of botched sexual relationships, a bad temper, or, as he was told, an anger management problem, and a question he repeated like the refrain of a song: "Just what the fuck you think you're doing?" Was he happy? He guessed so. He never thought about it. Was he depressed? Well, everything'd been fine till Susie left, so maybe it hadn't been fine after all. What else? Those few moments of terror in Iraq would sometimes pop back in his head and all he could see were flashing lights and explosions and, oh, yes, flying body parts. When he'd seen a therapist last week—still hoping to save his relationship—Dr. Nardone asked, "Where d'you see yourself in ten years?" He began to say, "In jail," then bit his tongue. *Where did that come from?* he'd asked himself.

What had he learned as a trooper? To keep his face absolutely blank, to express confidence and optimism, to expect the worst, to remain alert in incredibly boring situations, to go to the gym five days a week, to lie in moderation, to keep away from the bottle. He liked it. He liked the occasional adrenaline rush; he liked the routine; he liked the clarity; he liked a bunch of the guys he worked with, men and women. He liked being with people he could trust. This, more or less, was Woody Potter. All in all he was a pretty good guy, though, as he'd be first to admit, there was room for improvement. Oh, yes, he was tall, muscular, had short dark hair—more like a fringe than a haircut—dark eyes, a jutting chin, and a three-inch shrapnel scar on the left side of his neck. An eighth of an inch deeper and he'd be dead.

It was eight miles from Woody's small Cape in Carolina to Morgan Memorial, much of it through the woods on Route 2, a pause at the light on Route 1, and then three miles up Water Street—coming through a dark place and ending up at a three-ring circus, since cruisers and emergency response vehicles from half a dozen towns had seen fit to pay a visit. All were drawn up around the emergency entrance with lights flashing and radios chattering. Two ambulances and a rescue vehicle had also turned up. Some of the cops were off duty. Were they volunteering? No, they were here to see the fun.

More were inside the ER, but the only patient was a big South Kingstown cop being treated for a sprained ankle, which he'd twisted in his rush to see the snake. In an observation room was the nurse, Alice Alessio, who had been on duty in labor and delivery, and whose hysteria, Woody was told, was thought to be on the mend. Soon he was calling her Nurse Spandex like everyone else, though a few called her Alice Spandex and when Woody first heard the name, he thought she must be East European.

The two mothers in labor and delivery, including the Summers girl, whose baby had disappeared, had been moved to another floor. Bonaldo wanted to clear labor and delivery entirely. "The big problem," he told

Woody, "is the snakes. We found one sneaking through the nurses' station. I mean, Alice Spandex doesn't recall how many she saw. She said maybe five, maybe ten. But she's not thinking clearly."

This really is a circus, thought Woody. "Are they poisonous?"

Bonaldo was a balding middle-aged man with a red-faced, swollen look. He was tall, a little over six feet, though Woody was taller. His rimless glasses sat at a crooked angle on his nose; his blue shirt was half untucked. "Fucking corn snakes—'bout the nicest snakes you'd want to meet, and the one we caught was like doped up. Nearly a six-footer. And pretty? It looks like Halloween candy. But how many others are out there? Nurses, patients, doctors, everyone—they're seeing snakes all over the hospital. It's like a hysterical reflex."

Bonaldo said this in one long breath, and Woody felt he was having too good a time. He felt that Bonaldo was "acting" chief much in the way he might be called a "pretend" chief. Actually, he was a Realtor doing the town a favor. Quarrels in the department and friends in City Hall got him the job, but more of this later.

"And the baby?"

They stood by the triage desk. The woman on duty pretended not to be listening.

"There you've got me. Like it seems to be gone."

This was the first of many times that Woody thought the snake, or snakes, were taking precedence over the baby. Bonaldo would deny it, but it wasn't the missing baby making him flap his hands and roll his eyes, nor was the baby making his comrades in law enforcement dash around, look in closets and under beds with highly agitated startle responses as one after the other imagined that he, or she, had seen a colorful flicker at the corner of his or her eye. Woody had brought back a fairly active startle response from Iraq, so much so that Susie wouldn't walk up behind him without announcing her presence, but he felt like an absolute beginner compared to these guys. But then he'd always liked snakes.

"So who's in charge?"

"I am, I guess." This seemed to embarrass Bonaldo. "Though there's an off-duty South Kingstown captain who's been a big help, also a Westerly lieutenant. But it's my jurisdiction. Did I tell you an FBI guy's coming down from Providence or Boston? Abduction, you know, that's their bailiwick. And now you're here, too, Corporal. You're the trooper. That's why I called you."

"Great," said Woody, without enthusiasm. He felt lots of stuff had to be cleared away before he got to the actual baby. All these cops in the ER, outside and upstairs and more arriving—most he knew and a few were close friends, basketball buddies, fishing pals. It was like a convention with tabloid written all over it. Rhode Island was more of a big town than a state; it was a third the size of San Diego County, where his sister lived, with a third the population. Soon cops would be showing up from Woonsocket fifty miles away on the Massachusetts border, as far as you could get from Brewster and still be in Rhode Island. And the crime scene unit was driving down from North Scituate, also nearly fifty miles.

"What does Miss Spandex say?"

Bonaldo made a grunt that might have been a laugh and explained the confusion about her name, ending up, "Actually, I was in high school with her mother. Hot? You better believe it." He cracked his knuckles in emphasis.

Woody grasped that Bonaldo hadn't really talked to Alice except to learn the basic details—baby boy missing, snakes in crib—because she was hard to talk to: "It's the hysteria." Other nurses were trying to calm her down. South Kingstown had tried to talk to her, as did Westerly, but all they'd discovered was there might be, really, quite a lot of snakes. "Like a menagerie," said Bonaldo.

When Woody had been learning anger management techniques, one method had meant practicing three types of patience, one being the patience of voluntarily accepting suffering. He was, with a degree of irony, trying that now. The alternative was to start yelling.

"And the mother?"

"Oh, you know, she's taking it pretty well, considering."

"Maybe I'll talk to the nurse first."

"The problem," said Bonaldo, "is this Spandex girl was supposed to be on duty and she wasn't. I mean, she wasn't on the floor. The babies were by themselves, I don't know how long. It was the curse. . . . You know, her monthlies. She said she had the cramps something awful. My wife does the same thing. She was all knotted up in the toilet."

"For how long?"

"Long enough."

Alice Alessio was in a room across from the ER desk. A Brewster cop—Harry Morelli—stood at the door with crossed arms. With a shaved head, drooping mustache, and ferocious scowl, he looked like a Turkish harem guard shoved into a blue uniform.

As Woody began to enter the room, he saw two men and a woman from the crime scene unit hauling their stuff through the emergency entrance. Woody knew them well, and they nodded to one another. The corporal, Frank Montesano, came over to Woody, as a Brewster detective led the others to the elevator.

"Got a circus on your hands, Detective?" said Montesano.

"It's not my circus, I hope."

"Why steal a baby?" Montesano was as solid as a fire hydrant and about forty.

"Who knows? To sell it, have it, ransom it, trade it, you name it." It was a question that Woody hadn't given much attention to. Those damn snakes kept getting in the way.

"I guess the hospital doesn't use a baby LoJack system." Seeing Woody's disbelief, Montesano added, "It's a transmitter you put on the baby as an anklet. If someone takes the baby out of a designated area, all the doors and elevators lock down and bells ring. Some come with a GPS. Lots of hospitals use them."

"Well, Morgan Memorial's not one of them."

After Montesano went up to the nursery, Woody asked himself: *Why had the baby been taken?* Cops hurried through the ER on a variety of real or made-up errands, glad to break out of a routine. Boredom, Woody thought, was as dangerous to cops as risk-taking. But the trouble at Morgan Memorial was nothing Bonaldo could handle on his own—taking statements, gathering evidence, searching the hospital and nearby vicinity, assisting the transfer of patients to other floors and hunting for snakes. It was a logistical nightmare. Practically speaking, the whole hospital was a crime scene. It might take days to straighten it out. It wasn't the work Woody minded but the clutter. Here he found lots of clutter. But no matter how bad it was, it would get worse as the news spread into the world. By now the hospital's top medical and administrative staff were arriving, including the director, Dr. Joyce Fuller, who had degrees in business and hospital administration rather than medicine. In addition, somebody had put out calls to local psychologists and counselors to help with the general hysteria. A lot of patients needed calming down; some of the staff as well. Although the hospital had only fifty beds, it employed about two hundred people. Woody guessed every one of them had learned what had happened and all would call a minimum of five friends and/or relatives.

To complicate matters, an ambulance pulled up at the door with a real emergency. The tech and driver took an elderly man out of the back, a resident of Ocean Breezes suffering from chest pains. Several cops glanced at the old guy in irritation, as if he were a trespasser who should be sent someplace else. Woody knew the EMTs: Seymour Hodges and Jimmy Mooney. Hodges had got back from Iraq about four months ago and Woody had been interested in talking to him about it, though not enough to actually call him. But then he turned his attention to Nurse Spandex.

Alice Alessio lay on her back with her hands pressed to her cheeks and seemed focused on the ceiling light. She was rigid, but every few moments she began to shake so the bed rattled, and then she began to whimper. The older nurse sitting by her side stroked her forehead and aimed soothing noises at her ear. This was Bernie Wilcox, and she'd been a nurse for forty years. If she hadn't insisted on working part-time, she could have been a head nurse or a nurse supervisor, not in a podunk hospital like Morgan but in Providence or Boston. She didn't say this; other people said this. Everybody she worked with said she could have any job she wanted. She was that good. Years back, she'd had some of those jobs, but now she liked her loom, her weaving, and her thirty sheep as much as she liked nursing. So she split her time.

Woody Potter had never met Bernie, but he was struck by her empathy and calm. If he didn't have so much on his mind he might have guessed the empathetic calm was professional apparatus. It made her job go more smoothly. This didn't mean that Bernie was the opposite of calm, but she had little use for Nurse Spandex. What she wanted was to keep Nurse Spandex from running screaming through the hospital, because making scenes and pitching fits was what Nurse Spandex was all about. That and getting laid.

Woody knew none of this, but he knew the name Nurse Spandex, and he could see how her nursing scrubs had received a variety of tucks and taking-ins to set off her figure. At thirty-five, or thereabouts, she was on the cusp between overripe grape and fallen peach. *Windfall* was the word he was looking for, or was it *deadfall*? Then there was her makeup. Her eyeliner and eye shadow were distributed across her cheeks much like a flooded Mississippi River is often distributed across the Midwest.

At the foot of the bed, Woody tried to imitate Bernie's expression of empathetic calm. It wasn't easy for him, not because he wasn't empathetic but because a blankness of expression and varieties of anger were the only expressions he was good at. Or, as Susie had screamed at him recently: "You only look happy when you're playing with the dog!"

Woody leaned forward. "You've had a terrible shock."

Although he spoke in what seemed to be a melodious whisper, Alice Alessio responded with a wail. Bernie looked at him reproachfully. Alice heaved herself about the bed and Bernie had to take her arm so she wouldn't fall out. Woody lowered his head and folded his hands in front of him to look vaguely priestlike. He disliked hysteria; he didn't see the purpose of it. What he liked in life was unruffled affability with a touch of ironic humor, an easy male banter where he didn't have to explain his feelings. Men might worry, they might curse, they might weep, but they didn't get hysterical. What was the point of the upset? Emotionalism on one side and dirtbags on the other—surely, it was a narrow path through life.

After a few minutes, Nurse Spandex achieved a sort of nervous vigilance and Woody asked her to describe what had happened, which nearly set her off again. Then, with much faltering and stammering, she managed to collect the words to tell her story. She had been in the nursery until about two-fifteen, mostly at her desk but also seeing to the babies, the dear little things, but it was terribly difficult because she was torn up by her cramps. She should have called someone; she knew she should have. Instead, she ran to the bathroom down the hall, where she was again attacked by cramps. "Hard enough to make my teeth shake," she said. After five minutes, or maybe ten, she made her way back to the nursery, stumbled back, if truth be told, and right away she saw something wrong in the Summers baby's crib. He was struggling under his little blanket as if he couldn't breathe, struggling to free himself. She had run to the crib and yanked away the blanket, and then . . . Here she again began to wail.

Woody waited. Another thing he disliked was asking women about their periods. His embarrassment always showed; he might even blush. In high school he recalled how girls could just get up from their desks and walk out of the room unchallenged. Sometimes he knew for a fact the girl was leaving to smoke dope or to have a cigarette. It had struck him as unfair.

When Alice was relatively calm, Woody asked about the snakes. Could she give an idea of the number? How many had she seen? Her lower lip quivered. At first it was ten, then that number went down. After all, ten six-foot snakes would more than fill the crib. Even five would be difficult. Maybe four, maybe three. Could it be one? No, it had to be more than one. More than one but less than two? Again she began to weep.

During her story, Nurse Spandex glanced up at Woody, glanced away, wrinkled her brow, looked at the ceiling, rubbed her nose, bit her lip, wiped her eyes, sniffed, wrung her hands, and darted glances at Bernie Wilcox. Woody was sure she was lying. It seemed printed in block letters across her forehead. So he asked a few questions. When she'd been in the bathroom, had she heard anything? No, well, maybe she'd heard footsteps, she couldn't be sure. Had she seen anyone, another nurse, someone on the staff? No, nobody. Was she sure she'd been gone five minutes, or was it a little more?

When it grew apparent that Woody doubted her, Alice began to weep again and talk about the snakes, how they had reared up, how she thought they had eaten the baby. Then her whole body began to shake.

So Woody gave it up for the time being. On the other hand, she might have taken the baby herself. She had the best opportunity, and she clearly was lying about something.

As he left the room, Bernie Wilcox followed, and before he'd gone five feet she took his arm and pulled him back. "That slut's not on the rag. She had her period two weeks ago and told us all about it, just like usual."

Woody turned in surprise and Bernie winked at him.

In the next few hours, Woody talked to the head of the hospital, doctors, nurses, members of the maintenance crew, and people who had been in the hospital when the incident took place. Other police officers were also talking to these people, and Woody joined in with a few questions. In each case, the person either told him nothing he didn't know or nothing he could use. In addition, each was afraid of something occurring to put his or her job at risk. They were circumspect, they professed ignorance, they cast troubled glances at the TV truck from Providence parked outside. They said they'd do "whatever it took" to get the baby back. Their hesitation was understandable, but Woody didn't like it.

Mayor Grantland Hobart, whose position was mostly honorific, took Woody aside. "Any chance of keeping this out of the papers?" He was a developer. If Brewster were known as a town where nasty things happened, it could cost him a fortune. Woody nodded toward the television news truck.

The mayor tugged his lower lip. "I was afraid of that."

What struck Woody was that no one expressed concern for the missing baby. Oh, a few said, "What a shame, what a shame," but it was a matter of formality, something to get out of the way before returning to the subject of their innocence. No, it wasn't a matter of innocence or guilt—they were protecting their résumés. Was he being too cynical? But he was tired and his back hurt from the standing around.

The fact was a baby boy less than twenty-four hours old was missing. Between people's worries about their jobs and those damn snakes, it was like the kid had vanished twice: once in truth and once from people's stories. For crying out loud, the baby didn't even have a name yet. The mother couldn't decide between Brad, Clint, and Sean. Movie-star names. In the same way, his own father had been torn between Woody, Dylan, and Elvis. Can't there be a law to protect kids from stupid names? "Is it short for Woodrow or Woodward?" people asked him. Nope, just Woody. It was right there on his birth certificate. At least it wasn't Elvis.

What mattered was the baby. The snakes were frosting. But he was tempted to grab someone, anyone, by the arm and shout, "Don't you give a fuck about the goddamn baby?"

That was almost what Susie had said. "Don't you want to have a goddamn baby?" But he was working and she was working; they were never home at the same time and there was his temper and the marriage kept being put off and then she left. And there were other problems, or "issues," as she called them.

Up on the second floor everything was quiet. Lights had been set up in the nursery. Frank Montesano dusted for fingerprints and put small red arrows next to the ones he found—walls, cribs, cabinets, they were all over. Janie Forsyth was busy with her camera. Lou Rossetti moved crabwise across the floor with his nose six inches above the tiles, armed with tweezers, evidence tubes, glassine envelopes, and the rest. They eased around cribs, chairs, tables, sinks, and rolling carts like slow-motion dancers. They wore blue latex exam gloves and booties. Their "exhibits," as they were called, would be taken over to the state crime laboratory, part of the College of Pharmacy at the University of Rhode Island.

Woody stood in the doorway and kept his hands in his pockets. On the walls were watercolors of piggies and duckies, puppies and kitties—a free-for-all of the intensely cute meant for parents and staff, since to the infants they were scarcely a blur.

Montesano and his crew didn't look at him. Woody knew they could be busy till daybreak, hardly aware of the passage of time. It was like grade school—some kids spent hours fussing with model ships and cars; some preferred to rush through the world with muscles throbbing. Woody had belonged to the second group.

"Any more snakes?" asked Montesano, still focused on fingerprints.

"Shit," said Rossetti. "I'll bet ten bucks there wasn't more than one."

Looking at the cribs, Woody imagined how he would feel if one had contained his son, even a daughter. "And I bet you're right."

"I got some interesting mud," said Rossetti. "They must clean this floor at least six times a day, so this is interesting recent mud."

"I like good mud," said Woody.

"How's Susie been?" asked Montesano, still without looking up.

"Oh, she's fine, fine. You know, like always." *Why am I lying?* Woody asked himself, ashamed. But it was too late to say, "By the way, she's left me." Maybe he could say something to Montesano when they were alone.

"We'd like to have you both over for dinner some night."

"Sure thing," said Woody. "That'd be great."

"Yeah," said Montesano, "it's been too long. Maybe I'll invite Rossetti here if he swears to eat with a knife and fork. I've even seen him eat *soup* with his fingers."

The men laughed. Then Woody saw Janie Forsyth look at him questioningly and remembered she was friends with Susie's sister. That meant Janie already knew.

Jill Franklin parked her Tercel on Chestnut Street a block from the hospital. It was past six, and the sun would soon rise over the ocean. She grabbed her camera bag and notebook and climbed out, careful not to slam the door. A white frost hopscotched the nearby lawns; the leaves, past their peak, were sallow or brown. She had no wish to be where she was, but her editor had called, and if she wanted to keep her job she had no choice. He had given her a room number and a few instructions, adding, "Don't forget, I want art."

Jill was thirty and a single parent. Luckily, her own parents lived only two miles from her apartment in Wakefield, so she had been able to drop off Luke. He was six. Jill had been substituting in local schools before the job had come through at the *Brewster Times & Advertiser* at the beginning of summer. It wasn't perfect, but it beat substituting. She was a little under average height but athletic and had played field hockey in high school and college. Now she sometimes coached it and could still outplay any girl on the team. But she was tired of being a jock, tired of schools, and she hoped her job with the *Brewster Times & Advertiser* would lead to a bigger paper, like the *Providence Journal*. Really, she'd like anything where writing was involved.

Jill had straight blond hair, an angled bob that she believed made her round face look thinner, a slightly snubbed nose that her father liked to say was like Socrates's nose, and nice lips and teeth. She didn't spend much time looking in the mirror. "It is what it is," she said. But she was proud of her athletic ability and didn't mind her thick calves, a result not just of running but of broken-field running, the stops, turns, shifts, the abrupt changes of direction. Anyway, she mostly wore jeans, which she was wearing now—jeans, a dark sweater, a black leather jacket, and running shoes. At the last minute, she decided to leave the jacket in the car.

She went straight to the main entrance, walking quickly, as if she had a destination in mind, someplace that wanted her as much as she wanted it. She breezed past the cop at the door with only a brief nod, which said, *If I weren't in such a rush I'd stop to chat.* "Never look uncertain," her boss had told her. Ahead was the information desk, at which sat a volunteer, an elderly woman who looked up with a smile.

Jill smiled back as she made a no-no gesture with an index finger. "I'm late, I'm late." She turned right toward the stairs.

It pleased her to run up two flights of stairs and not be out of breath. Her vanity needed comforting, considering that she was behaving in a way she disliked. *Face it,* she told herself, *I'm behaving badly.* She opened the door to the hallway and turned left. Several rooms were being cleaned; a nurse and doctor were discussing a chart; a man in a wheelchair stared at the ceiling. Jill breezed by them, and at the end of the hall she turned right. The room she wanted—314—was halfway down. A policeman stood outside. Jill walked quickly forward and then turned into room 316. An elderly man was asleep in the bed. An untouched breakfast tray was on the swing-out table. Jill picked up the tray and left the room, turning right.

The policeman outside room 314 looked disgruntled and sleepy. Again Jill smiled. "I'll bring you a breakfast as soon as I get rid of this. You sure look like you could use a cup of coffee." As she entered the room, she saw he was trying to smile back, a rudimentary beginner's smile that made his face warp. Maybe she really *could* bring him a cup of coffee.

Peggy Summers lay in bed staring at her with an unfriendly expression, not suspicious, just unwelcoming. She was sixteen or seventeen, with stringy blond hair and a narrow face. Her mouth was slightly open and her two front teeth looked like a rabbit's. She held a white plastic spoon in her hands, which she was breaking into smaller pieces in a series of snapping noises.

"Would you like something to eat?" Jill asked cheerfully. "Coffee, eggs, French toast—looks awfully good."

The unfriendly expression didn't change. "I just want to get the fuck out of here."

Jill put the tray down on the table, trying to conceal her surprise. "I know you've had a dreadful shock. It must be terrible for you."

"How's it terrible? Tell me."

Despite the girl's tone, Jill found herself wondering if Peggy even knew her baby had been stolen. If that was the case, there was no way Jill wanted to be the one to tell her. "Well, your baby—"

"You ever seen the movie *Rosemary's Baby*?" interrupted Peggy. "It was like that, you know what I mean?"

Jill had begun to take out her camera; now she stopped. "I don't think I do."

"A Devil baby. I'm glad it's gone."

Before Jill could answer, a man hurried into the room followed by the policeman who had been at the door. It was Woody Potter, though this was the first time she'd ever laid eyes on him. Even so, despite his boots and jeans, she guessed he was a cop.

"Who are you?" demanded Woody.

Jill meant to say something about delivering the breakfast tray. Instead she said, "My name is Jill Franklin and I work for the *Brewster Times and Advertiser.*"

Woody's anger came as a relief, something like a breath of fresh air. He grew red in the face. "Get out! Don't you have any self-respect? This poor girl has had her baby stolen and you're sneaking around trying to ask her questions? What kind of person are you?"

THREE

The boy zigzagged his bike along Water Street through downtown Brewster in the absence of any early-morning traffic. In summer it was different, the street was full of cars and motorcycles heading to the beach, but right now at seven o'clock on a Thursday morning in late October he had the street to him self, or pretty much, because a delivery truck was double-parked in front of the Brewster Brew. The boy's name was Hercel McGarty Jr. and, as he told himself, he was the only Hercel in Brewster, the only Hercel in Washington County, and probably the only Hercel in Rhode Island. He liked that. His father's name was also Hercel. His father was from Oklahoma, and his father said that in Oklahoma lots of kids were named Hercel. It was as common as Joe-Bob, or almost. His father didn't know where it came from, except he guessed it was short for Hercules, but Hercel Jr. probably shouldn't go bragging about that. It was a secret between them. Hercules—the strongest man in the world. But now his father had gone back to Oklahoma, taking his name with him, and Hercel Jr. wouldn't see his dad until summer vacation. He wouldn't even see him at Christmas. Instead, Hercel was stuck with his stepdad,

Carl Krause, and it wasn't simply a matter of not liking Carl—or Mr. Krause, as he wanted to be called. He was scared of him, even though his dad told him never to be scared of anybody. Of course, he had his mother, but Hercel thought she had also got scared of Mr. Krause, though she wouldn't admit it.

Hercel was ten and in fifth grade, but right now he had serious business to take care of before he rode his bike over to Bailey Elementary on the corner of Gaspee and Bucklin: serious business concerning a snake. Hercel was tall for his age, blue-eyed and thin with blond hair. "You look like a hillbilly kid," Mr. Krause had told him, and Hercel didn't know if that was true or not, but he looked like his dad and his dad looked like him, so if they looked like hillbillies then they were like hillbillies together, which was okay by Hercel, though he'd have been hard-pressed to know exactly what hillbillies looked like and he sure wasn't going to ask Mr. Krause, because Mr. Krause didn't like questions. In fact, he'd get mad.

Why his mother had married Mr. Krause was one of those mysteries. Like just when Hercel thought he'd got stuff figured out, adults would do something absolutely ridiculous. His mom marrying Mr. Krause was like that. Hadn't they been getting along fine without him? Of course, it'd been hard for her taking care of him and Lucy—she was his sister and she was five—after his dad left, hard to take care of them and keep her job at CVS, but marrying Mr. Krause seemed a rash decision. After all, Hercel made some money delivering stuff and collecting returnable bottles and raking leaves. "You call that money?" Mr. Krause had said. "That ain't shit."

Hercel's bike was a twenty-four-inch Pacific Highlander mountain bike. It was bright green and could go flying off curbs with no trouble, hardly even bounce. His dad bought it at the police auction for thirty bucks when it was almost new. It had eighteen gears and a vortex suspension fork, which his dad called important, though Mr. Krause more than once called it a "hunk-a-junk." The embarrassing part was even though Hercel had had the bike for more than a year, he still couldn't ride "no hands." One hand was okay, but not no hands, except for ten feet or so, which didn't count. Since he didn't have a helmet, that was just as well—at least that's what some people thought, people like his mom. But Hercel, as he told himself, had limited funds, and given the choice between a helmet and lock, he'd bought the lock. Maybe he'd get a helmet for Christmas, who knew. Mr. Krause said he never wore a helmet as a kid, they were "sissified," but Hercel knew he wasn't a good advertisement. So far, knock on wood, Hercel had never had a serious accident, and lots of times he'd ridden to the beach and out to Burlingame and over to Charlestown, and he kept meaning to ride out to Tig's farm to see her sheep and two big dogs.

So riding down Water Street at seven a.m. with his book bag on his back and his Red Sox hat pulled down tight on his head, Hercel lifted his left arm off the handlebars, and then, once he felt comfortable, he slowly lifted his right. One, two, three, but then the bike wobbled and he grabbed for the handlebars and the bike swerved and a car honked, but he was really okay, and the bike straightened out. He was embarrassed, that's all. The trouble was that the bike started to wobble when he got nervous, like maybe he started to shake and the bike felt it and started to shake, too. So if he could take his hands off the grips without getting nervous, without worrying what might happen, he'd be fine. He was chicken, wasn't that the truth? He was afraid of falling and getting hurt, and that made him angry with himself.

But here he was at the police station, and he bounced up over the curb to the front steps. Should he lock his bike? Maybe he had better. After all, it was full of crooks. Thinking that made him remember why he had come, and he got angry. The damn crooks! And he ran up the steps.

The lobby was empty except for a policeman behind the desk reading a newspaper. "I want to report a crime," said Hercel.

The policeman lowered his paper but didn't speak. He looked tired, as if he'd been up all night.

"Someone broke into our basement and stole my pet. They broke the lock."

"Oh, yeah?" The policeman began to look amused.

"Yeah. They stole my snake, a corn snake, a really nice one."

Vicki Lefebvre awoke that morning on the couch. Her covers—two shawls and her winter coat—had slipped to the floor and she was cold even though the sun was just coming through the windows. It took her a moment to get her bearings. It was seven.

Quickly, she scrambled to her feet. Had Nina come home? She ran upstairs to Nina's room fearing the worst. But her daughter was asleep, her brown hair tousled on her pillow, her thick bangs nearly reaching her eyebrows like her favorite singer, Adele, whose posters hung on the bedroom walls.

"What time did you get home?" shouted Vicki.

Nina opened her eyes and looked at her mother. Vicki should have known right then that something was wrong, because Nina showed no expression. Usually her emotions were all over the map.

"Where were you? Don't you know I was worried sick? You were gone two nights. You lied to me. I'm going to call your dad immediately, see if I don't! Maybe he can deal with you." All this was delivered in a shout as her daughter got out of bed and made her way to the bathroom. She'd slept in her clothes, jeans and a sweater. There was mud on her cuffs, and her feet were dirty.

"Look at the mess you've made with your muddy clothes! Where have you been? I demand an answer, young lady. Have you been seeing some boy? If you get knocked up, I'm not raising your brat. I insist you tell me where you've been. Look at the time! Now you'll be late for school!"

Nina entered the bathroom, shut and locked the door. A moment later, Vicki heard the shower. She felt on the verge of tears. "I refuse to put up with this!" Then she felt foolish shouting at a locked door and returned to her daughter's bedroom. She didn't want to yell at Nina. She wanted to tell her how glad she was to find her safe and sound. Even to tell her she loved her. The girl's shoes were also muddy. Clothes were scattered across the floor, papers covered the small desk, along with socks, jars of makeup, dirty glasses, and cereal bowls. Vicki gathered up the dirty dishes.

When Nina came out of the bathroom, she didn't return to her room but headed down the stairs, not running, just proceeding at a steady pace.

Vicki ran after her while balancing the dishes, so as not to drop them. "Aren't you even going to change your clothes? They're an absolute mess. What's wrong with you, anyway? I demand you come home right after school. If you ever do this again, I'm calling the police. You're grounded, young lady. Until further notice!"

At the door, Nina picked up her backpack with her schoolbooks. She looked up at her mother who had paused halfway down the stairs. Vicki was too mad to think of anything except her anger and Nina's list of transgressions. Later she recalled the girl's expression and how sad she looked. And she also thought about how her daughter always shouted back, how she always gave as good as she got. But not this time. This time she slung her bag over her shoulder and left, even shutting the door behind her.

• • •

Ernest Hartmann's back hurt, and he blamed it on the queen-size bed in the Brewster Inn, a lousy bed with a dip in the middle from years of rough sex play, and his back had slipped into it like a burger into a bun and got bent out of shape. Now he walked in a crouch. Whenever he straightened up, a million volts of electricity shot through his sacroiliac or someplace like that. Absolutely the last thing he wanted was a back operation, a surgeon taking a knife to him. But he had messed up his back before and each time made it worse and someday his sacroiliac, or whatever it was, would be no more than silly putty.

At seven a.m., having been awake for several hours, he had gingerly crept from bed and dragged himself to the shower. This by itself nearly killed him. But the hot water had done some good, and despite the pain he managed to get dressed. The alternative was lying like a log until the maids found him. He put on his jeans, a blue aloha shirt with a chain of white hibiscus across the chest, and a dark blue blazer. Then he headed for the door.

Hartmann folded himself into his blue Ford Focus coupe—he called it a Mazda in drag—and sat, breathing heavily. If he had been able to afford something bigger like a Ford Escape, he could climb in and out without yanking his back, but he hadn't had the extra money, though he was paying for it now in back pain, that's for sure. Pulling out of the motel lot, he drove to the CVS for ibuprofen, aspirin, and naproxen—he would pop all three until he started feeling better. Then he drove to the Brewster Brew to dose himself with caffeine and maybe a pumpernickel-raisin bagel with cream cheese.

The coffee shop was in the middle of the block, and in its previous life it had been Henry's Shoes, but as Brewster Brew it was making more money than Mr. Henry ever made in his last few years, and the owner, Jean Sawyer, also got a break on the rent.

When Hartmann entered, Jean was talking to Florie Ligetti at the counter, talking so intensely that neither woman saw him. Florie, Hartmann thought, was a little too thin and had one of those flat asses he didn't like, flat as a board. Jean was more to his taste, plump and womanly. Both women were about his age. Not that Hartmann was interested; he was only window-shopping. Anyway, having sex with his back out would put him in his coffin, *muy pronto*. On two shelves behind the counter were old-time coffeemakers, and above them was a watercolor of a gentleman in a white wig who looked vaguely like George Washington, though more depressed. Beneath were the words: *Wrestling Brewster, Our Founder.*

Hartmann tapped a quarter on the glass and the women looked at him blankly, as if wondering what he was doing there. "Could I get a black coffee and a bagel, pumpernickel-raisin, if you have it?"

As the woman behind the counter took a cup from the shelf, she began to smile as if just waking up. "Haven't you heard about the snakes?"

The very question made Hartmann's back hurt. He decided not to answer it. "And cream cheese, low-fat cream cheese."

"The hospital's full of them. A baby was stolen. Abducted. Peggy Summers's baby, poor thing. I hope they don't ransom it, because Peggy doesn't have a dime. The town's absolutely packed with cops; they're all over at the hospital. My mom went over this morning for a flu shot and they wouldn't let her in. You said you wanted cream?"

"Black." Hartmann was positive he didn't want to get caught up in a wacko conversation, but then he asked, "Where'd the snakes come from?"

"Nobody knows. It's a mystery. The whole thing's a mystery. TV's been here, all sorts of people. It's going to put this town on the map. No way it's not going to be on CNN with that Wolf Biter, or whatever his name is."

"Blitzer," said Hartmann. "That a real picture up there, that Brewster picture?"

"The watercolor thing? No way. I had a contest to see who could paint the best old-fashioned picture of the guy they named the town for. The winner got five pounds of coffee of his choice. A kid from the high school won. It looks like George Washington, don't you think?"

"Was that his name? Wrestling?"

"That's right, Wrestling Brewster. He spent his life wrestling with the Devil."

"Doesn't look like he won," said Hartmann.

"He was eaten by a pack of wolves. They had wolves in those days."

During their conversation, the woman poured Hartmann his coffee and put the bagel in the toaster oven. "I'll bring your bagel over in a jiff. There's a newspaper, but it doesn't have anything about the snakes. I mean, it just happened."

Hartmann gingerly walked to the table; the wrong step sent a jagged lightning bolt through his lower back. He wondered how he had thrown it out. Maybe it was bad dreams about the twins, about street gangs in LA where they lived; heavy traffic. As he sipped his coffee, he looked out at the street. In the course of a minute, three police cruisers drove by in one direction and two drove by in the other. He guessed this snake business was something after all. He wasn't sure how he felt about it. If the person he was supposed to meet was trying to keep his business secret, then a town full of cops might put a scare into him.

The woman brought his bagel. "You look like you're walking on eggshells. It must be the weather. My mom says her bones tell her when a storm's coming."

Hartmann turned awkwardly. "It was the bed at the motel. I slept on it wrong, that's all."

"I never visit motels myself. They wash the sheets but not the bedspreads. Bodily fluids soak into them. Anyway, you should go upstairs. They got lots of ways to fix it."

"Beg pardon?"

"You-You, they'll take care of it."

Hartmann thought the pain kept him from hearing correctly. "I'm not following you."

"You're not from around here? The You Within You. They got classes all day long. It's an alternative place. They got a bunch of different massage people. Like a supermarket, I mean, you just pick the one that suits you best. You-You, get it?"

"Got it. Maybe I'll give them a try." It wouldn't do any harm, he thought.

"I've got friends that swear by it. Me, I got a back like a horse."

Moments later the woman was again talking to her friend. Hartmann had had massages in the past, though not for a while. He didn't dislike them, but neither was he a fan. They were intimate yet formal at the same time. Not like a dentist, who was purely formal. He knew he should think of it like seeing a dentist, but a massage had a faintly erotic element that was undentistlike. On the other hand, his back was killing him and he had a few hours to spare. Anything was better than being in pain all day.

Hartmann knew nothing about the different types of massage, so when he climbed the stairs to the You-You desk and the young man asked what sort of massage he wanted, Hartmann said, "I don't know, something like a health club massage. I pulled my back."

"I don't believe we have that sort of massage. Is it Swedish?"

As an insurance investigator, Hartmann had met lots of unpleasant people and he had learned to deal with them without animus, or at least without revealing his feelings. This young fellow had nothing wrong with him except he belonged to a world that Hartmann knew nothing about and he saw Hartmann as belonging to a world he had escaped. He was thin, thirty, fit, with a monkish appearance. From another room came the grunts and thumps of an exercise class.

Hartmann rubbed the back of his head and grinned. "I'll take whatever makes me feel better. Something conservative. Never mind the hot stones." Hartmann had noticed a flyer advertising stone massage, as well as shiatsu, reflexology massage, hilot massage, and ayurvedic massage. Other flyers announced classes in yoga and a number of offerings that made no sense to him, such as myofascial release, and some that made sense but which he didn't understand, like aromatherapy. Hartmann wasn't judgmental, but neither was he an easy believer. Toward everything he took a wait-and-see approach.

"Then we'll make it Swedish. I'll see who's available." The young man got busy on his iPhone.

Ten minutes later Hartmann was naked except for his shorts and a towel around his waist. His clothes were folded on a chair, as he waited in a small room painted in various pastels with posters of peaceful landscapes mostly indicative of spring and early mornings, nothing in black and white, nothing moody like Ansel Adams.

A young man entered who looked rather like the man at the front desk except he was blond. "Hi. I'm Gabe. May I call you Ernie?"

"No," said Hartmann. "I'd prefer Ernest, if anything."

"And are you earnest?" Gabe laughed. Hanging around his neck and across his red T-shirt was a gold chain with a circular red medallion of a serpent with its tail in its mouth. "I take it you're a virgin?"

Hartmann had been looking at the snake. "I beg your pardon?"

"This is your first time at You-You?"

"Right."

"Should I concentrate on the back, or do you want the full treatment?"

By now Hartmann was on his belly on the table, with his head in the horseshoe-shaped support, staring down at the tile floor. "It's the back that's bothering me."

"You seem pretty tense."

"Maybe it's because I'm a virgin."

They both laughed.

"Just the back," said Hartmann. "Maybe the shoulders if there's time."

Gabe put his hands on Hartmann's lower back; he winced.

"Touchy, touchy. Just relax. You've got nice hair. Do girls ever tell you that?"

"Not for a while."

"You do anything to it?"

Hartmann winced again. The back felt worse, not better. "I wash it and brush it. The rest is genetic."

"What are you, in your forties? You don't even have any gray."

Why's he asking about my hair? thought Hartmann. He decided to change the subject. "What's that red snake you've got around your neck?"

"Ouroboros, the snake with its tail in its mouth. It's the symbol of cyclicality and the Eternal Return," said Gabe, settling into his subject. "Everything repeats itself. What we're doing now we've done countless times before and we'll do countless times in the future. If matter is finite and time is infinite, then events have to repeat themselves. It's only logical. No telling how many times I've given you a massage. More than once, that's for sure."

"Just as long as your prices don't go up." Hartmann thought he should have guessed the snake meant something like that. He couldn't imagine having such ideas.

"Ouroboros is one of our oldest symbols. Many people think that when the first travelers left Africa seventy thousand years ago, they brought this symbol with them. You see, this isn't a European snake. It's huge; it's African."

Hartmann made a noncommittal grunt.

Gabe had stopped working on Hartmann's back; now he started again and again Hartmann winced. "Just relax," Gabe repeated. "You know what it means to 'go with the flow'? You gotta focus on it, think of it as the center of a bull's-eye."

After a moment, Hartmann asked, "So what does this snake do for you?" The man's hands were warm as he kneaded the small of Hartmann's back with long, firm strokes.

"It reminds me of beginnings and endings, where I've come from and where I'm going. It reminds me that everything I think's real is in fact an illusion, an illusion that occurs again and again through time—just like that movie *The Matrix* but different. Have you ever wondered where we'd be if it weren't for the snake in the Garden of Eden?"

"I've never given much thought to it."

"We'd still be in the garden, but we wouldn't know anything. We'd be ignorant. No, we'd be stupid. Have you thought how it'd be without knowledge?"

"No newspapers."

Gabe pushed down sharply and Hartmann grunted. "You're a funny guy, aren't you." It wasn't a question.

Hartmann apologized. "I don't mean to be disrespectful. We've all got to believe in something, right?"

"It's not that I just believe in snakes. I respect them."

"But you believe in Ouroboros." Hartmann wondered if Gabe knew about the business at the hospital.

"I don't *believe* in some big snake with its tail in its mouth. It's a symbol. I believe in what it symbolizes. Are you Catholic?"

"I was raised Catholic." Hartmann hadn't been in a church for twenty years except for weddings and funerals.

"Me, too, but then I moved on."

Hartmann realized his back had begun to feel better.

"Right now," said Gabe, "I'm a pantheist. Everything's part of the supreme being—you, this table, your shoes, me, everything. It's all energy and it repeats and repeats. It seems like many things all mixed up, but it's just one thing."

"Like Ouroboros."

"Exactly."

"As long as it makes you happy," said Hartmann diplomatically. What he didn't understand was why people made things so complicated. Even if you tried to keep things simple, they got complicated all by themselves. So why start with them already complicated? Then you had a mess.

In ten more minutes, Hartmann's fifty minutes were up. Gabe slapped him lightly on his rump. "There, that should do you for a while."

Hartmann got off the table. He definitely felt better. He'd paid at the front desk, but he wondered if he should give Gabe a tip. He reached for his clothes to get his wallet. Something fell from his pocket, clinked on the floor, and rolled. It was the brass coin the man had given him in Boston with a five-pointed star on one side and a goat standing on its hind legs on the other.

Gabe reached under a chair, picked it up, and looked at it. "Wow, where'd you get this? It's neat. Is it your good-luck coin?"

"Someone gave it to me yesterday." Hartmann reached out for it.

Gabe looked at the coin for a moment and gave it back. "And it's got those funny letters. Like ancient. This is really weird. D'you know what it means?"

Hartmann put the coin back in his pocket and continued getting dressed. "I've no idea. Some mystical stuff, most likely."

"That goat standing on its hind legs, that's the horned god. It's what later became the Devil. It's an image of Satan."

Hartmann finished tying his shoes. He was tired of these subjects and wanted to get busy. "It probably comes from Africa, too. Right?"

Gabe didn't hear the sarcasm. "Most likely. All this stuff's really old. Pan was a horned god, and he's one of the oldest gods we know—god of forests and trees. When we knock on wood we're asking for Pan's protection. We've been doing that for ten thousand years, at least."

Hartmann decided to forget the tip. He stretched out his hand. "Thanks for your hard work, Gabe. You've done me a world of good."

That morning another state police detective was assigned to the case—Bobby Anderson, an African American. "Hey, I'm their token black guy," he might say to someone he was questioning. It was disarming and made the other person—if he was white—more forthcoming just to show he was okay with black guys. White-guilt shit. "Can you say you're the token white guy?" Bobby Anderson would ask Woody. "You ain't token nothin', you the fuckin' *National Trust.*" And if Woody invited Bobby to go fishing on his boat, Bobby would say, "Fishin'! I'm the fried chicken and watermelon man. I don't look at no fish unless it's catfish. You goin' to promise me catfish? Shit, you know colored folks can't swim."

"Give me a break," Woody might say. "You spent six years in the marine unit. You're dive certified, for crying out loud."

Woody considered Bobby Anderson his best friend, but he didn't know what Bobby kept hidden behind the jive mask. He knew that whoever was back there was a careful observer, but he didn't know the reason for the jive; or rather, he could see how it worked when Bobby was on a case, but he didn't see why he used it with friends. It created an impression of breezy fellowship, but actually it was a distancing device, letting Bobby stay hidden while the person he talked to grew more open. Maybe it was no more than a bad habit, or maybe he wanted to keep the barrier up. But why that might be the case, Woody couldn't tell.

It was Bobby who got the call that morning from acting chief Bonaldo about the kid reporting his snake being stolen. Presumably Bonaldo could have sent his own men to the kid's house, but he wanted to diversify the responsibility to decrease the chance of messing up and getting criticized. Bobby said he'd meet him in fifteen minutes.

Bobby drove his own car, a magnetic black Nissan 370Z coupe with a rear deck spoiler. He wore a medium gray sharkskin suit, a charcoal-gray silk shirt, and a red silk tie. He looked good; he knew he looked good. He couldn't imagine being an undercover cop. His whole purpose in life was to be out in the open. And if a number of troopers disliked how he made a show of himself, they also knew he was better at his job than most of the rest. He was a very dark black man with a shaved head and teeth so white they seemed lit from inside.

When Bobby downshifted and drew to a stop in front of Carl Krause's bungalow, acting chief Bonaldo wondered if he'd made a mistake. He had meant to make a casual call—no point in riling up the street. With Bobby's rumbling muffler and slight screech of tires, Bonaldo saw curtains twitch in a few surrounding houses.

Hercel McGarty Jr., who was missing school after having reported the apparent theft of his corn snake, knew right away that somebody important had arrived, and what he wanted was a ride in that car. Even sitting in it would be cool.

Bobby was out of the coupe and standing on the walk next to Bonaldo before the acting chief had quite prepared himself. Already he felt rushed.

"Chief Bonaldo? Detective Anderson, you can call me Bobby." He stuck out his hand. "Hey, kid, that your green mountain bike? Very nice."

Hercel stood a little straighter and grinned.

It's a sunny morning in late October; the leaves of the maples are falling two by two. The retired guy across the street rakes his lawn. A yellow delivery truck slowly passes as the driver seeks an address. The two yappy dogs in the house next door express their disapproval of the group on the sidewalk. They spend all day looking out the window, looking for a chance to be indignant. A neighbor drives by in a small SUV, recognizes Bonaldo, considers tooting his horn and doesn't.

Bobby's full of energy, taps his foot, shifts from leg to leg, moves his hands, glances around. He looks like a single guy with a full dance card who leaves behind a trail of broken hearts. In fact, he's been married fifteen years and has two daughters. His wife, Shawna, is a radiologist at South County Hospital in Wakefield, and his daughters Rainey and Bessie are twelve and fourteen years old.

Then there's Fred Bonaldo; we haven't said much about him. He's four inches taller than Bobby and almost twice the weight. If you thought his red face suggested a cholesterol problem, you'd be correct. He's descended from Italian immigrants who moved into Washington County in the late nineteenth century to work the granite quarries. Local granite went into buildings from Boston to Washington, D.C. The grandfather worked in the quarries, the father had a grocery store, and the son, after time in the army, got into real estate, and other things, like uniforms. Fred Bonaldo loves uniforms.

He developed this taste as a Cub Scout, then it grew as a Boy Scout and fattened in high school in the Civil Air Patrol. In the army, he spent two years in the military police. Later he spent time with a volunteer ambulance squad and in a volunteer fire department, whose uniforms came out in parades—Memorial Day, the Fourth of July, Labor Day, Columbus Day, Thanksgiving, because almost as much as uniforms, Fred Bonaldo loves parades. Being a Master Mason, Scottish Rite, Thirteenth degree Master of the Ninth Arch, has allowed him to participate in even more parades while wearing a wide variety of regalia, fezzes and aprons accumulated over years of service. Stated plainly, it might be hard to imagine Bonaldo's passion for uniforms and parades, but they make his heart beat fast. He tells himself that it's the work he likes; actually it's what he wears to work. "You don't wear clothes, you wear costumes," his father said, when Freddie was seven and playing Superman with a cape made from an old blanket. And that was right.

Brewster's former police chief, John MacDonald, died of a stroke last March, and Fred Bonaldo used his Masonic and non-Masonic connections on the town council and police department to put himself forward. His time in the military police, his training as a volunteer ambulance attendant and fireman, the two courses he's taken in public safety at URI, even being a Mason, more than qualified him, he felt sure, to be chief. The pay was low, the applications few, and Bonaldo was named acting chief over the protests of many in the department. Fred Bonaldo's wife, Laura, also felt sure he deserved to be chief, and she had marshaled her friends and customers—she owns a baby boutique—to lobby for his appointment. Even so, the protests have kept up, and so Fred has remained acting chief until the whole business can be sorted out—that is, until he's made a real chief or is kicked out without offending a certain portion of the population, which means a large group who have known one another since grade school.

What's significant at the moment is that Fred Bonaldo knows this business with the snake and missing infant will either make him or break him, and he's terrified. His hope is that Bobby Anderson and Woody will help him in this matter, since most of the department's officers want him to disappear like a dime down a well.

Standing with Bobby and Hercel, acting chief Bonaldo keeps putting his hands in his pockets and taking them out again; and as he turns the sun reflects off his glasses, first exaggerating his dark brown eyes and then creating gleaming silver medallions. He knows Carl Krause, knows the trouble he can cause, and he wishes he was standing outside any house but this one.

As for Hercel Jr., he's glad not to be in school and he's glad his snake was stolen instead of just escaping again, because what a corn snake does best is escape and what it does second-best is slither into people's houses, and that has created a certain amount of fuss, which, considering the snake is totally harmless, is silly. But, as one woman said, when she reaches under her sink for the Clorox what she doesn't expect to find is a big snake. His stepdad, Mr. Krause, also hates the snake, but he hates the neighbors worse, and Hercel bets his stepdad has even freed the snake in the past so it can frighten people. In fact, this morning when he saw the snake was gone he suspected his stepdad of letting it go, but then he had seen the broken lock on the basement door. As to why his stepdad might want to frighten people, Hercel puts it down to meanness.

"So, Hercel," said Bobby, "what do people call you? D'you have a nickname?"

"They call me Hercel. My dad says it's short for Hercules, so it's already a nickname. His name's Hercel, too. He lives in Oklahoma. He says I'm probably the only Hercel in Washington County."

Bobby looked at Hercel thoughtfully, feeling he had just learned quite a bit about the boy. "I expect that's true. So you like snakes, right?"

"Not as much as I used to. They can be a nuisance."

Bonaldo made a "hrumph" noise to indicate he could say a lot about snakes being a nuisance if asked.

Bobby told the boy to show him what he'd seen that morning, and Hercel led him up the driveway. The yapping dogs next door resumed their racket. The bungalow was set on a slight incline so the basement door opened directly onto the backyard. On the concrete step in front of the door were splinters of wood and on the area around the lock were marks indicating the door had been forced with a pry bar. It was a simple lock and wouldn't need much forcing.

"You going to take fingerprints?" asked Hercel.

"Not right now." Bobby hadn't thought of it. "Show me where you keep the snake."

"You want to go inside?" asked Hercel.

"If that's what it takes."

Hercel hesitated. Mr. Krause hated to have people in the house, it made him angry and suspicious. It wasn't good when he got angry. But maybe Mr. Krause had gone out or maybe he was still up on the second floor and wouldn't hear them.

"Come on, boy," said Bonaldo. "We don't have all day."

Hercel led them into the basement.

On a table against the wall was a cage about five feet by four feet by four feet with branches, a shallow bowl of water, and cedar shavings. The top lifted up, and a latch kept it secure. The wire mesh had been patched in a few places, presumably where the snake had gotten out in the past. Also on the table were six bricks with which Hercel weighted down the top. On a nearby table, Bobby saw a smaller cage with a dozen mice.

"You feed those mice to the snake?"

"Not really."

Bobby lifted the lid of the snake cage. "What you mean 'not really'?"

"I raise these mice and I take them to the pet store and trade them for other mice. Stranger mice."

"What makes you think he doesn't give your own mice back to you?"

"It's a woman, and I don't think she'd do that."

"But you're not positive?"

"Pretty positive."

"Aren't you going to take pictures or anything?" asked Bonaldo.

"I'll give the crime scene unit a call."

A step was heard on the stairs and a voice shouted, "Put up your hands or I'll shoot!"

Bobby saw a nervous-looking man pointing a shotgun at him. He had always felt that if he were killed as a trooper it would be in a situation like this rather than by somebody on the highway. He took a deep breath. "My name's Robert Anderson, I'm a state police detective. This is Fred Bonaldo, Brewster police chief. Your son's snake was stolen; he's been showing us. I didn't know you were home. Why don't you put down that shotgun so I can show you my ID?" Bobby spoke calmly, but he didn't feel calm. The man on the stairs was over six feet and heavyset, with disheveled hair. He wore a stained T-shirt and jeans, and didn't look sane.

"The fuck you say. You expect me to believe the police chief and a trooper detective are going to hunt for a kid's missing snake? Keep your hands up!"

Hercel tugged on the pocket of Bobby's sharkskin jacket. "He's not my dad; he's Mr. Krause. He married my mom."

FOUR

DR. JOYCE FULLER JABBED a pencil at a yellow Post-it pad with the words *Have a nice day!* printed at the bottom. She jabbed till the black dots became a black blob, jabbed until the pencil broke. She was an attractive woman of the seamless variety, as if made from standardized parts, as if her hair, makeup, hands, feet, and sculpted aerodynamic figure spent the night in separate boxes rather than being joined together in bed. She was forty-three years old and had been head of Morgan Memorial for two years. Now her career was over.

Until early this morning she had done well. The hospital had an inadequate budget, and she economized where she could. Unluckily, one of her economies had been her decision not to purchase an infant protection system, the small tags attached to an infant's ankle that gave warning if the infant was taken from the unit. Providence and Boston hospitals had them, but Brewster had a fraction of their births, about eighty a year. That seemed too few to justify the expense. Local crime was almost nonexistent, except during the summer months, and other items had seemed more necessary. But that was yesterday. Since then the unthinkable had happened. Now it was eight-thirty Thursday morning and she had just put in a call to a company that sold such devices: locking the barn door after the horse had been stolen, people would say. And they'd be right.

She would resign, of course; or perhaps she could just offer to resign. Even so, the board of trustees would want her resignation. Surely her very presence would lead people to seek out other hospitals. An expectant mother would be an idiot to have her baby in Brewster after what'd happened, though given the new protection devices and heightened security, Morgan Memorial would be the safest hospital in the state.

Joyce Fuller had spent ten years in college and graduate schools for advanced degrees in business and hospital administration. She could have earned a degree in medicine, but she had wanted to run a hospital instead of being attached to one. What could she do with those degrees now? No other hospital would hire her with this tragedy on her record. Perhaps a job in a pharmaceutical company or a medical supply company; even teaching was possible—but she wanted none of those.

Normally two nurses were in the nursery at that hour, but one called in sick late yesterday, and that left Alice Alessio. Laboratory, service, and maintenance staff came on at four, with additional medical staff arriving soon after. So Alice would have been alone for only four hours. Indeed, Tabby Roberts, the nurse supervisor, had called yesterday afternoon to alert her to this problem and ask for advice. Instead of saying that someone else must be found, Dr. Fuller had said, "I'm sure it will be all right."

She even wondered, and she knew this was inexcusable, if she could predate her order for an infant protection system to last week so it would seem she was attempting to solve a problem before it became too late. She almost said something to the salesman on the phone—a promise to buy his device rather than another—but then she had bit her tongue. Better to be a fool than a fool and a criminal.

It was possible, according to Reggie Adams, chairman of the board of trustees, that litigation would result. It all depended on Peggy Summers. Reggie had said he would get on the phone with the hospital's lawyers right away. So it occurred to Dr. Fuller that she would not only lose her job, she might be sued as well.

What had the state police detective asked her? Who else knew? At first she had thought only three or four people knew Alice would be alone. But those few could have told others, and those others still more. "So," Woody Potter had said, "it could be fifty people." Of course she doubted that, but the detective made his point.

But for a month or two her job was secure. As Reggie had explained, to let her go right now would be an admission of guilt on the hospital's part. "But I *am* guilty," Joyce answered. Yes, but to admit it would be to invite a lawsuit. "We'd just be begging for trouble," Reggie said.

So she sat, jabbing a pencil at a pad as she waited for one more person—several had come already—to arrive with an expression ranging from disappointment to anger while she tried to placate and to some extent explain. Wouldn't putting a bullet in her head be better? Her father, an old military man, would have had no doubt about that. No hanging or car exhaust or pills for him; he'd use his service pistol, which, he had often told her, had served him well in the Pacific. But now, fortunately or not, he was gone and the pistol had been sold. So, for her, hanging, car exhaust, or pills were still options. Or she could drive to the beach and walk into the surf. She saw herself walking into the water as if in a movie and thought how cold it would be, going deeper until her head slipped under. How crudely melodramatic. Couldn't she do something? Couldn't she find a lesser penance than death?

First of all, she would talk to Alice and learn where she'd been during that fatal time, since she didn't believe that nonsense about Alice's period. What had she been up to? And didn't her nickname of Nurse Spandex suggest a range of questionable activities? Surely following these lines of inquiry was better than doing nothing.

Jimmy Mooney and Seymour Hodges had been up twenty-eight hours straight except for catnaps in the ambulance, which, for Jimmy, meant almost no sleep at all because Seymour kept screaming in his sleep. When Jimmy asked, "What the fuck you screaming about, Seymour?" Seymour would say, "Just stuff" or "You don't want to know." Twice he had screamed, "Get down, get down!" and twice more he had screamed, "He's burning!" What Jimmy knew for certain was that Seymour wasn't screaming about anything nice. Actually, Jimmy would like to hear a nasty story or two, and so he kept asking, "What're you screaming about, dude?" And Seymour would say, "Fucking stuff, man. Death and damnation." It made Jimmy glad he hadn't joined the National Guard after all.

Earlier, Jimmy had picked up a stiff at Ocean Breezes, the old folks' home, and took it to Digger Brantley, third-generation owner of Brantley's Funeral Home on the Hannaquit end of Water Street. Of course, his real name wasn't Digger, but Jimmy couldn't recall his real name, but it was Hamilton and those close to him called him Ham.

Picking up stiffs for Digger was the second of Jimmy's jobs. He called himself a first-call driver, though few in town knew what he meant, and sometimes he used the ambulance and sometimes he used Digger's white Chevy van: sliding the stiff into a black body bag and hitting the road. Or he might get a call to take a stiff up to the state medical examiner in Providence, or the medical examiner might call him to pick up a stiff and take it to Brewster. Mostly Seymour did the driving and Jimmy paid him from the money he got from Digger.

Jimmy did other work for Digger Brantley, such as being a pallbearer, driving a hearse, opening and closing doors for grieving widows, and helping Larry out at the Burn Palace. Jimmy did this not so much because he enjoyed it or because the pay was good, but for possible advancement. Digger was in his mid-forties and had no kids. But he and his wife, Jenny, were too lovey-dovey, as far as Jimmy was concerned. As he said to Seymour, "Old people fucking, it makes me queasy, like thinking of your folks fucking. Gray flesh, know what I mean?"

Jimmy had told Digger he was looking for a more serious job and had signed up to take a class in restorative art at a two-year college in Connecticut. Digger said if Jimmy passed the class he would take him on as an embalming intern. Jimmy was twenty-three years old and not getting any younger. He wanted to move up from transporting stiffs to packing them into the ground or even the fire, if that's what was called for.

Right now, Jimmy was telling Seymour about a woman he had helped embalm two days before. "A heart attack at forty, how do you like that? Arteries so packed with shit that Digger had to use those little needles they pump the juice into dead babies with. Digger said it was like squirting toothpaste through a syringe. You run into all kinds of dead people at funeral homes."

Seymour didn't respond; then he said, "You hear those coyotes last night?" He pronounced coyotes as a two-syllable word.

"When was that?"

"Shit, man, they were running all around the rig when we were parked at the hospital, yapping and clicking their teeth. I didn't know why until I heard about the stolen baby. That's what they were after.

They wanted to get that baby and sink their teeth in it. That's what they like. Soft stuff."

"The fuck you say. I didn't hear any coyotes." Seymour fired up the giggle weed every chance he got, so Jimmy figured he'd been stoned. Most days the rig reeked of it, and Jimmy had to keep the air conditioner blowing just to avoid a severe contact high. Jimmy never smoked himself. It made him paranoid.

"You were asleep. They were here right before the cops showed up. It wasn't a loud yapping. It was more like whispering."

"You were stoned."

"No, man. I might've been stoned, but those coyotes are always around. Every time we pick up a stiff I hear them. I mean at night. They're hanging around looking for meat."

It was bullshit, as far as Jimmy was concerned. Seymour hardly ever noticed anything, but when he did it was always something weird. He'd say, "Hey, d'you see that crow with a cigar in its mouth?" Not that Jimmy hadn't seen coyotes in town, but mostly he'd seen them near Burlingame or Great Swamp. Recently, he had rounded a corner late at night and there'd been a bunch in the road. They scattered when he'd hit the gas, but not right away. They had looked at him first with their eyes red in the headlights.

"At night in Iraq there were always dogs barking," said Seymour. "You'd be on patrol and hear them going at it. You just knew they were feeding on the bodies. Or a bomb would go off and there'd be body parts scattered all over and these dogs would be barking. They'd hear a bomb and it was like hearing the dinner bell."

After Ernest Hartmann finished his massage, he returned to the Brewster Brew. He was waiting for a phone call and he'd might as well be there as anyplace else. He bought the *Globe*, got another cup of coffee and a bagel, and settled down to wait. Now that baseball season was over the *Globe* wasn't as interesting. There was some trade talk and some guys were getting surgery, but that was about it. Hartmann had played high school ball in Worcester. It made him feel closer to the guys in the big leagues.

"How was the massage?" asked Jean, as she set another pumpernickel-raisin bagel before him.

Hartmann tentatively turned back and forth in his chair. "Seems to have done the trick, or pretty much. I had my doubts at first."

"How come?"

"The guy was a little flaky. He had this medallion of a snake with its tail in its mouth. Kind of a religious thing. He asked me where we'd be without the snake in the Garden of Eden. I couldn't quite follow it, what with the poking and prodding, but he thought we'd be worse off."

"They seem like nice people. They come in here often, though they're not big coffee drinkers. I had to order chai."

"What's that, a kind of tea?"

"A kind of sweet tea. It has spices."

Hartmann made a face. "Most people are nice people until you scratch the surface, then you find only some of them are nice people."

A young couple came in and Jean went to take their order, though she'd have preferred to talk about snakes with the man in the Hawaiian shirt. That's how she recalled him to herself: the man in the Hawaiian shirt. Snakes were a big subject with clients that morning. She thought of her customers as clients—her coffee clients. In fact, she had been worried that snakes being loose would scare them off until a policeman told her there'd been only one. As for where we'd be if it weren't for the snake in the Garden of Eden, she knew where her husband, Frankie, would be. He'd be licking his balls.

Jean was busier than usual till lunchtime. It was that baby that did it. People wanted to talk about it. They wanted to go to a public place and exchange their views. Like it seemed a sure thing the head of the hospital would be canned. Other people also. The story had been on TV, even in Boston. A girlfriend in Dorchester called to ask how she liked being at the center of the universe. "You're really on the hot seat down there," her friend had said, and Jean had said it wasn't so bad.

But why steal a baby? Maybe some poor mother who'd had a miscarriage and lost her baby got her wires crossed and decided to steal one. Adoption wasn't so easy, what with the abortion clinics. The young sluts got knocked up and had the baby scraped out. Then the pieces were sent to a laboratory for research. She'd read about it in a magazine. And somebody said there was a good market for stolen babies, especially white ones and especially boys with blue eyes. Though, if truth be told, any kid of Peggy's wasn't going to be college material. Even high school might be too much. One man said some people even *eat* babies, because they're soft and plump. Jean had been totally disgusted, and when she spilled the man's chai and a few drops ran into his lap it hadn't been an accident. He'd known it, too, because he'd given her a look. But she'd looked right back. Oh, there seemed to be lots of things you could do with stolen babies, and none of it was nice.

After that, Jean stopped talking to strangers about the stolen baby, because if a person had something nasty to say they took real pleasure in saying it.

It was five minutes to twelve when the man in the Hawaiian shirt got a phone call. Jean was exact about the time because she'd just looked at her watch. Ginger Phelps showed up and stayed an hour so Jean could rush home for a bite to eat and to feed the cats. So Jean had looked at her watch to see how soon she was coming. Ginger worked half-time at the library down the street but didn't need to be there till one o'clock.

The man's cell phone rang and he took the call. Jean was curious about him because he wasn't from around here and she thought he might be a reporter doing a story on the snake and stolen baby, which is why he pretended not to know anything about it. If he wrote a story for a big paper like the *Globe,* she hoped he'd say something nice about the Brewster Brew.

Mostly the man in the Hawaiian shirt just said, "Yeah-okay," but then he said, and Jean was positive about this, "Why all the way out there?" Then he went back to saying, "Yeah-okay," and then he said, "Why does it have to be so late?" Then there was more "Yeah-okay," and then he said, "You should've told me that before. I'll be stuck here all afternoon." He glanced at Jean and rolled his eyes. After that he lowered his voice and said something Jean couldn't hear. Then he hung up and Jean watched his face. First he looked worried, then he looked uncertain, and then he chewed his lower lip. When he saw Jean was still watching he said, "The wife," which she knew was a lie. Then he took his paper and left. That was the last she saw of him.

Bobby Anderson had large square fingernails, very pale and almost lemony. He studied them speculatively as he counted to five. Across the desk in an interview room sat Carl Krause, with his hands cuffed behind him. Bobby was trying to keep himself from slapping Carl upside the head, and he was already in a little trouble about something like that.

Bobby was pissed that Carl had scared him with the shotgun. Of course, once Carl hadn't fired, Bobby could argue with him—yell at him, was more like it. Like did Carl know the mountain of shit he'd be in if he shot a state trooper and a police chief, even an acting police chief? To say nothing of Hercel, who'd probably be hurt as well. Every cop in New England would come down on him like ten freight trains. They'd flay him alive. And if he resisted? They wouldn't shoot to kill.

These guys were top marksmen. They'd nibble him like a mouse nibbles a piece of cheese until there wouldn't be enough left of Carl to pack into a wet sock. Bobby said all this at the top of his lungs as Carl reconsidered. And as Bobby was shouting, he'd edged his way forward until, when Carl had lowered his head to partake of a thoughtful moment, Bobby grabbed the shotgun and whapped him upside the head with it.

"You didn't have to hit him so hard," acting chief Bonaldo had said.

"The fuck I didn't." Bobby glanced at the boy and realized that Hercel agreed, which said a lot about Hercel's relationship with his stepfather.

That was less than an hour ago, and now Carl was sitting on the other side of the desk. His stained T-shirt was torn and there was a red bruise on his cheek. For a relatively young man—his late thirties—Carl's face was severely lined, but they weren't age lines so much as creases that looked darker because he was unshaven, like a person might get from sleeping on his pillow wrong. Except in Carl's case they were permanent. And he had a cold look about him. He looked like he wanted that moment when he'd decided not to kill Bobby and acting chief Bonaldo back again, because now, given the chance, he'd waste them.

The trouble was Bobby didn't see how he could keep Carl locked up except for twenty-four hours. Sure, he'd threatened to blow their heads off, but a lawyer could argue that Carl had lowered his weapon once he learned the two men were peace officers. If he booked Carl, it would never go to court. Bobby would just be wasting people's time. On the other hand, Carl had wanted to kill him. Bobby had had plenty of angry men, even angry women, stare at him with murder in their eyes. But Carl was different. He stared at Bobby with a smile, and Bobby knew that he believed a time would come when he'd get even.

"Why do you make your son call you Mr. Krause?"

"He's not my son; he's my stepson."

"That doesn't answer my question."

"It's a matter of respect."

"D'you beat him?"

"You better ask him about that."

"He's afraid of you." Then it occurred to Bobby that Hercel wasn't afraid for himself but for someone else, maybe his mother or sister; or maybe he was afraid he wouldn't be able to visit his father in Oklahoma.

"No boy likes to be corrected."

Carl talked to Bobby like he was ignorant, and Bobby didn't like that. "Somebody broke into your basement last night and stole that snake. I don't know what time it was. Presumably after Hercel had gone to sleep."

"I was up on the second floor. I didn't hear anything."

"Who knew the snake was in the basement?"

"Half the neighborhood. It was escaping all the time."

"Do you know Peggy Summers?"

"Not to speak to, but I know who she is. She's a slut."

"Why d'you say that?"

"People talk."

"Do they say who's father of her baby?"

"If they do, I haven't heard it."

"What about Alice Alessio?"

"Doesn't ring any bells."

"Nurse Spandex?"

"Her neither. Is that a real name, or are you trying to trick me?"

"I wouldn't trick you, Carl."

Bobby knew that Carl had worked for a plumber in town but had been fired. He'd also worked for a construction company and had been fired from that as well. The plumber said Carl had an attitude problem. The construction company said Carl had hit another man. And Bobby could imagine more problems before that, a whole lifetime of problems. He'd looked to see if Carl had a record, but there had only been some speeding tickets. Bobby also heard Carl could be charming, but if true then Bobby hadn't seen it. Now Carl worked on his own as a skilled handyman, mostly on houses down at the beach during the off-season, but also for some businesses in town. He didn't drink; given his temper, it was just as well.

Carl repositioned himself in his chair. The handcuffs probably hurt—Bobby had put them on tight—but he didn't complain. "You going to lock me up or let me go?"

Bobby figured Carl already knew the answer. He didn't like Carl's little smile, his smugness, like he knew a secret that Bobby could never guess. As sometimes happened, he wondered if Carl would act the same way if Bobby weren't a black man. It wasn't something he actually thought, but it wandered through his brain. He hated having it there.

"So tell me, Carl, where'd you go last night?"

"I didn't go anywhere; I was home the whole time."

"Can you prove it?"

"Ask my wife."

"How long have you been married?"

"Year 'n a half, about. What's that have to do with anything?"

"You're practically newlyweds. That's surprising, seeing your wife made you sleep upstairs."

"Who told you that?"

There was a tightening around Carl's eyes. He was furious, but he wouldn't show it; he wouldn't show anything. Bobby didn't answer the question, and Carl didn't ask again. He knew perfectly well who had told him. This worried Bobby. He liked Hercel and didn't want him hurt. For that matter, even if he'd disliked the boy, he wouldn't want him hurt.

"Where're you from originally, Carl?"

"What business is it of yours?"

"Just tell me."

"Oswego, north of Syracuse."

"I know Oswego," said Bobby. "Why'd you leave?"

"I got the itch."

"You got family there?"

"Nope."

"Your parents alive?"

"Nope. You going to write my biography or something?"

Bobby mildly hoped Carl might explode so he could yell like he'd yelled in the basement. But Carl wasn't playing. He was keeping the door shut on himself. Still, Bobby meant to contact the authorities in Oswego. He would be surprised if someone like Carl had gotten this far in life without leaving serious traces behind, like serious violence.

"Okay, Carl, I'll let you go. You want a ride back to your house?"

"I'll walk."

"I'd be glad to take you."

"I said I'll walk."

Bobby went behind him to unlock the handcuffs. As he freed him, there was a second when he thought Carl might grab him. Bobby stepped back a foot, but then stopped. *Jesus, I'm getting paranoid*. But he couldn't convince himself that he had been wrong.

Carl got to his feet and rubbed his wrists. He still had his smile, but it was larger. Bobby's desire to hit the man made him almost laugh. Here he had tried to get Carl to lose his temper and he was nearly losing his own.

"Okay, Carl, but I'm not convinced I should let you go. I'll be keeping my eye on you, so don't do anything foolish." Bobby wanted to warn Carl not to take anything out on his stepkids and not to take anything out on his wife. But there had been no complaints about child abuse, no domestic disturbance calls, so Bobby didn't mention it. In any case, Carl was almost out the door by the time Bobby finished his sentence.

Acting chief Bonaldo had a son—actually he had five children, two girls and three boys—but it's the youngest who concerns us here. He was ten years old and named after his great-grandfather, who had come to Brewster from the village of Bonaldo in northeastern Italy: sun-baked, pancake-flat agricultural land just south of the Dolomites. The great-grandfather's name was Baldassare Bonaldo, and this was the name that Fred wanted to honor. But because he had the sense not to burden a baby with a name like Baldassare, he was baptized with his great-grandfather's nickname: Baldo. Baldo Bonaldo.

Baldo resembled his father, rotund and plodding, with a similar red-faced, swollen look, though he was more than a foot shorter, didn't wear glasses, and had all his hair. He loved his father and at times he was proud that he appeared as a smaller version of the acting chief, but at other times he saw it as an unpleasant destiny. If Baldo ever wanted to know what he would look like at forty-five, the answer was right in front of him, waving his hands in time to his arguments, complaints, and desires. The father was a gesticulator; the son was a gesticulator.

Baldo was an intelligent kid but shy and uncomfortable with his shape. His two older brothers were athletic and fit, but Fred Bonaldo had never been athletic and fit, and Baldo knew he was destined to follow that path—a lifetime of dieting and bingeing. But he wasn't gloomy; he had inherited his mother's sense of humor. Unluckily, his liveliness led to a love of practical jokes, and these led to trouble. He liked to save his money and order from catalogs, although he might regret the consequences. The detonations from the remote-controlled fart machine had seriously angered members of his fifth-grade class, and the fart spray had been worse, while the farting doorbell had led his father to chase him down the street. These setbacks failed to slow him. There was the pull-my-finger Santa and the green plastic monster that leapt out when you raised the toilet seat. The talking dog collar, the giant radio-controlled ant, the animated striking snake, and the 3-D striped bass that appeared to be smashing through your windshield—this, for Baldo, was what life was all about, and it gained for him a certain caution on the part of others. A little itch powder down the pants of the fifth-grade bully Butchy Dunn had made Butchy furious, but the innocent-looking red lollipop that caused him to fart uncontrollably inspired real fear. The difficulty, as with most shy people, was Baldo wanted to be liked, but given his passion for practical jokes he was a difficult kid to hang out with. It took courage.

The boy Baldo wanted most as a friend was Hercel McGarty Jr., who, of anyone in fifth grade, was the most serious and had the least developed sense of humor. These are the tricks life plays. The mouse wants to hang out with the cat. Hercel didn't dislike Baldo, he just didn't see the point of him, which was how Hercel felt about quite a few things. For instance, it would be wrong to say he didn't have a sense of humor, but a whoopee cushion, even the electronic variety, didn't interest him. He saw no point in it, and the same could be said of a pie in the face. Sure, he had an imagination, but he pushed it aside. An imagination made it difficult to concentrate; he saw no point in it.

In September, Baldo had talked to Hercel at recess and told him he would like to be a vampire, though he'd wait until he grew up so he wouldn't be a kid-size vampire. Hercel found this a strange ambition. Baldo said he knew vampires were unpopular; they had bad breath, couldn't sleep at night, and had bad habits. But what Baldo liked was that vampires weren't shy. "Whoever heard of a shy vampire?" asked Baldo. Hercel looked at him and walked away.

Baldo liked Hercel's evenness of temper. He didn't put it in those words, though it was what he meant when he called Hercel cool. He was curious about Hercel. But Hercel wasn't curious about Baldo. On the other hand, Hercel was well mannered. Even if Baldo bothered him, he wouldn't knock him down. His father, Hercel Sr., had told him never to punch somebody who was weaker than he was, especially in the face.

Baldo also thought Hercel had something odd about him. He knew *odd* wasn't the right word, but he couldn't think of anything better. That's a problem with being ten: feelings and ideas are still being sorted into language. And Baldo was well spoken. Because he was shy and spent a lot of time by himself, he had done a fair amount of reading. It would be nice to say he read Charles Dickens and Emily Dickinson, but no, he had read a book on hypnotism for beginners, a book on invisibility and levitation, books by people who had been taken up by flying saucers, a book called *How to Flirt 101,* also a book called *Forbidden Science,* which explained how to harness energy from outer space and the true function of the Great Pyramid.

Baldo's curiosity about Hercel had increased since the start of the school year to the point that he had begun to follow him. Not all the time, but sometimes. Baldo told himself that something might happen to let him do Hercel a small service, like pushing him out of the way of a speeding car or saving him from drowning. Really, there's something pathetic about these uneven relationships.

Baldo knew nothing about Hercel's snake, nor did he know why Hercel had missed school that day. There was a bug going around, and quite a few kids had missed a day here or there. Baldo had even heard kids after school talking about snakes in the hospital, a whole truckload of snakes and one fat nurse had jumped out of a window and three patients had heart attacks and died. There was no talk of a missing baby. That would come later. But Baldo in his insistent way wanted to know if Hercel was all right. Maybe one of the snakes had bit him. Like many ten-year-olds, the line between reality and possibility was a shifting frontier.

Though it was still a week until daylight savings time, by five-thirty it was nearly dark. Clouds had moved in, and there would be rain in the night. About that time, Baldo was making his way toward the corner of Newport and Hope, to the bungalow where Hercel lived with his sister, Lucy, his mother, and his stepfather. He didn't quite imagine himself looking through the windows, but if he ambled by slowly enough Hercel might come out and they could exchange a word or two. He didn't know about Carl Krause and wouldn't recognize him if he saw him.

Hercel wasn't hanging around the windows waiting for Baldo to walk by. A light was on in the two-window gable above the front porch, the first floor was dark, and a light was on in the basement. Baldo stood across the street, shielded by an old maple, and considered his options. The yappy dogs in the house next door gave a sporadic bark, more a generalized warning than focused indignation, but it was enough for Baldo to think that if he were to approach the house, he should do it quickly. There was little or no traffic, and no people were wandering around. Folks ate dinner early in Brewster.

Baldo didn't choose to look through the basement window; rather, he just found himself going in that direction. He wore jeans and a dark sweatshirt and had black hair. Fred Bonaldo's hair had also been black before it fell out. Dreading what lay ahead, Baldo already knew that someday he'd be called Bald Baldo Bonaldo and Baldy Baldo. These realizations can lead to bitterness or a teeth-sucking homespun philosophy.

Moments later, Baldo lay on his stomach behind a bush, peeping through the basement window. The first thing he saw was the empty cage where the snake had been kept, though he didn't know it had contained a snake. A pet gerbil, Baldo thought. At that moment, the snake was in the Brewster Animal Shelter. It was evidence, but acting chief Bonaldo had yet to decide what kind of evidence. It might be a weapon; it might be a perpetrator; it might be a victim. This remained up in the air. Anyway, when Hercel told him he wanted his snake back, Fred Bonaldo said it couldn't be done.

Edging closer to see more of the basement room, Baldo discovered Hercel lying on the cement floor. His first thought was Hercel had been hurt, but his eyes were open and his face calm, apart from a look of intense concentration. Hercel lay on his stomach with his arms crooked in front of him and his chin resting on the backs of his hands. His legs were bent and his feet were raised toward the ceiling as his heels tapped each other in a thoughtful way. A foot in front of Hercel on the cement were three marbles. These were what he was staring at.

Well, this was a mystery, and it was with regret that Baldo realized Hercel didn't need his help. Still, Baldo lay quietly and watched, though the ground by the side of the house was cold and rather damp.

Then it moved, the marble in the middle moved. It moved about three inches and Hercel hadn't touched it. Baldo got the shivers, but he guessed that Hercel had blown a sharp blast of boy breath to send it rolling. But Hercel's mouth was shut and his cheeks weren't puffed out. Baldo thought he must be wrong. It hadn't moved after all. Even so, he watched more closely.

Next the marble on Hercel's left began to roll. Hercel's mouth remained shut. Could he be snorting through his nose? The marble rolled forward about six inches and stopped.

In Baldo's small library were several well-thumbed magic books. He could make coins disappear and then reappear in a person's ear. He knew three card tricks. He knew the rigid-rope trick and the cigarette-through-a-coin trick. He could turn water to wine, but don't drink it. But he couldn't make marbles move by themselves.

Now the marble on Hercel's right began to move. Hercel was focused and straining, and his face had turned pink just as if, Baldo thought, he was trying to free a large turd. The marble rolled forward, and then turned and clicked the marble in the middle. No way could Hercel make a marble move sideways by secret blowing. Baldo crawled forward until his nose was pressed to the glass.

Hercel again pursed his lips, and his face turned pink. His folded hands curled into fists. The marble in the middle moved. Then, slowly, it rose in the air. Shaking with inner vibration, it rose three inches, and then up to about five inches. It hung there briefly until Hercel gasped loud enough for Baldo to hear and the marble dropped to the floor.

Then, unhappily, a man began to shout, "Hey, kid, what the fuck you doing?" It was Carl Krause leaning over the side of the porch.

Baldo turned and glanced back through the basement window. At that moment Baldo's and Hercel's eyes met. But it was the briefest of moments, because in an instant Baldo leapt to his feet and broke through the bushes as he heard Carl's boots clomping down the front steps.

"You fuckin' brat, I know what you're up to!"

Baldo wasn't much of a runner, but circumstances can erase any shortcoming. He ran as he'd never run before as he heard Carl behind him. He never even glanced back, nor did he know how far Carl kept up the chase. Six blocks later, when Baldo dropped to the ground exhausted and no longer caring if the man killed him or not, he looked back and Carl was gone.

FIVE

IT WAS EIGHT O'CLOCK Thursday night and drizzling when Ernest Hartmann drove out of Brewster in his Ford Focus. He had a map as well as written directions, but the first part of the drive seemed simple enough. Beside him on the seat lay his Browning Hi-Power. He'd been unsure about bringing it but then grabbed it at the last moment. Thirteen rounds in the magazine and one in the chamber—nine-millimeter, the King of Nines, as his father had said. Better safe than sorry.

Hartmann took Route 1 to Perryville, and then turned north on Ministerial Road to South Kingstown. There were few lights. Most of the road led him through woods with scattered houses back among the trees, and then farms and a park and more houses around Tuckertown Four Corners, then back into the woods again. For a two-mile stretch he saw nothing but the shadows of trees till he passed Larkin Pond and reached South Kingstown, where there was an Amtrak station. A mile to the northeast lay the University of Rhode Island campus; less than a mile to the west was the entrance to Great Swamp. He had passed few cars, had seen no people. At one point three scruffy dogs dashed out of the trees and across the road. On further thought, Hartmann decided they were coyotes.

He was uncertain about what he was doing. It was unwise, perhaps illegal, and possibly dangerous. Balanced against these considerations were his twin girls, living in LA with his ex-wife. If he turned a good profit on this current venture, he could move there. The money would give him something to live on until he found a job. That was one good thing about being an insurance investigator—they were always in demand.

So whenever he thought he was making a mistake driving out to the swamp, it felt like he was rejecting his daughters, pushing them out of his life. Yet if it weren't for them, there was no way he'd be doing what he was doing now. If it was as illegal as it sounded, then just the fact he knew something about it could make him an accomplice and, if nothing else, he'd lose his job and his investigator's license.

As for why Hartmann had to come out to Great Swamp, well, it had to do with Indians, at least that's what he had been told. It had to do with Indian claims and Indian burials. It had to do with the Indians' detribalization by the state of Rhode Island in the 1880s and their loss of fifteen thousand acres of land. After a century of trying to get their land back, the tribe was given eighteen hundred acres thirty years ago. Bad feelings continued about this, but how it led to grave robbery Hartmann didn't know. Possibly Indians had raided white cemeteries placed on those fifteen thousand acres, or possibly whites had raided Indian graves. But it also had to do with casinos and the Indians' desire to have a casino in Rhode Island and the exertions of the Connecticut Indians—who had a huge casino across the border—to keep them from having one. But Harrah's Entertainment backed the Rhode Island Indians, and they carried a lot of clout.

Hartmann was interested in the insurance angle. The village of West

Kingston, and a number of other villages, formed the town of South Kingstown: eighty square miles and thirty thousand people. In addition, South Kingstown contained Great Swamp and part of the Indian land. Vandalized graves, uncertain responsibility, international conglomerates, angry townspeople, as well as swamp Yankees: fiercely independent rural poor whose roots in South Kingstown went back several hundred years—what lay ahead, it seemed to Hartmann, was litigation. If it were all as he'd been told, insurance companies would be eager to pay Hartmann for his services. But the story he had heard in Boston didn't entirely jibe with what he'd heard this morning. For instance, the fellow in Boston said nothing about the Indians building a casino.

Hartmann turned left onto Liberty Lane, drove past a row of small houses and farms, and then the road came to an end at the train tracks, and another road, a dirt road, turned left along the tracks and half a mile later passed a few buildings and garages, all dark except for several outside lights. Now the trees thickened, and in his headlights he saw bushes of mountain laurel. Soon he passed a parking area and a raised barrier; the road narrowed to little more than a single track. Did he wonder why the barrier had been raised? He hardly noticed it.

Yet as he proceeded and the road grew narrower and bumpier, his doubts grew larger. He'd been told to drive to the old hangar on Worden Pond, still two miles ahead. But after going no more than a quarter of a mile, he slowed to a stop. He could easily bust an axle on one of these holes, and, of course, the Ford Focus didn't have four-wheel drive. Looking for a place to turn around, he saw nothing suitable. Trees, laurel bushes, and swamp blocked his way. Setting the pistol in his lap, he put the car in reverse and peered out the back; then he rolled down his window. The air was thick with the smell of wet, rotting leaves. Twice he nearly went off into the thick mud of the swamp. He moved at hardly more than a crawl, but his increasing fear caused him to speed up and then abruptly brake as he veered toward the mud.

After five minutes, he dimly made out the parking area. Something was wrong; the barrier was down. He slowed again and backed within a foot of the metal bar. Taking his pistol, he began to get out of the Ford. Then he saw someone walking toward him from the parking area. His heart took a leap until he realized the man was wearing a uniform. Presumably he was a park ranger and he'd been the one to lower the barrier.

The man held a flashlight, and the glare made it difficult for Hartmann to see as the man approached his door.

"I'm lucky I caught you before you left," said Hartmann, through the open window. Still, he kept his pistol just below the level of the glass.

The man bent down and raised the flashlight slightly toward his face. But there was no face. There was only a skull and great black holes where the eyes should have been. The mouth was a black gash.

Hartmann froze with his mouth open to speak, but instead of words he made only a long drawn-out "Aaaa." It was his last sound. The man at the window raised his other hand and shoved a long knife into Hartmann's chest, moving aside as his arm thrust forward to keep from being splashed with blood. Then he lifted the knife upward so the body wouldn't thrash off the blade. Hartmann's hands jittered and his feet kicked between the pedals, but then all movement stopped.

The man withdrew the knife and reached forward and put his hand in the warm blood. With his bloody fingers he drew a smiley face on the rear side window. He shone his light on the bit of artwork and seemed satisfied. Then he leaned into the driver's-side window and grabbed hold of the thick brown hair. Raising the knife, he cut a straight line across the top of Hartmann's brow.

. . .

Harriet Krause stared at the red bruise on her cheek in the bathroom mirror. She had a narrow, delicate face with a straight nose and dark eyes. The bruise took up her entire left cheek. Carl had struck her with his open palm when he had returned home from chasing the boy down the street. For that matter, he had nearly struck her when he'd come back from the police station that morning. In both instances he accused her of helping the people who were out to get him, whatever that meant.

"Why should anyone be out to get you?" she had asked. He'd looked at her as if she was an idiot and his expression changed to suspicion. Then he retreated upstairs, his feet clomping on the steps.

The blow had hurt, but what bothered her more were the changes that had come over Carl in the past months, changes with no explanation. They had been married a year ago April, and the first year had been wonderful. They had been hungry for each other, as well as loving. Although Carl had lost his temper more than once during that time, he had never hit her or the children. Then, in August, when he lost his job at Phelps Plumbing & Heating, he'd come home and kicked a chair, broken a vase, and smashed her mother's pottery lamp. And he'd been shouting, even growling, in his anger at Howard Phelps, who had criticized Carl's attitude, that Carl had gotten angry at a customer and it hadn't been the first time he'd been rude to someone.

Harriet had stood in the kitchen doorway, watching Carl smash up the living room. But she hadn't spoken. She'd been too astonished to speak. When he'd finished, he sat down on the couch and put his head in his hands, sitting as quietly as a statue.

"Are you all right?" she'd asked. "What happened?"

"Don't talk to me now." Carl said this with seeming calm, and she had returned to making dinner, even though her hands were shaking.

That night he told her he'd been fired, but it wasn't his fault. A customer had been rude and he was rude back.

Before that, in April, he had been fired from a construction company because of a "disagreement" with another worker. When she'd talked to him about it, he had said, "These things happen, I'm a new worker and I'm better than a bunch of the older guys. Some of them got pissed off."

She had accepted that as the truth, and she had accepted that Howard Phelps was wrong to fire him, though she hadn't accepted it as readily. But Carl was persuasive. He described what had happened and it seemed to make sense. Also she loved him and dreaded that something might go wrong between them. But the times he had gotten angry, according to Carl, had been the other person's fault. That morning when he pointed the shotgun at the two policemen, and at Hercel, too, for that matter, he said they had broken into the basement and he hadn't known they were policemen. Did she expect he'd do nothing? Anyway, he wasn't going to shoot; he was just putting a scare into them.

Harriet had said, "Did you have to threaten them with a shotgun? They were wearing suits and ties, and they were with Hercel. It's crazy to think they were burglars."

That's when he'd slapped her. He hadn't even warned her first, hadn't shown his anger. And her anxiety, which had been growing for several months, grew worse.

After Howard Phelps fired him, Carl had taken work closing up, caring for, and repairing half a dozen houses in Hannaquit once their owners had left at Labor Day. He also began working for Hamilton Brantley, mostly as a handyman, but whatever Carl did, he didn't like it. But whether it was Brantley he didn't like or the fact that Carl was around other people or because he was squeamish about working at a funeral home, Harriet didn't know.

So it was in August that she began to see a change. He'd grown quieter on one hand and short tempered on the other. They hadn't spent as much time together, perhaps because she had been busier with other work once the kids were in school. Lucy had started kindergarten and hadn't decided if she liked it. At least twice a week, she'd say, "I'll go today, but I don't want to go tomorrow." Harriet talked to her, even tried to bribe her, saying she'd take her to the park or to a movie or they'd have macaroni and cheese for dinner. Lucy was strong-willed, like her father, but that was another story. Hercel was easier and could amuse himself. But his very independence had come to worry Harriet. He didn't seem interested in having friends and spent too much time alone.

When she thought how good everything had been even in June, it made her weep. Carl had been happy; they'd all gone to the beach. Even though he didn't spend a lot of time with the children, he seemed to like them, and she hoped he would grow to love them. Then she realized when she first noticed the change. It was when Carl told Hercel he must call him Mr. Krause.

Harriet had protested, but Carl said he needed it as a sign of respect. When Harriet continued to protest, he got angry in a way she hadn't seen before: accusing her of being a bad mother, of letting the kids get away with stuff, though he didn't say what kind of stuff. A few days later he had apologized, but it wasn't long after that they stopped having sex. And it had been so good before then! Some weeks after that he had begun to sleep upstairs, first making excuses—she was too restless in the night; she woke him with her snoring—but soon he didn't even bother making an excuse. And when she had asked him what had gone wrong, asked what made him so angry and secretive, he had said, "Look in the mirror and ask yourself the same question." It made no sense to her.

But tonight that's what she was doing, asking herself what had gone wrong. Not that she was doing it on her own. After Carl slapped her, she had called her best friends, Anita Barr and Amy Calderone. They both said the same thing: "Call the police."

Harriet argued that Carl might change, that the first year had been great and she couldn't believe the wonderful man she had married had vanished completely.

"He won't talk to you," said Anita. "He's short-tempered with the kids and he sleeps upstairs. Now he's slapped you. Personally, I'd tell him to get his ass out of the house. But if you want, make him see a therapist, or you can go to a marriage counselor. But you have to tell him that if he doesn't do it, then he has to move out. Good grief, how can you live with him if you don't feel safe?"

Amy had seen no reason to expand on her original advice. "Just call the cops. Perhaps he'll see a therapist and things will work out, but have it happen with him out of the house. He needs to be away from you and needs to be away from the children. How simply do I have to say it? He's dangerous."

Looking at herself in the mirror, Harriet decided to follow Anita's advice. She would talk to Carl and tell him they had to see a counselor. And when would she talk to him? Harriet decided it would be best to do it tomorrow. She didn't want to do it when he was upstairs in that spare bedroom by himself. She was afraid to.

Thursday evening Woody left Brewster and drove to a tavern in Wakefield before going home. He'd been on his feet all day and was exhausted. How Bobby Anderson remained upbeat and energetic in all situations was something Woody could only watch with wonder. Then, in mid-afternoon, Woody had remembered Ajax and called a neighbor kid to take the dog for a walk. Ajax would rather die than pee in the house.

Woody had also made the mistake of engaging in Susie-think, imagining she was at home to take the dog out. Now that she was gone, Woody would have to hire the neighbor kid or bring Ajax along in the truck.

Woody found a table in the bar, ordered a cheeseburger and Diet Coke, and turned his attention to the football game being broadcast on four large televisions hanging from the ceiling. But his thoughts remained on Brewster and a day spent identifying dead ends, since nothing he had learned told him who might have taken the baby, nor was there any sign he had been kidnapped. At least no ransom demands had appeared. As far as Woody was concerned, Nurse Spandex was the chief suspect. Then two FBI agents had shown up in the afternoon. The best to be said of them was that they weren't too pushy. But even the best agents tended to treat the local police as idiots.

Some of Woody's time had been spent, or wasted, dealing with the media who had descended on the hospital like crows on roadkill, requiring ten cops just to keep them off the property. This began at dawn with Jill Franklin, the reporter from the *Brewster Times & Advertiser.* He had given her a tongue-lashing, but it hadn't fazed her. Instead, she'd been focused on what she heard from Peggy Summers.

"She's glad the baby was stolen," Jill had said. "She says he's the Devil's baby."

Woody hadn't believed her till he talked to Peggy, and although she said nothing about any Devil, the girl didn't seem to care that her baby was gone. Instead she seemed relieved and only wanted to go home. Woody, however, had held her in the hospital just to keep an eye on her, while police fanned out to discover whether she might be involved in the theft of her own child. One of the FBI agents suggested this was a possibility and reeled off statistics to prove it. While it might be true, no evidence had so far been found. Another difficulty was that Peggy wouldn't identify the father.

Later, when Woody found Jill leaving the hospital cafeteria, he had asked, "What did you mean by that remark about the Devil's baby?"

"She said it was like the movie *Rosemary's Baby*. Remember? The baby was the Devil's baby. Maybe DNA would show something about that."

"Is that a joke?"

Jill faced Woody with her legs slightly apart. Like a linebacker, he had thought. Though she certainly wasn't built like a linebacker. He had to make himself not look at her breasts.

"It wasn't meant to be funny. It might help to identify the father. Are you glad the FBI's here?"

"Are you asking as a reporter?"

Jill left the question unanswered.

Afterward he had sent Bonaldo to make sure the baby's placenta was still available. Maybe DNA would turn out to be an issue. Then he had meant to talk to Peggy Summers again, but she was with the FBI agents and he hadn't had the chance.

Woody was finishing his cheeseburger when he noticed a woman by herself glancing at him from a table across the room. He looked away but then realized he knew her. She was the head of Morgan Memorial, Dr. Joyce Fuller. When he looked back, she stood up, none too steadily, and approached his table.

"May I join you?"

Woody invited her to sit down, trying to look more welcoming than he felt. He had hoped his workday was finished.

Dr. Fuller brought her drink, something colorful with vodka, and sat without speaking, drawing a circle with her finger in the drops of water on the table's surface. She was older than Woody by about five years and not quite as perfect in her appearance as she had been that morning, which, to his mind, made her more attractive. He had never trusted women who never had a hair out of place.

"I'm sorry to disturb you." Dr. Fuller continued to look at the table. "I just need another human being right now."

Woody kept silent.

"You must think I'm a fool."

"Why's that?" The noise from the TVs made it hard to hear.

Dr. Fuller didn't answer his question. "My career's over. I'm grieving for my career."

Woody started to make a consoling remark, but what could he say, "Oh, you can get another"? He knew perfectly well that she had been wrong not to equip the hospital nursery with an infant protection system. Basically, it was bad luck, since the odds of having a baby stolen were maybe a trillion to one. But none of that helped now.

Dr. Fuller shook her head as if clearing it of dark thoughts. "Did you learn anything useful today?"

Woody began to say he couldn't discuss an ongoing investigation, but then he shrugged. "We learned where the snake came from." He told her about the theft of the snake from Hercel McGarty. The crime investigation unit had gone over the basement, and various bits and pieces were sent to the lab at URI to join the bits and pieces found in the nursery.

"Anything that helped?"

"I don't know, a bit of mud."

"You must be glad the FBI came down from Boston."

Why did everyone assume he'd be glad? "You bet."

She pushed her hair away from her forehead. "You know, everything's been easy for me. I think that's turned into a curse."

"I don't follow you."

"School, money, jobs—they've come easily. The curse is that because things have gone well, I made the mistake of assuming they'd keep going well. I guess I believed I was blessed with good fortune. But it's as if my whole life was ordained to lead to this one irreversible mistake: a baby was stolen. When I learned last night that labor and delivery would be understaffed for four hours, I decided it didn't matter. I believed nothing would go wrong because I felt nothing was fated to go wrong. Now a baby's gone. And like a fool I keep wishing I could go back and do it all over again, except this time I'd do it right. Isn't that stupid? I hear these words coming out of my mouth and I'm appalled."

"It's human," said Woody. It wasn't stupidity she suffered from, it was arrogance, but perhaps that in itself was a form of stupidity. He realized Dr. Fuller had had a lot to drink.

"Are you married?" she asked.

"No." Was it possible to tell her he'd been engaged, more or less, but his fiancée moved out a week ago? But Woody couldn't imagine telling such a thing to a stranger. He hadn't even told Bobby.

Dr. Fuller laughed without humor. "I've been nearly married three times. On each occasion, I put my career first. The last time was before moving to Brewster. I turned away from marriage, turned away from having babies. Isn't it ironic that my career should be destroyed by a lost baby?"

Woody didn't respond.

Dr. Fuller drank some of her drink. "I could really use a cigarette. Does it shock you that a hospital administrator still smokes?"

"I don't shock that easily."

"What do you think I should do?"

Woody thought she had nice eyes, almond-shaped and dark brown. "First off, you have to stop feeling sorry for yourself."

Dr. Fuller burst into tears. Woody frowned. Should he apologize? He saw no reason for it. "You won't be able to do anything until you do that," he added.

She wiped her eyes. "You're right, you're right. I just can't help it."

"Then try harder. You can't make this go away. You've got to come to terms with it and move on. Otherwise you're screwed."

Her anger made her eyes glitter. "Haven't you made mistakes?"

"Everyone makes mistakes. Yours is a particularly bad one."

Dr. Fuller leaned back and again pushed her hair off her brow. "I ordered those devices this morning—baby LoJacks, the nurses call them. The board of trustees wants my resignation. I was on my way home to write the letter, but I came in here instead. They can't decide whether to dump me right away or wait until the baby is found. They're worried about lawsuits, which is to be expected. I tried to talk to Alice Alessio to get a clearer idea about what happened, but I couldn't find her."

"She was sent home in the afternoon."

"I know. I went to her apartment, but she wasn't there. Then I went to her mother's, but she didn't know where she was. She said Alice had turned off her cell phone; either that or it was out of battery. I went back to her apartment, but she hadn't come home. Then I came here."

"Excuse me a moment," said Woody.

Before he was out the front door of the tavern, he had taken out his phone and punched in Fred Bonaldo's number. Bonaldo answered on the second ring. "Yes?" Woody heard a cringe in his voice, the tone of a man who expects to be yelled at.

"Were you keeping a watch on Alice Alessio, and do you know where she is?"

Bonaldo cleared his throat. "Yes, I assigned a man to it."

"And?"

Bonaldo made more throat-clearing noises. "He lost her."

"What the fuck's that supposed to mean?"

The acting police chief was silent, and then said, "He was parked in front of her apartment; then he left for a bit to go to the Subway for a grinder."

"So how long's 'a bit'?"

"I don't know how long. When he got back to her apartment, she was gone. He and some other men are looking for her right now. I really yelled at him."

"That'll do a shitload of good." Woody took hold of himself before he began to yell. "Call me if you find her. I want to know immediately." He cut the call and went inside to Dr. Fuller. As he'd said, people make mistakes, but that didn't make it better. Bonaldo deserved a serious dope slap.

The woman had stood up and put on her jacket. "What happened?"

"The nurse disappeared. Bonaldo doesn't know where she is."

"I think I'd better go home."

Woody had been afraid of this. "Sorry, you can't drive."

"Of course I can. I'm perfectly fine."

"Lady, I've spent years looking at the wreckage caused by drunk drivers." Woody lowered his voice. "If you get in your car, I'll arrest you. You want that in the newspaper, too?"

Briefly, she looked about five years old. "How'll I get home?"

This Woody had also foreseen. "I'll have to drive you."

"What about my car?"

"You'll have to get it tomorrow."

Woody paid his bill, and they walked out to the Tundra. He started to apologize for the dog hair on the passenger's seat, and then didn't. She wore a dark coat. The golden retriever's fur would make a mess of it. On the other hand, it wouldn't hurt her to be less perfect in her appearance. "Put on your seat belt."

"Are you always such a tough guy?"

He was surprised. "What makes you say that?"

"You're brusque and unsympathetic."

A range of answers occurred to him, beginning with "Do you like tough guys?" and ending with "Fuck you." Instead he said, "Sorry, I'm just tired."

She lived in Narragansett and gave him directions. "Who're Alice's friends?" This time he tried to soften his voice.

"I'm not sure she has many. The other nurses don't seem to like her, though I hadn't noticed she was inefficient in any way . . . until now. They call her Nurse Spandex. She flirts with the doctors."

She talked about the hospital on their fifteen-minute drive—the quality of the medical staff, the changes and improvements she had hoped to make. Left unsaid was that none of those improvements would happen now, at least on her watch.

Dr. Fuller lived in a new condo overlooking the bay. It was the sort of place Woody expected her to live in. "Would you like to come in?" she asked.

"I've got to get home. I've got pets." Woody felt foolish saying that last part.

"I'm sorry, you must think I'm terrible. I'm not making a pass." She paused, then added, "I'm afraid."

This, too, surprised him. "Of what?"

She didn't answer.

"Of other people or yourself?"

"Of myself, I guess."

The ocean, which Woody saw a piece of between buildings, appeared abruptly ominous. "Don't be silly."

She opened the door of the truck. "I'm sorry. I'm taking up too much of your time."

So he'd gone inside. Soon he was sitting at the kitchen table drinking ice water, while she made herself coffee. The kitchen and living room were like Dr. Fuller herself, classy and nothing out of place.

She talked about her fears, about her father, who'd been in the military, reaching the rank of colonel and ashamed he hadn't made general. She talked about the weight of failure, the oppressive feel of it. Whenever she thought she was descending into self-pity, she apologized. Woody said little about himself; briefly he described his years with the state police. At one point, he wondered what she'd be like in bed. *I'm an idiot,* he thought. He tried to tell her she could do other things. The words felt false in his mouth. She looked at him ironically.

"I can't say it right," he told her, "but it's true. Until you can make yourself believe you can still do something, your life's going to be a mess."

It was past midnight when he left. Bobby Anderson teased him about it later. "Dr. Woody," he called him. Then: "She's an attractive woman. Were you tempted?"

"Don't even think it," Woody had said.

That Thursday night Carl Krause lay in bed in his upstairs room with his hands at his sides and growled, a vibration in his throat, a liquid pulse at the back of his mouth. He hardly knew he was doing it. If Baldo Bonaldo had felt an affinity with vampires, Carl Krause had an affinity with werewolves, though he didn't realize it. Yet lying in bed remembering Bobby Anderson, he growled. Remembering the fat boy who he'd seen peeking through the basement window, he growled. If asked what he was doing, then he might say, "Thinking," since thinking for Carl had become like growling. Recalling his quarrel with his wife and how he slapped her, he growled.

It seems odd he should feel so aggrieved, as if Bobby, Baldo, and

Harriet were his tormentors, three names on a long list of tormentors. When someone thinks that, it's often because he feels he can't explain himself, that others just don't understand. This wasn't Carl's problem. He felt aggrieved because some people existed. Beyond the confines of his second-floor room, he knew those people were talking to one another. And who was the subject of their conversations? Why, it was he: Carl Krause.

If he lay still, he could hear them. At times his hearing was so sharp he could hear them outside on the sidewalk, even down the street. But tonight he heard them downstairs and at times on the stairs themselves as they neared his door: a single squeaking board, a scraping noise. Then Carl would leap from bed, run to the door, and fling it open. But he wasn't quick enough; they were gone. So he slammed the door to warn them he knew what they were up to and went back to bed to wait. Then he again heard the whisper of voices like the whispering of leaves, and again he growled. The whispering grew, the creaking of the stairs increased, and once more Carl rushed to the door and flung it open.

Did he think how it must sound to his wife and stepchildren downstairs, trying to watch television, and then later in their beds? How they stared at the ceiling in the dark of their rooms? No, never. These days he hardly thought of his wife and stepchildren as people, as human beings; rather, they were emanations flowing from an unknown source. They were the tentacles of some larger creature. To see them was like seeing fingers and imagining the hand, seeing claws and imagining the paw, imagining the coarse, furred arm and powerful shoulder. Oh, Carl knew how it was connected, just like the eyes shifting across the ceiling were connected. He wouldn't be surprised if the whole town was connected to make a single creature, a single monstrosity. He wasn't saying it was true; he was only saying he wouldn't be surprised.

Carl was lucky not to be plagued by doubt. Not always, but almost always. Had he doubted, he would have worried and been fearful. Being certain made him strong. Weakness was what he'd had ten days ago, two weeks ago, last month. He had worried something wasn't right, like that time in Oswego. He couldn't concentrate; he wept. He had imagined terrible things had happened. He'd seen a doctor. In that dark time, he lost his certainty. He'd come out of it like a child—weak and worried, depending on others. He had smiled and let them have their way. It was his long exile from himself.

But then the nervousness passed; the babyness, the girl behavior, the silly weeping was gone. He had felt his certainty growing like a fist within him. That's when he'd moved upstairs. He needed to be by himself in order to think, which meant to growl.

Each morning as day broke, as long as it wasn't raining, Steve Tovaldis took his two yellow Labs, Willie and Sophie, down Liberty Lane for a walk, past the small houses and turf farms to the railroad tracks and then along the tracks to the swamp. And each morning the Acela from Boston to New York would roar past and the dogs would bark their heads off. First they had been frightened, but now they liked it and waited for it to happen. The train roared and they barked back. It was a conversation.

Tovaldis liked to walk the dirt road into the swamp sometimes as far as Worden Pond, except in May, when the mosquitoes hatched and were particularly ravenous. The thousands of frogs ate as many as they could, but they just couldn't keep up. So Tovaldis bought about a gallon of Ben's Max 100 to keep them off. He slathered the stuff across his entire head, even when wearing a hat, because Tovaldis was as bald as a billiard ball, which let him, as he liked to say, save a fortune on haircuts—$15 every three weeks, $250 a year, $3,000 in twelve years. Just adding up the figures made him want to go out and buy something.

A short ways past the turnoff to the shooting range, Willie and Sophie ran ahead, barking like crazy. Tovaldis ran after them, calling their names. He was afraid they'd spotted a coyote and would chase it into the swamp. Willie had done that once by himself and came back bitten and torn. Tovaldis imagined one single coyote showing itself to lure the dogs into the swamp. Then a whole pack of coyotes would jump them. He knew that was true, but it was hard to convince anybody. On the other hand, when he had moved to Liberty Lane thirty years ago, there had been no coyotes. Then they snuck in. He didn't even bother owning a cat anymore. The coyotes had killed five of them, either the coyotes or fishers.

The dogs had stopped at a blue Ford Focus parked on the other side of the barrier, though how it got there Tovaldis had no idea, since the barrier was down ninety-nine percent of the time. He slowed to a walk as he called the dogs, then he shouted, "They're friendly!" Some people were scared of big dogs, but Willie and Sophie wouldn't hurt a fly. "They won't bite!" he added.

As he neared the car, Tovaldis saw someone in the front seat. Presumably the man had been asleep, at least until the dogs started their racket. Tovaldis thought those dogs went through life just looking for an opportunity to bark, as if it were their primary occupation. Perhaps the driver had got stuck on the other side of the barrier and had chosen to wait until a ranger showed up in the morning. Personally, Tovaldis had never been able to sleep in a car.

The car was backed against the barrier, a green metal bar extending across the road. Tovaldis stepped carefully around it so as not to step in the mud. "Down!" he shouted. The dogs were jumping up toward the open window. There'd be trouble if they scratched the finish.

His first thought was surprise that anyone could remain asleep with Willie and Sophie making all that noise. They were running around the car, barking their heads off, and the fur stood up on their backs. Then he noticed the rust-colored smiley face on the side window. He could make no sense of it. Tovaldis leaned forward. He saw the man had spilled more of the rust-colored paint all over his nice Hawaiian shirt. He bent down to see better and with surprise he saw the man's hair was the same color as the stuff on his shirt. No, that wasn't right. The man had no hair. He'd been scalped.

SIX

WHEN A TERRIBLE CRIME takes place in a small town, it's a tragedy. When a second takes place, it's a curse.

Ernest Hartmann's murder activated many people in many unexpected directions; people who felt sure they knew how their day would play out abruptly found themselves going elsewhere, while hundreds of other plans, hopes, dreams, whatever, were put on hold—all because of Ernest Hartmann. No, that's not quite true. The scalping had a lot to do with it. The scalping meant no dawdling, no long coffee breaks. More state troopers, police from South Kingstown, park rangers and officers, Indian tribal police, and then the Massachusetts state police and Watertown police—Hartmann lived in Watertown—and Boston police—Hartmann's office was in Boston—oh, quite a few were set in motion. They were appalled, indignant, angry, businesslike, hardworking, even a little excited. After all, none had been involved with a scalping before.

Then there was the smiley face. During the night the blood had dried and parts had flaked off, but enough remained to make its effect: a circle about six inches across with a big grin and googly eyes. Most killings are crimes of passion or cold calculation. This one seemed like madness. Certainly, it was preferable to see it as madness rather than as calculation, because what sane person would do such a thing?

If one thinks of these police officers as forming a great body, then the journalists formed that body's shadow. National networks and cable news sent helicopters. The print journalists came in cars, but they were fast cars. All assumed the scalping and the stolen baby were linked. Being equally outrageous, in the public mind, how could they not be connected? Though no evidence existed to link these crimes, this was no obstacle to flights of fancy about those responsible, fabrications ranging from a single madman to visitors from outer space. And beneath it was fear—for some it was like a tickling in the throat when getting a cold; for others it was a weight deep in the gut. For all, it formed the dread about what might happen next.

Through this Woody Potter and Bobby Anderson hunched their shoulders and plodded along, though five other state police detectives had joined them.

"Hey, boss," said Bobby, "you seen the CIA sent a team?"

"The fuck you say."

"Jes' kiddin', boss, jes' kiddin'."

"Wouldn't of surprised me any."

Jean Sawyer at the Brewster Brew had lots of new customers who drank gallons of coffee, ate pounds of pastry, and tipped well. To all who listened she described her conversations with Ernest Hartmann. These took on greater heft with each retelling. "He asked about Wrestling Brewster, our town founder. I told him Wrestling means wrestling with the Devil, which it does. He said he'd seen the Devil's work in his time and asked if I'd seen the Devil here in Brewster and I said I wouldn't be surprised. That's when he started looking scared. He sat drinking coffee for about four hours and looked scareder by the minute. Then his phone call really set him off. When he left, he could hardly walk, he was trembling so much." There was more. In fact, there was no end to it. Talk like that—it paid the bills.

Often there are too few police officers working on a case; in this instance there were too many, at least in Woody's opinion. Too many jurisdictions were involved, and at first there was no task force—a word whose weight seems to solve a problem by its very enunciation—to establish a clear chain of command. Woody and Bobby reported directly to the lieutenant in charge of the area detectives unit, but that was only at the start. Because the troopers involved in Brewster and the troopers involved in Great Swamp came from separate barracks, their lieutenants had to coordinate through the District B commander. And there were other local, state, and federal authorities. The result, to Woody's way of thinking, was a bunch of freelancers, which was a distraction. Five times he went to interview someone to find the man or woman had already been interviewed by the police or press or both. The first time a person says something it's a statement, the next time it's an art piece, and to separate the foundational material from filigree was time wasted.

Although these complications were most obvious in the adult world, some trickled down to a smaller one. Students at Bailey Elementary School were expected to be in their seats at seven-thirty sharp. At seven-twenty-five Baldo Bonaldo was still two hundred yards from the old school on the corner of Gaspee and Bucklin. The elms that once lined Gaspee were long gone, but the oaks, with which they'd been replaced, had reached substantial size and supplied the acorns that succeeding classes of students had used to pelt one another and had led succeeding groups of teachers to say, "Why couldn't they have planted maples?" Hercel McGarty Jr. stood behind one of these oaks.

Baldo was a dawdler, but his customary tardiness had worked its way up his own particular chain of command to acting chief Bonaldo, whose punishments had grown increasingly severe till they rested on the cusp of the physical. As Baldo hurried, he dwelled on a range of possible chastisements. Then Hercel grabbed him by the collar.

Hercel wore jeans and a dark blue hoodie. Baldo wore jeans, a blue-and-red flannel shirt, and a yellow crewneck sweater that his mother had insisted he wear even though it made him look ten pounds bigger.

Baldo fell back to the sidewalk. "Hey, cut that out! I'll be late!" Then he saw who it was. Hercel stood above him like Godzilla.

There followed a moment when each boy considered his options. Hercel wanted to beat Baldo black and blue, but he didn't want to hurt him. Still, he had to scare him.

Baldo was more calculating as he pondered his next move. At last he said, "That was a fantastic trick! Can you teach it to me?"

Hercel stepped aside with a sense of being outwitted. He knelt down by the other boy and pushed him back to the ground. "Have you told anyone?"

"Of course not. You never give away the secret of a magic trick. I mean, it's immoral. Do you think Houdini talked?"

Hercel didn't know Houdini. "This is serious. You can't tell anyone."

"Hercel, you're my best friend. I'd never talk."

Hercel narrowed his eyes. At most he had considered Baldo a mild fifth-grade acquaintance. Now friendship was being thrust on him. Still, Hercel understood the terms—friendship was being asked for silence. He didn't dislike Baldo, but, as has been indicated, he didn't understand him—all those weird jokes—and so he never thought of him. Baldo had been like an empty place in the air. Now Hercel stretched out his hand to that empty place and helped Baldo to his feet. "We'll see," he said.

"I'm late!" shouted Baldo, throwing up his hands, a gesture indicating a scale of punishments beyond comprehension.

"I'm going to visit my snake," said Hercel. "It's in the animal shelter."

The previous evening Baldo's father had told him about the snake that had terrorized the hospital and who owned it. It made Hercel even more important in Baldo's eyes. "What about school?"

Hercel shrugged. Compared to snakes, school didn't mean squat.

"Do you have a bike?" asked Hercel.

Baldo didn't. His mom had run over it in the driveway and it had to be fixed.

"We'll take mine."

Baldo understood that while being late to school was a serious crime, it was nothing compared to missing school entirely. On the other hand, he knew the offer of Hercel's friendship came with obligations.

"What about that trick with the marbles?"

"Later," said Hercel, whose bike was lying nearby on the ground.

When Baldo saw that sharing Hercel's bike meant placing his sneakers on the nubbin-like tips of the rear axle while standing erect and gripping Hercel's shoulders, he grew doubtful. He had many qualities, but courage was low on the list.

"Do you think I could run along at your side?"

The shelter was across town at the recycling center. Hercel looked at Baldo and didn't speak.

"Okay," said Baldo, "I can manage it." He hoped the terror of balancing on the axle's nubbins would be offset by the intimacy of clutching Hercel's shoulders.

They wobbled down Gaspee away from the school. The bike's spring suspension made them bounce. Baldo was impressed that Hercel could so easily blow off fifth grade considering his stepfather's temper.

Leaning over Hercel's ear, he described how Carl had chased him down the street yelling threats and how he'd barely escaped.

"Yes," said Hercel, "he's like that." This was said matter-of-factly, then, equally matter-of-factly, he said, "You want to see me ride no hands?"

Before Baldo could say, "Not today, thanks," Hercel raised his hands from the grips.

There followed a blessed second when gravitational laws were swept aside, then came another and a third, but during the fourth second the bike veered to the right. Baldo vice-gripped Hercel's shoulder's so powerfully that Hercel called out, "Hey, that hurts," and after two more swoops the bike straightened out.

"Maybe I don't have it down yet. Can you stop squeezing my shoulders?"

Baldo relaxed his grip. "Don't do it again, okay?"

Hercel didn't answer. He turned a corner and then another to avoid Water Street, which had become congested with traffic. This wasn't simply police and journalists, but included thrill seekers who wanted to tell their friends they'd driven through downtown Brewster safely.

After a few minutes, Hercel asked, "What do you think of wormholes?"

Baldo guessed that Hercel wasn't talking about the worms that robins ate, but ghouls were shot through and through with wormholes, and when it came to ghouls Baldo knew a lot, although they weren't as interesting as vampires and, indeed, he saw a class distinction between them, since vampires feasted on the living and ghouls preferred their bodies dead. But ghouls, like vampires, were shape-shifters and took the form of hyenas. If Hercel wanted to know about ghouls, Baldo would be an eager teacher.

"Ghouls?" Baldo asked.

The bike swerved.

"Wormholes," said Hercel, "connect one part of the universe with another part or even with a different universe. They can also be used for time travel. So you could step through a doorway made of exotic matter and end up billions of light-years away. Or, like, you could end up as a different age. I mean, I could walk through a doorway and be ten years older. I can't decide what I'd like best."

"Are they real?" Just as Baldo might roam in the gray area between the true and false, so he enjoyed the gray area between the real and unreal. Wormholes might be competitive with ghouls, even vampires.

"Sure, they're real. They have metrics, like a metric foot or a metric ounce. You use the metrics to work out their space–time geometry, but I don't know anything about that. Einstein helped discover them; he called them bridges. The only trouble is they're theoretical. I mean, you can't just go out and find one. Wouldn't it be cool to go through a doorway and wind up someplace incredibly far away? And if you didn't like that place, you could step through the doorway to another place, some new place. I mean, you could do it and do it till you found a place you liked. Wouldn't that be great?"

"I guess so." Baldo couldn't imagine not living in Brewster, despite its limitations.

"Where would you go first?"

"Maybe my grandmother's. She lives in Narragansett."

"My dad lives in Oklahoma. I could go there. But then I'd go to the farthest place in the farthest universe, no matter what it was. At least it'd be different."

After they had gone another block, Baldo said, "So what about those marbles? That was fantastic."

"I said later. It's not later yet."

By the time they entered the dump, they had grown suspicious of what lay ahead. They saw a lot of traffic that didn't look like dump traffic. Approaching the animal shelter, they saw two television trucks parked in front, as well as the cars of journalists and curiosity seekers. State troopers and a number of Brewster cops were also visible.

"It looks like they're interviewing your snake," said Baldo, as Hercel came to a stop and Baldo jumped off. "Awesome ride."

Hercel guessed he was making a joke about the snake being interviewed. He often felt he understood what his snake was thinking, but that was because he knew it. To other people it was just a snake.

Hercel leaned his bike against a metal barrel and they walked toward the shelter, a one-story cinder-block structure flanked by rows of cages in which a bunch of dogs were barking their lungs out. Some leapt against the wire mesh, which made a clanging sound. Baldo couldn't imagine how they'd get inside. Hercel's plan was to walk purposefully forward. After all, it was his snake. The dump had a thick, furry smell, like congealed meat soup with slices of lemon.

Hercel was about to push through the crowd when a woman saw him, looked once and then looked again. She ran to him and took his arm.

"Hey, I can help you. Come over here."

Hercel and Baldo found her familiar. She was blond, youngish, athletic, and had a pug nose. Then Baldo recalled she had been a substitute teacher when they were in fourth grade, but he couldn't remember her name. It had only been for a week or so. The woman was Jill Franklin, reporter for the *Brewster Times & Advertiser*, and she couldn't believe her good luck.

"You kids hungry? Come on, I'll buy you breakfast." She introduced herself and reminded them she'd been their substitute teacher.

"I don't want breakfast," said Hercel.

"Yeah, I know," said Jill, "you want your snake. But it's not going to happen. All those people will stop you. And if you get through them, then those cops will stop you. Aren't you supposed to be in school, or are you playing hooky?"

"It's my snake. I want to see how it's doing."

"It's doing just fine," said Jill. Now she remembered Hercel from last year—a very literal-minded kid, but he hadn't driven her crazy like some of the other kids. This Bonaldo kid, for instance, the chief's son, had put some kind of fart machine under her chair and once it had started detonating she'd kissed class discipline good-bye. "Believe me, you're not going to get in there. But I can help you. Now, let's get out of here before those vultures spot you."

"I've got my bike."

"We can put it in the back of my Tercel, I think."

So they put the bike in the trunk, securing it with a piece of clothesline. Baldo got in back and Hercel got in front. Jill drove to the Dunkin' Donuts at the edge of town. Even if they weren't hungry, she was. She'd been going since daybreak ever since news came over the scanner about a body found in Great Swamp.

She turned her head toward the chubby Bonaldo boy. "You still into farts?"

"Pull my finger."

Jill laughed so hard she nearly ran up over the curb. "He play those tricks on you?" she asked Hercel.

"He'd better not," said Hercel, "if he knows what's good for him." There was no threat in his voice, which somehow made it more threatening.

"And what would you do?" asked Jill conversationally.

Hercel was silent for a moment. "I'd think him into nothingness."

There was a grunt from the backseat.

"Well," said Jill, "we wouldn't want that, would we?"

A minute later she pulled into the parking lot at Dunkin' Donuts. "By the way, what do you call that snake? What's its name?"

"It doesn't have a name," said Hercel. "It's a snake."

"Don't you have pets? What d'you call your pets?"

"My mom has a dog and cat, but I only have the snake. Mr. Krause won't let me have any other animals. Do you know the difference between a snake and a lizard?"

"Sure," said Jill, locking the car and joining the boys on the sidewalk. "One crawls and the other slithers. They're both nasty, as far as I'm concerned."

Hercel ignored her remark. "Snakes don't have eyelids and they don't have ears on the outside."

"Snakes don't have legs and lizards do," said Baldo.

"There're a whole bunch of legless lizards," said Hercel. He went on to describe them as they entered the restaurant.

As they sat down, Jill said, "Perhaps we can name your snake. It would help me with my story. You want doughnuts, Cokes? Whatever you want, it's on me."

So they talked. To Jill's mind, if she got Hercel to name his corn snake, it would give her an advantage over the other reporters. It would be a journalistic coup. Hercel ordered a Coke and a plain doughnut. Baldo ordered a strawberry Coolatta and two doughnuts, both cream-filled. Jill had coffee and a breakfast sandwich.

"I say we name it Satan," she suggested.

They discussed this. Hercel didn't want to name the snake, but he was willing to go along if she really wanted to name it.

"Why Satan?" asked Baldo.

"It's a catchy name; people will remember it. It makes good copy." Then, to Hercel: "What color is the snake?"

It had large orange shapes, sort of like the shapes of Spain and

France, outlined in black with rivers of gold and tan in between. It was between five and six feet long.

"Wow, it sounds satanic," said Jill. "Don't forget. When anyone asks, it's Satan."

Then she went on to the standard questions. When did he last see the snake? Around nine o'clock Monday evening. Where was it kept? A cage in the basement. It used to be in Hercel's room, but Mr. Krause got mad. When did he see it was gone? About six-thirty Thursday morning. Someone broke open the basement door. The lock was busted. Where did he get the snake? His dad gave it to him for his birthday when he was six. His mom was furious; she hated snakes. His birthday was the fifteenth of March.

They talked for half an hour. Jill had known nothing of Carl Krause, but as Hercel talked she developed a sense of what life was like in the house—what she called the family dynamic. When Hercel told her about Mr. Krause threatening them with a shotgun and how Bobby had grabbed it from him, she began to take notes.

When she finished, Baldo asked, "What's your opinion about vampires?"

Jill laughed. "You've quite a range of interests between farts and vampires. Actually, I've no opinion about vampires. Reality can be horrible enough without worrying about what doesn't exist." She was thinking about Ernest Hartmann's murder and that somebody had scalped him, which the boys, as yet, knew nothing about.

It was around this time, nine in the morning, that Woody Potter came into Dunkin' Donuts looking for a friend of Alice Alessio's who, he had been told, worked there. The nurse still hadn't been found. Seeing Jill and the two boys, he guessed what was going on, and he felt his temper thrashing at its leash.

"What the hell you doing?" he said as he approached the table.

Other customers looked at Woody with alarm.

"What business d'you have taking these kids out of school? The law says they gotta be in school and you kidnapped them. That's a felony."

In the following pause, Hercel said calmly, "She didn't take us out of school. We were already out. I tried to visit my snake, but too many people got in the way. I want the police to give it back. It's wrong to punish it. It's only a snake."

Woody's anger faded. What he saw was a kid with a steady temperament, a small version of those people who go through life as if on railroad tracks, experiencing minimal doubt. Baldo, on the other hand, was on the verge of tears.

Woody scratched the back of his head. He had stayed up late talking to Dr. Fuller and had been woken early by the news of Hartmann's murder. That was the trouble with these all-consuming investigations, you never got enough sleep. He sat down next to Baldo and glanced at the crumbs on his yellow sweater.

"Okay," he said to Jill, "you'll catch a break this time, but things are hard enough without people muddying the waters. Come on, kids, I'll take you to school."

Jill looked at him with a slight smile. He thought she was being smug. She thought he was a handsome guy. She said good-bye to Hercel and Baldo as Woody stopped at the counter to ask about the woman he'd been seeking. He was told she worked only afternoons and evenings.

Getting Hercel's bike from the trunk of Jill's car, he wheeled it to his Tundra and put it in the back. ("Nice bike, kid. I like the green.") Woody's golden retriever was in the truck and tried to lick each kid a thousand times. "Hey, he's licking my face. Don't they have germs?" asked Baldo. But Hercel and Ajax got along just fine. Soon Hercel's dark hoodie was covered with dog hair. The only trouble with having a dog in the truck was it made it hard to talk. But at least Woody learned the snake was named Satan.

A breeze and the morning sun put some life into the last leaves. A flock of geese crossed overhead toward a salt pond. It was Friday, October 23. In two weeks it would be Susie's birthday. *Well, at least I don't have to get her a present*, thought Woody. *That'll be a saving.* He tried to smile, but it felt like a knife in his gut.

Woody led the boys to the principal's office to make sure they wouldn't get in trouble for being late. The principal was a stout woman of about fifty. Her name was Deborah Dove, and she thought herself as hard as nails.

"It's absolutely terrifying what's been happening." She had just heard about Ernest Hartmann. "Are you sure we're safe? I certainly don't *feel* safe."

Woody recalled Bobby Anderson's joke about the CIA sending a crack tactical unit to Brewster. He started to mention it, then didn't. "We're making sure you stay safe, ma'am." He said good-bye to the boys. As he left the office, he heard Baldo say, "When are you going to tell me?" Hercel hissed, "Later!"

Woody drove into town to Water Street. He wanted to talk to the guy at You-You who gave Hartmann a massage, which he heard about from Jean Sawyer at the Brewster Brew. She said Hartmann had hurt his back because terrible anxiety kept him tossing and turning all night. She said misery was written across Hartmann's face like a picture on a billboard.

Although the investigation was in its early stages, Woody knew certain details already. For instance, the baby's placenta, which had been placed in a freezer to wait for the hazardous waste pickup, was also missing. Nobody could explain it. Acting chief Bonaldo suggested it might have been stolen, which seemed ridiculous. Who would steal a placenta? Yet Woody recalled that somebody had spoken of the possibility of DNA testing. He tried to remember where the conversation had taken place and realized it had been with the Brewster reporter in the hospital cafeteria. The mother had said her baby was like the creature in *Rosemary's Baby*, and Jill had suggested that DNA could help identify the father. Woody had thought Jill was making a joke.

Searching Hartmann's apartment, Watertown police had discovered, along with the address of Hartmann's daughters and ex-wife in LA, a permit for a Browning Hi-Power. The pistol wasn't in Hartmann's apartment or in his office in Boston, nor was it in his room at the Brewster Inn, nor was it on his person or in his car. Unfortunately, a fifty-round box of Winchester nine-millimeter cartridges had been found in the motel room with fourteen rounds missing.

Along with telling Woody that she had sent Hartmann to You-You for his back trouble, Jean Sawyer described her talk with Hartmann about Wrestling Brewster and wrestling with the Devil. Woody supposed the Brewster reporter had learned this, which is why she had named the snake Satan. He expected that soon the news media would have Devils all over the place.

It took Woody only several minutes to find Gabe. The fellow at the reception desk said that Gabe was with a client but would be free in a half-hour if he'd like to wait.

"I either see him right now," said Woody, "or I take him to the cop house. You choose." *Cop house* was a term Woody had never used, but he thought it would get the ball rolling, which it did.

Gabe stood before him two minutes later. "Pushy, pushy," he said. He wore a dark purple cotton turtleneck. The red medallion showing the snake with the tail in its mouth gleamed in the overhead light. Woody couldn't take his eyes off it.

He took Gabe into an empty office and shut the door. "You gave a massage to an Ernest Hartmann yesterday morning. What do you remember about him?"

"Did he complain? It was a perfectly normal Swedish massage."

"No complaints. What do you remember about him?"

"He had beautiful hair—thick and brown."

Not anymore, thought Woody. "He was murdered this morning."

Gabe pressed a hand to his mouth. "He was such a nice man. How? Where did it happen?"

"I'm the one with the questions." Then he shrugged. "Out in Great Swamp. Somebody stuck a knife in him. We don't know who."

Again Gabe put his hand to his mouth. "I've always said that was a dreadful place. Full of mosquitoes and who knows what else. Did he suffer?"

"I doubt it. What's that thing hanging around your neck?"

Gabe looked down as if surprised by its presence. "You know, Ouroboros? The snake with its tail in its mouth? It symbolizes the Eternal Return. Ernest was interested, so we talked about it. Then we talked about the snake in the Garden of Eden. Like, the Devil? I didn't know anything then about the snakes in the hospital, or the missing baby. Horrible, absolutely horrible. But you know what they say, there's no such thing as coincidence. Our talking about snakes, I mean."

The two men stood facing each other. "So why do you wear it?"

"Well, for me, it's a symbol of our destiny. Not just our death but also the rebirth that awaits us all. That's what's meant by the Eternal Return. We go round and round. Like this conversation, we've already had it in other lives, other emanations, though the words might be a little different."

Woody studied Gabe's earnest expression. "So what about Hartmann?"

"Oh, he'll be back. I don't know how, but he'll be back."

A flake, thought Woody. Still, he'd run a check on him. There was no reason a flake couldn't be a murderer. "Anything else to say about him?"

Gabe put a finger to his lips and looked thoughtful. "Oh, yes, how could I forget? He had this awesome coin. Or peculiar, you know what I mean? It fell out of his pocket when he was getting dressed and I picked it up: a brass coin about the size of a silver dollar. Let me see, on one side was a five-pointed star with a circle around it and some mysterious writing and on the other side was a horned goat standing on its hind legs. You know what that means, don't you?"

"Tell me."

Gabe put his hands on his hips. "Satan! Isn't that a coincidence? The horned god. Of course, it's also Pan, and we talked about that. Did you know that *panic* comes from Pan? It's what happens when Pan screams. People panic. Can you blame them? It seems we have a lot of panic in Brewster right now. *Pandemonium*, that's the same thing. People are very upset. Anyway, witches use the coin to identify one another. A secret talisman. Isn't that peculiar? I heard that, and a chill ran up my spine, like a goose had just walked across my grave."

Gabe's talk was exhausting. No way could Woody last through a massage without running from the room. "Who told you about the coin?"

"A man I know."

"Does he work here?"

"I'd like to talk to him first. If he wants to talk, I'll give you his name."

Woody felt anger rising in his throat. "Either I get his name or I throw you in the drunk tank." Did Brewster have a drunk tank? Woody didn't know.

"You're not at all as nice as I first thought you were, d'you know that?"

"I can live with it. Now tell me."

After further huffing and puffing Gabe gave him the name of a yoga instructor at You-You. "I'm not saying he's a witch, mind you. He's very smart."

Woody wrote down the name. "One other thing: don't go out of town."

Gabe was appalled. "Am I a suspect? I was home all night; I've got witnesses."

"Just don't leave town."

Before Woody went to this next interview, he called the units who'd searched Hartmann's car and motel room to ask if they'd found a coin or medallion with a star on one side and a goat on its hind legs on the other. They hadn't. He asked them to search again. One of the troopers from the crime scene unit, Lou Rossetti, said, "Hey Woody, that guy who found the body had two big Labs that were running around the car. But we found other prints there, too. We first thought they were dogs, but they were probably coyotes. A whole bunch of coyotes were running around the car during the night."

The man Woody went to see was Todd Chmielnicki. Woody found him in his office on the third floor—a white room with a white desk and bookcase, a white floor, and a red rug. The walls were bare; one window high up on the wall, too high to see out of. Chmielnicki stood up to shake hands. He was a tall man of about forty, taller than Woody, and very fit—not a pound too many, not a pound too few. He had short black hair, an angular face with high cheekbones, and wore a black T-shirt and black jeans. The effect of room and man was dramatic—too much so, to Woody's taste—as if Chmielnicki, like an actor, had seized a persona rather than earning one. His bright blue eyes reminded Woody of a Siberian husky.

Chmielnicki had a foreign accent that Woody couldn't place and spoke in a calm whisper. He invited Woody to sit down. The choices were a couch set against the wall or a chair by the desk. Woody took the chair. Already, he felt distrustful—the way Chmielnicki carried himself, the control of his body language, those eyes, his physical strength, and the quiet voice Woody had to strain to hear all made him uneasy.

"And what do you do here?" asked Woody.

"I teach various types of yoga and meditation, mostly to other teachers, but I also teach a master class in Raja."

"Is that a kind of yoga?"

"It's a system that attempts to control the mind."

Woody knew little about yoga, although Susie had gone to a yoga exercise class—violent activity in a room well over one hundred degrees. She'd come home with her face as red as a beet. "And how does it do that?"

"By inhibiting the mind's modifications." When Woody didn't respond, Chmielnicki continued: "Most mental activity leaves its mark, its muddy footprint—thoughts, feelings, memories, prejudices, ideas. These determine how you behave. Raja yoga sees these as impurities. Through its practice we seek to erase these modifications to allow us to regain our free will and experience our true selves."

"And you've done this?"

"It's a long process. We also study ways to change the modifications in others."

"What's left when you take them away?"

"Just the self, pure unadulterated self, free of deterministic restrictions."

"So you can see modifications? You can see mine?" Woody had asked the question before he'd known he'd ask it.

"They're all over you. The way you dress, the way you hold yourself, the way you speak. For instance, you clip your words, you hurry them out of your mouth, you put them under tight control. You keep your hands close to your body but your feet apart as if ready to jump. D'you think you were born like that? They express your relationship with your anger. You control your language in order to contain it. But your temper is a determinant factor in your behavior. It's a modification. It expresses a defensive reaction, and you'd be happier without it." Abruptly, Chmielnicki clapped his hands and watched Woody jump. "And you've got a pronounced startle response. Were you in the service?"

Woody thought this had gone far enough. "So you're a witch?"

Chmielnicki's laughter was of the booming variety, the very reverse of his manner of talking. "Now, there's a serious modification. Most prefer to be called Wiccans rather than witches. They practice Wicca, which means they're neopagans practicing a nature religion."

"Do they worship the Devil?"

"Not necessarily. Wiccans aren't Satanists, though there are some of those—the Church of Lucifer, the Temple of Set, LaVeyan Satanism—and some dabble in black magic. There's also a wide range of gray magic—shape-shifting, for example. They follow the Left-Hand rather than the Right-Hand Path of conventional religion. Wiccans, in their various manifestations, are the largest group, though plenty of old-fashioned witches lurk about. The coin Mr. Hartmann dropped is a Wiccan symbol. Had the star been upside down, it would have indicated Satanism. I'm neither witch, Wiccan, nor Satanist, though I'm acquainted with adherents of all. To eliminate one's modifications requires a certain neutrality."

"Are there Wiccans in Rhode Island?" It seemed to Woody a silly question. Was it the subject that made him uncomfortable or the man defining the subject?

"We have several hundred divided into a number of covens. There are even Satanists. I should say that most Satanists don't actually believe in Satan, or such is their claim; rather, Satan is a symbol of what they hold important, their carnality, and what they call our basic nature—extreme egoism, selfishness, self-indulgence. Their philosophies derive from Friedrich Nietzsche and Ayn Rand; their practice is taken from Aleister Crowley."

Woody found it hard to imagine witches without broomsticks and pointed black hats. "So how d'you find them?"

"You may Google them. Most have websites. And many prefer to be called Neo-Heathens. They practice what they call pagan virtues. Some are also interested in shape-shifting. With spells and certain unguents they claim to be able to change into animals or birds: wolves, cats, coyotes, fishers, owls, ravens. No one cares to be a rabbit or chicken. They prefer carnivores with conflicted personalities."

"Why change into an animal, and why would you want to?" The subject chipped away at Woody's sense of reality. Not that he believed it, but it worried him that others believed it.

"We've known these stories a long time. Circe turns men into pigs. Daphne turns into a laurel to avoid rape. Gregor Samsa turns into a cockroach. They're found in every culture—it's risky to reject them out of hand. Sometimes a person is changed into a beast as a punishment. Sometimes a person changes himself. Or it's something a person has no control over. As to why they choose to change their shapes—it gives them the animal's strength and frees them from human inhibition. It's said to be liberating. As for how, that's a good question. They might be lying. It might be a form of mass hysteria. It might be self-induced hallucination. Witches once smeared themselves and their broomsticks with unguents composed of belladonna, opium poppy, poison hemlock, monkshood, and animal fat, which created hallucinations. They called it flying ointment. And there's a final possibility: they might actually do it."

"That's ridiculous."

Chmielnicki laughed. "Those are your modifications talking. Ninety-two percent of our genome contains the basic genes for all vertebrates; the rest carry the differences *between* all vertebrates. Half of one percent separates us from Neanderthals; three percent separate us from other mammals. But within a chain of DNA are inactivated intragenic regions called introns whose purpose isn't understood. We also have disconnected genes that are to the DNA what the appendix is to the body—useful once but useful no longer. Some believe that within them lie the secrets to alternate forms and to activate them might make shape-shifting possible."

"By cutting open the brain?"

"Not necessarily. Chemicals might do it. Even the control available in forms of yoga might affect it. A teacher said, 'Yoga limits the oscillations of the mind.' Through yoga one can control one's involuntary muscles, one can control pain, pierce flesh, and close the wound. One can walk on burning coals and not be burned. So why can't we activate our dormant genes to change into another creature?"

Woody's discomfort with the subject made him feel as though he was on precarious ground. "So what's the animal of choice in South County?"

"Coyotes seem most popular."

"Could they commit murder?"

"Woody, anybody can commit murder. Haven't you learned that? But if, through shape-shifting, one becomes a predatory animal, the terms change. Do we call it murder when the cat kills the mouse?"

"Could you commit murder?"

"I like to think not. My teaching attempts to free me of those desires. But you surely have known people you wanted to kill."

Woody could almost feel the touch of those blue eyes on his face. He was sorry he hadn't turned Chmielnicki over to the FBI agents to question.

"Like most people," Chmielnicki continued, "you have a conflicted nature and are vulnerable to the emotional changes brought on by unexpected circumstance. You seem to have recently had a loss. Everything you look at you see through the fog of that loss. Your anger today has been increased by it. Is it a death? No. A great rejection? Possibly. Woody, did your wife just leave you, or possibly a girlfriend?"

And so it went.

SEVEN

NIGHT WAS APPROACHING. The sun was already low in the west when clouds began to move in. Harriet Krause stood at the living room window, watching Hercel bike out of the driveway and turn down Newport. Seeing him disappear filled her with worry. He seemed strange to her, but she knew that wasn't the right word. *Introspective* was what she meant, *clear-sighted*—it seemed too much for a ten-year-old. Whatever it was, he didn't take after her, or his father, either, for that matter. Maybe he was like her grandfather, who was said to be moody and too smart for his own good. Harriet had never known him. He had disappeared when she was still a baby. Some people said he'd walked into the ocean.

Hercel spent too much time by himself, although that Bonaldo boy had come with him after school. But was he a suitable friend? She was sure he was the one who left the rubber dog mess on the living room rug. If Carl had seen it, he'd have absolutely killed Randy, her miniature dachshund. It was pure luck he hadn't, because he had come home early from work for some reason. Now he was upstairs banging around, opening the door and slamming it. She knew she had to talk to him, but she didn't know where to begin. At least he wasn't drinking. When she'd met him at church two years ago, he had seemed kind and intriguing. Now he didn't go to church anymore.

The door slammed open again. Harriet waited for it to slam shut, but instead she heard Carl's heavy feet on the stairs, coming down fast. She braced herself.

"Stop her screaming!" he shouted. "If you don't make her stop, I'll do it myself!"

He had begun shouting halfway down. Now he was in the living room, facing her. He hadn't shaved, and the deep creases on his cheeks formed dark gullies. The gray cat took one look at him and ran from the room. He swung a foot at it and missed.

Harriet tried to stand her ground but could hardly look at him directly. "What do you mean? Who're you talking about?"

"Your kid! She's screaming! Are your making her do it?" He had stopped shouting; when he spoke it was almost a growl.

"Lucy? She's watching TV in our bedroom." *What used to be our bedroom*, Harriet thought.

Carl strode down the hall and threw open the bedroom door so it crashed against the wall. Lucy was sitting on the floor, watching *The Electric Company*. She jumped up. The sound was turned low; nobody was screaming.

"What the hell are you doing in here?" Carl shouted.

Harriet hurried to get between Carl and her daughter. She could see Lucy was frightened. She was a thin girl with short brown hair, wearing jeans and a green T-shirt decorated with light green frogs. She had kicked off her lighted sneakers—the heels flashed red with every step—which lay some distance from each other. Harriet hated to see her frightened. It made her angry.

"She's not doing anything. Can't you see you're scaring her?"

"She was screaming. She's hiding it now." Carl bent toward her and spoke with ferocious conviction.

Harriet turned to Lucy. "Sweetheart, were you making noise?"

Lucy shook her head and kept glancing at Carl.

"What's happened to you?" Harriet took a step toward her husband. "We're supposed to love each other."

Carl opened his mouth to speak and Harriet was sure he was going to deny it, deny that he loved her. He looked almost sly. Then his anger came back. "You always defend her—she and the boy. You don't see what they're up to."

"And what are they up to?"

"The boy sneaks upstairs at night. He sneaks up and down the stairs. He thinks I can't hear him, but I do."

Harriet put out a hand to touch his arm, but he pulled away. "Carl, we need to see someone, get some professional help. We can't go on like this."

"What are you talking about?"

"I'll get the name of a counselor."

"No way I'm going to go to someone. No fucking way. Been there, done that. Tricks, that's all. You think I don't see what's going on? I got eyes. People tell me stuff, lots of stuff. And that fucking cat. I know all about cats."

With that, Carl walked down the hall. The dachshund yapped at him and then yelped and came dashing into the bedroom. In another moment, Harriet heard Carl climbing the stairs. Then she burst into tears.

As Hercel saw it, he wasn't frightened of Mr. Krause, but Mr. Krause scared him. The first was a more or less permanent condition; the second happened now and then, like that afternoon when Mr. Krause had growled at him. Hercel understood that Mr. Krause was still mad because he'd brought policemen into the basement, but it was, after all, Hercel's snake. It wasn't like Mr. Krause had had a snake stolen.

Hercel had come home after school with Baldo, and after they'd had a snack and watched some TV, Baldo had gone home. Hercel had been taking the milk from the fridge when Mr. Krause came quietly into the kitchen and growled. Hercel nearly dropped the carton.

"I know what you're doing," Mr. Krause had said.

It had taken Hercel a few seconds to understand that Mr. Krause didn't mean the milk. He also understood it wouldn't do any good to ask Mr. Krause what he meant. It would only make Mr. Krause mad. So he'd just stood there facing Mr. Krause but not looking at him too much, because Mr. Krause didn't like that, either.

"How'd you like somebody standing outside your door at night. Would you like that, boy?"

Hercel said he wouldn't.

"You got a lock?"

Hercel shook his head.

"That's a shame, boy. You hear what I'm saying? It's always good to have a lock." Then Mr. Krause had left the kitchen and gone back upstairs.

Hercel had decided he didn't feel like any milk right then, and he put the container back in the fridge. Then he went to find his mother. He explained he was going to visit Tig. She had invited him. It wasn't very far, and he'd ride his bike easy. He was surprised when she agreed, surprised she didn't ask a lot of questions. She had just looked sad.

"Be careful," she'd said.

He had said okay. Then he got a sweater, put his toothbrush in the back pocket of his jeans, and was on his way.

Antigone, or Tig, lived six miles from town, and by the time Hercel was halfway there the sun had set. Several times she'd invited him to see her sheep. He could stay the night and help her feed the chickens in the morning. He didn't like to think this was an inappropriate hour to arrive, the dark coming on and almost dinnertime. Anyway, his mom had said it was okay.

And he didn't want to see Baldo; he'd had enough of Baldo for one day. Hercel had told him he had done his trick with magnets, that the marbles were really ball bearings that looked like marbles, that the magnet was a short rod he hid in his palm, and he added something about positive and negative poles. Baldo hadn't believed a word, but he didn't want to call Hercel a liar. These were qualities Hercel admired—skepticism and loyalty, but it didn't mean he'd tell Baldo anything. At last Baldo had gone home, but Hercel knew he would ask his dad about magnets and positive and negative poles. But Hercel didn't care about that, because now he was out of the house.

As for his "trick," as Baldo called it, Hercel didn't know how it worked, except it gave him a headache. He looked really hard at the marbles and pushed them somehow with his thoughts. He concentrated, imagined one of them moving, imagined it rolling and lifting, and then one rolled, then another. How could he explain it to anyone, much less a kid? Anyway, rolling a marble three inches or lifting it three inches, what was so special about that? Small potatoes, as his dad used to say.

Few cars passed, which was just as well, because Hercel had no reflector on the back of his bike and no light on the front. Whenever a car came, he would pull onto the dirt. The road was lined with trees, and he thought it would be just his luck to hit one. It meant he had to go slower, which was too bad, because soon he wouldn't be able to see anything. Some houses were set back in the trees, and their lights helped. He just had to make sure he saw the turnoff to Tig's farm. Otherwise, he'd be stuck.

Luckily, another car passed as he neared the turnoff. It passed and blared its horn, which nearly sent Hercel into a ditch. Then he got moving again and made the turn. By this time, it was dark. No lights anywhere. He figured he had a mile to go, but after he'd gone about twenty yards his front tire slipped off the road. He pulled hard to the left, but the tire slid along the lip of the pavement and he went down, scraping his hands on the gravel and knocking the wind out of him. He picked up the bike and rolled it a few feet. It seemed okay. He limped beside it, because he had banged his knee. Hercel wasn't happy, but he figured what happened was what he would expect might happen, all things considered, and he had to put up with it. He was only sorry he hadn't brought a flashlight, but he'd been in too much of a rush to leave.

It was then he heard the yapping. At first he thought it was a dog, but it was higher than a dog's bark. He heard one, then a second and a third. He moved more quickly; he couldn't tell if he was moving straight until he stepped off the road and almost fell. He put the bike back on the pavement and got moving again.

The yapping grew closer. At times it was almost a scream, like a siren or cat. Hercel jogged forward, pushing the bike. Next time he went off the road, he yanked the bike back and jumped on. He wobbled forward in the darkness, trying to stay parallel to the edge of the road, or where he imagined it must be. The yapping grew louder. Had it been light, he would have seen them.

He had seen coyotes before, and a week earlier he had seen two in the tall grass down by the beach. And he knew they took people's pets; kids talked about it in school. They got in people's trash and skulked around at night. But he had never heard of them chasing anybody. He pedaled hard, keeping his hands evenly spaced on the grips, trying to go straight. He thought he saw the shadow of a tree and turned away from it. The coyotes' yapping was almost like singing.

Moments later, Hercel saw a light ahead of him through the trees. The coyotes were right behind him. In the bits of silence within their yapping, he heard the click of their nails against the road's hard surface. Hercel stood up and pedaled harder, slipped off the road but kept his balance and yanked the bike back on the pavement. The muscles in his thighs ached, and his fingers hurt from clutching the grips. The light was brighter. Ahead, to the left, he saw a stone wall and then a gate. It had to be the farm. He heard the coyotes panting. Trying to quiet his terror, he aimed at the wall.

Bobby Anderson accelerated up Water Street from the police station, as his black 370Z made a growl a little like the growl made by Carl Krause. He had just spent twenty minutes with that jerk-off Freddie Bonaldo, and it felt like twenty days. He had asked the acting chief to call the police in Oswego to see if they had anything on Krause. But Freddie had forgotten. He had been too busy with the press, too busy getting his picture on the front page of a bunch of papers. He also made provocative statements, such as, "I wonder if any baby is safe in this town." What had gotten into him? Bobby knew Freddie was just dying to announce there had been a scalping, thinking it would get him a spot on Jay Leno. Get him tossed out of his job, more likely.

At least the so-called task force had been announced and a chain of command established. The state police detective commander was in charge: Captain Tom Brotman. Bobby had exchanged only a few words with him in the past, but he knew his reputation, which was tough, smart, and photogenic. It was the photogenic part that might be a problem if it interfered with his relationship with the press. Bobby distrusted a boss who liked to have his picture taken. If the situation got worse, the deputy superintendant might take over; but now it was Brotman, and the town cops—including Bonaldo—took their orders from him. The

FBI was another story; they told Brotman only what they wanted to. Now, however, the governor had got into the action. Rhode Island had a population of about a million, meaning the governor could stick his nose into everything. He had already put his press people at Brotman's disposal, and the helicopters and a bunch of reporters had gone up to Providence for a press conference.

Tonight, after the excitement, the town was shutting up early. Ronnie McBride had unrolled his sleeping bag in the alcove of Crandall Investments, hardly eight o'clock and already pickled. Howard Phelps was locking up at Phelps Plumbing & Heating. No telling where Woody was. Bobby had run into him early that afternoon, and Woody had given him the job of finding Nurse Spandex. *Thanks a lot, Woody.* But Woody had got a lead from a guy at You-You that he wanted to check out. He hadn't seemed happy about it, and Bobby had asked him what was wrong.

"A guy I was interviewing, a yoga teacher. I should of let the FBI handle him."

Bobby had asked why.

"The fucker kept reading my mind. That's what I need on top of everything else, a new-age clairvoyant."

From Janie Forsyth, the trooper doing the photography in the hospital, Bobby had learned that Susie had moved out. At first he'd been angry that Woody hadn't told him, but then he realized it showed how much pain Woody must be in, because Woody dealt with pain by locking it inside him. If it came out at all it was as steam puffing out his ears. The last Bobby had heard from Woody about Susie was that they were getting married in December. Now Susie had split. Still, Bobby was supposed to be his best friend. How could you not tell your best friend that your girlfriend had dumped you?

Bobby had felt he knew them well. He and his wife had gone out with them a bunch of times—dinner, movies, dancing, fishing, the good stuff. Susie even babysat his kids. She was finishing a graduate degree in social work at URI, with nothing left but a few papers and fieldwork. She and Woody had met four years ago, started dating, and then Susie had moved into Woody's place in Carolina two years ago. When had he last seen her? Maybe three weeks back. The four of them had dinner at an Italian place in East Greenwich. She'd seemed fine, but on the ride home Bobby's wife had said that Susie had looked a little low. "You're always looking for drama," Bobby told her. "She looked great."

He didn't look forward to telling Shawna he'd been wrong.

Bobby hadn't found Nurse Spandex. She wasn't in any of the usual places. Yesterday she had called Dr. Fuller at the hospital and said she wouldn't be coming in for a few days. Then Dr. Fuller had unsuccessfully tried to find her. So she was either hiding because she'd fucked up or hiding because she was guilty of something. Or she might be dead. That seemed unlikely, but then Bobby would have said scalping was unlikely. Bobby would keep looking tomorrow, but now he meant to see Peggy Summers to try to loosen her tongue about who the father had been. Bobby had heard all that *Rosemary's Baby* stuff, and to his mind Peggy was pretty messed up. On the other hand, she was only seventeen.

Peggy lived with her parents in a house near where the knitting mill had stood—a worker's house on Williams Street, except the mill was gone and the house remained. In fact, a whole street of identical narrow, two-story clapboard houses remained, as if at loose ends, not knowing what to do with themselves. Peggy's father, Ralph Summers, had emphysema and was on oxygen—stretching behind him were decades of smoking and taking in plaster dust from hanging Sheetrock. So the family lived on his Social Security and what the mother, Mabel Summers, made at the Stop & Shop. Two cops were watching the house.

Bobby waved to them, climbed the front steps, and gave an energetic knock.

Entering their living room, Bobby saw he wasn't welcome, partly because he was a cop, partly because he was black. This amused him. He was a handsome guy, and if they didn't like him, it was their loss. But maybe it made him push them a little.

"I'd like to speak to your daughter, if I may."

"She's gone to bed," said Ralph Summers.

Bobby showed his shiny teeth. "So why don't you trot upstairs and ask her to come down." Summers sat in a tan Barcalounger that a bunch of cats had used to sharpen their claws. A TV table was on either side of him, one with Budweiser, one with the last of a pizza. Bobby guessed Old Ralph hadn't trotted anyplace for a while. His cheeks were flushed pink; the rest of his face was the color of concrete.

"Don't worry," said Bobby, "I'll find my own way. Just sit tight; take a load off your feet." By the time he had finished his sentence, he'd reached the top of the stairs. He heard the couple downstairs angrily whispering to each other. Bobby figured he had done them a favor. He had broken up their routine, giving them something to grouse about in the days to come. The upstairs had two rooms, plus a bathroom; only one had its door closed. Bobby knocked.

"Hey, Peggy, it's me Bobby. We gotta talk." He pushed the door open.

Peggy was propped up in bed, smoking and watching an *American Idol* knockoff on a small TV.

"So, Peggy, how you feeling?"

"Get the fuck out." With her narrow face and overbite, Bobby thought she looked like an angry rodent.

"Now, Peggy, let's be nice. Either we talk here or someplace where it's not so nice. You got an extra cigarette?"

She tossed him a pack of Marlboros, which he snagged out of the air.

"Light?"

She tossed him a yellow plastic lighter. Bobby lit the cigarette, tossed back the pack and lighter, and took a deep drag. He had been trying to quit, but he felt he needed one.

"So what's up with this missing kid of yours? He's disappeared and you don't care? You hard-hearted? Why don't you love him?"

Peggy stared at the TV. "Because I never wanted it in the first place. Why should I give a fuck about a baby I didn't want?"

"So who was the father?"

"I don't know."

"You don't know, or you don't want to tell me?"

She turned toward him angrily, and Bobby saw she was close to tears. "I don't know. It was dark. I didn't see his face. There were a lot of people, but they weren't wearing regular clothes. Like they were dressed like Batman, you know, capes and shit. It was a party in the woods late last March. There was a fire. Nobody was drinking, but they had, you know, some pills, some mushrooms."

"Was it your first time?" Bobby was prepared to be sympathetic.

"Fuck, no. That was when I was thirteen. Some boys got me after school. One boy, a year later, I nearly bit his prick off."

"You're a tough cookie."

"I can be nice sometimes." Peggy went back to watching the TV.

"So what can you tell me about the guy you had sex with?"

"Nothing, he just grabbed me. I was pretty stoned. He's lucky I didn't puke on him. Would've served him right."

"How'd you get out there?"

"Somebody drove me out, and somebody else put a blindfold on me. I was in the backseat. Maybe it took a half-hour to get there. They said I had some friends there, but there wasn't anybody I knew."

"What's this business about *Rosemary's Baby*?"

Peggy started yelling. "Don't you see? The fucking mushrooms and people stamping their feet like some kind of dance. The guy who did it, he could have been anybody. He could have been the Devil himself." She put her hands to her eyes and began to sob. Bobby watched her. The sobs seemed real enough.

"How come you didn't get an abortion?"

"They told me not to. They kept calling, sometimes ten times a day. They called my parents. They made a bunch of threats."

"What kind of threats?"

"That they'd tell, that I could get hurt."

"Who made the threats?"

"You think they gave their names? I didn't know anybody."

"They offer money?"

"They gave my dad some."

"How much?"

"He didn't say. That son of a bitch, he'd give me up for ten bucks."

Peggy was again watching the TV. Bobby thought about what she'd said. "Okay, I've bothered you long enough, at least for now. Get some sleep. I'll talk to you tomorrow."

"Fuck you."

When Bobby got downstairs, Ralph Summers shouted at him, "You satisfied? You got her all upset!"

Bobby gave him a smile. "How much money'd you get so she'd have the baby?"

Ralph's face turned purple. "I never got a penny."

"You're lying to me, Ralph. It's not nice to lie. I'm going to keep coming back until you tell the truth." Bobby headed for the door. "Have a nice day."

He was halfway to his Z when he heard the house door open and close behind him. Mrs. Summers hurried down the steps. "Did she tell you?" She seemed both excited and frightened.

"She said she couldn't see his face."

"Yes, but did she tell you why?"

Bobby wondered if this was some sort of game. "She said it was too dark."

"That's not the reason. She told me he was wearing a mask. It was dark, but not *that* dark. He was wearing a mask of a skull, a human skull. That's why she's upset. It nearly drove her crazy at first."

And with that, Mrs. Summers hurried back to the house.

Seymour Hodges and Jimmy Mooney were in their ambulance parked out by Dunkin' Donuts. Seymour liked to mix up his weed with jelly doughnuts, and they had a box of a dozen balanced on the dash. By morning it would be empty. Some nights, when the passion was on them, they'd splurge on a second box. "It's all business expenses," Jimmy would say. "It's not like it's costing us anything."

It was ten o'clock Friday night and business was slow. A few chest-pain runs and a stiff to the Burn Palace, that was it. Seymour was ready for his nap, and Jimmy yammered to keep him awake. He was sick of Seymour screaming at night, and he talked to postpone the evil moment.

"A scalping," Jimmy said. "I've never seen a scalping. You seen a scalping?"

Seymour tended to be slow in answering, as if the words percolated into his head like water seeping into clay. Then he spoke so slowly that sometimes a minute would pass between one word and the next. Occasionally, when the next word came, Jimmy would have totally forgotten what Seymour was talking about.

"A guy in another company was into scalping. Maybe a sniper."

"What'd he do with them?"

"Dried them out. They all looked the same. Iraqis aren't like us; they all got the same color hair. Black, some gray. He'd try to sell the scalp back to the family, you know, a memento. He got some sales, but it's not like the families got the right scalps. He'd reach into a box and grab the first scalp he saw. Like I say, they all look the same."

"Maybe we'll get the scalped stiff when the ME lets him go," Jimmy said, referring to the medical examiner. "Nah, he'll go up to Boston. That's where he's from, right?"

Seymour didn't answer, and Jimmy was afraid he'd nodded off. It was warm in the cab and thick with the greasy smell of good dope. Leaves blew across the lot; sometimes, to Jimmy, they looked like darting creatures.

"It'd be neat to have your own scalp," said Jimmy. "I mean, like somebody else's scalp. You think the Indians ever used them like, you know, toupees?" There was no answer. "Hey, Seymour, what d'you think?"

After a moment Seymour said, "I've never seen a bald Indian. I don't think they come bald."

"Shit, I think you're right. My dad's as bald as an egg. I been combing my hair with my fingers, 'cause when I use a brush it gets full of hair. Those hairs are what you call irreplaceable. They're like brain cells; you only get a certain number. Did I tell you about the Indian stiff I helped Digger bury last summer? A whole bunch of them were drunk as lords. Honked all the way to the Indian burial ground off Route Two, throwing bottles out the window. We got down that dirt road and they'd dug a round hole. Trouble was, a big boulder was at the bottom. No way could we put the casket in there. Well, they hooted and hollered till Digger said he sure wasn't taking the stiff back. So the Indians took the body outta the coffin and stuck him in the hole, just bent him around the stone, looked like he was hugging it. A youngish guy—green as a pickle. Then they dumped dirt on him. One of the Indians put the casket in the back of his truck and took it home for his chickens to roost in. Later he said he'd got the best eggs he'd ever eaten."

Seymour was silent. Jimmy heard him breathing regularly, right at the edge of snoring. Jimmy tugged his arm so he grunted. "Hey, Seymour, you still interested in a job at Digger's? I don't think Carl'll last much longer. Crazy as a shithouse rat. He was upstairs whispering to a stiff this morning, almost growling at it. Digger asked what was up, and Carl said he was clearing his throat. Fuck he was. Digger don't like oddness in people. I have to act like a fucking choirboy around him. I figure Carl just needs a push. I tell you the story about a guy putting a stiff's hand in another guy's lunch box? Fuckin' Carl would go tearing down the street if that happened. You still interested? It'd also mean time at the Burn Palace. There's money out there."

Seymour made no answer.

Jimmy tugged his arm. "You interested or not? I mean, I got other friends I can ask. Fuckin' Carl gives me the creeps."

"Sure," said Seymour. "Sure, I'm interested."

Vicki Lefebvre stood at her daughter's door and tried not to breathe. She tried to will her ears through the wood and into the room with the Adele posters. She might have opened the door and taken a peek, but when she'd done that an hour ago at nine o'clock, Nina had shouted, "Will you leave me the fuck alone! Why don't you ever trust me?"

But at least her daughter was home and didn't smell of dope. Three times Vicki had gone out to the yard to see if her daughter's light was on, but that didn't mean anything. Nina could sleep through a brass band if she set her mind to it. When she'd gone into her daughter's room, it was because she had heard Nina weeping. Vicki had stood in the hall, trying to make up her mind, but she didn't see how she could hear the weeping and not do anything. After all, it wasn't like her heart was made of stone. But Nina had stayed home last night and she'd stayed home tonight, so that was progress. But she still wouldn't say where she'd been, and when Vicki asked, Nina became angry and frightened at the same time. She would yell at her to "get the fuck out."

Three times Vicki had called her ex in Groton, and this evening, she had gotten him. He must have been in a hurry to go somewhere, because he hardly paid attention to what she was saying. "She's a kid," he had said. "She's sowing her wild oats. I did the same thing; you, too. Remember?"

Vicki tried to say it wasn't the same, that Nina was hysterical one moment and abusive the next.

"Maybe she got laid and didn't like it," said Harold. "You know how these girls talk each other into it. They dare each other. You should keep a closer eye on her. I'll talk to her about it, if I come up this weekend. I don't know; I got a pretty full schedule. How's her boyfriend? Do you like him?"

"She doesn't have a boyfriend," Vicki said, which was true enough, as far as she knew. Then Harold said he'd keep in touch and that was it. And who was he kidding? Harold had never kept in touch his entire life. But it occurred to Vicki that she could talk to some of Nina's friends. She didn't have many, but there were two or three that went back ten years or so.

Larry Rodman had gotten home at about nine o'clock, earlier than usual, but he'd had only one client. He put a couple of TV dinners into the microwave and pushed the button. Macaroni and cheese was his favorite. Afterward, he'd have a little maple-walnut ice cream and catch some ground-and-pound, sprawl-and-brawl on the mixed martial arts channel. He liked the girl bouts best, especially with Cyborg Santos, who looked the meanest. Rodman lifted the four stoneware cookie jars down from the shelf and set them in a row; then he dug in his pockets.

This ring was twelve carats. He dropped it into the twelve-carat jar and it made a little clink. By itself, it wasn't worth much, but they added up. But tonight he had a special treat. Digging into his pocket, he withdrew an engagement ring: eighteen-carat white gold and a one-and-a-half-carat diamond that sparkled under the ceiling light. He dropped it into the fourth jar. Often the family wanted the rings returned, but sometimes they were too upset to ask. If they came back later, he'd say it was too late. The deed was done. Larry didn't bother with the rest of the stuff—watches, necklaces, bracelets, pins, brooches, cuff links, tie clips—unless it was top of the line. And pacemakers, he had a barrel of them waiting to go to the dump. No, he saw himself as a specialist. Gold wedding rings were what he liked, with a few diamond rings for their sparkle—"To put a little light on the subject," he liked to say.

When the microwave dinged, Larry got himself a Coors and a fork. Then he checked his fingers for gray flakes. Sometimes a dozen or so would get under the nails—little gray crescents. He would make a joke of it. "I wonder who's coming to dinner tonight?" he might say. Or, "Who's going to sleep with me tonight?"

Larry saw some gray and went to the sink, scrubbed his hands with Borax and a nailbrush. It was probably the old lady who'd given him the ring, the one brought in early that evening from Ocean Breezes. He gave a little salute as the water swirled down the drain: "Thanks, sweetheart."

Acting chief Fred Bonaldo was home in his smoking room, wearing his new chief's uniform with its gold braid. His attitude was that he might as well wear it now, because pretty soon he'd be out on his ass. Like he'd be the first to admit he was in over his head, which meant if he got fired he would never march as a cop in the Memorial Day parade. He'd be stuck with the Masons again, not that they weren't a bunch of great guys.

It wouldn't be so bad to admit he was in over his head if a lot of other people—even women, like his wife—didn't also keep telling him he was in over his head. He had liked Woody Potter, but now Woody was barely polite. Had Fred forgotten to do this; had Fred forgotten to do that? Was it his fault Alice Alessio had vanished? Hopper had been watching her and slipped away to grab a grinder. They didn't call him Whole-Hog Hopper for nothing.

Then the Oswego business—what did Carl Krause have to do with anything, anyway? Reporters, FBI, helicopters—this was a quiet town. Fred had never counted on abductions, and although the scalping had happened in South Kingstown's jurisdiction—thank God for that—Hartmann had been hanging around in Brewster, and so people kept thinking it was *his* business. Well, he had two men watching Peggy Summers's house. No way could she sneak off. Whole-Hog would be fine as long as he had someone to keep him from the trough.

On top of everything else, the Krause kid kept calling him—though he wasn't a Krause; he was Hercel something. Somehow Hercel had gotten his private cell phone number and kept calling to ask when he'd get his snake back. How the heck should he know? The snake was the center of the whole investigation, just like a gun in a murder investigation. So he couldn't just give it back, no matter how much the kid asked. And the kid had a voice like a robot: "May-I-have-my-snake-back-please." It made Fred want to tear his hair that had gone south long ago, because every fuckup was another nail in the coffin of his career.

And Krause was another sore spot. Fred had almost dropped a big smelly load when Krause pointed that shotgun at him. He thought he'd just bought the farm. He had meant to call over to Oswego, like Woody told him, but he plain forgot. And how was he supposed to think with helicopters buzzing around and a hundred reporters crowding him and asking if there'd been new developments? He should have taken a lesson from Baldo and said, "Pull my finger."

It seemed the only way Fred could save his job was to do something dramatic, like grabbing a kid from a burning house or shooting it out with crooks. But no way would that happen. At times he might be dramatic, but he'd never been brave. And it could get worse. That evening Woody said he was chasing down some witches. Fred laughed till he saw Woody wasn't making a joke. So the witch business might go someplace, but the trouble with stuff going out of control was everyone ended up hating everyone else, which made it hard for someone like Fred, whose single purpose in life was to be well liked.

In Brewster the wind picked up and the sky cleared as clouds headed off elsewhere, blowing across the face of the partial moon as if the moon itself were in a hurry. By midnight the town was mostly dark. Woody Potter was finishing some paperwork in police headquarters, which meant filling out the forms of the National Incident-Based Reporting System, breaking everything into categories, numbers, and capital letters, but which did not, as Fred Bonaldo had observed, tell you whether a snake was a weapon, perpetrator, or victim; and scalping could only be listed as "other."

Elsewhere, Sister Chastisement had come over from Narragansett to spank a lawyer, whose buns were like bowling balls from hours in the gym. "This hurts me more than it hurts you," she said. Father Bob at St. Michael's watched *High Noon* on Turner Classic Movies. He recalled how half a century earlier Katy Jurado's décolletage had led him to masturbate, and on Saturday he'd confessed it to Father Joseph, whose answer was always "boys will do that," as he doled out Hail Marys and Our Fathers.

Ginger and Howard Phelps were again playing gin rummy, and Ginger was winning. That's because Howard kept thinking of Carl Krause, who'd passed him on the sidewalk that afternoon and growled. When he had fired Carl, he'd been unsure whether or not to call the police. He'd never heard anybody shout at a customer like that. Howard had been in his office and heard it from that far away. When he went to speak to Carl, the customer fled, though other people had also been there and all looked at Carl as if he were crazy. Once Howard had learned what'd happened, he had no choice but to fire him. Even then he had thought Carl was about to go berserk and strike him. But then Howard tried to put it behind him. No point in letting Carl rent space in his head. And he had hoped the same was true of Carl, that he'd put the whole business behind him. But then came the growling, and what was Howard to make of it?

Harriet Krause was asleep, and so was her daughter, Lucy. Carl was upstairs, watching the knotholes move. Three times he'd heard the cat out in the hall, but when he had flung open the door the cat was gone.

Jean Sawyer was lying in bed next to her sleeping husband, reading a romance novel, *The Virgin's Debauch*. Every time she tried to sleep, she pictured poor Mr. Hartmann lying scalped out there in the swamp, and it gave her the shivers. Twice she'd nudged Frankie, hoping for some solace, but he lay there dead to the world, the pig.

Todd Chmielnicki sat on a small rug, staring at a bare white wall in his apartment, more of a monk's cell than a home. Although his eyes were open, he saw nothing. What does it mean to be liberated from reality? And why would anybody do it? Chmielnicki was focused on the first of the upper limbs of Ashtanga. His mind had turned from the world to concentrate on a spot between his eyebrows; his brain and senses were deep in communication with one another as he moved into his interior. Were an explosion to occur in his room, he wouldn't notice. He will stay this way all night.

Jill Franklin was proofreading her story for Saturday's paper, in which the snake's name, Satan, figured prominently. She had also learned from "a source" at URI that the mud found on the floor of the hospital nursery had most likely come from Great Swamp. This, too, was information that other papers didn't have. If she could rack up more of those, it might be a pathway to a job at the *ProJo,* a real paper.

From the other room her six-year-old son muttered in his sleep. Some nights Luke called out "Daddy!" at times as a cry of help, at times in yearning. Each time was like a knife through Jill's gut. Luke had never known his daddy. She and Derek had split up two months before Luke had been born. "I don't want to be tied down," he had said. As far as she knew, he was still tending bar in Boulder. He'd never shown any interest in getting to know his son.

It was about time, Jill thought, that Luke had a real father, or at least a gentle and loving stepfather. All day she'd been thinking Woody would be a perfect candidate for the role. The only problem was that he hated her.

Of course, other people were also awake—Vicki Lefebvre; Dr. Fuller; Mayor Hobart; Harriet's best friends, Anita Barr and Amy Calderone—as well as hundreds of others in South County, a name that contains Washington and part of Kent County. Winter's approaching; Halloween's almost upon us. High above town a flock of geese noisily flies south, looking like fleeting insects across the moon. It's doubtful they look down. What do they know of the complexities of human emotion beneath them—the guilt, ambition, fear, joy, and rank desire?

It's ridiculous to think that they might notice the alcove in front of Crandall Investments is empty except for a tattered sleeping bag. And where is Ronnie McBride, who sleeps there on most nights? He seems to have disappeared.

On Woody's drive home there was a moment when he almost turned toward Dr. Joyce Fuller's condo in Narragansett. Last night he had helped her and tonight she could help him, though it wasn't conversation he wanted but to climb into her bed. And it wasn't Dr. Fuller in particular he wanted, but the embrace of another body. Dr. Fuller was just the one he felt he stood the most chance with. Mostly Woody's self-discipline held him together in adversity. Now it felt weakened. But it wasn't one thing that bothered him but a whole collection: Susie's departure, the inexplicable missing baby and murder of Ernest Hartmann, the missing Nurse Spandex, Todd Chmielnicki's unsettling observations, his own fragile emotional state and temper. He felt hanging on to a warm female body could help him with this. Almost any female body would be a huge improvement over Ajax, who sensed something was wrong and kept leaning over the center console to lick his face.

That evening Woody had met Sister Asherah MacDonald, who taught meditation and holistic health at You-You. She was a fifty-eight-year-old lesbian, plump and wearing a loose ankle-length blue dress, and kept her long gray hair in a ponytail. Woody realized he had seen her before, or rather he'd seen her car—a light blue Prius with about twenty bumper stickers, such as FAT PEOPLE ARE HARDER TO KIDNAP, GOD IS COMING AND SHE IS ANGRY, MY OTHER CAR IS A BROOM, A DAY WITHOUT FAIRIES IS LIKE A DAY WITHOUT SUNSHINE, TREE-HUGGING DIRT WORSHIPPER, and WE ARE EVERYWHERE.

With a round, beaming face, she seemed, Woody thought, militantly benign, but who knows how deep it went. She lived with her partner, Sister Isis, in an old farmhouse at the edge of town. That afternoon she had greeted Woody with seeming delight, which, he guessed, was how she greeted everyone. The hard part in listening to her was he had to be careful not to filter her words through his cynicism.

She belonged to a coven of thirteen women who met with other covens for the eight Sabbats—two solstices, two equinoxes, May Day, Halloween, August 1, and Groundhog Day, also known as Candlemas; and the Esbats, which occurred on each of the year's full moons. Wiccans appeared to be great partiers, with lots of dancing, singing, and the casting of benign spells. As Sister Asherah described it, the gatherings sounded like good clean fun and a little dull. She, too, spoke of the Eternal Return, the cycle of birth and rebirth. Woody couldn't tell if it was a lesbian thing, and he didn't know how to ask her. As for shape-shifting, she had heard of it being done, but her own coven had been unsuccessful in those areas. Sister Asherah said she was appalled by the baby's abduction and Hartmann's murder. Perhaps that was true. She had heard of Satanists in Rhode Island, but she knew none, nor was she interested in meeting any. Wiccans condemned selfishness and self-indulgence, and, like Christians, favored reciprocity: Do unto others as you'd have others do unto you. Finally, she gave him the names of several other Wiccans. Woody said he'd be in touch.

The only link with Wiccans, Woody thought as he drove home, was the coin. Hartmann had also shown it to another investigator in his Boston office and had said it had something to do with graves, perhaps Indian graves—the man had hardly paid attention. Woody hoped to keep its existence silent. To add witches to the subjects of snakes, abductions, and scalping would bring back the helicopters with a vengeance.

He reached home at twelve-fifteen, fed the animals, and tumbled into bed half dressed. All night, it seemed, he dreamed of fleeing through a forest at dusk; something was pursuing him, but he never got a good look at it.

EIGHT

When Hercel awoke Saturday morning he had no idea where he was. The room was suffused with the faint red light of dawn that reflected off the glass of the picture frames and slowly moved down the spines of the books in the bookcases. He didn't recognize the curtains, with their red stripes and vertical trellises of red roses, or the red-and-blue rug with geometrical designs. The people in the pictures were strange to him, and who had this many books? Then he remembered the coyotes and leapt from bed.

Immediately he yelped and fell to the rug. His ankle felt like spikes were being driven through it. By the time he had rolled over onto his knees, the door had opened with a bang. A tall balding man with a gray ponytail stood in the doorframe, supporting himself on an aluminum walker wound with colorful ribbons from which hung silver, red, and gold balls like Christmas ornaments. Hercel looked at it with surprise as he pushed himself up on his good leg and fell over on the bed. He saw that his right ankle had been wrapped with tape.

"We're both crips now, aren't we? We should have a race." The man shuffled into the room and stuck out his big hand to Hercel. "I'm Barton

Wilcox. We haven't met yet. You had a nasty scare last night. You want some breakfast? You must be hungry. I've got an old crutch of Bernie's we can probably adjust if you want to try it. Tig's been asking when you'd wake up."

As Hercel shook the man's hand, Tig appeared in the door, followed by Bernie. She was the one who'd wrapped his ankle. They wore startled, expectant expressions, which relaxed as they saw Barton and Hercel shaking hands.

"I know where that crutch is," said Tig, and she disappeared.

"How do you feel, other than your ankle?" asked Bernie.

She wore a long green skirt and a loose white blouse, and her gray hair was in a bun. A variety of silver rings were on her fingers and thumbs, a variety of silver bracelets and silver chains hung around her neck, and she even had a variety of silver earrings. Hercel tried to calculate how much it must weigh.

He rubbed his shoulder. "My shoulder's sore. Otherwise I'm fine."

"And how's the psychological damage?" asked Barton cheerfully.

Hercel looked at him questioningly.

"He's trying to find a polite way of saying you were nearly eaten," said Bernie, "and so it might have messed with your head."

Hercel tentatively touched his forehead. "My head feels fine."

Barton laughed. "Good, that's all I cared about."

Tig reappeared in the room with a crutch, and Bernie fiddled with the screws to make it shorter. In a moment, Hercel tried it, taking a step or two, and it seemed okay. In fact, he rather liked it.

"That's great," said Barton. "Let's go eat breakfast, and then Bernie can take you home. Or you can help Tig feed the chickens if your ankle can stand it. Bernie called your mother last night to tell her you were fine."

Hercel hobbled down a pine-paneled hall to a large kitchen. From the wooden beams hung strings of peppers and garlic, as well as bunches of thyme, basil, rosemary, and many other herbs. Hercel stared up at them. "Wow, do you cook with all these?"

Bernie laughed. "Only some of them. Barton has been growing herbs for the nine herbs charm. There's mugwort, fennel, thyme, mayweed, lamb's cress, nettles, chamomile, and the rest. I promise he'll make a big mess in my kitchen."

Hercel turned to Barton. "Are you a witch?"

Now it was Barton's turn to laugh. "I'm a retired professor of English—Old English, as a matter of fact. The charm is from the tenth century, probably before. It protects against poisons and snakes. But what we need is a charm against coyotes. But here's a bit of my translation.

"Nine herbs have power against nine poisons.
A serpent came crawling, he ripped a man in two
then Odin took nine Glory Twigs,
hit the adder and it flew into nine parts.
Thus the apple stopped the poison,
so the snake would never again enter this house.

"They used apple juice and grease to mix the herbs into a salve. Of course, we don't know if it helped anybody, but it couldn't hurt, that's the main thing. But eat, eat, before your breakfast gets cold."

Bernie put pancakes on Hercel's plate. There was real maple syrup. The others had already eaten, but they sat with him at the table. Barton drank coffee; Bernie and Tig had cups of tea.

"Can you tell us what happened last night?" asked Bernie. "You were hurt and dazed when we found you. I suppose I should have called an ambulance, but the trouble with being a nurse for thirty years is I think I know best. I fixed you up the best I could and put you to bed. I had to sit with you for quite a while before you'd let me leave."

Hercel had a faint memory of Bernie's soothing voice talking to him as he lay in the strange bed. If he had dreams, he didn't remember them. He told them of bicycling out of Brewster to visit Tig and see the farm. She had invited him, he thought, about a week ago.

"You should have called," said Bernie. "I'd have picked you up."

No, he wanted to ride his bike. He'd never gone that far out of town before, though he had ridden down to the beach and out to Burlingame. As to why he'd chosen that particular hour, Hercel only said that Mr. Krause had been mad at him, but he didn't explain the difference between being frightened and being scared.

"And who's Mr. Krause?" asked Barton.

So Hercel told them. He tried not to tell too much, but it was enough for Bernie and Barton to exchange looks.

"And why do you call him Mr. Krause?" asked Tig.

"He says it shows respect."

"None of this tells us what happened," said Barton, changing the subject. "So you began riding your bike out here. And then . . . ?"

"It got dark," said Hercel.

He described how in the increasing darkness it became hard to stay on the road. So he began to walk the bike, but soon he heard the coyotes and began to hurry.

"You must have been terrified," said Bernie.

Hercel thought about it. "All I thought about was staying on the road. I think I didn't have time to be scared, at least not then."

Soon Hercel had found himself running beside his bike, but he still went off the road. At last it seemed his only hope of getting to the farm was to ride. Even then he slipped off the pavement as the coyotes got closer. Then he had seen lights ahead through the trees, which enabled him to keep the bike going straight and to ride faster. The coyotes were right behind him, and he knew they'd try to cut him off. He swerved a little to block their advance as they snapped at him. Then he saw the stone wall and gate of Barton's farm a short ways ahead and heard the barking of his dogs.

"I pedaled as hard as I could. I've outrun big dogs before, but these were different. I knew I wouldn't be able to stop and jump over the wall, so I stood up on my pedals and ran into it. I flew right over your dogs. Then I hit the ground."

Bernie had run outside when she heard the dogs, taking a shotgun with her. The coyotes were yapping on the other side of the wall, and she fired into the air. "I didn't hit any, but it scared them. Then I found you and carried you inside. You muttered the whole way."

"My head hurt," said Hercel.

"I should think your whole body hurt," said Bernie. "It's a good thing the ground's not frozen yet, or maybe you fell into a nice pile of sheep manure."

There was more laughter, but it was nervous laughter. Tig said it couldn't be manure, because Hercel didn't smell. Barton said he was lucky he hadn't broken his neck. Bernie didn't say anything. It was hard to imagine that a boy or anyone would have ridden a bike straight at the wall.

"The coyotes get meaner as their numbers increase," said Barton. "Not long ago a man was attacked in Massachusetts, and a number of children have been attacked here in Rhode Island. People might as well kiss their pets good-bye if they leave them outside. A bunch of coyotes pulled down a Rottweiler last month. New England coyotes are bigger than the ones out west. They've got more wolf in them. You're lucky you didn't end up like Wrestling Brewster."

"How so?" asked Hercel.

"He was killed by wolves when he went out hunting sometime in the 1760s. There weren't many wolves left by then, but they got him just the same. You know, he got his name because he was supposed to be wrestling with the Devil and people said the Devil had got him, that the Devil had taken the shape of wolves."

"Barton, they don't need to hear this," said Bernie.

"You're right, you're right. You think you can get around on that crutch okay, Hercel? Your bike must be on the other side of the wall, unless the coyotes ate it. I expect it's pretty banged up. I'll see if I can fix it."

Twenty police officers and state troopers, as well as an FBI agent, filled a conference room in the Brewster police station at eight o'clock Saturday morning for a briefing chaired by Captain Tom Brotman, state police detective commander, with Phil Hilkavich, District B commander as vice-chair. Woody, Bobby Anderson, acting chief Bonaldo, a lieutenant and several detectives from South Kingstown, park police, a tribal policeman, and others were gathered around a rectangular table. Bonaldo supplied coffee and doughnuts. A secretary took notes; the tone was somber.

Captain Brotman was a thirty-year veteran of the state police and held graduate degrees in public safety, criminology, and psychology. Like many in positions of authority, he understood that the higher he rose, the more he was watched—press, TV, colleagues, friends, enemies, everyone. The trick was to know it but to seem unaffected by it, and surely he had known people ruined by professional paranoia, people who'd maneuvered themselves into positions where it became impossible to act because every possible consequence became threatening. Tall, imposing, and with a strong baritone voice, Brotman saw a series of dangers that could cover him in mud. The barbaric nature of the crimes, the yet to be publicly mentioned subject of witches, the possibility of human sacrifice and black magic—these were a recipe for hysteria, and with hysteria would come the question "Why aren't the authorities—and Tom Brotman, in particular—*doing* something?"

Captain Brotman showed no sign of this concern. Maybe he drank more water then usual, licked his lips, shifted from foot to foot, touched his hands to his gray suit coat more than usual, and those who knew him well recognized it.

He began by describing the two crimes while admitting that no clear evidence linked them. In the public's mind, what linked them was a shared viciousness, but that might mean nothing. The one link was the bit of mud found on the floor of the hospital nursery that most likely—but not certainly—came from Great Swamp. Consequently, they had to work harder—no days off and no excuses. Then he passed out photographs of the nursery, which were mildly interesting. Next came photographs of the snake, including one of Chucky Stubbs, the sergeant at the animal shelter, raising it up to show its length. Chucky was about five-foot-seven; the snake was two to three inches longer.

Next, Brotman passed out photographs of Ernest Hartmann dead in his Ford Focus; then lying on a stretcher, with front, back, and side views of the scalping; and then naked on a table at the medical examiner's, which also revealed the knife wound in his chest. But for the men and women in the conference room, all they could see was the scalping. As Bobby said later, "I'm fuckin' glad I saw it before lunch and not after lunch." The scalping photographs underlined the gravity of their undertaking, not that they needed reminders. It wasn't worse than a fatal shooting in a bar, but it was more horrible. So here was the victim and here was the horror, and the one stood beside the other like a man next to an elephant.

Last were photographs of the smiley face, which was like a comic hat on the elephant; like putting bells, whistles on the elephant. It was as appalling as the scalping itself, though of a different category—the scalping was an act of barbarity, the smiley face an act of madness. Seemingly, it had been done by dipping a hand into the blood, but since no fingerprint was found, Brotman assumed that the artist—presumably the murderer—had worn latex gloves.

Captain Brotman went on to describe what had been done so far. People living in the vicinity of the hospital had been questioned, but no one had seen anything unusual. One man reported hearing coyotes barking. An ambulance driver parked behind the hospital, Seymour Hodges, had also heard coyotes and claimed to have seen them running around the ambulance—something not witnessed by the tech, Jimmy Mooney. Residents on Liberty Lane, the road to the swamp, were questioned, but again nothing unusual was seen. One woman had noticed a small blue car driving past to the swamp on Thursday evening, somewhere between eight and nine, but then she had put the kids to bed and didn't know whether it had returned.

Steve Tovaldis had been questioned. A junior high school teacher in South Kingstown, he was married with three children between the ages of nine and fifteen; he was popular with his neighbors and eager to help whenever asked; he'd lived in the same house for fifteen years. He hadn't been questioned about Wiccans, and Brotman asked the South Kingstown police to get busy with it.

The medical examiner calculated that Hartmann had died sometime between eight and ten o'clock. For dinner he'd had three pieces of pizza—cheese and sausage—at Rudy's Pizza in downtown Brewster. This had been washed down with a Diet Pepsi. He'd eaten by himself and paid his bill at six-twenty-three p.m.

In Hartmann's motel room had been found hair products from

Anthony Logistics for Men: shampoo, conditioner, and hair cream, with fragrances of coconut oil, jojoba oil, chamomile, peppermint, and aloe. These were used to wash and groom a custom hair system, presumably Hartmann's.

A criminalist from the state crime lab, as well as a forensic scientist and doctor from the medical examiner's office, had joined the crime scene unit. Casts were taken of the footprints of Hartmann's killer, or prints they believed belonged to the killer—size 11D Timberland Pro Terrenes with slightly worn SafeGrip, slip-resistant rubber soles. Although other prints were found about the blue Ford Focus, these were the most recent. However, casts were taken of four other prints. The crime lab criminalist passed out a piece of paper detailing the five types of shoes, with the Pro Terrenes at the top. Also attached was a list of stores carrying the Pro Terrenes, though with Internet shopping this was probably a waste of time.

There were also the prints of Tovaldis's yellow Labs and the prints of three or four coyotes, drawn by the smell of blood.

The driver's-side window of the Focus had been fully opened. Hartmann had been killed by a long blade thrust upward into his heart's right ventricle, which was then twisted to slice through the pulmonary valve, the right atrium, and the aorta. The same knife was probably used for the scalping, cutting a horizontal line through the skin at the top of Hartmann's forehead.

The crime scene unit in the hospital had identified half of the fingerprints lifted from the nursery. They had obtained Alice Alessio's prints from her apartment, since she still hadn't been found. Analysis of the soil and organic matter in the bit of mud found on the floor pointed to a freshwater wetland environment, while the organic matter's mixture of Atlantic white cedar, black gum, and laurel suggested Great Swamp.

Profiles were compiled of the nurses, doctors, aides, hospital staff, patients, and visitors who either had recently visited or whose work might have taken them into the nursery. Profiles were also compiled of the people who worked in the swamp and resided along Liberty Lane.

Woody described his talk with Sister Asherah MacDonald, and it was agreed there should be a concerted effort to talk to other Wiccans, as well as men and women employed by You-You. Woody described differences between the Wiccans, neopagans, Neo-Heathens, and Satanists, adding that these were just general categories. Wiccan and neopagan websites suggested there might be five hundred within the state. Most seemed nonviolent, well meaning, and idealistic. He added that he knew nothing about the Satanists. As police officers, it seemed their interest lay with the more extreme groups. "Actually," said Woody, "they start pretty extreme and get extremer."

Captain Brotman pointed out that Wicca was recognized by the courts as a valid religion. It had been active in the United States for more than fifty years and had an estimated two hundred thousand members. Wicca was protected by the First Amendment, and there were Wiccan chaplains in the military. Consequently, they had to be careful not to be seen as persecuting or profiling. A few police officers responded to this with "now I've seen everything" expressions.

Bobby described talking to Peggy Summers and her mother. "It appears she was pretty much raped by a guy wearing a skull mask. She thinks there were lots of people; all had been downing mushrooms and various illegal substances. She's very vague about the whole event, but she thinks the others danced around her as she was being raped. It's not that she was fighting or anything. The guy took advantage of her when she was stoned. She said she'd gone there because it was supposed to be a party. Either she won't tell me or she doesn't know who suggested it to her in the first place. She'd been told some people she knew were there, but she didn't see them. Free food, free drugs—it sounded good to her, except on the way out she was blindfolded."

The matter of the missing placenta was discussed. Who had the opportunity to take it? Could it have been taken at the time when the baby had been abducted? Why was it taken? And, again, who knew that Hercel owned a corn snake? Well, everybody in the neighborhood did, as did a lot of kids at school, because Hercel had taken it to show to his class in September. Woody explained that the snake in fact had no name, and the name Satan had been invented by a local reporter.

"We've got different issues here," said Brotman, "and we shouldn't confuse them. The abduction and murder may or may not be connected. Then, what's the reason for the snake and the scalping? We assume they're part of some ritual, but they might have been done to throw us off the track. What do we know about Hartmann?"

A Boston cop and a Massachusetts state police detective again described that Hartmann had told an associate something about graves and Indian graves and Indians in general. However, the associate had hardly paid attention. A dozen of Hartmann's friends and acquaintances had been questioned, as had his ex-wife in LA, but none had information as to why Hartmann had driven to Brewster, nor had they known he was gone. However, it seemed clear he'd brought a Browning Hi-Power and the coin with the Wiccan symbols. Brotman passed out a drawing of the coin made by Gabe Strauss at You-You.

"It's possible," said Brotman, "that Hartmann didn't have the weapon with him. But if he did, it's now most likely in the hands of the killer." He passed out photographs of an HP. "This is a single-action nine-millimeter semiautomatic pistol with a thirteen-round magazine capacity with another round in the chamber. It has an effective range of one hundred fifty meters."

The Indian tribal policeman expressed concern that the scalping and mention of Indian graves had occurred to throw suspicion on the tribe. Brotman had spoken to the chief sachem and members of the tribal counsel as to how they should proceed, but he wanted to remind the officers that neither crime had occurred on tribal land nor directly implicated Native Americans. That being said, tribal officers had interviewed Native Americans who lived within a few miles of the Hartmann murder, and would interview more if necessary. But he wanted to point out that most scalping in the latter part of the nineteenth century had been done by white bounty hunters.

He then gave a few facts about the Great Swamp Massacre of December 19, 1675. First, the Narragansetts were not at war with anyone at that time. Second, of the more than one thousand Native Americans who were killed, most were women, children, and the elderly. Those who escaped had retreated deeper into the swamp; those captured were sold into slavery in the Caribbean.

"Since the time of the massacre," he said, "a few people have said that the ghosts of dead warriors haunt the swamp. Now they're saying the ghost of a warrior did the scalping. This is not only foolish, but it's slander, and you can see how it might also affect the investigation."

"How?" asked a South Kingstown cop.

"You can't handcuff a ghost and stick him in prison. You blame it on ghosts and everyone else goes free."

Bobby described the behavior of Carl Krause, while Bonaldo said he had a call in to the police chief in Oswego, something he hadn't done as yet. Bobby said he also meant to talk to Hamilton Brantley, owner of Brantley's Funeral Home, who employed Krause part-time as a handyman.

Additional troopers and policemen were assigned to help Woody track down Alice Alessio. Her description had been sent to other police departments, hospitals, and the medical examiner's office.

There was more; there is always more. The FBI agent discussed possible reasons for abduction, including human sacrifice. This didn't sit well with the police officers, who tend to be a conservative lot. Snakes, baby theft, witchcraft, scalpings, and the ghosts of Indian warriors stripped back the covers to a world they had always worried might exist. All had seen terrible things; now they were promised things even more terrible, or such was their thought.

"Be careful," said Captain Brotman in closing, "that you don't talk to reporters. If news gets out about witches and the rest of it, our workload will triple and the town will fill up with sightseers."

As Woody and Bobby left the building, Bobby said, "An absolute cluster-fuck."

"You've been a little cynical recently, don't you think?"

"I get that way when shotguns are pointed in my direction. It's a personal thing. I end up considering my mortality, which is a subject I like to avoid. I should move to Tahiti and grow breadfruit trees."

"You wouldn't like Tahiti," said Woody. "It's full of tourists. Try Pitcairn Island. It's got under fifty people. You could expand the gene pool."

"Do they like black folk?"

"What choice would they have?"

They walked out to the parking lot. It was a bright fall day; a stiff wind was shaking the trees. It was shortly after eleven, and morning light brightened the nineteenth-century church steeples. A crow voiced its monosyllabic opinion, and nobody answered to prove it wrong. Leaf blowers were active and somewhere a chain saw.

"You think there're a lot of coyotes around here?" asked Bobby.

"As compared to what?"

"Well, when I was a kid, there weren't any. Then some people said they saw them and others said they were wrong. Then everybody said they saw them, and now they're saying they've seen a lot of them."

"You know there're two thousand coyotes in the city of Chicago?" said Woody.

"Man, I don't care about Chicago, I care about here. We got a shitload."

Each thought he saw fear in the other man's eyes and each hoped it didn't show in his own.

After the meeting, acting chief Fred Bonaldo walked to his office down the hall. He walked slowly, in case anyone wanted to talk to him. He was making it easy for them to catch up. But nobody wanted to talk to him; they wanted to talk to one another. He could hear them laughing and talking energetically. They were part of a select fraternity, and he wasn't a member. He was only *acting* chief. And even if he was named chief—which felt ever more unlikely—he still doubted he'd be admitted to their fraternity. He told himself he had no good reason for thinking this; it was just a bad feeling.

It wasn't that Fred didn't have friends, but most of his friends were Masons. He admired them, he even loved them, but they weren't policemen. Fred was friends with his doctor, his dentist, and his lawyer; he was good friends with Tony Caprio, owner of Caprio's Toyota. He was good friends with Father Pete at St. John's; there was nothing he wouldn't tell him. He was even friends with the husbands of his wife's friends, which were a pretty mixed crew. But none were cops.

This was partly why he hadn't called the Oswego police chief. Even if Fred didn't identify himself as acting chief, he was sure the man or woman would hear it in his voice, would hear he was more of a Realtor than a cop. Fred imagined how the Oswego chief's voice would grow cool. He just didn't need that in his life right now, he really didn't. People knocking down his door, clamoring to speak to him, and then letting him know in just so many words that he was a lightweight. No, he didn't need that from an Oswego cop, who didn't even have the ocean to turn to when he was feeling low.

On the other hand, Fred knew he had to make the call because of his son Baldo, his favorite, the one who looked like a miniature version of himself, poor kid. Baldo had come home from school all excited, his round face lit up like a hundred-watt bulb. Fred loved seeing his son happy. It made his day. Then Baldo said, "I've made friends with Hercel. He's great! He's going to be my best friend. He knows neat magic tricks."

Fred remembered Hercel. He was Carl Krause's stepkid. So he had said, "Are you sure that's a good idea?"

Baldo heard his father's caution. "Sure, it is. It's fantastic. Why shouldn't it be a good idea?" His excitement had turned to watchfulness.

What could Fred say, that Carl Krause was a nutcase? That he was uncontrolled and potentially violent? These were not adjectives that Fred wanted to trickle back to Carl. He also knew that Baldo would laugh at them. So what other reason could he give? The family's social position? They weren't Roman Catholics? They hadn't been born in Brewster? They drove the wrong kind of car?

"Maybe you're right," Fred had said. "He looks like a good kid. Just remember, when you meet a person, they're on their best behavior. It's only when you start knowing them that the funny parts show up."

"That's not true with Hercel," said Baldo eagerly. "He hated me at first. It took a long time before he got to like me. I kinda grew on him."

So Fred decided to call Oswego. Maybe Carl Krause would have an outstanding warrant for his arrest or something useful like that.

The Oswego police chief was Matthew McGarrah and it had taken several calls and a lot of explaining before Fred had been given his home phone number. At first they indulged in a certain amount of chitchat before they got to the business at hand. "Do you know old so-and-so?" "We already had eight inches of snow." Then Chief McGarrah came to the important part: "Carl's a great guy if he takes his meds."

Fred felt a chill. "How d'you mean?"

"He gets paranoid, a little violent. He beat up a guy in a bar. If he's on his meds, he's a real charmer. He'd do anything for you; you only have to ask. But three times he's been down to Benjamin Rush for ECT treatments. Did him a world of good. For a while."

A request for clarification revealed that Carl had gotten shock therapy in a nuthouse in Syracuse, just like Jack Nicholson in *One Flew over the Cuckoo's Nest*. *Zap, zap*, and your brain vanished into the local power grid. No wonder Carl acted so funny. It made Fred feel almost sorry for him.

They chatted some more, and Fred got the names and phone numbers of an Oswego shrink who'd seen Carl, and some shrinks at Benjamin Rush.

"Carl was fine for at least two years before he moved east. I figured he'd been cured. Is he doing okay?"

"Maybe," said Fred. "We're just curious, that's all."

Next Fred put a call in to Captain Brotman and passed on the information. To his mind, it'd be better if Brotman contacted the New York shrinks. He had more clout and wouldn't be stopped by the confidentiality business. For crying out loud, it wasn't as if shrinks were priests. In fact, most of them were atheists or Jewish.

• • •

Leaving Woody in the parking lot around eleven-thirty, Bobby Anderson climbed into his Z, revved it several times to get the squirrels jumping, and drove to Brantley's Funeral Home at the other end of Water Street. Although he'd seen a lot of dead people, he disliked the transitional phase between death and the cemetery or crematorium, when the makeup was dished out and the dead were made to live again, all in good fun. He had seen guys mushed in car wrecks who had been put back together and looked the picture of health, as long as you squinted. He found it creepy. "People need closure," Shawna told him. "As far as I'm concerned," Bobby had said, "being dead is closure enough. It's like they bring a guy back to life, then whack him again."

The funeral home, like many in the East, had begun as a Victorian mansion owned by a local bigwig: an asymmetrical gray house with a turret on the left, wraparound front porch, and a single, three-windowed gable at the third floor. The roof was patterned slate. It was only in the South, Bobby figured, that you found funeral homes in bungalows, even mobile homes.

Bobby parked in back and checked his smile, and a few minutes later, he was sitting in Brantley's quietly modulated office—soft chairs, soft music, muted colors, and a polished mahogany desk and file cabinet. Only the computer monitor was modern.

"Call me Ham; everybody does," said Digger Brantley.

As with Fred Bonaldo and Chief McGarrah, a few minutes were given to chitchat. "Yes, I grew up in this house, though we've moved to something more modern on James Street. Jenny, that's my wife, wanted more privacy. It wasn't until I went to school that I learned other kids didn't have to maintain absolute silence whenever the telephone rang. I still keep a small apartment up in the turret to use if we're really busy."

Brantley was a well-groomed gray-haired man in a three-piece blue suit. His round, close-shaven face was a healthy pink; his voice was assured and muted. Though not quite stout, he presented the impression of enjoying his creature comforts. As he gave a short history of his career, he happened to mention that he'd embalmed his father and had helped in the embalming of his grandfather. "I felt it a great honor," he said.

It was then Bobby realized that, unlike himself, Brantley would never find embalming your old man creepy. He saw that while Brantley surely had a keen sense of his mortality, he viewed death differently than Bobby. The funeral of someone who had lived into old age was, in most cases, an act of quiet celebration for a life well lived. For the sick and suffering, their torment was blessedly at an end. For the young, one's duty was to help the family grieve and move on. Brantley's occupation, as he described it, had civic, social, and religious responsibilities. He hoped to make the survivors his friends. Many were friends already. After all, he and Jenny had grown up in Brewster.

"Sad to say, these days family funeral homes are a dying breed," said Brantley, "what with the spread of the corporations. Service Corporation International is the largest. They operate over fifteen hundred funeral homes and own over four hundred cemeteries here in the U.S. You mostly don't deal with a licensed mortician but with a salesman who knows all a salesman's tricks. SCI trades on the New York Stock Exchange, and they have to keep their investors happy. Sorry to go on about it, but it gets my dander up, as my grandfather used to say. But the business is changing in other ways. It used to be only one out of ten was cremated; now it's over half. In twenty years less than a quarter will choose burial. Fortunately, we have our own crematorium near Hope Valley that's able to fill the needs of a few other funeral homes in South County. Keeps the home fires burning, you might say."

Bobby shot him a quick look, but Brantley maintained his benign expression. So far Brantley hadn't asked Bobby the reason for his visit, and Bobby guessed that the practice of patience was part of Brantley's business, to give the impression he had all the time in the world to spend on Bobby's needs.

"I'm curious about an employee of yours," said Bobby. "Carl Krause. We're not investigating him for anything and, as far as I know, he's not guilty of any crime. I don't want to get him in trouble."

Brantley smiled benignly, and behind the smile, Bobby thought, there could be anything, not necessarily anything bad, just anything.

"Carl's been a big help, though he only works part-time. As you can imagine, an old place like this requires a lot of upkeep, and Carl's the sort of handyman who can do almost anything: plumbing, carpentry, electrical work, painting, and plastering. We're fortunate to have him. He's not a socializer, but then it's not necessary for him to socialize. Whenever we have a viewing, he stays out of the way. I've four full-time employees and two other part-timers. None have made complaints about Carl. Is there something in particular you're interested in?"

It seemed to Bobby that he'd learned a lot and learned nothing. "Has he shown any signs of a temper?"

Brantley laughed. "Don't we all at some time or another? But seriously, I've found he can be irritable at times, but I've chalked it up to, well, he's not a socializer. He's certainly not quarreled with anyone here. I hope to give him some training—in a small way—in the preparation room. It's always quiet there, but some people are squeamish, as you might imagine."

There followed a tour of the funeral home. Brantley's wife had decorated much of the downstairs. "Jenny has a wonderful eye for details. It's a gift." Bobby liked the rental caskets for those who were cremated and was appalled that some families spent twelve grand on a casket that went up in smoke. He liked that some people were buried with their golf clubs, fishing tackle, and Barbie dolls, and was appalled that a woman had her two cats put to sleep so they could be in her casket. He found the preparation room and embalming table chilling.

Ham Brantley laughed. "The dead hold no mysteries for me."

Woody was reading the completed profiles of men and women who had access to the hospital nursery during the week before the Summers baby's abduction, when there was a tap on the door.

"Come on in!" he called.

Dr. Jonathan Balfour entered and shut the door behind him. His face was by turns arrogant and sheepish. "I have a confession to make," he said.

Dr. Balfour was a willowy, almost delicate young man with thick blond hair, a wave of which fell across his forehead. He had the long fingers of a basketball player or pianist. Dressed in khakis, a white shirt, blue V-necked sweater, and Sperry Top-Siders, he couldn't have been more Ivy League if he had had the words stamped across his forehead.

"Oh?" said Woody, noncommittally.

"Alice was with me when she should have been in labor and delivery. We were having sex. It's clear you'd find out about it, so I wanted to tell you first. I don't know whose fault it was. It was something we both wanted. I'd been watching her for weeks. When I found out she felt the same way, it seemed we had no choice. Now I'm sure it'll lead to my dismissal. Hers too, most likely. I don't suppose you can keep this a secret? Of course you'll do what you have to. I feel extremely guilty about the missing baby." Dr. Balfour stood with his hands folded in front of him in apparent humility.

"Is that the best you can say?" Woody was furious that Balfour had put the babies at risk. "A baby disappeared because of you."

"You're right to despise me. I despise myself. It was bad luck all around. I doubt that Alice was away from the floor for more than ten or fifteen minutes. She was very worried about it. Basically, she's a great girl. You've got to believe that."

Woody was hardly civil. "It doesn't strike me as a matter of bad luck."

"I mean, I should have stopped myself when I first realized I was looking at her inappropriately. At the time, it seemed very simple and uncomplicated—two adults exercising their desire. But there was nothing ordinary about it. For weeks I watched how her thighs moved; I'd watch her breasts. To learn that she felt the same way was the only spark we needed. We fed on each other like animals."

"So what was it? A burning passion, or were you knocking off a quickie?"

Balfour looked at Woody with dislike. "A bit of both, actually."

"Are these things common in hospitals?"

"I've known of it happening, but never to me."

"Do you realize we've been searching for Alice Alessio all over the state, that hundreds of man-hours have been spent looking for her?"

Dr. Balfour began to speak and then shook his head.

"Do you know where she is?"

"Yes, I do, as a matter of fact. Right now she's probably sitting in my living room, crying her eyes out."

NINE

FOR A WOMAN OF NINETY-FIVE, Maud Lord was in exceptional shape. Or, as she put it, she had the figure of a girl of seventy. She'd buried three husbands and was still ticking. At the moment, she was single, but if a chance for romance had again presented itself, she would gladly have buried husband number four as well. She had three children, nine grandchildren, twenty-two great-grandchildren, and, so far, five great-great-grandchildren.

Maud attributed these successes to walking around the block.

She had a small apartment in the assisted-living section of Ocean Breezes on Oak Street. Ten years ago she still had her own house, a large colonial, but it had led her children, grandchildren, and great-grandchildren into temptation. All lived in South County, and all wanted things of her. The fact that Maud lived in a twelve-room house excited their domestic ambitions. Didn't she want to get that old furniture—expensive antiques—off her hands? Would she mind if Hank or Tom or Sarah or Betty stored a few small items in one of her unused rooms, attic, or garage, but not the basement, it was too damp?

These suggestions/requests came nearly every week, and when she turned them down it didn't sit well with her loving family. They developed aggrieved, even spiteful, expressions. Little Bill, her favorite great-grandchild, said she didn't love him anymore. Her grandson's Maltese, Mr. So-Soft, growled at her.

So Maud gave it up. Sold the house, sold the majority of the antiques, and put most of the money in trust funds for the college education of her great-great-grandchildren, who were young enough to learn some manners.

To be sure, the walks had begun long before her move to Ocean Breezes. Many times, in the course of her three marriages, she had developed a powerful need to just get out and perambulate. This had taken her to the Appalachian Trail, the Swiss Alps, the fjords in Norway, and halfway across Patagonia. Now she limited herself to walking around the block, sometimes more than once.

Living where she did, she had several walks at her disposal, whether she turned left or right or went straight. On this particular Saturday morning in late October she chose to turn left, a simple choice that changed her life.

Maud was no longer an early riser—what was the point?—and it was nearly ten o'clock when she left her assisted-living apartment. On rainy days or in winter when it was icy, she would take a cane, but she liked to extend the state of being unassisted to all areas, and so on a mild fall morning with the sun bright in the sky, she left her cane at home.

She was thin, as might be expected, and relatively tall, though four inches shorter than she'd been at fifty. She needed glasses for reading, but not otherwise, and she didn't need to pad and puff up her thick white hair, as did a few of her contemporaries in Ocean Breezes. She imagined herself as straight as an oak, but that was no longer the case. Still, the slight bend in her back was no worse than it might have been in a woman of seventy. She had sharp blue eyes, and she saw everything. But she wasn't a gossip. Later she said the air had had an ominous quality she couldn't quite articulate, but doubtless that was said for effect.

Reaching the corner of Lark, Maud again turned left. She saw little traffic—an oil truck, a UPS truck, Father Pete in his Buick on his way to the Brewster Golf Club for nine holes before lunch. If she chose, Maud could walk quite quickly, but she enjoyed noting the differences from one day to the next, the gardens, the turning of the leaves, what the birds were doing and which remained, who was having his or her windows washed, who got a lot of mail, who got little. In this way, she saw herself as reading the block as one might read a book.

On this particular Saturday morning, because the weather was warm and she wore comfortable brown oxfords, she decided to branch out into new territory, relatively speaking, and when she reached the corner of Hope she turned right, which would add an extra block to her walk. She saw this block as one of newer homes. Maud had been born in Brewster and recalled when these houses were built in the 1930s, recalled the mules used to dig out the foundations. Before that the land had been part of a farm belonging to George Flocker, and the Flocker farmhouse, a brick colonial, was now in the middle of the block, set among Capes and bungalows.

So her pace was leisurely—an old snoop, people sometimes said. On some days she might meet another pedestrian and stop to chat, but this happened rarely. You'd think a few other residents of Ocean Breezes would also take walks, but mostly they watched TV or chatted and drank decaf or took part in lunchtime sing-alongs. As far as Maud was concerned this led to an early death, relatively speaking. God knows people had been dropping like flies in the past month, even some of her friends, and it wasn't even winter yet.

One house had red curtains and flickering crystals in the window. Another house needed to have the leaves raked. A third had half a dozen *Brewster Times & Advertiser*s scattered about its front porch—they must be away. A fourth had something odd hanging in a juniper, odd enough to stop Maud in her tracks, odd enough—and this was something she never did—to walk up the front walk for a better look. It was dangling close to the trunk and mostly concealed by the other branches, something gray. Maud tried to determine what it was, and as recognition flowed into her mind, her back, which had been bent as she leaned forward, began to straighten.

This was the moment the mail truck pulled up in front and Tommy Cathcart hurried up the walk with a package for Hercel McGarty Jr. from Hercel Sr., for this was Hercel's house.

"Hi, Maud. How're you doin'?" said Tommy. "Nice enough for you?"

Usually, Maud felt that at ninety-five she deserved to be called Mrs. Lord and she disliked how the girls at Ocean Breezes, as well as men and women in the bank, market, pharmacy, and flower shop, called her by her first name. But right now the mild discourtesy didn't faze her.

"Whatcha lookin' at, Maudie?" said Tommy, coming to a stop.

Maud Lord turned with a look of severe distaste that Tommy at first thought was directed at him. But it wasn't. "Somebody," she said, "has hung a gray cat by a piece of yellow twine from a branch, and it appears to be dead."

Tommy walked quickly across the grass. "Holy shit, Maud, you're right! Dead as a doornail. Poor thing."

Jill Franklin drove her Tercel slowly down Water Street to police headquarters, but her speed was due to thought rather than safety. She had reached a point of crisis concerning her chosen career, and she wondered if a job with less risk might be more to her taste, something like bronco-busting or bull riding, for it wasn't physical danger that worried her but ethical danger. Even that might not have bothered her, if it weren't for her son, Luke. At six, he was full of questions, and how could she answer them if she saw herself as a shit-heel?

She had gotten pregnant in the spring of her senior year at the University of Colorado in Boulder. It had been entirely her own fault; she'd been too lazy or cheap to renew her prescription of birth control pills, and Derek, her live-in boyfriend, hadn't pulled out in time—a small interior spill that resulted in Luke. Derek had vaguely offered to marry her, but Jill hadn't been that rash. He was a short-term rather than a long-term pleasure. Hiking, skiing, camping, and sex—he was great, but for how long can one dedicate one's life to fun? Besides, he was a complainer.

It wasn't till the baby had been born that Jill realized she had seen Luke as the answer to the question: What do I want to do after college? Do I want to teach, try journalism, join the Peace Corps, get a job in publishing, work in a bookstore, coach girl's soccer, lacrosse, basketball, or softball? No, I'll have a baby.

So after graduating, Jill had returned to Wakefield and moved in with her parents, who, fortunately, loved her. At first Derek had flown east twice a year to visit Luke, who he saw more as a curiosity than a son; but once Luke had stopped being a curiosity, the visits slowed. He had offered her child support, but since she felt entirely responsible for getting knocked up, she had turned him down. The money would also increase a sense of obligation that she didn't want.

Once settled, Jill had a series of boring part-time jobs that didn't interfere with being a mother. As Luke got older, the quality of these jobs increased, but they remained jobs of convenience, jobs she had fallen into. None had she hated; they were just dull. Of all of them, being a reporter for the *Brewster Times & Advertiser* was the most interesting, especially once she got past covering anything but social news.

Now, however, she worried her interest came at an ethical price. It had been fun sneaking through the hospital and locating Peggy Summers. It had been fun practically kidnapping Hercel McGarty and Baldo Bonaldo, and getting Hercel to name his snake Satan, but perhaps it hadn't been good clean fun. Now something nasty had occurred, and Jill, whose sense of morality had been developed on playing fields, didn't approve of putting it in the newspaper, which is why she was driving to police headquarters. It is rare, however, that an action has a single cause, and perhaps Jill was motivated in part—she would deny it—by the chance of seeing Woody.

As with most conflicted desires, she both hoped to find Woody and hoped to find him gone. Yet when the dispatch officer told her Woody was upstairs and he'd give him a buzz as soon as Jill said what it was about, she felt a surge of pleasure, along with lesser surges of embarrassment, timidity, and desire.

"Tell him it's about Peggy Summers," she answered.

A few minutes later, she was ushered into Woody's office. It was not long after Woody had concluded his conversation with Dr. Balfour, and at the moment his faith in humanity was at a low point. He glanced at Jill without pleasure.

"I've got nothing for the press. What's this about Peggy Summers?"

Jill left the door open as she approached Woody's desk. "First of all, I saw Alice Alessio this morning going into that little market on Ash Street, around nine-thirty."

"I already know about it. What about Peggy?"

"I talked to her this morning. I thought you'd want to know what she said."

"Shoot."

"Can I sit down?"

"Can't you stand and talk at the same time?"

Unpropitious was one of Jill's favorite new words, and recently she'd been giving it a workout in her interior monologues. Woody had just given her another chance to use it. This was the best to be said of his question.

"I more or less pushed myself into her house and wangled my way into her bedroom. She didn't want to talk, but I got her to."

Woody had learned much of what followed from Bobby Anderson, but he let Jill tell her piece. Mostly he asked himself what she was doing here, why she wanted to talk to him, what favors she'd ask in return. If that were so, she would be unhappy.

Jill spoke of the party in the woods and that Peggy wouldn't say who had invited her or who had taken her there. She spoke of the music—flutes and drums—the dancing, and what must have been drugs, because there wasn't alcohol. She'd been blindfolded for part of it and didn't know how many people were there. Maybe twenty. Some wore masks; all wore cloaks. She didn't recognize anybody, nor did she see the friends she had hoped to meet. The only light came from a bonfire.

At some point, Peggy realized she was the reason for the festivities. Probably it happened "when I was getting fucked," Peggy had said. People made a circle around her; it wasn't the fucking she minded so much as being watched. After all, wasn't fucking what life was about? The man had been neither gentle nor rough—it had just been an unwanted, impersonal fuck.

Some of this, Woody realized, Peggy hadn't told Bobby Anderson.

The other thing Peggy hadn't liked was the guy was wearing a mask of a human skull. She found it "creepy."

Woody took Jill through the story again. There was another detail Bobby hadn't known.

"Peggy said she'd had to walk through water, about a foot or so. She couldn't see, and two or three people held her hands. Whatever she walked on was hard, but it didn't seem like stone, because it bounced a little. She wasn't sure how far she walked like this—maybe fifty feet or so. They went very slowly."

When Woody was satisfied that Jill had nothing else about Peggy's story to convey, he asked, "Why are you telling me this?"

Jill felt embarrassed. "I didn't think I could report it. I mean, it would send people into a tailspin. A girl raped during some awful ritual? She already said it reminded her of *Rosemary's Baby*, and this sounds just like it. It's pure witchcraft. I don't report witchcraft. In fact, I'm not sure anymore *what* I report."

Woody studied her for a moment. "And you believed her?"

"Pretty much. I mean, the details seemed true: walking through the water and maybe the skull mask. The rest seemed basic horror stuff, which doesn't mean it didn't take place. But my reason for not wanting to report it isn't because I find it true or false. I just don't want to help create mass hysteria. People are already having fits about the snakes and the scalping."

"So what d'you plan to do?" Her admission surprised him, and it went a little way to balance out his irritation with Balfour. Maybe she was a person, not a problem.

"I'm not sure. I can't just report what the cops tell me to report." Jill laughed. "I've even thought I should quit. Something nasty's going on, and I don't want to frighten people. Maybe I'll write about it when it's over, if I have a job. Or maybe I'll write about stuff not directly tied to it. I liked those boys yesterday, Hercel and Baldo, even though you think I kidnapped them. I could write something about Hercel's dad giving him the snake. That doesn't seem too dangerous."

Woody had a difficult relationship with sincerity, meaning other people's. He tended to distrust it. It embarrassed him. Was he expected to respond with something equally sincere? After Jill had disclosed her ambivalence about her job, Woody found himself ready to say that he liked how her blond hair framed her face. Where had that idiotic idea come from? Luckily, before he embarrassed himself, a Brewster cop, Harry Morelli, burst into the room and began to blather.

"Maud Lord just found a dead cat! Somebody hung it by the neck with twine. Tommy Cathcart the mailman was with her. He's the one who called. You want to go down there?"

Woody Potter, as Jill said later, went ballistic.

"You think I'm here to go chasing after dead cats along with everything else? What d'you mean busting in here with that crap. Don't you have anything better to do?" This went on a bit longer, but then Woody came to a stop. He wondered what had gotten into him. He felt embarrassed at making a fool of himself in front of the girl reporter, who would probably rush off to tell the world about his rotten temper. He felt embarrassed about yelling at another cop, even a small-town cop.

Morelli stood in the doorway, wincing. Two other people stood out in the hall, staring at Woody in surprise.

"Sorry, Corporal," said Morelli. "Fred told me you were interested in Carl Krause. It was his cat, or maybe his kid's cat, you know, Hercel McGarty? I mean, I wouldn't tell you about any dead cat."

Woody sat with a hand to his forehead, partially covering his eyes. He didn't want to look at the girl reporter, didn't want to look at Morelli, didn't want to see the people in the hall. He took his cell phone and punched in Bobby's number. When Bobby answered, he tossed the phone to Morelli, making him jump for it. "Tell him. He's on cat detail this week." Woody began fussing with some papers on his desk. He didn't look up until the door closed; then he saw the girl reporter was still there.

"What's your name again?" Woody remembered her name perfectly well.

"Jill Franklin. Could I buy you a cup of coffee, or would you like a soothing martini?"

Woody processed this information and then got to his feet. "Coffee's good enough, and I'll buy my own. We're not allowed to take bribes."

Bobby Anderson was leaving police headquarters to hunt down Carl Krause when he ran smack into an older woman with lots of silver earrings wearing an oversized denim jacket over nursing scrubs. It was shortly after two o'clock.

"Hey, watch out," he said.

"Why?" said Bernie. "Are you going to hit me again?"

Bobby burst out laughing. In fact, he hadn't hit her. It had only been a nudge.

"So how're things at the hospital?" he asked.

"Nervous."

Bobby introduced himself. It was the least he could do since he'd nearly knocked her down. He also figured she must be curious about the identity of this handsome black dude. Hip-hop star? Famous actor? No, just your humble state police detective.

Bernie introduced herself as well. She mentioned working part-time at Morgan Memorial, having returned several years earlier after a ten-year absence. "When I left, the nurses dressed in white. Now they're dressed like clowns."

"What do you do in your time off?"

"Raise sheep and study weaving. We've a farm outside of town. In fact, maybe you can help me. It's why I was coming here. What do you know about coyotes? A boy was nearly killed by a pack of them last night."

Bobby, as we know, had a growing interest in coyotes. He and Bernie had moved to the side of the steps as others entered and exited the building. When Bobby learned the boy was Hercel McGarty, his interest increased. He liked the part of the story where Hercel ran his bike at full tilt against the stone wall, standing up on the pedals at the last moment so he could be thrown forward.

"Damn, I don't think I'd have the guts to do that even in the best of times."

"But coyotes don't attack people. These acted more like wolves." Bernie described how the coyotes wouldn't cross the wall to get at her sheep. "They're scared of the two dogs, and with reason. But in the past six months some have tried it. Anyway, I wanted to report what'd happened to Hercel. If he hadn't made it across the fence, I think he'd have been killed."

"How many were there?"

"I couldn't tell. Maybe half a dozen. Maybe less. I didn't really see them."

Bobby said he would contact the Division of Fish and Wildlife in Wakefield and also tell acting chief Bonaldo. Rhode Island had little history of coyote attacks, but there had been several in the past year. Even so, he doubted Bonaldo could handle it by himself.

Bobby had talked to Bonaldo within the past hour and learned about his call to Chief McGarrah. Much of it gave Bobby food for thought, but one sentence stuck out above the rest: "Carl's a great guy if he takes his meds." Otherwise he got paranoid, "a little violent."

"Did Hercel say anything about Carl Krause?" asked Bobby.

"No, but something's not right at home. He didn't say what, but he was biking out to our place to get away from it. He's friends with Tig—that's Antigone, our granddaughter."

Bobby considered telling her about the hanged cat, but he decided it wasn't her business—sharing information with civilians was something he had been warned about—nor did he tell her he was on his way to talk to Carl.

Harriet Krause had a part-time job at the CVS on Water Street. Bobby found her just as she was going on her lunch break and asked where he could find Carl. She knew nothing about the hanging of the cat, and Bobby lacked the nerve to tell her. Maybe he'd do it later, or maybe somebody else could do it.

Harriet said Carl was doing some painting in a summer home in Hannaquit. She described where it was, adding that Bobby would see Carl's red Ford F-150 in the drive. When Bobby had mentioned Carl's name, Harriet had tensed; or maybe she'd tensed when he had introduced himself as a detective. He guessed it was the business with the shotgun that bothered her. But then what had sent Hercel biking through the dark to Bernie's farm?

"What does this concern?" asked Harriet.

"Just a question about the shotgun business. It's nothing to worry about."

But Harriet *was* worried, though whether it was specifically directed or free-floating, Bobby couldn't tell. To quiet her a little, Bobby said, "You've got a great kid there in Hercel. Smart dude. I really took a liking to him."

"Yes," said Harriet. But the worry didn't go away.

Ten minutes later Bobby pulled his Z into a sandy driveway next to Carl's Ford pickup. Then he revved his engine to let Carl know he was there. The house was on stilts about thirty yards back from the water at high tide, with a staircase going up the side and four balconies facing the ocean—gray shingles, maybe ten rooms on three floors, and worth several million, or at least until the next big hurricane.

He made a fair amount of noise ascending the wooden steps. "Hey, Carl, you in there?" His pistol was in a small holster attached to his belt and under his suit coat. Bobby had a fearful desire to put his hand on it, but he controlled himself. He didn't know what was worse: his surprising Carl or Carl's surprising him. "Hey, Carl, okay if I come in?" Bobby pushed the door and entered. The whole first floor was an open area, with comfortable couches and a kitchen area set off by counters. The huge picture window facing the water made Bobby feel he was standing on the edge of a cliff. Hunks of driftwood did the work of art.

There was no sign of Carl except for several paintbrushes on the kitchen counter. The house was silent. Bobby could hear the slosh of the waves hitting the beach, the cry of a gull. In the distance, he could see Block Island. Bobby didn't like feeling scared, so he told himself he felt only nervous. Just a tad. If Carl was here, he was upstairs.

"Hey, Carl, where the fuck are you?" He crossed the living area to the open stairs, then went up to the second floor, banging his feet heavily on the treads. In a sitting area, another great window faced the ocean.

He went through two bedrooms with minimal furniture. Then, as he stood in the middle of the master bedroom, he heard a noise behind him. He spun around, putting a hand on his pistol but not drawing it. Carl stood in the doorway.

"Shit, Carl. You trying to mess with my head?"

"I didn't hear you."

"The fuck you didn't."

Carl raised a small pair of headphones. "I was listening to my iPod and doing some painting on the third floor." He spoke without expression.

Bobby reconsidered. Maybe he was telling the truth. On the other hand, he hadn't heard Carl come down the stairs, so Bobby still thought he was lying. In the bright, reflected light from the ocean, the deep creases on Carl's face looked black. He probably hadn't shaved for three or four days. Carl's unruly black hair reminded Bobby of the Greek woman with snakes instead of golden locks—what was her name? Medusa.

"So what d'you want?" asked Carl. He wore a carpenter's belt that included a hammer and pry bar.

"Did you hang your gray cat?"

"What're you talking about?"

"Your cat was found dead this morning. It was hanging from a piece of twine from a branch of the juniper just off your front porch. Did you do it?"

"What the fuck would I hang a cat for?"

Bobby was struck that Carl wasn't surprised by what he'd said. "You tell me."

"Well, I didn't do it. Anything else you want to bother me about?"

"Are you taking your meds?"

Very briefly, Carl had a sly look; then it vanished. "What meds are those?"

"The ones prescribed for you at Benjamin Rush."

"Sure. Sure, I've been taking my meds. Anything else?"

"What meds are they?"

"You tell me, you're so smart. I don't have to tell you shit."

Bobby figured he could get that information later. "Who'd the cat belong to?"

"Harriet."

"Did it have a name?"

"Yeah, it was Sooty. Something like that."

"You buy it?"

"Harriet's had it a few years. What the fuck are you bothering me for?"

Even this was said calmly. *Maybe he's taking his meds after all*, thought Bobby. Maybe it was flattening him out. But though his voice was calm, the rest of him seemed tense.

"Don't you care who found the cat?"

"Why should I? It wasn't my cat. Maybe Harriet found it. Maybe the kids."

"Did you want your wife or kids to find it?"

"There you go again, talking junk. Anyway, they're my stepkids."

Bobby turned away toward the window. "You've got a great view here. It's a great place to work."

Carl took a few steps into the room. There was a rug, and Bobby barely heard him. He turned, and Carl was five feet closer.

"If you like views," Carl said.

It occurred to Bobby he might not be safe here. Not that he was afraid of Carl, but he realized it would be dangerous to turn his back on him. He still had a mark on his cheek where Bobby had smacked him with the barrel of the shotgun. Carl wouldn't forget anytime soon.

"We might have to give you a lie detector test about the cat. You ready for that?" Brotman would pitch a fit over a polygraph test about a cat.

"Feel free," said Carl. "I got nothing to hide."

He's lying to me, thought Bobby. *The whole thing's a lie. Either he's a wack-job or I'm a wack-job, and I'd like it better if it was him.*

Vicki Lefebvre went out around noon to find Nina's best friends. One was still in school; one was working; one was a freshman at URI. The one in high school was out of town; the one at URI might be hard to find. That left Betty Hanchard, who worked at a Dollar Store in Hope Valley ten miles away. It was eleven o'clock when Vicki got there and another half-hour before Betty could take a break. Betty was overweight but had beautiful brown eyes and thick, shoulder-length chestnut hair. She was eighteen; Vicki had known her since she was six.

Vicki could see that Betty had mixed feelings about talking: on the one hand, it was a betrayal of Nina; on the other, she needed someone to talk to. In fact, she'd been worried sick. She had tried Nina's cell phone at least a dozen times, but Nina hadn't picked up.

Vicki and Betty had gone out behind the store so Betty could smoke. When Betty asked how Nina was doing, Vicki said, "Awful. She stays in her room and weeps. I'm really scared."

So Betty decided to reveal the text message she had received last night. It had kept her awake, it was so bad. That was when she'd started calling Nina. Betty scrolled through her cell phone until she found it. Then she showed it to Nina's mother: "Ive bin raped dont tell."

All of Vicki's worst fears seemed realized. She questioned Betty but learned nothing more, except Betty said Nina had often been busy in the last month and hadn't wanted to go out. "She was just no fun," said Betty. "I tried to come over, but she didn't want me to."

Vicki, who knew that her daughter had often been out, and often quite late, said nothing. She thanked Betty and drove back to Brewster.

Vicki meant to drive home and confront Nina with what she had learned. But the closer she got, the more she thought she should go to the police. She felt sure the rapist was one of Nina's new associates. She didn't want to go home and hear Nina defend them and talk Vicki out of doing anything. So when she reached Brewster, she went to the police.

Vicki Lefebvre first talked to a dispatch officer, who sent her to a patrolman, who sent her to a detective, Sarah Muller, who specialized in domestic issues. In explaining what had happened, Vicki mentioned that Nina had been returning home late at night with mud on her shoes. Muller had attended the briefing that morning, and the word *mud* caught her attention, which led her to think about Nina's "new friends." A minute later, she called Woody.

So it was that thirty minutes after entering police headquarters, Vicki was sitting in Woody Potter's borrowed office. It was shortly before one o'clock.

Vicki was in her mid-forties. She had never been beautiful, but she was relatively athletic, practiced yoga at You-You, and was in good shape. She had no chin to speak of, and her lips were like a pair of dimes pressed together, but her eyes were nice—a gingerly brown, though a little red from weeping. She had hoped to speak to somebody important, such as the police chief, and was disappointed by what she'd got. Woody wore jeans and a blue plaid shirt flecked with dog hair, and needed a shave. His short brown hair looked like something had been chewing it. Sarah Muller had told her Woody was a state trooper, so Vicki thought he was probably more accustomed to pulling over speeders than dealing with rape.

Despite her doubts, she told him about Nina's text message to Betty: "Ive bin raped dont tell." Then she said Nina had been coming home late, that she had these new friends, that she'd come home late Wednesday night with mud on her shoes, and that she'd refused to tell what had happened but was scared. Vicki spoke of standing at Nina's door, listening to her weep.

Woody got up. "Let's go see her." He phoned Sarah Muller to meet him there.

They left Vicki's car parked on the street and went in Woody's truck. Ajax had been sleeping in the small backseat, and Vicki saw right away where the dog hair had come from. Now she'd be covered with it, and it made her mad that Woody should be so insensitive. Vicki's own car was a pristine Honda Civic in which no animal had ever ridden. She meant to keep it that way. When Ajax licked her face, she shoved him away.

As Woody drove, Vicki described her ex-husband, Harold Lefebvre, who lived in Groton with his new wife. Vicki and Harold had been divorced when Nina was twelve. He'd never been worth much, but at least he paid the bills. Now it was hard to get him on the phone; maybe he saw Nina once a month, maybe less. Sometimes he'd call her or send a funny e-mail. Thinking about it, she couldn't imagine why she had married him, except he had been handsome. Nina had inherited his good looks.

Woody said little; at times he asked a question and if she could describe Nina's new friends. Vicki found him inattentive and expressionless. Then, pulling up in front of Vicki's white colonial, he wrote down the phone numbers of Nina's friends, as well as descriptions of the new friends and where Vicki had seen them. *Maybe he's not so bad*, Vicki thought.

Sarah Muller had already arrived in a Brewster patrol car. She was about thirty, with short dark hair, and wore gray slacks, a gray striped blouse, and a blue jacket. She understood she was the token female. Vicki led the way inside.

The house was silent except for the hum of a refrigerator. To Woody the interior looked like a house in a magazine, not because it was expensive but because it looked unlived-in. On the tables were ceramic figurines and half a dozen vases with silk flowers: yellow tulips and blue hydrangeas. There was also a collection of silk Japanese bonsai—cypress and Japanese maples—but Woody didn't realize the trees were made of silk and plastic. He was struck by the thick carpeting, even on the stairs, which masked their footsteps.

Vicki stopped at her daughter's door and rapped twice. "Nina, are you decent? I'm coming in. I've some people with me." Without waiting for an answer, she pushed the door open. "Excuse the mess," she said over her shoulder. "My daughter's a slob."

Nina had been asleep, and she quickly pushed herself into a sitting position. She wore a man's white shirt buttoned to the neck. Her thick brown bangs nearly concealed her eyes; Woody at once linked her bowl haircut to the posters of the young singer with the deadpan expression—muscular melancholy, he called it. The floor was layered with clothes, shoes, papers, books, CD cases, and PowerBar wrappers, so little of the rug was visible.

"These are policemen," said Vicki. "I know you were raped. You have to tell them about it."

Sarah put a hand on Vicki's arm. "Why don't you let us handle this?"

Woody drew a chair up to the bed and sat down. Nina stared at her lap, though Woody had seen the angry glance she'd shot at her mother. Sarah stood next to Vicki to keep her from interfering.

"Will you tell me what happened?" Woody asked. He tried to speak gently, but he only spoke quietly.

Nina kept staring at her lap. She was a pretty girl, but her mixture of anger and misery was what struck Woody most.

"Do you know who did it?" he asked.

Nina didn't answer.

"Did he hurt you?"

No answer.

For twenty minutes, Woody repeated his questions. Sarah also asked several questions. At one point, Woody sent Vicki from the room. At another point, he decided to keep quiet for five minutes—five minutes was his limit—and he had to look at his watch, because the time seemed so long. Through this Nina neither moved nor spoke. She seemed to be in a trance. Woody wondered if he should turn the whole business over to Sarah, that a woman officer might be more successful, but he couldn't see he was doing anything wrong.

He glanced at Sarah, and she shrugged. *All right,* Woody said to himself. *Let's go for the throat.*

"Let me tell you how it was," he said. "You were taken by some people in a car out into the country. Then they led you through the woods. Maybe you were blindfolded; maybe you walked through some water. Then you joined some others by a fire. They all wore long cloaks. Maybe they were smoking weed; there was dancing. You started feeling light-headed. A man pressed you down onto the ground or onto a blanket. The others formed a circle around you. The man removed your pants. This was the man who raped you. But you don't know who it was. He was wearing a skull mask. All you could see was the skull."

At this point, Nina began to scream.

TEN

WHEN DARKNESS FELL on Saturday night it was an unsettled dark, not the velvet dark of restful sleep. Too many stories were afloat, too many anxious speculations. One might think the baby's abduction, the snakes, and the scalping would be enough to disrupt the dark, but there was more. Some people had heard what Peggy had said about her baby, and some had heard something about the circumstances of its conception. How could they keep that information to themselves? Tig had told her friends that coyotes had chased Hercel, while Hercel's crutch lent credence to her story. When kids told the story to their parents, they were rarely believed—after all, they were kids—except in those cases where nurses at the hospital passed on remarks of Bernie's. It gave the story credibility. It gave it legs.

Then came the disappearance of Nurse Spandex and even the discovery of the hanged cat, which Maud Lord described to everyone at Ocean Breezes and which Tommy Cathcart talked about at the post office. Did something link these different events? Maud would say that was surely the case. And what was the cause of these events? This too generated theories—insanity, Indians, kidnappers, black magic, free-floating malice—all sorts of theories, and none of them comforting. What was lacking was a single theory to bind them together. That would come soon enough.

At first Hercel and Lucy didn't know the cat had been hung. However, other kids were eager to tell them, each hurrying to be the first. Lucy had cried so much that Harriet could hardly console her. Hercel hadn't cried. He believed that Mr. Krause had hung the cat, and it made him angry.

Harriet also suspected her husband, who hadn't liked the cat. It had been a gift from her first husband, Hercel Sr. He'd first planned to give her an armadillo, and Harriet had thought it was a victory as big as the battle of Gettysburg to convince him to get a cat instead. Because the cat was gray, Hercel named it Sooty. But it had been Harriet's cat, and maybe Lucy's. Hercel said he didn't need a cat; he already had his snake. The dog, Randy, Harriet had bought six years before. She'd never imagined having a menagerie. And now Lucy wanted a goldfish.

When Carl got home from work Saturday afternoon, Harriet had asked, "Did you hang Sooty from the juniper?"

"You fucking kidding me? Why should I hang a cat?"

"You don't seem too surprised about it."

"That colored cop told me."

"Why'd he tell you about it?"

Carl grinned. "He wanted to know if I'd hung it. I told him just what I'm saying to you: Why should I hang a cat?"

"I think you hung it."

Carl had been taking off his jacket. Now he threw it at her. "You're getting to be a real bitch, you know that? You're always suspecting me of something. You're lucky I don't give you what you deserve." He went on like this for another minute and then made for the stairs.

Harriet called after him. "Carl, what's wrong with you? We need to talk to someone about this. We need to talk about your anger. Why're you always suspecting me and the kids?" Harriet spoke rapidly to get it all out before Carl disappeared upstairs.

Carl paused with his back to her. "I know what you're doing." He grinned at her over his shoulder, the sort of devious grin without a trace of humor. "You want to get me locked up. You want to go off on a fuck trip with that colored cop."

Harriet opened her mouth to speak, but nothing came out, as fear, surprise, and indignation wrestled for her tongue.

Saturday afternoon Nurse Spandex returned to her own apartment, but she didn't like it. Although she hadn't had sex with Dr. Balfour in the two days she had stayed at his place, she'd thought it might happen soon, despite the fact he had made her sleep in the spare bedroom. She'd thought he'd grow so horny with her walking around in front of him—sometimes half-naked—he would just jump on her. That's what had happened in the past. But if she was home, she hadn't a chance. Hope on one side, no hope on the other—it was that simple.

"I bet you're gay," she had told him, but he only laughed.

"I bet you're afraid of women," she said, and he laughed again.

The worst was when she had said, "My pussy's wet for you." He had tossed her a towel.

She'd sulked and was ignored; she'd wept and was ignored. At last she had said, "What's wrong with me?"

"I just don't want you, that's all."

"Can't I fix it?"

"No. This is permanent."

So she'd tried anger. "I'll tell them you seduced me, you dragged me into that room!"

Again he had laughed. "I'm the doctor, you're the nurse. Who're they going to believe? You've already got a reputation. Nurse Spandex, remember? You've made your moves on lots of doctors. I may be weak, foolish, and irresponsible, but they'll see me as victim and you as predator. Tell me who's not going to believe it?"

After lunch, Dr. Balfour had driven her home. Maybe he was a bit friendlier. "They're not going to arrest you, don't worry about that. Even if you get fired, you can find another job. There's a nurse shortage, remember?"

A little later, Bobby Anderson had shown up at her door. She hadn't wanted to see him, and at first she didn't think he was a cop. He wasn't driving a cop car, and in his gray sharkskin suit he wasn't dressed like a cop. But in another minute he was in her living room. She hardly knew how it had happened.

"So, Alice, if you weren't sitting on the can, what was going on?" Bobby wanted to know more about her involvement with Dr. Balfour, not the gory details but the general picture and how long she was off the floor. Alice had wept, which was always the wisest course when she didn't want to talk. She was on the couch, and Bobby was walking back and forth in front of her. Bobby had been really rude.

"Give me a break with the tears, okay? Tell me what happened."

She explained she hadn't wanted to have sex, that Dr. Balfour had talked her into it. Some doctors were real predators, and she'd been unable to stop him.

"Were you raped?"

No, she couldn't say she was actually raped.

In that case, Bobby explained, you can't say it's just one person's fault.

So she told Bobby what he wanted to know. Dr. Balfour had said to meet him outside of room 217 at two a.m., and the business had taken exactly fifteen minutes.

"There"—Bobby put his notebook in his pocket—"that wasn't so bad, was it?"

Smart-ass black bastard.

Bobby had seen Carl Krause immediately before seeing Nurse Spandex, and immediately afterward he went to check on his cat detail: six Brewster cops who had talked to Carl's neighbors in the vicinity of Newport and Hope. None had seen anything suspicious. Some had seen the cat in the neighborhood and knew its name was Sooty. Some said Carl used to be real friendly, but in August, more or less, he'd stopped being friendly. They didn't know why.

Then Bobby had visited Maud Lord at Ocean Breezes. Two other policemen had already interviewed her, but that was okay, because Maud liked the attention. She had also described her experience to everyone at Ocean Breezes, and she had called the *Brewster Times & Advertiser* to see if they meant to send out a reporter. She hoped there might be a headline to send to her children, grandchildren, great-grandchildren and great-great-grandchildren to indicate she wasn't entirely safe. Nasty business was loose in Brewster, and if a cat could be hung, no one was secure. Maud Lord didn't believe this, but she saw no harm in stirring up her family.

What she liked about Bobby was that he called her Mrs. Lord. Regrettably, she had little else to tell him, so she told him about her walks. Bobby said he also liked walking. Maud explained that some days she went this way and some days that way, but it had been several months—probably last spring—since she'd walked past the gray craftsman bungalow on Hope Street, if at all.

"You'd be doing us a big favor, Mrs. Lord," said Bobby, "if you'd include that house in your daily walk." He knew there was almost no chance of anything coming of this, but he was a firm believer in extra eyes, especially sharp eyes like Mrs. Lord's.

Maud said she'd be delighted. She had served on eight juries in her time as well as reading a bunch of John Grisham novels, so she knew the sort of sharp eyes that Bobby required. She, too, knew there was almost no chance she would see anything, but even a useless task would add purpose to an otherwise long day.

"Should I get a cell phone?" she asked. Maud had never used a cell phone.

"Good idea. I'll get you a phone and a phone card at Walmart."

Maud beamed. At ninety-five there was little left on her face but wrinkles on top of wrinkles, but Bobby thought she was pretty when she smiled.

Woody had called Bernie Wilcox when Nina Lefebvre became hysterical, and Bernie had got permission from the hospital to come over to the house. Bernie seemed a no-nonsense sort of nurse, and Woody liked that. Bernie's job was to stay with Nina and keep an eye on her.

When Nina had started screaming, her mother had rushed into the room and blamed Woody for everything. Woody had thought Nina was faking, but then he decided nobody could fake terror like that. Sarah Muller had tried to calm the girl, but Vicki pulled her away, sat on the bed, embracing her daughter tightly, while Nina tried to pull herself free. That was when he had called Bernie. As for Nina, she had said nothing else once she calmed down, but she only continued to weep as her mother held her hand.

But at least Woody knew that what had happened to Peggy Summers had also happened to Nina, and if it happened to two young women it might have happened to more. He'd hoped that once Bernie had spent time with Nina, he could talk to her again. Surely, she'd recognized someone from that awful night. It might also be helpful if she and Peggy Summers were brought face-to-face. Woody was full of new plans, and it seemed that progress was being made.

In return for Bernie's help, Woody agreed to drive Tig back to the farm—she was at the library—since her husband wouldn't be driving for a while.

"Barton's got himself a brand-new knee," said Bernie, "and he's promised to take me dancing once it's healed."

Bernie had called the library to say that Woody would pick up Tig, and at four o'clock he had been outside in his Tundra. Bernie had described her granddaughter—tall, thin, black hair—but it was the fact she was accompanied by Hercel and Baldo when she came down the steps that led Woody to recognize her. Hercel was using a crutch. So he gave rides to all three.

"I'm going over to Hercel's house," said Baldo.

"No, let's go to your house instead," said Hercel. In Hercel's voice, Woody heard a firmness that he guessed came from not wishing to see his stepfather.

Hercel and Baldo sat in the small backseat with Ajax. Few things give a golden retriever more pleasure than the undivided attention of three ten-year-olds.

After going three blocks, Woody slammed on his brakes and pulled to the curb. "What the hell's that?" he shouted, staring in his rearview mirror.

A bullet had pierced the rear window on the passenger's side, and the glass was broken.

Woody leaned over the seat. "I swear it wasn't there a minute ago. Are you kids okay?"

After a moment of silence Baldo and Tig burst out laughing. It was a decal that Baldo had stuck to the window when Woody had been looking elsewhere.

"You could be real trouble," said Woody humorlessly. In the mirror, he saw Hercel nodding.

After dropping off Hercel and Baldo, Woody turned onto Water Street toward Barton Wilcox's farm. "So what was it like last night with Hercel?"

"He knocked himself out." Tig said this as if it were an act of indescribable courage. She told how she and Bernie had heard the yapping of the coyotes and how they had hurried to the door when Gray and Rags started barking. Bernie had grabbed the shotgun. Running into the yard, Tig had seen something fly over the wall more than fifty yards away. It had been Hercel. "Bernie said he flew ten feet. He hit the wall as hard as he could. His bike's a real mess. Could you crash into a wall like that? I could never do it. And this morning he didn't even complain."

Woody asked how she liked having sheep. Tig said she liked the lambs best; the sheep themselves were smelly. What she really liked was the wool. She told Woody how she helped wash and card the wool and then helped Bernie spin it. Some yarn they used for weaving and some for knitting. Tig said she'd already knit two sweaters and she had promised to knit one for Hercel. Tig also said she wanted to weave something from Gray and Rags's fur, but Bernie said it was probably too fine. Wouldn't Woody like a nice sweater made out of Ajax's fur?

Woody said no, thanks. "I've already got what sticks to me off the furniture."

As the road out to the farm grew narrower and the woods thicker, Woody thought of Hercel biking in the dark with the yapping coyotes behind him. Had a pack of coyotes really come rushing out of the trees? Just how many coyotes had there been? But Bernie and Tig had also heard yapping. Yet coyotes weren't supposed to behave like that. And he also wondered why the coyotes hadn't caught Hercel, no matter how awful that would have been. Surely they could outrun a boy peddling through the dark.

When they had nearly reached the farm, Tig said, "What do you think of telepathy?"

"You mean reading people's minds?"

"Yes, I think that's it."

"I think it's hogwash. Sometimes a person's expressions and body language tell you stuff so it seems you're reading their mind, but you're not. They're just little signs, little tip-offs about what they're thinking."

"And what d'you think about making something move by just thinking at it, you know, bombing it with your thoughts?"

"You mean telekinesis?"

"I don't know what it's called. Is that moving things with your thoughts?"

"Yeah. That's hogwash, too. It's what people wonder about when they don't have anything better to do. Why're you asking?"

"Just curious, that's all."

Woody felt there was more to it than that, but now they had reached the farm and the two Bouviers came galloping out to great them.

Later, at five o'clock, Woody had driven out to the field headquarters of the Fish and Game Division in Great Swamp. Hercel's bright green mountain bike was in the back of his truck. Barton had decided it was unfixable, and in a flash of altruistic stupidity—as Woody saw it—he had at first meant to buy Hercel a new bike. Then he thought it better to drop it off at a bike shop, despite its bent frame, handlebars, and front wheel. The seat, Woody sarcastically told himself, was still in good shape.

Fish and Game's field headquarters was a large cabin set among the trees along with half a dozen other buildings at the swamp's entrance. One of the division's coyote specialists, Gail Valetti, had come in specially that Saturday to talk to him. She was in her mid-thirties, with straight dark hair and a severe expression.

"It's absolutely impossible," she said, "that a pack of coyotes would have pursued a boy on a bike. Coyotes don't do that."

"Then what were they?" They were sitting in Valetti's small office, the walls of which were covered with wood paneling.

"They were probably dogs, a pack of dogs running loose. I *do* know that a lot of people who are completely ignorant about coyotes want to eradicate them, because of a bad and undeserved reputation. Coyotes serve a useful purpose within the environment and help to reduce the growing populations of smaller animals—foxes, raccoons, skunks . . ."

"And house cats?"

Valetti gave him a sharp look. "If you want your cat safe, keep it indoors."

Woody started to ask why coyotes were preferred over house cats, but he knew it would lead to an argument. To his mind, coyotes were like rats but bigger, cuter, and dumber.

"Bernie Wilcox and her granddaughter also heard them. Bernie said they were coyotes, not dogs."

"Whatever," said Valetti, raising her eyebrows in a way Woody didn't like. "I've talked to Barton and Bernie many times about their coyote problem. Obviously, the coyotes are attracted by their sheep."

"I guess you think they should get rid of the sheep and raise bicycles."

"Your attitude," said Valetti, "is less than helpful. It's also typical of most people's attitude. Coyotes are a necessary part of the ecosystem and do little harm. Perhaps twenty people are bitten each year, whereas a million people each year are treated for dog bites. Are you suggesting we euthanize dogs?"

"A coyote dragged off a seven-year-old girl on Prudence Island in December. Luckily, she was saved by her dog." Prudence Island was in Narragansett Bay, north of Newport.

Valetti's voice took on a metallic quality, no emotion, all business. *Like Robby the Robot*, thought Woody.

"That was terrible, admittedly, but people leave out food, leave their garbage cans open; they have compost heaps and bird feeders; they have lots of overgrown shrubbery; they don't take care of their rodent problems; they let their cats wander around outside. Stop coyote feeding in a neighborhood and the coyotes will go away. There's no reason we can't get along with them through passive coexistence. Wherever we have a coyote problem it's because people subsidize them."

Woody's mind was brimming with wisecracks, and he turned away from her gaze. On Valetti's desk were photographs of three children, miniature versions of herself. He also saw a picture of a man in uniform wearing captain's bars. "Your husband's in the service?"

"Yes."

"Where's he stationed?"

"Right now in Iraq."

"It must be a worry for you." Valetti's cool expression indicated it was none of his business and why was he talking about her husband? "So," said Woody, "what's the size of the coyote population in Rhode Island?"

"That's hard to calculate, since they increase quickly. Five thousand, we think, but it could be twenty thousand more—it's hard to say."

"Could these coyotes have been rabid?"

"There are very, very few cases of rabid coyotes."

"Do they have any predators?"

"Wolves."

"Great. So what about Hercel's coyotes?"

"I've already told you; they were dogs, perhaps feral dogs."

"They looked and sounded like coyotes." Now it was Woody's turn to sound like a talking robot.

"Who saw them? Didn't you say it was dark?"

Woody recalled what Chmielnicki had said about shape-shifting. What if he asked Valetti about it? He could guess her response. And what would it do to his reputation if it got around that he'd asked Valetti about shape-shifting? Captain Brotman would order him to take a rest cure, and afterward he'd go back to pulling over speeders on 95.

It was at this point that Woody's cell phone made its irritating twitter. He dug it out of his pocket. It was Bernie Wilcox, and her voice was high and frantic.

"Nina's gone! She climbed out the bathroom window. I feel awful. What should I do?"

"Stay where you are."

Woody was on his feet and out the door, leaving Gail Valetti to stare at his back in surprise at what she judged as rudeness. *Not even a good-bye,* she thought.

Woody punched in the numbers of Bobby's cell phone and then hardly gave him a chance to say hello. "Get over to Vicki Lefebvre's. The girl's escaped. Take a bunch of Brewster cops. I'll be there as soon as I can."

Bobby had clicked shut his phone and rolled his eyes. He'd been planning a quiet dinner at home with Shawna and their daughters. Good old Woody must have known he had been looking forward to something nice. No kids himself and no compassion—then Bobby grinned and headed for his Z.

He had still been on cat detail, scouring the neighborhood with some Brewster cops, looking for anyone who might know something about the hanged cat. Nobody did. Now he sent his Brewster cops over to Vicki Lefebvre's house on Market Street. Twenty minutes later Bobby was talking to Bernie on the front steps.

"She went to take a shower and I waited in the hall," said Bernie. "I should have gone into the bathroom with her, I know I should have. After a while, I thought Nina was taking too long, even though I heard the water running. I knocked on the door and called to her, but she didn't answer. So"—Bernie shrugged—"I used my shoulder."

Bobby figured Bernie outweighed him by twenty pounds and nearly matched him in height. He felt sorry for the door. "And?"

"She'd climbed out the bathroom window onto the garage roof. I don't know what happened to her after that. I ran outside. There was no one in sight. She could have had a ten-minute head start. I drove around for a few minutes and then called Woody. I wish you'd just take me out and shoot me in the head."

"Maybe later." More police cars were arriving, including three state police cruisers from the Alton Barracks. "What was Nina wearing?" he asked Bernie.

"Jeans, sneakers, a purple sweatshirt. She'll be cold."

Bobby had called the canine unit only to find that Woody had already called them. They would be there by seven. The police and troopers had fanned out in all directions, knocking on doors and driving up and down the streets. Nina had now been gone for a half-hour. If she was a runner, she could be four miles away. Bobby talked to Vicki to get the names of Nina's friends and anybody else who might have helped her. Vicki was wild with anger.

"That fat bitch was supposed to be watching her? Keep her out of my house! I've already called my ex-husband. If anything's happened to

Nina, we'll take you to court. You just wait to see what the newspapers say about this!"

Within the hour, fifty men and women were searching for Nina. A Belgian Malinois and its handler were also busy. The police sought out Nina's friends and schoolmates. This was both a benefit and a disadvantage, because soon everybody in Brewster knew that a sixteen-year-old girl had vanished. More people joined in the search, until it seemed that crowds of people were filling the streets. A command center was set up at police headquarters under the nominal control of acting chief Bonaldo. These searches begin eagerly, but as time passes optimism decreases. People remain energetic, but it's a grindingly obstinate and cheerless energy. In any case, on that Saturday evening, Nina wasn't found.

Hercel spent the afternoon and early evening with Baldo Bonaldo, first having called his mother to say where he was. "Do you have homework for Monday?" she asked. Twenty vocabulary words and little else, which was true enough, but they were hard words: *malevolent*, *portentous*, *caliginous*. When would he ever use them? As for Hercel's mother, she knew that by staying away from the house, Hercel was choosing to stay away from Carl. This frightened her. She had no idea what to do about Carl and was afraid to speak to him. Her friend Anita Barr kept saying, "Kick him out" or "Call the police," but Harriet felt if she did, then nothing could be patched up afterward.

Hercel had begun to ask his mother about Sooty, but then he didn't. It would be dealt with like most of their domestic difficulties: with stubborn silence. Yet Hercel grieved. Most nights the cat slept at the foot of his bed. It kept him company when he read or watched TV. Sure, it liked Lucy almost as much, and his mother most of all, but Hercel was okay with that. What he didn't like was the cat being dead.

"Your cat kicked the bucket," said Baldo.

Hercel didn't tell him to shut up, but he gave him a look that meant much the same thing.

This silenced Baldo for a bit, but what interested him was Hercel's trick, not a dead cat.

Hercel shook his head. "I'm not talking about it. Ever. If you want to be my friend, don't ask about it. I don't want lots of people going on about it."

"I thought you said it was done with magnets," said Baldo in an Aha-I've-caught-you tone.

Hercel had forgotten the magnets. "They are magnets, very special magnets. My dad gave them to me. But I put them away and locked them up. They scare me."

This interested Baldo. "Why?" But Hercel wouldn't answer. "I won't tell anyone about them, really." Baldo's wheedling tone became a nasal whine, but it was a suspicious whine.

"If you talk about it to anyone, you're not my friend. Maybe you're not my friend anyway; maybe you're just interested in my trick."

This hurt Baldo, and he fiercely shook his head. "I don't believe it's magnets. It's something else and you should be proud of it. You're like David in David and Goliath, but you don't need a slingshot. You'd be a hero."

They were in the basement rec room. There was a Ping-Pong table, and Baldo had promised to teach Hercel how to play. "Would David still be a hero if he went looking for Goliath?" asked Hercel. "If he hunted him down?"

"Sure," said Baldo, "I guess so. Like if he just snuck up and murdered him?"

"Yeah."

"He's David, right? He can do pretty much anything."

Baldo's mother gave Hercel a ride home at nine. He disliked not having a bike. For some reason a lot of people were on the street. He hadn't heard about Nina Lefebvre. He thought about David killing Goliath. He wondered if David had felt bad about it afterward.

At midnight Seymour and Jimmy were driving down Water Street toward the hospital. They had had an accident on Route 1, a couple of cardiac arrests, and an oldster for the Burn Palace, so it'd been a good night. Seymour was smoking weed, and Jimmy had the windows open. Every so often he'd cough dramatically, but Seymour didn't seem to notice.

As they passed Crandall Investments, Seymour said, "Hey, look at that. Ronnie's not there. Second night in a row. I wonder where he's sleeping."

"How can I look at something that's not there?" Jimmy thought Seymour was always saying dumb things like that. "It's like staring at the hole in a doughnut."

"Where d'you think he is?"

This was another dumb remark. "He's probably getting a haircut."

"At midnight? You're fucking with my head."

Jimmy found the subject boring. "I was out at Digger's Burn Palace. Guess who I saw?"

"Ronnie McBride."

"Fuck you, can't you ever be serious? It was Carl. I didn't know Digger had Carl working out there. Larry was showing him shit. Carl didn't say how long he'd been there. He was in a bad mood. So what else is new, right? You just gotta stay away from him when he's like that. You think you could work out there? Like if Carl gets canned?"

"What's so hard about it? They're stiffs, right?"

"You gotta frisk them for rings and shit. I don't know if I could do that. Now they want to pass a law that you gotta pull their teeth because of the fillings. Like they're full of mercury. No way I'm yanking a stiff's teeth. It's not religious. If a stiff's got teeth, he should take 'em into the furnace. I mean, they're his teeth, right? Then you gotta grind the bones. They put them in this thing that's like a big food blender with bells and whistles. I told Larry I wanted to use it to whip up a batch of margaritas, and he gave me that dead look of his. Me, I want the dirt—a nice casket, not too expensive, not too cheap. Larry was packing some chunks of bone into the grinder and smoking a cigar. You think ash wasn't dropping onto that dead guy's bits and pieces? Digger told me that from one stiff to the next you can never get out all the ashes, so everybody's boxed up with some ashes belonging to someone else. How'd you like to be boxed up with a fat old colored woman? Nah, I want the ground."

By now Seymour had parked the ambulance by the hospital. He leaned back and began rolling another joint. Jimmy kept chatting to keep Seymour awake.

"You know these classes diggers take, I mean, guys training to be diggers? They got this class in the restorative arts and they got all these digger students in a classroom and you know what they do?" Seymour didn't answer, and Jimmy raised his voice. "You know what they do?"

"Tell me." Seymour decided against the joint. Maybe he'd take a little nap.

"They bring in a bunch of aluminum roasting pans like the ones you use for a Thanksgiving turkey, except each pan holds a head, like cut off at the neck. Isn't that cool? Each one of them gets to work on a severed head."

Seymour grew more alert. "Where do they get heads?"

"The school buys them. They cost about seven hundred dollars each. You can buy all sorts of shit; you wouldn't believe the sort of shit you can buy, legal or illegal. But for the legal shit there's a price list, though you need some sort of license: hands for five hundred dollars, wrists for five hundred, elbows for five hundred, then the whole leg for up to a thousand dollars. And fuckin' skin, man: ten dollars a square inch. You're a walking gold mine. It's like the gooks eating a chicken: they use every bit. Those student diggers powder up the heads, put on lipstick and rouge, just like with fashion models, and all right in the turkey pan."

There was a pause, and then Seymour asked, "You got plans about Carl?"

"Hey, I got lots of plans. I only gotta pick one. We could scare the shit out of him; do somethin' to drive him right around the bend but we don't let him know it's us. That's the main thing. He's got a wicked temper. Maybe it's better if I do it by myself so nothing gets fucked up. Then he quits or gets fired and Digger says to me, 'We gotta replace Carl. You got any ideas?' And I say Seymour Hodges is the man for the job. How's that sound?"

"Fine by me." Seymour was quiet for a bit, then said, "If Digger starts burning more people than he buries, you gonna call him Digger or you gonna call him Burner?"

"Nah, I don't like that. Maybe the Cooker. No, I'll call him the Chef. It's got a classy ring to it. The Chef."

One o'clock Sunday morning and a pair of coyotes can walk down the middle of Water Street without a care in the world. Sniff a little here, sniff a little there. When Ronnie McBride is sleeping in the doorway of Crandall Investments, the coyotes go by on the far side of the street. Maybe they don't like how he smells. But tonight Ronnie's off someplace else, and the coyotes have the whole street to themselves.

All those people searching for Nina Lefebvre have gone home by now, though cops have her picture taped to the dashboard of their cruisers. Bobby Anderson's home in bed with his wife. Shawna hasn't seen Bobby for a while and she'd like a little romance, but Bobby's sound asleep after hurrying through people's yards all night.

Amy Calderone, Harriet's friend, is wide awake. First she turns one way and then the other. She tells herself if she's not asleep in ten minutes, she'll take a sleeping pill. Then ten minutes go by and she gives herself another ten minutes. Most nights she and her husband, Marty, sleep in each other's arms; they're close like that. But tonight she keeps pushing him away. These embraces, tonight they're oppressive. Amy keeps thinking of Harriet. Why doesn't she call the cops on that Neanderthal? *But maybe I'm the one who should call the cops.* Harriet would be furious. But isn't her safety more important? Even more important than her friendship? And the Neanderthal, wouldn't he be furious as well? Amy pushes Marty away and turns over with her back to him. Ten more minutes and she'll take a pill for sure.

Larry Rodman is watching a skin flick. No rings tonight; the families wanted them back. Larry likes to watch the classics from the forties and fifties. These white bitches gotta be dead by now; the studs, too. If they're alive, the bitches' tits are flabby as used rubbers. But Larry thinks they're dead. That blond bitch with the colored guy's fat cock in her mouth—Larry thinks he's already toasted her, sent her to the oven. He must have burned a bunch of them. It's just statistics, that's all. He's carried them over the welcome mat like a bridegroom. Then he's burned them. It's this that turns him on, not the titties and slick pussies. And when he's hard enough, he'll rack off. Shoot his wad onto the TV screen. It's like pissing in their faces.

Ginger and Howard Phelps are playing gin rummy, but they're not giving it the usual attention. Ginger thinks about that missing Lefebvre girl. What could have gotten into her? She's known Vicki for years, and though she's not a close friend she would never want anything to happen to Nina. Howard was out searching with some other guys for a while. A snipe hunt, Howard called it. Neither Ginger nor Howard likes how things are going, but they don't talk about it; rather, it's like they have a sour taste in their mouths, a sensual discomfort, and they know lots of people who feel the same way. It's not a feeling that has a name yet, but quite a few are lying awake, trying to figure what to call it. *Disquietude* is a word on Hercel's vocabulary test on Monday. Maybe it's disquietude.

At one o'clock Woody Potter is sitting at his kitchen table with a cup of chamomile tea with a little honey and a moderate amount of Jack Daniel's. He promised himself he would go to sleep no matter what. He imagined counting coyotes jumping over a wall and laughed.

A dog from the canine unit had followed Nina's scent for six blocks, and then it vanished. The consensus was someone had picked Nina up in a car. Her friends were contacted, but all denied seeing, helping, or hearing from her. She was in eleventh grade at Brewster High School, and so other classmates were also contacted. Nothing. Then Vicki said that Nina's cell phone was missing, so she had probably called someone; or maybe she had run into someone or flagged someone down.

Whenever Woody brooded, Ajax would come, sit at his feet, and stare at him. If Woody looked back, Ajax would look away. Sometimes Ajax would bring Woody one of his toys—stuffed things, rubber tug toys, and a rubber Santa Claus now faded and with punctures from the dog's teeth. It squeaked when it was squeezed. It was the Santa Claus that Ajax brought now. He sat at Woody's feet with a perky expression, squeaking the Santa over and over, defying him to snatch it away. It made Woody want to give the dog a well-meaning smack.

"Go lie down. I don't feel like being cheered up right now."

Instead of retreating to his bed, Ajax lay down a few feet away and continued to stare at him with worried eyes.

"You can be a real pain, you know that?"

Ajax's tail thumped on the carpet.

Woody turned aside so he wouldn't have to see him. He was reviewing the various events in Brewster to try to form a pattern, but he kept being distracted by their outrageous details. Why would you scalp a person in the twenty-first century? Why would you put a snake in a hospital crib? Then came the rapes of Peggy Summers and Nina Lefebvre, with their trappings of Satanism. Why? And was Nina pregnant? If she had conceived on Wednesday night, that was three days ago. It would take maybe two or three more to show up on a pregnancy test. Woody knew that much from Susie, who had twice hoped she was pregnant and would fuss with pregnancy strips and a Pyrex measuring cup of piss from four days until her period. Woody had thrown away the measuring cup and got another. Every time he'd seen the cup in the cupboard, it reminded him of the difficulties—by which he meant the failings—in their relationship.

Sitting at the kitchen table, he thought of Susie again. It irritated him to miss her so much, since he'd known for a long time that their differences were irreconcilable. To marry her would mean quitting his job as a trooper, and he couldn't imagine doing that. They had discussed this so often he could repeat their discussions verbatim, twenty pages of dialogue that he could put on stage as a one-act play called *The Incredibly Dull.*

But then Woody had a surprise. As he conjured up Susie's face, he instead saw Jill Franklin. He jerked back his head. "Good grief, what a pathetic dope you are," he said out loud.

Ajax got to his feet, wagging his tail, and Woody scratched his ears.

"Relax, I'm just being dumb again." But he kept thinking of Jill—her short blond hair, her round face and snub nose. Didn't she look ridiculous? He didn't think so.

When he had coffee with her that afternoon, they didn't talk about what had been happening in town. Jill hadn't wanted Woody to think she was pumping him for information. Instead, she talked about her six-year-old son and how she felt bad about not spending more time with him, even though her parents were glad to take care of him. But her son—was his name Luke?—wanted a dog and her parents didn't want a dog in the house. So that was that.

Woody hadn't said much; rather, he mentioned things instead of talking about them. He mentioned growing up in Pawtucket; he mentioned being bored by it; he mentioned hunting trips to New Hampshire; he mentioned Iraq and Operation Desert Storm, a silly name, since he had spent months doing nothing. He didn't mention being scared shitless by a missile attack on an army barracks in Dhahran, when he'd just been passing through and had stopped for something to eat. After that it seemed he heard the shouting and screams every night. Even now it sometimes happened if he was particularly stressed. Why should he tell her bad news like that? Nor did he mention his temper or his marriage to Cheryl or his time with Susie. He didn't like talking about himself. It meant revisiting a place that either bored him, scared him, or made him fell guilty. Nor did he say he liked the state police, because everything was clear—not the stuff you dealt with but how you dealt with it, the protocol.

The series of rationalizations in which Woody next immersed himself hardly bear describing, but they concerned Jill's work as a reporter and Woody's questions about how she would write about the hanged cat, Hercel's flight from the coyotes, and Nina's disappearance. The more he considered it, the crosser he got, forgetting, it seemed, Jill's own reservations about writing on such subjects. As he thought of her journalistic responsibility, or lack of it, he also thought about what she looked like—the smoothness of her skin, her muscularity. But he tried to pretend he wasn't thinking about this. It was only an irritating distraction.

The pretext that began as wisps of smoke gained substance, or perhaps one might say the bad reason hid itself behind an apparent good reason. Whatever the case, at two o'clock in the morning Woody called Jill Franklin, ready to read her the riot act for irresponsible journalism.

Jill picked up after the third ring with a mumbled hello. "What're you doing?" His gruff tone suggested that he hoped to catch her engaged in mischief.

"Is this Woody? Well, I'm sleeping, oddly enough. I take it you're not?"

Woody again grew suspicious that she was in the midst of writing irresponsibly about events in Brewster. But as he spoke, he realized how ridiculous it sounded, and his aggressiveness faded to an apologetic monotone.

"You don't have to worry about that," said Jill. "I was fired." She explained how that afternoon she had told Ted Pomeroy, the owner of the paper, that she wanted to return to writing social news because she questioned the ethics of helping to create mass hysteria. Though a reporter for only a short time, she had already fallen victim to the solipsism of thinking an event didn't exist until it was reported in the paper or on a news program. Pomeroy wasn't sympathetic. He'd seen a surge in sales over the past days and he wanted it to continue. "You think you're irreplaceable?" he had shouted. "I'm the only one who's irreplaceable!" So he'd fired her.

"It seems to me," Jill told Woody, "that I should blame you for this. After all, you're the one who's been yelling at me all week."

Woody considered apologizing, but instead he returned to his original question: "So what're you doing right now?"

There was a pause. Jill considered his question, as Woody listened to her breathe. "Well, I'm talking to you on the phone. Before that I was sound asleep, and in a few more minutes I hope to be asleep again, if you'll let me."

"Okay, okay," said Woody, sounding gruff again. "What are you doing for breakfast?"

"I'm spending the day with Luke and my parents. Are you free Monday?"

ELEVEN

IT'S NOT JUST POLICE OFFICERS, firefighters, rescue squads, and ambulance techs who come upon awful events; more often than not it's those we might call innocent of the world's darker parts. Some time ago in Detroit an eight-year-old boy poked open a garbage bag he had noticed in a playground for two days. What he first thought he had found was the leg of a deer. What he really found was the dismembered body of a murdered prostitute. Hard to get over something like that, hard to push it from the mind.

On Monday morning two fourteen-year-old ninth-graders at Brewster Junior High decided to skip school to go squirrel hunting, though they'd be happy to shoot anything bigger if it got in their way. Davie Bottoms was armed with a Daisy DY880, a bolt-action rifle that held fifty BBs; ten pumps sent a BB at its target at seven hundred fifty feet per second. It had cost fifty bucks, which he'd saved in no time by mowing lawns. The previous week it had come in the mail, and Davie was eager to get busy. His mom hated it, but his dad had one as a kid and just laughed. For a boy, it was part of growing up: such was his argument.

The other boy, Alex Milbank, had a Crosman 1377C multi-pump

pneumatic pistol, fourteen inches long. With ten pumps, it could shoot a pellet at six hundred feet per second. It held one pellet, and he had to reload after each shot, but this was done quickly. He'd "borrowed" the pistol from his brother Mikey, a senior in high school, who'd be seriously pissed if he found out.

Alex carried the weapons in a duffel bag, along with a box of doughnuts, a six-pack of Coke, and a plastic bag for whatever they managed to kill. They rode their bikes south out of town on Whipple Street, through half a dozen blocks of houses ranging from old to new and then passing the last house, an old farmhouse belonging to Sister Asherah MacDonald and her partner, Sister Isis Perry. In another quarter-mile Whipple Street reached a dead end at Trustom Pond National Wildlife Refuge, eight hundred acres of forest extending inland from a two-mile barrier beach and Trustom Pond. The boys pushed their bikes about twenty yards into the woods and then unpacked their weapons.

There is a transformative moment when a boy puts a gun in his hands. He doesn't necessarily change from good to bad or from cautious to reckless; rather, he takes on gravitas, a new significance, usually marbled with fantasy as a steak is marbled with fat. Davie and Alex immediately felt older, more mature; they had become hunters, potential breadwinners; they were able to live off the land. This wasn't something they especially saw in themselves as individuals, but each thought he saw it in the other. They had heard, of course, of Hercel McGarty being pursued by coyotes, and they felt if they were lucky enough to run into a coyote, they could handle it no problem.

"Lock and load," said Davie.

"Rock and roll," said Alex.

They wore dark sweatshirts and baseball caps. Davie wore camouflage pants, which Alex envied. He only wore jeans. They walked quietly into the woods.

There had been sun earlier; now it was getting cloudy. The weather was warm for late October. Indian summer, people said. The trees had mostly lost their leaves except the oaks. They didn't follow a path, and bushwhacking was difficult. If they'd known sweetbriar was also called Pilgrim's curse, they would have understood the reference. There were also canes of prickly rose. Thorns caught on their sweatshirts and snatched away their caps. Then, after a few minutes, they saw a squirrel high in an oak and they let loose. Perhaps they fired fifty BBs and a dozen pellets. After the first shot, the squirrel darted to the other side of the tree and waited.

"Did you hit it?" asked Davie.

Alex would have liked to say yes, but he shook his head. They looked around at the trees. Crows were calling, and they would have shot a crow if the opportunity had arisen, but none did. They'd have even shot a seagull.

"We need to be more quiet," said Alex.

Davie nodded, but this was hard to do as they pushed through the brambles. Still, they had been in these woods before and knew the vines wouldn't last forever. Again they saw a squirrel, and again they fired and missed.

"Maybe if we wait for them," said Davie.

This seemed better than being scratched to pieces. After another ten yards or so they came to a small open area, where they lay down to watch the surrounding branches.

And so they waited. The woods were quiet; not even the crows were calling. The breeze through the branches made a faint whispering. Occasionally, they heard a rustling noise, but then it passed and silence returned.

After ten minutes, Davie joked, "D'you think that first squirrel could have told the other squirrels?"

Alex considered this. "Either that or the crows." They were getting bored.

A few more minutes went by, and then Alex crawled about twenty feet beneath the brambles to get a better view of what lay ahead. A few seconds after that he hissed at Davie and motioned for him to move forward.

Alex pointed to something through the trees. "What's that?" he whispered.

A long, dark shape seemed to protrude from the side of an oak about twenty yards away. The brambles kept them from seeing it clearly.

"Maybe a branch's leaning against the tree."

Alex sighted his pistol with its barrel resting on his forearm. He fired. The pistol made a noise like *"Pffft!"*

"Did you hit it?" asked Davie.

"I think so." Alex inserted another pellet and began pumping his pistol.

Then Davie fired. After a moment, he said, "I hit it for sure."

Alex aimed again and fired. Pause. "So did I."

Then Davie fired again. They went on firing for another couple of minutes. There was no sound of the BBs or pellets hitting anything.

"Let's get a little closer," said Alex.

They crept forward and stopped. The object was clearer, but it still seemed part of the tree. Davie saw a white growth at the bottom. He aimed at it and fired. Then Alex fired and Davie fired again.

"What is that?" asked Alex.

"Some kind of fungus." Davie fired and pumped, fired and pumped.

Alex fired a pellet and then another. "I got it for sure."

"Like shooting pigs in a barrel," said Davie.

Once more they crept forward, and for maybe half a minute the dark shape vanished behind the brambles growing above them. Then they saw it again and stopped. Neither spoke. It wasn't a fungus after all. Alex dropped his pistol.

The dark shape hung from a branch. The white growth was two bare feet dangling about three feet off the ground, but they had been chewed. Some animal, surely more than one, had leapt up, tearing at the feet and calves, ripping the jeans, so the feet were ragged, a big toe was missing. Once their first shock began to diminish, Alex saw where his pellets had pocked the white ankles. The boys realized they had been shooting at somebody's feet and at the dead body that rose above it.

Davie shouted, leapt up, and began pushing his way back through the brambles. He hardly felt how they tore at him. Alex was right behind him. The more the vines grabbed at them, the harder they pushed. Their hands and faces were scratched. After a minute Alex saw he didn't have his brother's pistol. He sure wasn't going back for it.

Woody Potter and Jill Franklin had agreed to meet at the Brewster Brew at eight o'clock Monday morning. From the moment he got out of bed at six, Woody had been telling himself he was being foolish. He arrived fifteen minutes early. Jean Sawyer said later he'd had a hangdog expression.

He had a cup of coffee and picked up the *Providence Journal*. Then he recalled Nina Lefebvre, and he asked Jean if she remembered seeing Nina in the coffee shop last week with an older man and two women. Her response was so eager it was as if Woody had invited her to sing at Carnegie Hall. She pushed back her hair.

"Why, yes, I *did* see Nina with two older women and a man. Of course, by older I only mean they were older than Nina. I'm sure the man was in his thirties—handsome in a rather coarse way. He wore a black shirt, which drew my attention, and he had black hair. He had a double espresso. Of course, I love Brewster, but not many people drink espresso, so I'm always glad when they do. And the two women had cappuccinos. They were quite fit. One wore capri pants, dark with an athletic stripe down the side. I believe she had short blond hair. The other wore solid knit gray pants with a drawstring. Her hair I think was brown, sort of a pixie cut. She wore a tank top, dark blue or green. The other wore a light-colored V-neck. Both were too thin for my taste. I prefer Rubens. Do you know Rubens?"

"I've never met him." Woody immediately saw that was the wrong answer, and he stopped before saying, "Does he live here in town?"

"Anyway," added Woody, "you've a good memory for clothes."

Jean gave a little laugh. "I always remember their clothes better than their faces. I suppose it's because I'm so fashion-conscious. They certainly weren't wearing anything expensive, more like workout clothes. I'd thought they'd all come from a class at You-You."

"And when was this?"

"A week ago, and it must have been Saturday, otherwise Nina would have been in school."

"Had you seen them before?"

"One of the women was familiar. The blond. And I might have seen the man before. I'm really quite fortunate You-You is so close. Many people who work there or take classes often come here. And after a class, they're quite hungry. I sell far more pastries than I ever thought I would. And croissants! I hardly knew what a croissant was before I opened up. I'd always called them buns. But so many of them come here it's hard to keep track of them. And they all look alike, you know, like sailors."

"How d'you mean?"

"They're all fit and are dressed for yoga or some jumping class. Most are between, oh, twenty-five and forty. Of course, there're older people—yoga for seniors, Pilates for seniors. I really think they need to be more careful. Some of them come in after class all red-faced and breathing hard. It'd be terrible if one of them keeled over before paying their bill." Jean gave her little laugh. "But seriously, last spring an ambulance had to come for one of them. It was only palpitations, but it could have been worse. Her friend called nine-one-one. My friend—she's a librarian—said I should keep a nurse on hand. She was joking, but still . . ."

"Can you say anything more about the ones you recognized?"

"You mean with Nina? The blond was about Nina's height. That's not very tall, is it? Maybe five-five or five-six. Very fit, not an ounce of fat. Maybe a pointy face. Do you ever look at someone and think he or she looks just like a cat or a bird, even a fish? This girl reminded me of a greyhound, a blond greyhound. And the man? He had a little gray in his hair and needed a shave. He might have been about six feet, certainly taller than the blond. A squarish face—he reminded me of a bulldog. Or maybe a pug—his eyes were wide apart in that pug way, and his chin and mouth were mushed."

"Mushed?"

"A square chin and thin, downturned lips—you know what I mean."

Woody didn't. "And what was their mood? How did they behave?"

"Oh, they were quite jolly. Laughing and telling jokes. Quite noisy."

"Nina, too?"

"I don't know if she said much, but she laughed as much as the others. . . ." Jean stopped and looked at someone over Woody's shoulder. She had glanced in that direction two or three times, but now she frowned as if an intruder was trying to eavesdrop. Woody turned and saw Jill Franklin looking at him with a slight ironic smile.

"Mixing business with pleasure?"

Each person in life has a cross or two that he or she must bear. An annoying cross of Woody's was that he blushed—not much, but always at moments of slight embarrassment with a woman.

"I'm at that table over by the window," he said, "with the paper and coffee." He spoke somewhat brusquely to counteract the blushing.

"Your coffee must be cold."

"Have you been here long?"

"Perhaps a minute."

He felt a twinge of irritation. "Have you been getting good information for another article?" Then he remembered that she had lost her job.

Jill's eyes lost their humor.

"I'm sorry," said Woody. "That was a stupid thing to say. Let's sit down."

Jill ordered a cappuccino; they both ordered bagels with cream cheese. Jill also got an orange juice. They said little during these transactions. Jill had on jeans and a black leather jacket; underneath she wore a maroon tank top. She also wore a silver chain with a lapis pendant in a silver setting.

"Nice necklace," said Woody.

Jill understood this was further apology for his remark. Perhaps it was in his nature to be brusque. If so, then it was too bad. On the other hand, he'd blushed, so maybe he was just your typically conflicted male. So she smiled.

"Yeah, I know you told me you were fired," said Woody, hanging on to the subject. "A whole lot of people have been asking me questions, reporters from Providence and Boston, TV guys, people who've no right to be asking me questions."

The humor again went out of Jill's eyes. "I simply asked if you were mixing business and pleasure. Did you think I was grilling you?"

Woody realized he had again said the wrong thing. He liked her eyes when they grew serious, although the expression wasn't in his best interest. He glanced out at the street. The clouds had moved in with a hundred varieties of gray. It would rain later. He looked back at Jill and raised his hands, holding his palms up toward her. "Let's start over," he said.

Jean Sawyer arrived with Jill's cappuccino and the toasted bagels, one plain and one multigrain. Woody's was plain. The interruption eased the tension.

"Did you leave your dog in the truck again?" asked Jill.

"Ajax? He likes it. He always knows I'm coming back."

Gradually they moved to other subjects. She liked to kayak in the salt ponds along the coast, and so did Woody. They calculated that at some point they had been kayaking in Trustom Pond at the same time. It seemed a benign coincidence. Woody liked hiking; Jill went running, usually along the beach at low tide. Woody said he'd have to get back to running. Then they talked about movies.

Someone overhearing their conversation would have found it dull. But it was the subtext that was important, their gestures, how they glanced at each other and were unable to look at each other for too long. Doesn't it seem foolish that someone is reassured when another person likes the same—often very silly—movie? They both liked *The Lord of the Rings,* the movie and books. Jill had read the trilogy three times and had read *The Hobbit* out loud to Luke. The connection gave them a sense of comfort. Neither would have been outraged if the other had disliked Tolkien, but it was better they did. Woody wasn't much of a reader, but he'd read *The Catcher in the Rye* and *Of Mice and Men,* both of which he'd liked, as had Jill. She had read quite a few mystery novels. Woody hadn't—they were too much like being at work, a preposterous and exaggerated work—but he'd read *The Shining* and *Cujo* and *The Dark Half.* This, for some reason, led Woody to look at his watch. It was ten minutes after nine. He leapt to his feet, and his chair tipped over with a crash.

"Holy shit, I'm late! I've got a briefing! D'you mind if I call you later?" Here he blushed again, only a trace of pink, but Jill saw it. Then he rushed out the door, leaving it open behind him.

I guess I'm paying, thought Jill. She took out her wallet. She didn't mind.

Woody was the last to arrive in the conference room in police headquarters. The same men and women from Saturday were there, as were a detective from Westerly, another from Charlestown, a detective from the Violent Fugitive Task Force, another from the criminal investigation unit, a lawyer from the attorney general's office, and several Woody didn't recognize. No more room was left at the table, though a place had been saved for him. Six people were squeezed into chairs against the wall. Everyone looked up when he entered. This morning there were no coffee and doughnuts.

"Glad you could make it, Corporal," said Captain Brotman tonelessly.

Bobby Anderson winked at Woody from across the table.

On Sunday there had been further interviews with people in and around the hospital in regards to the missing baby. Neighbors reported seeing vehicles on the streets or arriving at the hospital after midnight, but nothing was particularly suspicious about this. In no case had the descriptions been detailed enough to lead to an identification, except for a black Mercedes belonging to one of the doctors. Woody's arrival had interrupted this report. It resumed once he sat down.

A South Kingstown detective, a DEM investigator, and a CIU detective described their progress in and around the swamp. Again a number of people and vehicles had been seen, but none appeared necessarily suspicious. However, detailed descriptions—as much as possible—had been gathered and the people and vehicles were being sought. Seven had been located, but either they weren't in the swamp at the right time or it seemed absurd to suspect them—two nuns from St. James had gone for a walk. Thirty officers and volunteers were attempting to search the entire swamp, but they hadn't finished. Where they had found footprints, the footprints had been photographed and casts had been taken. They had also collected a number of bottles and beer cans. A trooper had fallen into the water.

Nina Lefebvre had not been found, but reports of her being seen were coming in from all over the state, as well as from Connecticut and Massachusetts. Some could be discounted; others had to be investigated.

"Why were they discounted?" asked a South Kingstown lieutenant. His name was Joe Doyle. Red-faced, oversized, and a thirty-year veteran, he was known as Joe "I do things by the book" Doyle. To Woody's mind, Doyle never contributed to a meeting; he simply lengthened it.

Two had been African American, one had been Hispanic, and one Polynesian. Of the others, either the age difference was too great or they lived too far from the scene.

Several at the table glanced at Doyle as if he'd asked a silly question. He resettled himself in his chair and looked belligerent.

Acting chief Bonaldo and Bobby described the search for Nina Lefebvre within Brewster. Everyone in her eleventh-grade class was being interviewed, as were her other friends and people who lived in the vicinity of her mother's house. These interviews were still going on. Nina had been presumably picked up in a vehicle on Water Street, where the dog had lost her scent. People in the area were questioned—including Jean Sawyer at the Brewster Brew.

Woody mentioned talking to Jean that morning. Perhaps he made it seem as if this was why he had been late to the briefing. The descriptions he received from Jean were similar to what had been learned before, although the earlier interview hadn't disclosed the information that the vaguely familiar man looked like a pug dog and the vaguely familiar woman looked like a greyhound. Woody hadn't wanted to mention this, and then he did. There was a certain amount of coughing and harrumphing. Unvoiced wisecracks hung in the air like dissipating smoke. Woody then asked if the people at You-You had been questioned. Captain Brotman said it would begin this morning.

"I'd like to be part of that, sir," said Woody.

A forensics criminalist said the mud on Nina's shoes and clothes had a similar consistency and mixture of organic matter as that found on the nursery floor and in Great Swamp. This caused a slight stir. It seemed connections were being made between separate elements of the investigation.

Nina's bedroom had been searched. A few additional names had been found but no address book. Neither had there been a journal or diary. On the other hand, an unused pregnancy kit had been discovered.

The FBI agent described what the agency had done to locate the missing baby, mostly out of state. A number of leads were being investigated. He spoke of cases of babies being sold for adoption. There was also much cross-border abduction from Mexico. He also mentioned reports of clandestine clinics in Tijuana and Juárez that performed transplants of kidneys and corneal tissue from abducted Mexican children to the children of wealthy Americans. He went on to describe other Mexican clinics that harvested organs from abducted children.

"I don't see how any of that affects us in Brewster," said Captain Brotman. "We've enough problems without dealing with Mexico's."

A Massachusetts state police detective said that people who knew

Hartmann were still being sought, especially those who Hartmann had dealt with in the previous two weeks, to see if they knew why he might have driven down to Brewster.

Lieutenant Aaron Hammond, head of the area detective unit, had talked to Carl Krause's doctor in Oswego and to doctors at Benjamin Rush in Syracuse. It had been difficult to get information because of privacy issues, but Hammond had been helped by several calls from the governor's office. Carl had been in Benjamin Rush on three different occasions, the most recent being a little more than three years ago. Each time he had had a course of ECT treatments: twelve treatments, three times a week for four weeks. He had greatly benefited from these visits, but if they hadn't seemed to last, it was because he had stopped taking his medication. Carl said the pills made him feel stupid. Each day he had been taking, or should be taking, 900 mg of Lithobid, a slow-release form of lithium, and 300 mg of Lamictal, an anticonvulsant used as a mood stabilizer. His doctor in Oswego said he hadn't talked to Carl since April, when Carl had told him everything was going great. He had a new doctor he liked, had a great wife and a good job. Everything was fine.

"I asked the Oswego doctor what happened when Carl went off his meds," said Hammond. "He was reluctant to talk about it, saying it was a matter of privacy. Then he told me Carl tended to 'act out,' that he had 'violence issues.'"

Bobby rolled his eyes.

Still to come were reports on Alice Alessio and Peggy Summers, and discussion on the subject of coyotes. At that moment, however, the door slammed open and a Brewster police officer burst into the room. Seeing acting chief Bonaldo, he ran to him and whispered something. Bonaldo reacted as if he'd been slapped.

"A girl has been found hanging from a tree in the woods." The chief could hardly keep his voice steady. "It might be Nina Lefebvre. Some kids with BB guns were using her for target practice."

The rain that threatened earlier had now begun with a vengeance, one of those cold fall rains whose purpose seems to be to tear the last leaves from the trees and flush the grime from the earth. Wind rushed through the branches and the whole forest was in motion, a moaning and creaking nothing like language but full of protest nonetheless.

With water dripping down his face, Bobby stared at the body of Nina Lefebvre swinging back and forth, turning first one way, then the other, as if she were looking for something. Her ragged feet, coyote-bitten and pocked by BBs and pellets, were terribly white next to her dark jeans, as if scoured clean by the rain. Bobby's response to grief was not tears but the desire to hit something. He kept his fists in his pockets.

"Cut her down," he said.

"We need to go over the ground," said Frank Montesano. He had arrived with the crime investigation unit at the dead end of Whipple Street at the same time as Bobby, and together they had slogged into the woods. A doctor from the medical examiner's office was expected shortly.

"I don't give a fuck. Cut her down. Now!"

The body hung from a branch about fifteen feet off the ground. The rain had slicked down Nina's dark bangs, concealing her eyes, which was a blessing, thought Bobby. Her mouth was open, as if she were thirsty. Her clean and purposeless hands seemed to be floating. Water dripped from the fingers.

Janie Forsyth trotted to the tree, jumped and grabbed a low-hanging branch. Then she pulled herself up and grabbed the branch above her. In another second, she was sitting on the branch to which the rope was tied.

Bobby and Montesano stood beneath her. Ten other police officers remained back so as not to muddy the crime scene. Probably all of them wanted to urge Janie to be careful, but nobody made a sound. The body continued to turn this way and that.

Janie had a pocketknife, and she opened the blade. Briefly, she looked down at the men staring up at her. They reminded her of hungry baby birds. Bobby's wet black face seemed almost a vacancy into which the whites of his eyes were placed. Janie slipped the blade between the rope and the branch and began to cut.

Bobby stood under the body. Nina's feet hung three feet from the ground, and, reaching up, Bobby could touch her waist. When the rope was cut, Nina fell toward him, and he let her fall across his shoulder. He was surprised at how heavy she was. Her thick sweatshirt was saturated with water. Maybe it's no more than that, he thought. BBs fell to the ground, a little splash of golden rain. Bobby lowered her so he could hold her in his arms. When her wet hair brushed across his face, he thought he'd scream. He was careful not to look at her. He didn't want to see her eyes. He carried her to a stretcher back by the other officers. The rope trailed behind him. Like a snake, they all thought.

Bobby stayed in the woods for another two hours. He had no cap, but he wore a leather coat. Still, he was drenched. The uniformed troopers all had rain gear. Someone offered Bobby an umbrella, but he turned it down. He felt he deserved to be drenched, no matter how stupid that was. He was also cold, though not half so cold as Nina, not a tenth so cold. Any age was a lousy age to die, but sixteen seemed particularly harsh. After a while, the medical examiner took her body back to Providence, but Nina still seemed to hang in the air, so much so that Bobby tried not to look up. Her cell phone was missing, and no bag was found. Montesano said there were no obvious footprints other than Nina's and the police officers', but that wasn't conclusive. There were also paw prints. Slick leaves covered much of the ground, which still might reveal traces of footprints; they would be hard to detect. It seemed Nina's death was suicide rather than murder.

"I can't swear to it," said Montesano, "but everything points in that direction."

Bobby could only speculate about what had happened. When Nina escaped from her house, she'd either called someone or ran into someone she knew on Water Street where the dog lost her scent. Then she had either stayed with that person or met up with someone else. Somewhere she'd gotten a rope; somewhere she'd left her cell phone. Presumably her phone had an address book and would contain a list of her calls. He could get her calls from the phone company, unless Nina had used a prepaid phone. A lot of kids used those nowadays.

As Bobby considered these possibilities, his anger returned. Whoever Nina was with hadn't tried, or sufficiently tried, to save her from suicide. Had the person encouraged her? Had she been with the person Saturday night and all day Sunday? Had the person given her the rope and taken the phone? That suggested he or she had been involved in the rape and was trying to protect himself or herself. If so, Bobby thought, Nina's death hadn't been suicide but murder, though a court might not see it that way.

So what did this anonymous person stand to gain? Continued anonymity. And how had he or she convinced Nina to end her life? The person could threaten to publicize the rape and could exaggerate Nina's role and willingness. Or Nina might be convinced she was protecting her friends; she was saving her parents from embarrassment. The person could have encouraged Nina's despair as one might encourage a runner in a race.

The similarity between what had happened to Nina and Peggy Summers had to be looked at: the bizarre ritual, the chanting and dancing, the hallucinogens, the man with the skull face. Could Nina be convinced she was carrying the Devil's baby?

A trooper shouted to Bobby and he jumped. The pellet pistol had been found among the brambles about fifteen yards from where Nina had hung. There was no sign that the boys had come any closer but plenty to show they had bushwhacked their way up to that point. Davie Bottoms and Alex Milbank sat in the backseat of a cruiser parked in the turnaround at the end of Whipple Street, their faces and hands patched with Band-Aids from the brambles. They didn't talk; they were abject and miserable. They knew they wouldn't get any sympathy from anyone and couldn't imagine what lay ahead. They knew nothing would be forgotten, either by them or by others.

Sitting in Dr. Joyce Fuller's office, Woody was amazed he had ever thought of having sex with her. It wasn't that she was unattractive, nor was it that she was five or six years older than he. She was just so tidy, so consummate in her arrangements, so determined that nothing be out of place—not a hair on her head, not a pencil on her desk.

"Certainly, I expect that staff members—medical, clerical, whatever their position—have had sex with one another, though it's rare. It would also cost somebody his or her job."

"Would a doctor be more protected?" asked Woody.

"Nobody would be protected. It would be a breach of hospital regulations."

It was late Monday morning. Through the closed door, Woody

could hear the business of the hospital continuing—phones ringing, announcements over the PA system, secretaries talking and laughing.

Woody had told Dr. Fuller about Dr. Balfour and Alice Alessio. It turned out that Balfour had already talked to Dr. Fuller earlier that morning. She had notified Reggie Adams, chairman of the board of trustees, who had urged her to do nothing about dismissing Dr. Balfour and Nurse Alessio until the police had made an arrest and the guilty party had been convicted. In the meantime, the relationship between Balfour and Alessio should be kept quiet.

"Once everything is settled," said Adams, "they can be sent on their way."

And me, too, Dr. Fuller had thought. *I'll be sent on my way, unless I resign first.*

"To tell the truth," said Dr. Fuller, "I'm surprised by Dr. Balfour. There's always a certain amount of flirting, and people might see each other—sexually, I mean—away from the hospital, though it's discouraged, but there's never been any hint of that in Dr. Balfour. He's never seemed interested. Of course, that's not the case with Nurse Alessio. I doubt this was her first time, though we've no proof. Perhaps Dr. Balfour had never been sufficiently tempted. Do you find . . ." Here Dr. Fuller paused. "Do you find Alice attractive?"

Woody looked up abruptly. "She's not my type." She was a quickie, and he didn't go in for quickies. He didn't care to explain this to Dr. Fuller. "She's not the sort of woman you go to for conversation," he added. Then he wondered if he was saying too much. It would be easier to talk to a man.

"No," said Dr. Fuller, "I expect Nurse Spandex's conversational abilities are few, whatever her others might be. Have you learned anything at all about that poor baby? It seems I spend most of my time thinking about him."

"Descriptions have been sent all over the country. The Summers girl has been no help." Woody decided not to tell Dr. Fuller about the man with a skull instead of a face, but he expected she already knew. "She says she's no idea who the father might be. What about you? Do you feel any better? I'm sorry, I know *better* isn't the right word."

Dr. Fuller's smile was ironic and sad. "I want to thank you for the other night. I think I no longer feel sorry for myself, or only a little bit, though my guilt, if anything, has increased. As you said, I can still be useful. I need a new approach to seeing myself, some way in which my pride plays a smaller part. But as soon as possible I need to get away from here. I don't know if I'll be able to stay until there's a conviction, if it ever happens."

Bingo Schwartz was a state police detective who often worked with Woody and Bobby Anderson, but he felt creaky and looked forward to retirement, although he was only fifty. Still, he'd been a trooper for more than twenty-five years, and enough was enough. He was overweight and had a bad leg, his wife hated him, his kids were spread out across the country, and, well, he wanted some enthusiasm again. Some joie de vivre. He didn't think he'd find it in the state police, which wasn't a complaint. He was just tired of cop thoughts, as he called them, tired of standardized cop procedure.

When Bingo had been young and foolish, he had wanted to be an opera singer. He had been sixteen and it had taken maybe no more than two weeks to see it was an impossible desire. But the choirmaster at St. Luke's in Warwick, Mr. Pasero, had said he was a natural basso, and Father Michael agreed. Mr. Pasero had played Bingo records of Ezio Pinza. These, Bingo told himself, had changed his life. Soon he had learned to sing "Some Enchanted Evening," and his mother had invited neighbors into the living room to hear him. One woman wept and said he was even better than the original. This is when Bingo thought he'd be famous.

Then, luckily, common sense prevailed. Bingo had still sung in the choir and in local theatricals, but it was amateur stuff. Even so, he spent many hours listening to Pinza, and other bassos—Samuel Ramey, Jerome Hines, Boris Christoff, and the greatest of them all, Chaliapin. He studied Chaliapin's roles and could sing parts of *Boris Godunov*, as well as parts of Gounod's *Faust* and Boito's *Mefistofele*. His favorite was Leporello in Mozart's *Don Giovanni*, and the aria he liked best was "Madamina, il catalogo è questo," in which Leporello brags that Don Giovanni had fucked one thousand and three women in Spain, and another thousand elsewhere.

Of course, in retirement, Bingo wouldn't be a singer, though he might join a choir again, but he would like to work part-time in a theater helping to build sets, ideally for operas. He was a first-rate carpenter and had friends in the theater, even singers, so it didn't seem an impossible ambition. And he was humble. As he liked to say, "I only want to swing a little hammer."

Bingo was known among his colleagues as the "Mumbler," because he would sing or hum his favorite arias under his breath. This Monday afternoon, as he made his way along the sidewalk in the rain from the Brewster Brew to Crandall Investments, he hummed the aria about the thousand and three Spanish victims of Don Giovanni's passion.

Ma in Ispagna son già mille e tre.
V'han fra queste contadine,
Cameriere, cittadine,
V'han contesse, baronesse,

Marchesine, principesse.
E v'han donne d'ogni grado,
D'ogni forma, d'ogni età.
Nella bionda egli ha l'usanza
Di lodar la gentilezza,
Nella bruna la costanza,
Nella bianca la dolcezza.

Bingo was hardly conscious of this, but it gave him comfort and made his walk more than simple plodding. As for the reason for his short journey, it had happened, in the search for a person who might have seen Nina, that somebody had mentioned Ronnie McBride. If Ronnie had slept in the doorway of Crandall Investments, as he did nearly every night, he might have observed something. Then it turned out that Ronnie hadn't been seen since late Thursday.

So Bingo Schwartz was on his way to talk to George Crandall, head of Crandall Investments. Walking with a distinct limp, Bingo hardly felt the rain. "In winter he likes fat ones, in summer he likes thin ones," he sang in Italian, though no one could hear him. He wore a brown suit and black raincoat. On his head was a Greek fisherman's cap.

George Crandall had been born and bred in Brewster, but he did his best to look like a Wall Street mogul, and his suits were knockoffs of five-thousand-dollar originals. He was forty years old, and most people still thought of him as Georgie. When first introduced to a person, he exuded weighty solemnity, but then he would giggle at some silly thing or make a foolish remark and all his seriousness would be overthrown.

"Ronnie's been sleeping in my doorway for about two years," Crandall told Bingo, "ever since his wife died. He has a house; he just doesn't want to use it. He's a little touched in the head, though he's as gentle as a lamb. I've known him all my life. The grieving process hits everyone differently, I suppose. At first it bothered me to have him sleeping out there. After all, it's *my* doorway. But then I grew used to it. He wasn't doing any harm and he didn't make a mess, just some crumbs now and then. He'd be gone by seven and take his sleeping bag with him. I'm not sure where he went, but he'd often be in the library during the day."

Bingo wondered where this was leading, but he was patient and believed in letting whoever he was interviewing tell their story at their own pace. It was a mistake to hurry them. They tensed up.

"That's why I began to worry on Friday morning. Ronnie's sleeping bag was still here. I couldn't leave it in the alcove, so I brought it inside. Then I took it over to West Cleaners to have it washed—purified and sanitized is more like it. It was absolutely filthy. I thought Ronnie would be pleased. It'd be a treat to have it all smelling lemony. But Ronnie hasn't been back, not Saturday night, not Sunday night. So I called the police. I hope that's all right." Crandall gave a nervous laugh.

"Has he done this before?" asked Bingo.

"Absolutely never. I mean, he'd miss a night, but he'd never leave his sleeping bag behind. And I thought with all these awful things—the baby being stolen and the snakes—better safe than sorry. I was in school with Ralph Summers, Peggy's dad, though he was a few years ahead of me, and I met her mother when I was Peggy's age. And then the scalping. I even imagined poor Ronnie might have been scalped. And now Nina's disappeared. You see, Ronnie being gone a few days, it's never happened before."

Monday night it was dark by six and the rain fell as hard as ever. The wind continued to pluck the last leaves; on a few streets there was flooding. It was a night to stay home, a night to have a fire in the fireplace.

At eight o'clock two cars drove out Whipple Street past the farmhouse, where Sister Asherah and Sister Isis lived, to the dead end, where they turned and slowly made their way back. As they reached the farmhouse, the cars cut their lights and their doors opened. Four men hurried across the lawn, while two others sat behind the steering wheels and waited. The sound of the rain probably concealed the sound of the motors. Lights were on downstairs and several were on upstairs, but the women weren't visible, which was just as well. Sister Asherah's blue Prius was parked in the driveway. Sister Isis's Civic was in the garage.

Each man carried several bricks. They approached the windows, ducking down so they wouldn't be seen. The men stopped and then one gave a whistle. Each began throwing his bricks. There is nothing subtle about a brick through a window. There's no development, no buildup. The violence is immediate. The glass crashed and crashed. Bricks bounced across the floor and broke things. Windows in the living room and dining room, windows in the kitchen—they all shattered. A woman screamed.

Then the men ran back to the two cars. The doors slammed. A man shouted, "Get fucked, bitch!" The cars squealed and fishtailed back down Whipple Street.

TWELVE

IT RAINED ALL NIGHT and into the morning, steady and unrelenting. Shortly after six, Woody and Bobby Anderson sat in Woody's Tundra out at the beach. Woody had a permit to drive on the sand, though he did little fishing, and he'd pulled up almost to the high-tide mark facing the ocean. Ajax sat in back. He didn't like the rain and had a wet-dog smell. Woody had gotten muffins and coffee from Dunkin' Donuts. It was barely light, a lighter gray against the dark. The waves seemed to come in from nowhere, invisible until they crested and broke in a white rush. The windshield wipers whapped lazily back and forth.

Woody and Bobby often communicated in a light banter, jokey and jivey. It was like a separate language, heavy with gesture, and resonated with multilayers of irony, cynicism, and gravity. They had developed it over years of working together, and very few people could catch its nuances, hear meaning in its seeming foolishness, or had a sense of its complexity. Bingo Schwartz understood it and found it exasperating. Frank Montesano understood it and found it too exclusive, with slang only Woody and Bobby understood. "We de bullen," Bobby might say.

"We la flic," Woody might answer. No more than "We're the cops." Pure silliness.

After Nina Lefebvre was found hanging in the woods, the banter disappeared. They didn't stop out of respect or a sense of seriousness. They weren't even aware of stopping. It just stopped, and who knew when it would begin again, if at all.

"Has it occurred to you," said Woody, "there might be a third girl, even a fourth and fifth, who had a baby? They might not have been born in a hospital."

"How d'you find out about them?"

"Start by talking to teachers at the schools, I guess. Maybe Nina's friends. Or start with Peggy."

Bobby stared at the ocean. He tried to find comfort in the waves' steady repetition, but no comfort came. Back in May he'd borrowed Woody's truck and he, Shawna, and the kids had come to collect stones to line the walk from their driveway to the house. They were rounded, many colored, and weighed anywhere from ten to forty pounds. It seemed a hundred years ago.

"You know, things are getting incredibly messy," said Bobby.

Woody didn't answer. He had said much the same thing a few minutes before.

Last night they had gone to the farmhouse belonging to the two Wiccans. Police had already talked to them, and now the women were sweeping up the glass. Sister Asherah had been crying: big, honking sobs, for which she kept apologizing. Sister Isis couldn't see why anyone should hate them. "We're perfectly harmless," she said.

A few people had seen the cars rushing down Whipple Street—Ford and Chevrolet four-door sedans, a few years old, dark colors. Though the descriptions weren't clear, Woody knew they were clear enough. Fred Bonaldo and the Brewster police had been charged with finding them, and in a day or so the men would probably be arrested. Since the status and legality of Wicca had already been established by the courts, the men were in serious trouble. Whoever broke the windows would be charged with hate crimes and violent assault, among other things. Woody wanted this to happen as soon as possible.

"This whole fucking town's about to explode," he said.

It was clear the window breakers weren't unique in their anger, even if, for now at any rate, they were the most violent. News of Nina's death had spread through Brewster, and people already knew of the rape of the two girls, the strange ceremonies in the woods, and the skull mask. Many approved of what the men had done, and Woody and Bobby knew the violence could worsen, which was why the men had to be caught right away.

Monday afternoon, one of the officers searching the swamp had found a silver triangular amulet hanging from a black cord. Within the triangle was a complicated knot formed by more triangles. Woody had shown it to Sister Asherah, who recognized it.

"Brighid's knot, the exalted one," said Sister Asherah, "Irish priestess of poets and healers. The Celtic knot confers these gifts on the bearer. Her day is February second, one of the Sabbats. Among pagans, it's the feast of Imbolc; among Christians, it's the Feast of Saint Brighid. She was an absolutely wonderful woman. A role model."

"Was she, you know, violent?" Bobby had asked.

"The very opposite; she's the protector of hearth and home." Sister Asherah had glanced at the wreckage around her. "Not that she helped us very much."

News of the amulet also spread through town as further evidence of witchcraft. As he had sat with the two women, Woody imagined people phoning one another and talking about the amulet in the woods. Already Woody had called Bonaldo and asked that a patrol car be stationed at the women's house all night. "And make sure the guys stay awake," he had said.

The two women had reminded Bobby more of worried hens than witches. As neopagans or Neo-Heathens they believed in animism, that every living thing, every object, the rain, the wind, the clouds, had a soul, which would pass on to other creatures, plants, and inanimate objects after death. They believed in gods of the forest, gods of fertility; they believed in the power of the matriarchy. Talking to them and trying to see into their deception, Bobby had seen only self-deception. But wouldn't he say the same about most believers, whatever their religion? It was clear the two women would be pleased to talk about Wicca for hours, much like Jehovah's Witnesses and Mormons who went from door to door seeking converts.

With prodding, Woody had got the names of others in their coven and some men and women in other covens. Even if the police didn't question them, they should be warned about what had happened. Only one other lived in Brewster; the rest were scattered between Westerly and Newport. Still, he intended that all would be questioned.

"How d'you define matriarchy?" Bobby had asked.

Sister Isis, who was thin to the same degree that Sister Asherah was fat, and about the same age, was happy to answer. "I see it, and I'm sure Sister Asherah would agree, as a woman-centered society with an emphasis on goddess worship. Many of the oldest societies were matriarchal, and many think the world would return to its natural balance if those societies came back again. Less violence, if you know what I mean."

As Sister Isis had talked, Bobby thought that nothing seemed harmful about the women's religion. Surely it was less harmful than many of the more conventional ones.

Sitting in the truck, Woody said, "You know that guy I was telling you about, Chmielnicki, at You-You? Maybe you could come with me to talk to him later. He kept guessing things about me that gave me the willies, like true things. Anyway, he might straighten out some of this Wicca stuff. You can't convince me that the Wiccans are connected to anything we're doing, but Chmielnicki also mentioned Satanists. Maybe they're the ones we need to locate."

Bobby was unable to take his eyes off the ocean. With the approaching daylight, he could see past the breaking waves to a farther gray. "I keep thinking of when that girl was cut loose, when Janie cut the rope. She fell onto my shoulder. I still feel the weight of her. I can't explain it. She felt incredibly heavy. Then her wet hair pressed against my face and I nearly lost it. I don't know how to say this—like my whole world disappeared, everything I love. It all went right out the window. In its place was just darkness. I can't get it out of my mind."

Woody didn't know what to say to this. He and Bobby never talked about emotional stuff, were never affectionate, and rarely shook hands. But none of that came to mind when Woody reached out and put a hand on the other man's shoulder. What he felt was that all his words had been taken away and only his hand on Bobby's shoulder could help. He kept it there for a few seconds. The waves crashed and crashed.

Hercel McGarty Jr. sat at the breakfast table poking at his Cheerios in a bright orange bowl, his favorite. Some floated on the surface of the milk and some sank. Some clustered together; some floated alone. He poked one with his spoon and then another and watched them bob. All this was of interest. He wasn't very hungry. It was six-fifteen, and in an hour he would leave for school.

He could hear his sister in the bathroom down the hall splashing in the tub, while his mother kept saying, "Are you sure you aren't clean yet?"

Randy, his mother's miniature dachshund, sat at Hercel's feet with an expression that swore he hadn't eaten in several days. Randy loved Cheerios, but then he loved all cereal, and almost everything else, except celery and mustard.

Outside, it was dark and raining hard. Hercel was sorry about that. The previous evening Tig's grandmother had brought him a new bicycle. Well, actually, it was a very old bicycle, but it was new to Hercel. "An English bike," Bernie had called it. The bike had Sturmey Archer three-speed hub gears, a chain case, a generator headlight, and a spring carrier over the rear fender. It was black but pretty rusty, and the chrome on the flat handlebars was pitted and flaked. Both fenders were dented. But the tires were new and the brakes worked. It was a Raleigh and heavy. Bernie said that Barton had bought it as a student in college. "And that was several centuries ago," she said.

But Hercel had yet to ride it, though he'd sat on its leather saddle in the garage. He wanted to ride it to school, but maybe he wouldn't. He didn't mind getting wet, but he hated to get the bike wet. After all, it was a new bike.

Hercel was still poking at his Cheerios when Carl came downstairs: *thump*, *thump*, *thump*. Hercel and his stepfather glanced at each other but didn't speak. Mr. Krause didn't like Hercel to talk unless Mr. Krause initiated the conversation. Carl went to the refrigerator and removed a large Virginia ham, from which he planned to cut a few slices. He liked ham, and he liked to fry the slices a little and eat them with buttered toast.

He set the ham on a cutting board across the table; then he sharpened the chef's knife, maybe ten strokes on a steel sharpener. Hercel glanced at him and glanced away. Carl positioned the knife at the top of the ham, eyed it, repositioned it, and eyed it again. Slowly he eased the knife into the ham, cutting a thin slice that peeled away like a wood shaving from a plane. Carl stood back and looked down at it, satisfied. Then he again positioned the knife at the top of the ham, eyed it again, positioned it again, and cut an even thinner slice.

"Do you know about flaying, boy?"

Hercel looked up from his Cheerios. "No, sir."

Carl didn't say anything right away. He repositioned the knife again at the top of the ham and went through the process again. He held up the third slice toward the ceiling light; it was thin enough to let the light shine through.

"I'm talking about human flaying, cutting the skin off a man or boy." Carl began to cut a fourth slice. "D'you know a man has eighteen square feet of skin on his body? But a boy like you? I expect only ten feet. Some people are flayed when they're dead, some are flayed when they're alive, like a punishment. There're books covered with human skin taken when the man was alive. You like books, boy. How'd you like one of those?" Carl paused for a beat before saying "boy." He kept doing it.

Hercel stared at the knife slicing the ham. "I don't think I'd like it, sir." He heard the bathroom door open and his mother say, "I'll help you get dressed." Then the sound of Lucy running down the hall to her room.

"They can be very pretty," said Carl. "Like works of art. Cutting the skin off a man, or a boy, that's delicate work. You don't want to cut into the meat, so you slice very slowly, maybe one-hundredth of an inch." Carl held the fourth slice of ham up to the light. "Maybe less. You don't want fat slices if you're covering a book. If I was going to slice the skin off a man, or boy, I'd start up at the neck. I'd cut a line from one side of the neck to the other, around the back. Then I'd ease my way down. How'd you think that'd feel, boy?"

Hercel's mouth was dry. "Not nice, sir."

"No, not nice." Carl was cutting a fifth slice. The other slices lay on a plate, pink and fresh. "I'd cut from one shoulder to the other. You'd want a substantial piece of skin for a book. You don't want bits and pieces; you don't want pieces of skin you'd have to patch together. It wouldn't look right. What's your favorite book, boy?"

Hercel didn't answer. He couldn't take his eyes off the knife.

"I said, what's your favorite book?"

Hercel looked up. Carl was staring at him. The dark furrows on Carl's cheeks looked like long gouges. "I don't know, I guess Harry Potter, sir."

Carl smiled. "Wouldn't it be nice if you had your favorite book covered with a nice soft piece of skin, boy?"

Hercel didn't answer.

"I said, wouldn't it be nice?"

"I don't think I'd like it, sir."

"How'd you know unless you tried it?" Carl smiled again. "And your own skin, boy, wouldn't it be nice and soft? How'd you like it if someone flayed the skin from your back? You think you'd scream? I bet you'd scream bloody murder."

Hercel didn't speak. He thought of the skin being sliced away from his shoulders and how it would feel. He thought of himself screaming.

"What d'you say, boy?"

Hercel jumped up, knocked the table so a little milk slopped over and pooled on the surface. "I got to go, sir." He hurried to the door.

"You spilled your milk, boy," said Carl behind him. "It's not good to spill your milk."

Hercel grabbed his coat and backpack, and ran out onto the porch. It seemed to be raining harder than ever. He ran around to the garage to get his new bike, his new old bike. He didn't like to get it wet, but he wanted to get away faster than Mr. Krause could run. As he pedaled down the driveway in the rain, he saw Mr. Krause staring at him through the kitchen window.

The previous day Woody had imagined he would again have breakfast on Tuesday with Jill Franklin at the Brewster Brew. But as the events of Monday unfolded he saw the likelihood of that prospect diminish until at midnight he gave up the hope entirely. So he phoned her, and when she answered he again realized he had woken her up. It was stuff like this, he thought, that made Susie call him insensitive.

"You keep long hours," she had said, the sleep muffling her voice as if she were speaking through a sock.

As he listened, Woody imagined what she looked like in bed—what the room looked like, what the bed looked like, what she was wearing or not wearing. It took his breath.

"I've been busy all evening." He briefly told her of the bricks thrown through the windows of the two Wiccans. As he talked he listened to her breathe and continued to imagine her room. He wanted to ask if he could come over but was unable to summon up the courage. It was a stupid idea, in any case.

"That's terrible," she said. "Those poor women."

"It could get worse." He tried to think what else to say. "How's your son?"

"He's great. He's sleeping right now, as a matter of fact; otherwise I'd let you talk to him. We watched a DVD earlier and he loved it. Have you seen *WALL-E*?"

"What's it about?" The movie didn't sound familiar.

"A garbage-compacting robot who's the last creature on earth. He falls in love with another robot named EVE who shows up on a spaceship. Actually, I don't think you can call a robot a creature. But this one moves and thinks and feels."

Woody liked hearing Jill's voice. "Any sex?"

"None to speak of. Maybe a little oiling."

"That'll work. It sounds like you had a good time. I mean, anything different from what I'm doing sounds like a good time."

"D'you always work such long hours?"

"It's pretty rare. But this business is unusually nasty, and there's no clear way into it. Just a bunch of separate bad things happening. The colonel's afraid of everything going down the tubes. That's Colonel Schaeffer; he's head of the state police."

"So we're not going to have breakfast?"

Again Woody felt momentarily out of breath. "I'm afraid not. But I'll call you later."

"That's what you said last time."

At eight o'clock Tuesday morning, Woody and Bobby Anderson went to You-You to question Todd Chmielnicki. They found him in his small office on the third floor. He looked, Woody thought, as if he'd never left. His blue eyes seemed bluer than before. After the usual introductions, Woody took the straight chair by the desk and Bobby sat on the couch. Chmielnicki's desk was bare and Woody couldn't imagine what he had been doing before they'd arrived. He himself got bored easily. If he was in a small room like this and didn't have at least a magazine, he'd be climbing the walls in no time.

"You know those two women?" asked Bobby. "Sister Asherah and Sister Isis? You know some guys threw bricks through their windows last night?"

Chmielnicki leaned forward with his elbows on the desk and the tips of his fingers pressed together to make a little tent. "I heard about it. One could have anticipated this."

"How?" asked Bobby.

"The popular mind takes a small threat and turns it into a large threat. That's not to denigrate the popular mind, or to reduce the extremity of the threat. It's small because it's unlikely many people are in danger. Perhaps just a few."

"Do you know who?" asked Bobby. His voice remained businesslike, with no trace of emotion.

"How could I possibly know that? The abduction of the baby, the scalping, the raping of the two girls, the snakes and strange ceremonies in the woods, and the girl's apparent suicide. These suggest extreme threat and imminent social collapse. Six days ago, however, everything looked fine. But was it fine? Think how termites eat their way through a timber, perhaps a beam supporting a house. Then the house collapses and people say it 'suddenly' collapsed. But it wasn't sudden; it was the next step in a steady progression. All that happened was the progression came into view. Something popped to the surface. The same thing may be said of Brewster: the progression is continuing and we only see its advance as elements pop to the surface. You look at the surface and seek a cause, but the cause lies within the crisscrossing tunnels underneath. You look for evidence and expect to find it in the surface manifestations, but what you need is not evidence. You need to discover an inference; you need to know what questions to ask."

"What questions would you ask?" said Bobby.

Woody turned from Bobby to Chmielnicki as he followed the conversation, but he had no wish to join in. No way could he have sounded as calm as Bobby.

"This isn't my area of expertise. But I expect I'd examine each of these manifestations and strip away all but the basic event."

"Like what?"

"Look at the baby's abduction as just an abduction. Look at it without the snakes, without the hospital, without the mother, without the circumstances of the baby's birth."

Bobby kept his eyes on Chmielnicki's face. He didn't necessarily like him, but he was impressed, and not necessarily by what he was saying but by his self-containment. Actually, he was also interested in what Chmielnicki was saying, but he would have to think about it. What he understood was nothing would be gained by threatening him. Chmielnicki might know everything about the whole business, though Bobby doubted it, but they wouldn't get it out of him unless Chmielnicki chose to give it.

Woody was less impressed, but the man made him uneasy, which was why he'd brought Bobby. He'd hoped Chmielnicki would read Bobby's brain just like he'd read his, just so Bobby could see what bothered him. Not that he believed in telepathy, of course.

"What about the Satanists?" asked Woody abruptly.

Chmielnicki turned his blue eyes in Woody's direction. "What about them, Woody?"

"Could they be doing this?"

Chmielnicki permitted himself a small smile. "I know no Satanists personally. There are rumors of a group that meets in the woods, but nothing specific. They may or may not be involved. But, Woody, the Satanists are always among us. You yourself must know that, being a police officer."

"I don't follow you."

"Among the Gnostics two thousand years ago the forces of good and evil, light and dark, were evenly matched. Like the left and right hand fighting one another, neither could claim victory. That paradigm was replaced by a paradigm based on the circle. At the center is total goodness: Jesus, Buddha, Mohammed—take your pick. Spreading out in concentric circles are saints, religious figures, the charitable and philanthropic, and so on. Farther from the center, we find our friends and ourselves. We believe in what exists at the center, but, unluckily, we have our imperfections. Farther on we begin to find the ethically and morally compromised, the hedonistic, the gluttons, the lustful, the greedy—those driven only by appetite and ego, who use or destroy others to achieve their ends. Then, in the farthest circles, we find the Satanists, though they rarely call themselves Satanists. They may not even call themselves evil, but their pride and self-deception let them justify any barbarity. They prey on each other; prey on all the rest. What lets us resist them? Our resistance derives from a belief in what exists at the center: a collection of values often symbolized by a specific name—Jesus, Buddha, whatever. Those values let us live within a society and with ourselves; they're what those farthest circles lack. Their only center is within themselves. They're always among us, feeding on the rest. You may call them Satanists or something else. They have many names."

As Woody listened, he tried to follow what Chmielnicki said, but it was difficult to think analytically because Chmielnicki irritated him. All this talk, maybe it was no more than a smoke screen. He decided to cut it short.

"What's your shoe size?" he asked, thinking of the footprints found around Hartmann's Ford Focus. But even Bobby was surprised by the question.

"Size nine-B. I expect you'll be fingerprinting me as well?"

"Right you are."

Chmielnicki gave another small smile. It seemed almost kindly. "You're looking better than you did the other day, Woody. I'm glad of it."

"Don't start," said Woody. "Just don't start."

. . .

As Woody and Bobby Anderson spoke to Chmielnicki, police officers were going through the three floors of You-You, talking to teachers and students alike. The officers had descriptions of the man and women who Jean Sawyer had seen with Nina, including her belief that one looked like a pug dog and the other like a greyhound. They also asked people what they knew about Wicca or any other neopagan group, as well as Satanists. Every man was asked his shoe size, and if it turned out to be 11D, or more or less, he was fingerprinted.

Of course several refused to answer, not because they were guilty or knew anything in particular but because they disliked being asked. These were whisked off to the police station, where they were fingerprinted and left in a holding cell to consider their options.

The information on each person's driver's license was taken down, as well as the names and addresses of others who taught or took classes. Again there were protests, but the nature of the crimes was such that the protests were ignored. If the person continued to protest, he or she was taken to police headquarters.

Finding the man who looked like a pug dog wasn't difficult. A state police detective, Bruce Slovatsky, asked the secretary at the reception desk if Nina had taken a class and was told she had taken a class in Kundalini yoga during the summer and signed up for it again in September. The teacher, Sam Lazar, was in the building teaching a class at that moment. The secretary asked Slovatsky to wait until the class was over. Instead, he took Lazar to police headquarters. As he said to himself, *He really* does *look like a pug dog*. Eyes far apart, thin downturned lips, a square chin. On the way, Lazar gave Slovatsky the names of the women he had been with on that Saturday when they had had coffee and pastry with Nina at the Brewster Brew. Slovatsky made a call and the two women—both yoga students—were picked up, brought to police headquarters, and questioned by two female detectives.

One of the women, Julie Turner, had a long, pointy face, and was tall, thin, and bony. The consensus was she looked like a greyhound, sort of. All three were relatively friendly and eager to help. Lazar and the two women said they knew Nina only from class, while the two women didn't even know her last name. They had never seen her outside of class except for that one time in the Brewster Brew, though Lazar said he had also seen her twice on the street and once at the beach, maybe more, he couldn't be sure. Although they knew of Wicca, the only Wiccan they knew personally was Sister Asherah. They expected there were others; they just didn't think of it much. They knew no Satanists and had never heard anyone talk of Satanism. They found the whole idea too kinky. They explained where they had been at the times of the various incidents; they had their fingerprints taken. Sam Lazar's shoe size was 10C. In each case, the interviews took about an hour as the questions were repeated. Their stories were pretty much the same. Julie Turner hardly remembered having coffee and pastry that day; she had coffee and pastry with lots of people.

Information about these three was fed into computers to see what more could be learned. But the results for everyone connected to You-You amounted to very little: a number of unpaid parking tickets, a warrant for two unpaid speeding tickets, a DUI five years earlier, an old shoplifting arrest, a drunk-and-disorderly suspended sentence, skipped child-support payments, a few bad credit ratings—these formed the extent of their bad behavior, if it could be called that. None of the fingerprints could be matched with the prints from the hospital nursery.

Nina's friends were again contacted and asked what Nina had said about You-You—she liked it, the exercises wore you out, she thought her friends should take it, et cetera. Peggy Summers was shown pictures of Sam Lazar and the two women. She didn't recognize them. She'd never been to You-You and had never taken any classes. "I can't be bothered with that shit," she said. "Get a life."

The women whose names were given to detectives by Sister Asherah and Sister Isis were located and questioned. These gave the names of others, both men and women. Woody and Bobby Anderson assisted in the interviews as officers drove to Warwick, East Greenwich, Narragansett, Westerly, Stonington, and other towns. This took them all day and into the evening. The third Wiccan in Brewster, Sister Hathor—otherwise known as Beverly Arkun—was much like Sister Asherah and Sister Isis, except that outside of coven work she preferred to be called Beverly. A patrol car with a Brewster officer remained parked outside her house on Walcott Street on Tuesday night.

Baldo Bonaldo had had a complicated relationship with the Brewster Library ever since he had put his remote-controlled fart machine, with the twist-out speaker for increased bass volume, under Ginger Phelps's chair. Ginger was a part-time research librarian and unlike Jill Franklin, who had also been a victim of the remote-controlled fart machine, she was humorless. She also worked at the Brewster Brew at the noon hour so Jean Sawyer could go home for lunch.

The small transmitter had a button that worked from fifty feet away, even through walls. With a repertoire of fifteen sounds, the fart machine had almost symphonic depth. Baldo had inflicted it on Ginger Phelps the previous March on a very busy Saturday. When the tuba-like sounds began to erupt from under the librarian's chair there followed a sequence of disbelief, discomfort, and hysteria as Ginger tried to locate who was doing this to her. Seeing no one with a guilty smirk, she grabbed the machine, threw it on the floor, and stamped on it. Black plastic scattered in all directions.

A brief silence was at last interrupted by the words "Oh, no," as Baldo realized she'd busted his good machine. Even so, he might have gotten away without more trouble if he hadn't gone to Ginger and asked to be reimbursed for the damage. He was still in fourth grade and had a deficient sense of causality.

In response, Ginger banned him from the library. "Get out and don't come back!"

During the next months, delicate negotiations were conducted between the library and acting chief Fred Bonaldo as Fred tried to have his favorite son readmitted. As he said to whomever would listen, Baldo's education was at stake.

At last the library, and Ginger Phelps, relented. The head librarian, Mary Michaels, was neither vindictive nor cruel. She was simply practical. Apart from the embarrassment, the fart machine was counterproductive to studious pursuits. A list of inevitable punishments—no TV for a year, no movies, fifty hours of community service at the library (sweeping, emptying wastebaskets)—was typed up and signed by Baldo, acting chief Bonaldo, Mary Michaels, and Ginger Phelps. Baldo was then readmitted.

But he wasn't welcome; in fact, he was watched like a hawk. He was ten years old, with a dim sense of the future. A year of deprivation was beyond the scope of his imagination. Even next week was a vague quagmire of possibility and promise.

Tuesday after school Hercel bicycled to the library through the rain and arrived sopping wet. Sympathetic librarians dried his hair with a towel and lent him a man's sweatshirt out of the lost and found. His wet clothes were draped over radiators, where they steamed peacefully.

Hercel had been assigned to write a short paper for fifth grade—no more than two pages—using ten more vocabulary words—*consequence, contumacious, despicable, dire, incoherent, melancholy, picturesque, solitary, tenebrous, vehement.* He had chosen to write about the town's founder, Wrestling Brewster, being eaten by wolves. His plan was to get rid of the vocabulary words all at once, giving him the chance to expand on his subject. With that in mind and with the aid of a dictionary he wrote his first sentence:

"In the tenebrous dark of a picturesque forest the despicable wolves crept from the melancholy bushes with incoherent growls."

Having used five words at one go, Hercel felt giddily liberated. He celebrated with a trip to the drinking fountain. This was situated next to the staff lounge, in which were two coffeepots—decaf and regular. Between the drinking fountain and the door to the lounge, he found Baldo Bonaldo, who was wondering if he could get away with putting a powder into the coffeepots to cause the library staff "to burp uncontrollably," as the little packet promised. Would they blame it on him? Baldo asked himself.

Seeing Hercel, Baldo drew him aside to ask his advice.

"You must be nuts," said Hercel.

They discussed this in energetic whispers. Hercel reminded Baldo of what he had to lose. Baldo described the ferocity of his desire and his conviction that they'd never suspect him.

"They'll think it was something they ate," said Baldo.

"All of them?" Hercel asked.

"Burping's not as bad as farting."

"'Uncontrollably' means you can't stop."

Their discussion continued. Over the past few days, Baldo had become a better friend to Hercel than he'd been before. Although Hercel still didn't understand him—this was one reason for the attraction—

he saw Baldo as harmless, intelligent, and kind, as well as being in the thralls of an addiction. They agreed at last that Baldo would forgo the burp powder in the coffeepot if Hercel showed him a trick.

"But I can't really control it," said Hercel. "I don't know how it works."

"That's okay," said Baldo. "I mean, great!"

So they separated. Baldo also had a paper to write using ten vocabulary words, and he'd better get busy. Before Hercel returned to his work, he removed a yellow tennis ball from his backpack and set it on the table.

These were the facts that kept Hercel busy into the late afternoon:

On the morning of November 3, 1762, Wrestling Brewster set out toward Great Swamp to hunt deer. Winter was almost upon them, and he needed to top off the family larder. His friend Moses Clinton meant to go with him, but the previous evening Moses had twisted his ankle carrying wood and was unable to go. Known for his stubborn and contumacious nature, Wrestling Brewster set off by himself, armed with his musket. The results would prove dire.

When Brewster failed to return that night, the neighbors were alerted. Some felt they should set out in the dark; others said to wait till morning. They argued with one another as minutes slipped away. At last it was decided to wait till daybreak.

At sunrise, the men set off, following Wrestling Brewster's solitary path into the forest. Then at the edge of Great Swamp they made a dreadful discovery. Brewster had been attacked by wolves. His clothes were shredded; his musket lay by his side; little was left but bones. Three wolves lay around him: one had been shot, two clubbed. The men gathered up Brewster's remains as best they could and returned to the village.

Brewster was a deeply religious man and quick to censure his neighbors for their shortcomings. If someone failed to go to church, Brewster would appear at his door and escort him. Drinking, dancing, ribald singing led to the arrest of the guilty party. Because of this and because of his name—to wrestle with the Devil—the rumor began to circulate that the Devil had taken the shape of wolves and eaten him.

Around four o'clock Detective Bingo Schwartz entered the library, hoping to find Ronnie McBride. He was not optimistic, but at least he could ask Ginger Phelps and Mary Michaels when they had last seen him. Ronnie had not returned the previous night to the alcove at Crandall Investments. Bingo Schwartz had also searched Ronnie's small house on Oak Street.

"It's like a museum," he told Captain Brotman, who had put Bingo in charge of finding Ronnie. "It's so clean you could eat off the floor. He's got pictures of his dead wife all over the place. The bed's immaculate, and it's got ten teddy bears lined up across the head, right across the pillows. Weird. I felt they were staring at me."

As Bingo approached Ginger's desk, he hummed Boris's final aria from *Boris Godunov,* the words of which began: "Farewell, my son, I am dying." The rainy weather bothered his knee and he limped more than usual, but he wouldn't use a cane. As he might say, "I refuse to be debased by the indignities of age." Such remarks were another reason his wife disliked him. They struck her as operatic, as if Bingo were constantly quoting from librettos.

Although Bingo had been brought up in Warwick, he had known Ginger for many years. "Hey, Ginger, seen Ronnie lately?"

"McBride?" Ginger thought for a moment. "Not since Thursday. Why?"

"Just wanted to ask him a few questions."

Ginger was sharp-witted and, besides, these were matters widely discussed in Brewster. "You think he saw poor Nina Lefebvre kidnapped off the street?"

Bingo decided not to answer. "How'd he seem when you saw him?"

"Same as ever, not too bad, not too good. He read the papers, left for a while, then came back and read the papers some more, then took a nap. Just like always."

Bingo was going to ask at what time Ronnie usually left when a yellow tennis ball shot across the room, hit the farther wall, shot back in the opposite direction, hit the wall, shot up to the ceiling—at least twenty feet above the floor—hit the ceiling, and then shot down toward the floor. At this point, Bingo snatched it out of the air.

"Odd," he said.

After the first bounce, Ginger had fastened her eyes on Baldo Bonaldo, but he had been staring at the ball with as much amazement as anyone else. Several people jumped to their feet, and old Mrs. Muldoon put her hands over her head.

"This has never happened before," said Ginger.

"No, I suppose not." Bingo put the yellow tennis ball in his coat pocket and left, humming more of *Boris*: "I have attained supreme power. . . ."

Half an hour later, Baldo casually strolled past Hercel's table. "You're scary, you're really scary."

Hercel didn't look up from his school report. "Pull my finger," he said.

Tuesday afternoon Vicki Lefebvre drove to Brantley's Funeral Home to talk to Ham Brantley about her daughter's funeral. Nina's body had not yet been released by the medical examiner's office in Providence, but Vicki wanted to steal a march on her ex-husband, Harold Lefebvre, from whom she had been divorced for nearly five years. Vicki was afraid Harold would try to have the funeral and burial in Groton, where he lived, just out of spite, and Vicki felt that since she had had custody of Nina she should also have custody over the funeral service and burial.

Ham Brantley agreed. He and Vicki had known each other since grade school. They'd been friendly but not friends, because Vicki was uncomfortable that Hammy "lived with dead people," as she described it. Later, in high school, she had been sure he even "touched" dead people, so she'd avoided dancing with him at sock hops and proms, because she was squeamish about having his hands "on her person," as she said. Anyway, starting in tenth grade, Hammy had dated Jenny Genoways, who he'd eventually married. Jenny had evidently liked those cold clammy hands on her person, and Vicki concluded that different people liked different strokes, or whatever it was. After graduation, Vicki and Ham had become better friends, since all chance of physical contact was over and, in any case, Vicki wasn't as squeamish as she used to be.

They sat in Brantley's carefully restrained office, and Vicki told him what she would like.

"We're really not churchgoers, Ham, though I was brought up Catholic. But there's the way Nina died. The police say it's suicide—I don't believe it for a minute—but if Father Pete makes a fuss, he might refuse to do a service at Saint John's."

Brantley sat in a tall leather chair behind his mahogany desk in his three-piece suit. Although Vicki had never thought him particularly good-looking—his eyes were too close together—she now found him quite distinguished, with his silver hair combed back over his head and his pleasant, reassuring voice. Even his weight suited him, and he appeared, to her mind, not stout but robust and self-assured.

"I don't believe that'd happen, Vicki. The church is far more liberal in those matters than in the past. But I've got a very nice nondenominational chapel right here in the building that I can put at your disposal if you'd like."

They went to look at the chapel. Vicki thought it was very nice.

"Excuse me for asking, Vicki, but were you thinking of cremation or a cemetery burial?"

Vicki didn't like the idea of cremation. It seemed so violent. And if Nina was buried in Brewster Cemetery, then Vicki could always put flowers on her grave and even, perhaps, be buried at her side, though it was much too soon to think of that. So they went to the display room to inspect the caskets.

"Did you have a price range in mind?" asked Brantley. "I understand how hard this is."

Well, Vicki didn't want anything too pricey. It wasn't like she had lots of money.

"So you're looking for something fairly cheap?"

Inexpensive had been the word Vicki was considering, and she felt that between the words *inexpensive* and *cheap* there lay a wide expanse.

The poplar wood casket cost $1,800; with its highly polished surface, it offered a rich yet subdued presentation. It was the least expensive except for a pine casket often used in cremations. Eco-friendly cardboard was also available. On the other hand, a more Christian-oriented poplar casket had antiqued hardware, hand-cast Last Supper lugs, and pietà corners. This cost $3,200. There was also a mahogany casket made of inch-and-a-half-thick boards with a fully adjustable bed and hand-tailored velvet bedding. This was $4,200. Vicki soon learned that *tasteful* and *subdued* were synonymous with *cheap*. She settled on a $4,000 mahogany casket in a Florentine design with an Eterna-rest adjustable bedding system in champagne velvet with matching pillow and throw, and a split and double-locking lid. The bottom half would be

THIRTEEN

MABEL SUMMERS, Peggy's mother, called the Brewster police station early Wednesday morning. After a lifetime of smoking, her speaking voice had been reduced to a gargle. "My baby's disappeared. She's not in her room." It took another minute to figure out that Mabel was talking about Peggy, who was seventeen.

"No, I don't know when it happened. I peeked in her room around five minutes ago and she was gone."

Patrolman Malone had taken the call. He contacted acting chief Bonaldo, who was home eating scrambled eggs and bacon. Whole-Hog Hopper had been watching Peggy's house. No telling what'd happened to him, though Bonaldo could make an educated guess. He called the troopers as well as half a dozen of his own officers. Then he wiped a bit of raspberry jam off his lower lip and got dressed. He felt he carried the weight of the entire town on his shoulders.

Ten minutes later he drove over to the Summers's house, where he met one of his detectives, Brendan Gazzola, and two patrolmen. Gazzola, at fifty, was tall, thin, and a chain-smoker, with yellow fingers, gray skin, and a cough as loud as a quiet Harley. At the moment, he was munching on a handful of Nicorettes.

Mabel Summers stood in the front door wearing a lavender housecoat. The rain had stopped in the night, the sun was low in the sky, and everything was shiny and clean. Whole-Hog Hopper sat in his patrol car across the street with a hangdog expression and eating something. He gave a little wave to Bonaldo; Bonaldo didn't wave back.

"She was up in her room last night, watching her little TV. I asked her to turn it down because Ralph was trying to sleep. She turned it down, then turned it up again. She's always been a brat, I don't know who she gets it from. Not that she can't be nice now and then."

Mabel took Bonaldo and Gazzola up to Peggy's room. Ralph was at the kitchen table eating pancakes. When he saw the acting chief, he said, "Baldy Bonaldo!" Then he went back to his pancakes. A drop of syrup clung to one of the oxygen tubes inserted in his nose.

Peggy's room was a mess, with clothes and shoes on the floor. Bonaldo stepped delicately over a pink thong. Like Nina's room, the walls were covered with posters of singers: Justin Timberlake, Beyoncé, Jay-Z, a poster advertising the album *I Am . . . Sasha Fierce,* and—strangely, Fred Bonaldo thought—a poster of Mount Fuji at sunrise.

"Can you tell if anything's missing?" asked Gazzola.

Mabel lit another cigarette. She wasn't supposed to smoke in Peggy's room and took spiteful pleasure in lighting up. "It's hard to tell. Her backpack's gone, I'm pretty sure of that. She usually keeps it right there on that chair." She pointed to a straight chair by a small desk.

"What about a jacket or sweater?" asked Bonaldo.

Mabel poked around on the floor with a foot. "Her green jacket's not here, and I didn't see it downstairs. And her blue-and-yellow sweater's missing, 'less it's in the wash. Maybe some shirts are missing, a pair of jeans with the knees cut out. She sliced up a perfectly good pair of jeans, can you believe it? Her iPod's not here."

"What color's the backpack?" asked Gazzola.

"Blue. It's a big one. Kinda ratty."

By the time they left, Bonaldo and Gazzola had a list of Peggy's friends, most being names the police had gotten before. It also seemed that if Peggy had disappeared, she had done it by choice, rather than being abducted. That didn't mean she wasn't in danger. Soon troopers all over the state as well as in Connecticut and Massachusetts had her photograph and description. She didn't have a car, and there were no buses out of Brewster. The Amtrak stopped in Kingston and Westerly. It was impossible to tell when she had left. Her mother had seen her in her room at eleven o'clock last night, so it could have been any time after that. The only time Peggy had gone out of the house since she had returned from the hospital had been the previous evening, when she'd driven with her mother to CVS. She'd worn a hat and dark glasses because "she didn't want to answer a lot of questions from a lot of assholes."

"You'd think she'd be ashamed," said her mother, "but she didn't act it. I know I'd be ashamed, if it was me."

Whole-Hog Hopper was no help. He'd had a large pepperoni, sausage, and cheese around midnight and conked out.

Woody Potter got the call about Peggy at home. He'd been asleep, having been up late because of the rocks thrown through Helen Greene's windows. A man walking his black Lab had said the two men had been in a blue Chevrolet Malibu, maybe four years old. "They were driving like they didn't care if they hit anybody or not," he told Woody. Two others had also seen the car, though they didn't know it was a Malibu.

One said the car had a bumper sticker on the back, but he couldn't see what it was.

Woody decided he could leave Peggy and the Malibu to acting chief Bonaldo for the time being. Instead, he had breakfast with Jill over in Wakefield—or Historic Wakefield, as it liked to be called. They met at a Friendly's on Main Street. Jill brought Luke. He was out of school that day because of some sort of teachers' meeting.

"Who are you?" asked Luke.

"I'm Woody Potter. I'm a new friend of your mother's."

Luke looked at him skeptically, as if he didn't see why his mother needed any friends. He looked away and began drawing on his place mat with a crayon. He was in first grade.

"I already told you who he was, honey," said Jill. She glanced at Woody and glanced at her son. She hoped it wasn't going to be one of those mornings.

"Can I have pancakes?" asked Luke. "And hot chocolate with whipped cream?"

Jill didn't normally let Luke have both pancakes and hot chocolate—too much sugar—but she knew he was offering her a deal: feed him right and he'd behave. "We'll see," said Jill.

"'We'll see' means 'No,'" said Luke.

Jill again glanced at Woody, this time with the beginnings of embarrassment.

"You like dogs?" asked Woody. "I got a dog in my truck."

"Does he bite?"

"Only if you shove your fingers down his throat."

"What kinda dog?"

"A golden retriever. He likes thrown sticks almost more than anything."

"I'm not a very good thrower."

"Gotta learn sometime, right?"

The waitress took their order. Luke got his pancakes and hot chocolate. Woody ordered the same. Woody asked Luke if he wanted strawberries on his pancakes. He did. So they both had strawberries. Jill ordered a vegetable omelet. She looked at Woody and her son with mild exasperation. Actually, she was feeling pretty good. Luke was telling Woody that his grandparents wouldn't let a dog in the house. "They say they have germs. Does your dog have germs?"

"I've never seen any. Maybe a tick now and then."

"What's your dog's name?"

"Ajax. He's named after a hero who was the tallest, strongest, and one of the dumbest of the Greek heroes."

"Is your dog dumb?"

"I tried to teach him to read all summer, but he still doesn't get it. Can you read?"

"I'm getting there. My mom helps me."

Their food came. Luke counted his strawberries and saw he had three more than Woody. He was torn between giving one to Woody and eating them himself. He gave the three extra to his mother. As they ate, Luke shot quick looks at Woody. If he thought Woody and his mother were talking too much, he'd ask a question—Do you think people live in outer space?—or show her something neat—like how he could make a tower of ten jelly packets. Woody taught him how to hang a spoon from his nose. Spoons clattered noisily onto plates and people gave them irritated looks.

After breakfast, Luke met Ajax in the restaurant parking lot. Woody had to hold the dog back to keep him from licking Luke's face.

"He's big," said Luke.

"Yup, I bet he outweighs you by twenty pounds."

"Can I ride him?"

"They don't like that. It hurts their backs. Is it okay with you to sit with him in the backseat when we drive to the beach?"

"Is he going to lick my face?"

"You just push him away and say 'No.' He's just being friendly."

"Why's he have so much hair?"

"He's getting his winter coat."

They drove over to Narragansett Beach. Woody parked and put Ajax on a leash. They walked down to the tide line. Like the bass harmony of a song, Woody's anxiety about the events in Brewster was always in his ears.

"Brewster's got a great beach," said Woody. "Sometimes it seems I can see all the way to France."

Luke was torn between keeping an eye on his mother and running as fast as he could. "What's France?"

"It's a country. There's a little poem about it. 'I see London, I see France; I see Mommy's underpants.'"

"Did you *have* to tell him that?" said Jill, laughing.

"Cool," said Luke. "D'you know any others?"

"Sure. 'Hasten, Jason, bring the basin. Urrp, slop, bring the mop.'"

"You're a very dangerous man," Jill told him. Then, to Luke, "Okay, honey, go run."

Woody let Ajax off the leash. He and Luke raced down the beach.

"He likes you," said Jill.

"He likes the dog. I just come with the dog."

"Do you find it hard to take compliments?"

"Yup."

Jill was interested in why Woody's fiancée had dumped him two weeks earlier. She didn't want to be picked up on the rebound. Instead of asking him about Susie, she mentioned Luke's father. "His main ambition was to tend bar and be a ski bum. In that, he was very successful."

When it was Woody's turn, he said, "She didn't like I was a cop; she didn't like the odd hours; she was afraid I'd get shot by some nutcase on 95; she didn't like that I didn't talk about my feelings; she didn't like living in the boondocks; she wanted to get a Ph.D. in social work and didn't want to do it at URI; she wanted to have a baby. Other than that she was great, pretty much. Oh, yeah, she didn't like to cook, and sometimes I thought she didn't like Ajax. She was a cat person, but when she moved out, she left the cat." Woody laughed.

"So why'd you stay with her so long?"

"Sometimes you hang on to something because it's better than having nothing."

He talked about his ex-wife, Cheryl. They'd been divorced more than a dozen years. "We were kids and I was drinking a lot. I was drinking a *whole* lot. I'd just come back from Iraq and was pretty fucked up without knowing I was fucked up. Like I thought nearly everything was lousy. That seemed smart thinking. And when someone yelled at me for thinking everything was lousy, then I thought *they* were lousy. That went on for a long time. Then I met Bobby Anderson. He yelled at me for thinking everything was lousy and I didn't mind it. So we became best friends. Then he told me to get a dog and I did." Woody laughed. "Maybe all that time when everything was lousy I only needed a dog."

Late Wednesday afternoon Bobby Anderson learned that Carl Krause's psychiatrist, Sheldon Frank, had moved from Brewster in early May to join a practice with two other doctors in Belmont, Massachusetts. And where did that leave Carl? Bobby had asked himself.

With the help of the Belmont police, Bobby managed to get Dr. Frank's home phone. He called him Wednesday morning.

"I arranged with Carl to see a psychiatrist in Wakefield before I left—Dr. Maddox. I thought Carl would like him."

"And did Carl see him?"

"I'm afraid I've no idea. I rather lost track of him when I moved to Belmont."

"Rather?"

"Okay, I lost track of him."

"So how'd you describe Carl?"

"Oh, he's fine if he's on his meds. Without them, he's a little, well, fragile. I really can't say any more because of privacy. . . ."

"Yeah, yeah," said Bobby, ending the conversation.

So Bobby contacted Dr. Timothy Maddox in Wakefield.

"Carl Krause? No, I don't have any patient by that name. I remember Dr. Frank contacting me about someone in April, but I never heard any more about it. It's difficult to keep track of these matters. I could ask my secretary. . . ."

"That's okay." Bobby ended that call as well.

Next Bobby drove over to the craftsman bungalow on Hope Street. Harriet answered the door and said Carl was at work. He could pretty much make his own hours. She thought he was over at Brantley's Funeral Home.

"Has Carl been taking his pills?" Bobby had been about to say "funny pills" but thought better of it.

"I believe so. I know he's been seeing his doctor in Wakefield."

"Dr. Maddox?" They were standing on the front porch. Through the door, Bobby saw Lucy sitting on the floor and shaking her finger at a doll with yellow hair.

"Yes, that right."

"Any bills or paperwork?"

"Carl takes care of all that himself."

"So how's he been lately?"

Harriet opened her mouth to speak and then shook her head. "Not so good, actually. I was going to call Dr. Maddox this week." Her eyes began to well up, and Bobby hoped she wouldn't cry.

"What do you mean 'not so good'?"

"He's been moody. Yelling at the kids. Me too, for that matter. I'm sure it's nothing. And he's been sleeping upstairs. I . . . I'm not sure what to do. He won't talk to me. He was wonderful earlier in the summer. Then, I don't know . . ."

"Did he ever say anything about the cat?"

"He said he'd nothing to do with it."

"Did you believe him?"

"I can't just go questioning everything he says. I mean, he's my husband."

So Bobby drove over to the funeral home. He didn't see Carl's truck.

"No, I haven't seen Carl this morning," said Brantley. He again wore his three-piece suit. *As if he slept in it*, thought Bobby. They stood in the front hall of the funeral home.

"He was here on Sunday," Brantley continued. "That's the last I've seen him. He's supposed to be here tomorrow morning. Can I give him a message?"

"I hope to see him before then. How's he been behaving?"

"Fine, as fine as ever. Anything wrong?"

"Nah, it's just some routine stuff. Could he be over at your crematorium?"

"I very much doubt it. He's never done any work over there."

Bobby drove down to Hannaquit to see if Carl was at the house on stilts where he had been painting the previous week. There was no sign of him. So Bobby drove around for a while, hoping to see Carl's truck. But he didn't. As he drove back to Brewster, he considered putting out an APB, but Carl hadn't *done* anything. Not yet, at least. Maybe he'd mention it to acting chief Bonaldo when he got to the police station. But then Bobby learned about Peggy Summers.

Early Wednesday morning Barton Wilcox heard the barking of the two Bouviers, Gray and Rags—a frantic, angry bark. Barton knew it meant coyotes.

Bernie was at the hospital and he was in his bathrobe. Even so, he pushed himself up from his chair with his walker and slowly made his way to the door. Outside he saw two coyotes running for the wall with the two dogs behind them. The coyotes had only once before crossed the wall in daylight and never crossed when the dogs were on guard, which was pretty much always. What surprised him most was something at the other end of the field. A third coyote was dragging a sheep toward the wall. That meant the two coyotes were acting as decoys. They had a plan. A shiver of fear ran through him.

"Hey, stop that!" Barton shouted, and tried to hurry forward. The other sheep were milling around in their foolish way, terrified but not knowing what to do. The legs of the walker caught in the grass and Barton fell forward, landing hard so the wind was knocked out of him.

"Granddad!" Tig came bursting out of the house.

Barton waved her back. "Get the shotgun and some shells! Be careful with it."

The two dogs were now tangling with the coyotes. They were big coyotes, fifty or sixty pounds, but they wouldn't be a match for the Bouviers. The third coyote tugged and dragged the sheep, one of the ones born in April. The ground was wet from the rain and cold. Barton repositioned the walker and began to drag himself up.

The shotgun was a twelve-gauge Remington pump. By the time Barton was standing upright, Tig was running back from the house. He took the gun, loaded it with two shells, and put a third in the chamber. He aimed at the coyote dragging the sheep. He didn't expect to hit it—it was too far away—but he hoped to put a scare into it. He had to take his hands off the walker to shoot, and when he fired he lost his balance and fell to the ground. He pulled himself into a sitting position. The coyote had stopped dragging the sheep and was looking doubtful. Barton aimed high and fired again. The coyote fled over the wall.

He looked the other way and turned cold. "Tig!"

His granddaughter was running toward the dogs. One of them, Rags, was limping. One of the coyotes lay dead on the ground. Three others were now circling Gray. "Tig!" he shouted.

Barton again pulled himself onto the walker and began to hobble after her. He had one last shell in the shotgun. The coyote that had attacked the sheep had come back and was tugging at it, but Barton couldn't be bothered with that now.

"Tig, stop!"

If she got too close, a coyote might attack her. Barton hobbled forward, furious with the walker, furious with his knee. Gray was able to hurl himself at the remaining coyotes and grabbed one by the neck. The others fled toward the swamp. The coyote dragging the sheep had made it to the wall, but Barton didn't want to fire his last shell.

Tig had reached Rags and was hugging him. There was blood on his back leg, shiny dark in the thick dark fur. Tig's yellow sweatshirt became smeared with it. Gray stood nearby, barking. A burst of coyote yapping came from the other side of the field. Barton saw the coyote and sheep had disappeared. Coyotes weren't dumb. They knew they'd gotten away with something. That meant they would be back. *Next time,* thought Barton, *I'll have the rifle and I'll be wearing a revolver as well.* He had a Colt Python locked in the hall table, a .357 magnum with an eight-inch barrel. In his study, locked in the gun case, were his rifle and a side-by-side.

But wouldn't it be better, he asked himself, just to sell out and move to town? I'm getting too old for this nonsense.

Tig was leading Rags back to the house. Barton met her in the middle of the field. "Never do that. Those coyotes would eat you just as quickly as a darn sheep."

"Rags's hurt," she said, as if this answered everything.

"You're more important than the dog."

Tig seemed to doubt this but didn't answer. The coyotes were still yapping. Barton wanted to call the vet and a neighbor down the road who sometimes did work for him, but he had left his cell phone inside. He felt like an old fool tottering across the grass with the walker and wearing a bathrobe. Tig was talking to the dog in a soothing voice, almost baby talk. Gray stayed at their side but kept looking around.

I'll get more dogs, Barton thought. *I'll get an army of dogs.*

When he'd nearly reached the house, he aimed at the spot where the coyote had dragged the sheep across the wall, aimed at the yapping. He fired his last shot. This time he managed to keep his balance. The coyotes were quiet for a moment, but then returned to their yapping and snarling as they tore apart the dead sheep.

Wednesday morning Woody was again late to the briefing, which had started at eleven, but it didn't seem to matter. In any case, he felt his time had been better spent with Jill. Even so, he had been unable to get Brewster out of his mind. He had an unsettled feeling, as if he were catching a cold, that he realized was fear. This was a new emotion for Woody. He'd felt terror in Iraq when the missile had struck, but never fear. He didn't like how it clung to him, how it fucked with his thinking.

The interviews with men and women connected to You-You were continuing, as were interviews with the neopagans and Neo-Heathens. Several had mentioned the possibility of Satanists but knew nothing specific. Just rumors. By now fifteen Wiccans were receiving some sort of protection from the authorities.

The search of Great Swamp had been hindered by the rain but still moved forward. However, an inspector from the Office of Criminal Investigation of the DEM said that Hancock Pond, half a mile from the swamp, had a small island that could be reached by stringing together ten or so boards. This would give the effect of slightly bouncing while walking through water. Captain Brotman assigned a group to check it out.

There was still no idea as to who, if anyone, had picked up Nina on Water Street Saturday night. More people were interviewed. The Massachusetts state police and Boston police were still trying to discover the man that Hartmann had talked to ten days earlier, though they had learned he was someone with whom Hartmann had had lunch.

Acting chief Bonaldo spoke of Peggy's disappearance, which everyone already knew about, and what was being done to find her. The fear, though no one voiced it, was that she would be found hanging in the woods. Bonaldo also described the window-breaking and the search for the two cars—a Ford sedan and a Chevrolet Malibu. He was optimistic they'd find the Malibu relatively soon.

"What do you mean 'relatively soon'?" asked Brotman.

"Today. We've got some leads."

"I should hope so."

Others, such as the FBI and the Brewster sergeant in charge of interviewing people in and around the hospital, knew nothing further. Alice Alessio was hiding out in her apartment. At first they had had the hope that discoveries would come quickly; now they were settling down to basic police work: collecting little bits and pieces of information to see if anything added up. Set against that process was the increased fear in town, which had led to the smashing of the windows. If any of the women had been near the windows when they had been broken, they could have been hurt. And might such a misfortune lie ahead?

"Not a misfortune," said Captain Brotman, "a disaster."

Bobby spoke about Carl Krause and the fact that his doctor had moved from Brewster in May. So Carl was presumably off his meds. He had looked for Carl for much of the morning but hadn't found him.

"What's this guy Krause got to do with anything?" asked Joe Doyle, the South Kingstown lieutenant.

Bobby scratched his head. "I really don't know. I just think they're linked in some way. Anyway, this guy flies out of control and it seems smart to watch him. I'm positive he hung the gray cat."

"You're still fucking with that cat? We got abductions and murders and you're fucking with a cat?" Doyle made a sarcastic, throat-clearing noise and shook his head.

Bobby started to get to his feet and Bingo Schwartz grabbed his arm.

Bobby sank back to his chair. When he spoke it was in a metallic whisper, as if anything louder would lead to fury and insult. "Krause is increasingly violent and mentally unstable. He threatened me and Bonaldo with a shotgun. The snake belonged to his stepson, and he had access to it. I think he's mixed up with something bigger."

"So it's a hunch, right?" said Doyle. "What's this, African intuition?"

In a nanosecond, Bobby leapt across the table. Only Bingo grabbing his ankles kept him from going further. Doyle threw himself backward; his chair tipped over, and he fell to the floor. Everyone else was standing.

"Out, out!" shouted Captain Brotman. "Everybody out! Not you, Doyle."

Twenty men and women filed out of the room and into the hall. Woody and Bingo stood on either side of Bobby, not holding him but ready to. The last one out shut the door. Some of the officers went for coffee; some went to the Coke machine; some stayed in the hallway far enough from the door so they wouldn't seem to be listening. Bobby, Woody, and Bingo belonged to this third group.

What they heard was a lot of muted shouting, all from Brotman. Certain words could be made out, ranging from "inexcusable" to "shit for brains." After five minutes Brotman came to the door and told everyone to come back in. The officers filed silently into the room. Nobody looked at anybody else. Woody snuck a look at Joe Doyle. His face was scarlet, and he stared at the table.

Soon everyone was seated, and Captain Brotman again stood in front of them. "Doyle," he said.

Joe Doyle got to his feet. "I'm sorry I said that, Bobby. I guess I've been under a lot of pressure, like all of us most likely."

Bobby gave Doyle a cool stare. "Apology accepted."

Woody knew that Bobby would prefer to black Doyle's eye. He wondered what would happen to the investigation if they all started fighting with one another. Well, even Ajax knew the answer to that one.

Brotman turned to Bobby. "Find Carl Krause and ask him about his meds."

Bingo Schwartz spoke next. He said he hadn't been able to locate Ronnie McBride. Nobody had seen him since Friday. He mentioned searching Ronnie's house and the ten teddy bears sitting in a row across the bed's pillows.

"Who's this guy, anyway?" asked Joe Doyle. Behind his question was the boast that even though he'd been slapped down, he wasn't broken.

"This is a small town," said Captain Brotman, "and we're dealing with a number of highly unusual events. There seems a chance they're in some way connected. We'll continue exploring that possibility until we discover evidence to the contrary."

When the meeting ended a half-hour later, Woody asked, "You really think Carl's connected to the missing baby?"

"You going to insult me, too?" asked Bobby, half seriously. "Yeah, it's a hunch. African intuition, straight from the witch doctor. Carl's connected in some way. And I want to make sure nothing happens to Hercel. I like him. I've also got bad feelings about those coyotes, and I don't like how they chewed up that girl's feet, and I don't like how they run through town as if they own the place. It's not coyote-like."

Mackie McNamara lived in a world with no gray areas. He saw things in black or white and that was it. But he wasn't a bad guy. He just couldn't see what the trouble was; he couldn't see why everyone was fussing like a bunch of old hens. If you had a problem, you fixed it. Simple as that.

He drove a bulldozer for a demolition company in Warwick, but he lived in Brewster, and his family had lived in Brewster for a hundred years. Now it was all fucked. He had a wife and two kids in a relatively new ranch house at the edge of town. He liked to listen to talk radio going to and from work, and a lot of stuff pissed him off. He liked to say that if you read the Bible fifteen minutes a day, you could finish it in a year. He was on his fifth go-round through the Bible, though it's hard to know what he had learned from it. He was forty years old.

When the baby had been stolen from Morgan Memorial, Mackie had been as upset as anybody else. He had known Ralph Summers—Peggy's father—nearly all his life, and he knew Mabel, too. And he'd known Harold Lefebvre, not well, but he'd known him. Then there was the scalping and other shit. Mackie knew for a fact it all came out of the

You-You place. He didn't like lesbians, didn't like queers, didn't like coloreds, didn't like liberals, and he didn't like anyone who disrespected the flag. But this is exaggeration, because Mackie knew specific lesbians, gays, and blacks who he didn't mind at all. What he had were bad feelings, and You-You was at the bottom of it.

If he had been by himself, these feelings might be chalked up to social peevishness of the "there's a lot of assholes out there" variety, but Mackie had a bunch of friends who felt as he did, some more, some less. If they were downing beers at Tony's just off Water Street, they might think it a lot. If they were at work, they'd think it less. But, basically, they thought the whole town was going to hell in a handbasket. They weren't dumb guys, but they weren't long on education. It was as if each had part of an idea, put them together, and it became a complete thought. Each had a dislike, a feeling that stuff wasn't working as it was supposed to. Put them together and it became a certainty. But they weren't bad guys; they just felt sure the cops weren't dealing with stuff, like the cops weren't doing their job.

So when it came out on Saturday that witches were involved with what had been happening, they were appalled. No, that's not quite right. Singly it upset them; together they were appalled. And since, like Mackie McNamara, they tended to see a world with no gray areas, their anger increased. No, that's not quite right, either. Singly some might see gray areas; together they didn't.

There were six of them, but their names don't matter except that they tended to be diminutives: Dickie and Jackie and Chucky. They were pissed off on Sunday and *really* pissed off on Monday. They were pissed off that the cops weren't doing anything. They were pissed off that witches lived right here in town. They were pissed that stuff was getting worse.

So doesn't it make sense they would want to toss bricks through windows? They weren't going to shoot anyone, for shit's sake. They were going to put a scare into them. So they drove to the house at the end of Whipple Street, the old farmhouse where Sister Asherah and Sister Isis lived—even their names were awful—and they did what they did.

The next day three of the men were upset by what had happened. The bricks caused more damage than they had expected. A single stone is one thing, but eight bricks is something else. The other three felt pretty good about it. They'd taken a stand; they'd done what the cops wouldn't do, were too scared or lazy to do. Mackie McNamara was one of those three, and he owned the blue Chevy Malibu. The bumper sticker said STOP GLOBAL WHINING.

None of the three had had Helen Greene as a teacher in grade school, though they knew she was a teacher. They also knew she wore long colorful skirts, peasant blouses, and lots of silver jewelry that looked silly on an old woman. In fact, she dressed just like Sister Asherah and Sister Isis, like it was a witch uniform or something. So it stood to reason she was one of them. That nurse, Bernie Something, also wore the witch uniform, and they meant to give her a scare as well, once they learned her last name and figured how to do it, maybe smash her car windows.

So on Tuesday night, after lubricating themselves with a little beer, Mackie, Chucky, and Dickie had driven over to Bucklin Street and threw stones through Helen's windows. It was as simple as that.

Then, late Wednesday, when Mackie was sitting at home in the den with his friend Chucky after work, they had visitors. Acting chief Fred Bonaldo, Detective Gazzola, and eight patrolmen came down on them like gangbusters, busting through the door with their weapons drawn and shouting obscenities. That's what Fred said a dozen times afterward: "We fuckin' came down on them like gangbusters." The only regret was that Mackie and Chucky hadn't offered resistance but let themselves be dragged out to the cruisers like bad pups to the pound.

Acting chief Bonaldo called Captain Brotman to tell him the good news. "They never knew what hit 'em," he said. When Brotman praised his work, Bonaldo beamed liked a blushing bride.

Within an hour all six were in a cell in police headquarters. Later on Wednesday they would be taken to the Department of Correction's Adult Correctional Institutions, or ACI, a cluster of eight buildings in Cranston, where they would be jailed in the intake service center as pre-trial detainees. Because of the nature of the charges—hate crimes and the rest—bail would be high, meaning they wouldn't be back on the street anytime soon. ACI held four thousand men and women in minimum-, medium-, and maximum-security facilities, as well as in a glorified county lockup.

"Like gangbusters," acting chief Bonaldo told his wife, Laura.

But they weren't bad guys.

Around dinnertime on Wednesday, Peggy Summers, in her green jacket and lugging her backpack, was picked up by a patrol car as she walked along Taunton Avenue in East Providence, a lower-middle-class city across the river from Providence. It had a number of poor areas and a large immigrant population, mostly from the Azores and Cape Verde Islands. The cops in the patrol car didn't think it was a safe place for a girl to be walking. They also had Peggy's picture stuck to their dashboard.

Two troopers brought her back to Brewster, and at seven o'clock she was in an office in the police station with Woody Potter and a female state police detective, Beth Lajoie. Peggy was scared, and Brewster was the last place she wanted to be.

"If you think I want to end up like Nina, you're fuckin' nuts." Peggy's stringy blond hair needed washing, as did her sweatshirt. In fact, thought Woody, she could use a long plunge in a tub of sheep dip.

Detective Lajoie was barrel-shaped, gray-haired, and had the benign look of a kindergarten teacher. She also had a second-degree black belt in tae kwon do. Woody thought she could probably take him out in three seconds. "There's no way we can protect you," she told Peggy, "unless we know what we're protecting you from."

Peggy's protests following this remark shrank to moderate whining and complaint as she came to see the wisdom of what Detective Lajoie had said.

Peggy stuck a finger in her ear, wiggled it, and studied the results. "I saw him."

"Saw who, dear?" asked Detective Lajoie.

"One of the guys out in the woods. Not the guy who fucked me, one of the others. He helped hold me down. First I saw him in the hospital, but he didn't see me. Then I saw him in CVS. He threatened me."

"How?" asked Woody.

Peggy drew one finger across her white throat. "Just like that," she said.

"Does he work at the hospital?" asked Woody.

"Yeah, sure, he was wearing a white coat."

"A doctor?"

"How the fuck should I know? It was a white coat, that's all."

"What's he look like?"

"I don't know, just average. Not too fat, not too thin, not too tall. You know, regular. And he's got brown hair. He's not young, that's for sure. Maybe your age. Oh, yeah, he's got no ears. They're stuck flat to his head."

Woody then called Dr. Fuller and asked her to get to the hospital as soon as possible. He needed to see the employee files.

Woody, Detective Lajoie, and Peggy Summers met Dr. Fuller at her office at ten o'clock. She wasn't pleased to be there but tried not to show it. With her was Paul Garcia, head of personnel. They went down to Garcia's office to look through the employee files.

"You know, this is highly irregular," said Garcia.

"Cry me a river," said Detective Lajoie.

Garcia concentrated on the files of white males between the ages of twenty-five and fifty. Several times Peggy picked up a file as if she had found the right one, only to put it down again.

After half an hour, she picked up the file of Benjamin Clouston, a clinician in anatomical pathology.

"That's the one," she said. "The prick."

FOURTEEN

Wednesday night Carl Krause knew something was wrong. He lay in his bed fully dressed in the second-floor bedroom and stared at the ceiling. Why had he thought the knotholes had been moving? He looked at them, shut his eyes, and looked at them again. Nothing. And the cat, what had gotten into him? It was like the blackouts he'd had when drinking. He'd wake up in the morning and wonder where he'd parked his car or, worse, who the girl sleeping next to him was. Like he couldn't trust himself. He had been ready to punch Harriet in the face. And that job with Brantley, he had to tell him he couldn't do it anymore. It was fucking with his head. And he had to call that shrink whose name he had got from Dr. Frank. He had to take charge. That was funny. He had to become boss, boss of himself.

But wouldn't it be dangerous to take the pills? It was hard to notice shit when he was on them. He got that cotton-head feeling. He got too relaxed, too stupid. He'd be taking it easy and the bad guys would be out doing push-ups in the parking lot. They never relaxed. At times he could hear them, like when he heard them in the trees, or those times on the stairs. What if he hadn't been paying attention? For shit's sake, he knew exactly what would have happened. For one thing, he wouldn't be here in his comfy bed; he wouldn't be anyplace. He'd be a zero in a sky of zeros. And they sneak into people. Like they turn them into their personal robots. He's seen it. That colored cop, for instance; he could see them in his face, in his white teeth. And if he hadn't been paying attention, he would probably be in jail, or dead. He could even see them in Hercel. Hadn't that little fuck let the cops into the basement? Talking about a snake; they weren't looking for any fucking snake, they were looking for him, and he was lucky not to wind up in their jail. No, it wasn't luck. He'd outsmarted them, at least for now.

The bad guys didn't care who they took over. They could take over a dog or a cat. Hadn't he seen it? And he knew for a fact they could take over dead people. He'd seen them move; he'd seen them turn and look at him, like it was his fault, like he'd done it to them. That one dead guy he'd had to stab to make him quiet down, stuck a knife right in his heart. Oh, yes, they could take over people. Hadn't he seen them outside his window at night, standing on the lawn, looking up at him?

Carl heard a noise at the side window; he turned to look. Nothing. When he turned back, the knotholes began to move. He wasn't positive at first. He looked at them, shut his eyes, and looked again. They were moving. Over his bed were nine on this side, nine on the other, and nine at the end. Three, three, three, three. Sometimes it would be twelve and twelve. Sometimes it would be six, six, six, six. Sometimes they were eyes; sometimes they were little doors, sometimes little nozzles pumping out gas. But they couldn't do it if he kept an eye on them. He had to watch 'em like a fucking hawk. That's why he couldn't let himself go to sleep. They'd be pumping stuff down on top of him, like some kind of acid. It would make his skin flake off, like he could grab a piece of it and yank it away. They'd turn him into a puddle, into a piss spot.

Carl began to growl.

He could feel his fingers getting stiff, just the tips, like he was getting claws, like he was getting little slicers at his fingertips. When he growled, the knotholes slowed down. He knew their tricks. They were mean, but they were little. They were nasty, but he could manage them. That's why they had to wait until he was sleeping, wait until they could sneak into his head thoughts, sneak into his dreams and make him cry again, cry like a brat.

Again there was a noise at the side window, a bumping. He turned to see what it was. Nothing. But they were out there. He'd seen them on the lawn. He'd heard them on the stairs. Now they were at the window. The knotholes began to jitter. They knew what was happening. The jittering was like chuckling. Could he hear them? He could hear only the wind.

He had to trick them. They were small; they were scared of him. One by one by one, they were scared of him. Get them together and they'd sweep over him like a flood. They wanted to make him part of their awful whining—whining in the trees, whining under the door. He even heard them at Brantley's. He had put his ear to the chest of a dead guy and heard the whining inside him. He stuck his hands into the guts of a dead guy and felt the vibration, the little motor of the dead.

Again at the window. *Bump, bump*. Carl turned out the light; he got out of bed. He knew how to trick them; he knew how to sneak. In the top drawer of the bureau was a small flashlight. Sometimes he used it at the Burn Palace to look into the oven to see who was left.

Bump, bump.

Carl moved quietly. The side window was small, smaller than the front ones, about the size of a regular TV screen. Carl knelt by the window.

Bump, bump. Carl turned on the flashlight. Then he toppled backward. He crawled backward, never taking his eyes off the window. It was Ronnie McBride. His nose bumped the glass; his forehead bumped the glass. His eyes were stupid and gray. He turned this way and that, as if looking for him. *Bump, bump.* Ronnie wanted to whine at him. In the flashlight's beam, the inside of Ronnie's mouth was gray as plaster dust; his tongue was as gray as one of Carl's gray socks. He wanted Ronnie to leave him alone. He wasn't the bad guy. Carl shouted and crawled back to the wall. It was Ronnie's head, just the head by itself and a bit of the neck ending in a clean cut. Ronnie's mouth bumped the glass as if he wanted a kiss, as if he wanted to press his lips against Carl's, as if he wanted to stick his gray tongue into Carl's mouth, stick his tongue deep into Carl's throat and suck the life out of him, like sucking the last bit of Coke through a straw, but it would be Carl sliding down Ronnie's gray throat into the nothingness of his sliced neck.

Carl scrambled to his feet. He had to yank Ronnie's head out of the tree and stamp it into the sidewalk, beat it until it became gray mush, turn its tongue to burger. Carl fell against the wall, but he kept the light pointed at Ronnie's head bumping the window with little kisses, turning this way and that. Carl threw open the door and rushed down the stairs, stumbling and grabbing the banister, smashing into the wall at the bottom so a picture fell and broke.

A light burned by the chair next to the fireplace, but the room was empty. Carl stumbled toward the front door. He heard a noise and turned.

"Carl."

It was the bitch.

"Carl, where are you going? It's past midnight." She moved into the living room, tentatively, in her nightgown. He could hear his step-brats rustling.

"We need to talk," said Harriet, coming toward him. "I don't understand what you're doing."

Carl knew she meant to make him weak; she would make him see the doctor, try to lock him up. She reached out a hand to him.

"Carl, what's . . ."

Carl lunged at her. With one hand he grabbed her throat and squeezed; with his other hand he grabbed a fistful of her nightgown. Carl shoved her back and lifted her. Harriet's eyes grew fat and white. He heard a screaming from the hallway. Carl lifted Harriet off the floor so her bare feet kicked against his jeans. Her hands fluttered at him. He lifted her high and threw her toward the stone fireplace. She hit the chimney; her head hit the mantelpiece. She fell against the iron tool set and crashed to the floor. Carl turned toward the hall. He saw his step-kids. He lurched toward them. He would be a wolf; he'd eat them.

Bernie Wilcox had had a busy night. The emergency room was generally quiet on a Wednesday night, except in summer, but tonight there had been an accident right at the corner of Water Street and Route 1 by the convenience store. There had long been talk of upgrading the existing blinker to a regular light. Now maybe they'd do it. Nobody had been killed, thank goodness, but a car from Brewster had pulled out without looking. Stupid kids. No seat belts, of course. Now five people were in the hospital. The pickup coming from Charlestown managed to swerve so it didn't hit the kids broadside, but it took off the front of their car, probably their dad's car: a Passat. The ambulance tech said the front end had been sliced like it'd been cut with a knife—two people in the truck and three in the Passat, a lot of blood and broken bones, squashed bones was more like it. Anyway, the ER had been busy. The ambulances had started bringing them in at eight-thirty, and Bernie worked four hours straight. Now they were in the ICU.

At some point she heard that Barton had called, but she'd been too busy to talk to him. Maybe he would get up when she got home and they would have a few words, maybe he'd have a glass of warm milk and honey, which he liked. Anyway, she would be glad to get back to the farm and take off her shoes, glad to get out of Brewster. Those poor women, Sister Asherah, Sister Isis, and Helen Greene. She knew them all; not well, but enough to exchange a few words at the Stop & Shop. And Nina, she could barely think of it. She'd be glad to get back to the farm and civilization.

Bernie retrieved her VW Bug from the lot and drove down Cottage Street. It was when she turned onto Water Street that she saw them—two children dashing from between two buildings, the bigger dragging the small one by the hand. What were they doing out so late? Didn't they have parents? Then she got a closer look. The boy was Hercel McGarty; the girl must be his sister. What was her name? Lucy. Her little shoes had little lights in the heels and sparked red when she ran.

Bernie stopped and lowered the window. "Hercel! What're you doing out at this hour?"

Hercel began shouting when he was twenty feet from the car. "He's coming, he's coming!"

Bernie shivered, scared by whatever they were scared of, scared because this was the first time she had seen Hercel anything but calm. She jumped out as fast as she could, given her size, and pushed the seat forward so they could get in back.

Hercel shoved Lucy into the backseat. "Go, go! I see him!"

As Bernie accelerated, she looked in the rearview mirror. She saw a shadow back by the two buildings where she had first seen Hercel and

Lucy. It was something on all fours, maybe a coyote, but it was way too big for a coyote.

The telephone on Fred Bonaldo's bedside table started ringing at one o'clock. Fred didn't hear it. Nothing could get to him once he was sleeping. But Laura heard it, and there was just so long she'd let it ring. She rolled over and jabbed her husband in the ribs.

"Fred, get the phone."

It was Harvey Lopes at the police station. "Something's gone wrong at Carl Krause's house." He explained that Bernie Wilcox had just called with a story about Carl beating up his wife, of picking her up and throwing her. Then he had gone after the kids. The boy had got into his bedroom with his sister and blocked the door. Then they climbed out the window. Carl had run outside and chased them until Bernie saw them on Water Street. Now she was taking them to the farm.

"She said Carl was running around on all fours," said Harvey. "I thought you'd want to know."

Bonaldo almost dropped the phone. On all fours? He really *didn't* want to know. He wanted to go back to sleep. But he'd told everyone in the police station, every cop in Brewster, to call him if anything strange or criminal took place. So Fred had only himself to blame. Briefly, he considered telling Harvey to call someone else, but then who else was there? After all, wasn't he chief—or, rather, acting chief?

"I'll be there in five minutes."

"D'you really have to go out?" mumbled Laura from the other side of the bed.

Bonaldo pulled on his pants. "It's my job."

"I thought being chief meant telling other people to do things."

He wanted to say that wasn't true of an *acting* chief. Instead, he said, "It's more complicated than that."

"You poor thing," said Laura, snuggling into her pillow. "You work too hard."

When Bonaldo arrived at the bungalow on the corner of Newport and Hope, he knew he had made the right decision. Drawn up at the curb were two Brewster patrol cars and Bobby Anderson's 370Z. A pussy wagon, Brewster cops called it. Bonaldo couldn't see how Bobby had got there before him, considering he lived ten miles away. A Brewster cop smoking by his car waved his cigarette at him, making a red *S* in the air.

Bonaldo hurried up the front steps, and Bobby met him at the door. "It's pretty messy. The CSI truck's on its way; so's the medical examiner."

"Where's the ambulance?" Bonaldo had assumed Harriet was alive and couldn't see why there wasn't an ambulance.

Bobby nodded toward the fireplace. "She's dead, been dead almost an hour."

Bonaldo felt as if Bobby had slapped him. He took a breath and entered the living room. Two Brewster cops, Harry Morelli and Whole-Hog Hopper, stood by the stairs with their hands in their pockets. From somewhere came a high yapping.

"Had to lock the little dog in the bedroom," said Whole-Hog. "Nearly took my arm off."

Then Bonaldo saw Harriet on the floor by the fireplace. Blood surrounded her head like a halo. He walked toward her. She stared back with dull eyes. No, she didn't need an ambulance. He felt his stomach turn over, took a deep breath, and turned away. "Where's Carl?"

"Gone," said Bobby. "Bernie said the kids told her Carl'd done it."

"Shouldn't the kids be here? We got to talk to them."

Bobby's eyes got harder. "They just saw their mother killed by their stepfather. Carl was clawing at Hercel's bedroom door, growling like an animal. Hercel and Lucy are hysterical. You really want to bring them to police headquarters? They're better off with Bernie."

Bonaldo saw his point. "So what's being done about Carl?"

"You're the chief. You gotta tell your men what to do. Detective Gazzola is out with a couple of cars. I called Lieutenant Hammond and he called Alton and Exeter barracks for backup. An APB on Carl's been sent out. There was a wedding picture here on the table. I told one of your guys to make copies and fax it all over the place. I hope you don't mind."

"No, of course not." Bonaldo didn't like Bobby's tone, didn't like Bobby doing his job for him, though he would probably do it ten times better. "Anything else?"

"Yeah, I called Woody."

Batman and Robin, thought Bonaldo.

The CSI truck arrived. Frank Montesano, Janie Forsyth, and Lou Rossetti dragged their lights and equipment into the living room. "We got to stop meeting like this," said Montesano.

"I'm working on it," said Bobby. Janie Forsyth looked at him sympathetically.

Woody arrived five minutes later, looking half awake. He'd driven fast with the window open, occasionally slapping his face to take the place of the gallon of coffee he needed. Crossing the living room, he looked down at Harriet and winced. "So this is the distraction Joe Doyle was worried about?" He was furious, but he didn't know what to do about it. Maybe just swallow hard and find Carl.

More people arrived. Montesano pushed everyone out of the house except for his team and the medical examiner.

"I guess we better get busy and find him," said Woody. "It makes me wish I'd never met Hercel. I don't like bad stuff getting into my gut."

Bobby just looked at him. Personally, he felt glad he knew Hercel.

He and that Baldo Bonaldo kid made him laugh. "Let's get busy," he said.

Carl squatted down behind the convenience store at the corner of Water Street and Route 1. He'd run out the whole two miles from downtown and he felt good. He'd loped out; he'd galloped. Now he wanted something to drink. Beer was sold only at the liquor stores, and they were closed. He knew he could get something else inside.

Carl had seen who had picked up Hercel and Lucy; he recognized her yellow Beetle. He knew where she lived. He'd get out there and finish his work. He didn't have a gun; the cops had taken his shotgun, but he had a sheath knife. A knife was like a single claw. He'd catch the brats and end it. They were little, but they'd be big someday. That's when they got dangerous. He'd get them before that happened. Then he'd have peace in his head.

But he wanted to drink something. He had a bad thirst, not a water thirst or a soda-pop thirst. Carl walked around the side of the building. The door buzzed when he went in. A fat woman sat behind the counter eating from a bucket of popcorn. Her chin was shiny with grease. Maybe she was thirty; maybe she was fifty. She looked like a swollen tick.

"You heard about the accident?" she said.

Carl thought she was talking about what he'd done to the bitch.

"I didn't do it," he said.

The fat woman laughed.

Carl got two medium-size bottles of Listerine, all they had. He got a Coke and four little bottles of vanilla extract, all they had. He'd make a Listy Cooler. He grabbed a loaf of Wonder Bread to clean his mouth afterward. He took a drink cup. Then he went to the counter. He stood looking at the fat woman. She looked at him and looked away. He stuck his hand into the bucket, grabbed a handful of popcorn, and shoved it in his mouth.

"Hey!" she said.

Carl leaned toward her and slowly opened his mouth so the half-chewed popcorn dribbled across his chin. He leaned toward her and growled.

The fat woman fell back off her stool onto the floor. She scrambled up to her hands and knees, and stared at Carl. "I can have the cops out here in two minutes flat, just see if I can't!"

Carl threw some bills on the counter. No more games. It was time to eat some baby cake. Once outside, he crossed the highway, walked a bit, and stopped to fix his drink. He poured a mix of Coke, Listerine, and vanilla into the paper cup. He drank, gagged, threw up, and then he drank some more. He refilled the cup with Coke, Listerine, and vanilla. This time when he drank he kept it down. He finished the cup, drank another, and tossed it aside. He dropped the empty bottles onto the road. He stuffed his mouth with soft white bread, chewed, swallowed, and stuffed his mouth again. Then he began loping along. The road was dark, with only a few outside lights from a few houses. Carl began to feel good. After several minutes, he heard the distant yapping of coyotes. But the coyotes didn't bother him. He was a wolf. He had a claw.

As Bernie had driven out to the farm, she listened to Hercel describe what had happened. At first he had been unable to talk, he'd been breathing so heavily. Lucy was curled up in the backseat, weeping and weeping. Hercel was also crying a little, but he was trying to stop. He described how his mother had been talking to Carl, how she had been talking perfectly nice, but then Carl grabbed her and threw her against the fireplace. Hercel wanted to help her, but Carl had turned toward them, growled at them. It was only because he tripped over the fireplace tools that he hadn't caught them.

Hercel had dragged Lucy to his room and started shoving stuff against the door, like the bed and bureau. Then he opened the window. Carl tried to open the door but couldn't. Hercel lowered Lucy and told her to sit still. Then he got up on the windowsill. At that moment Carl smashed through the door, falling over the bureau. Hercel jumped to the ground and grabbed Lucy's hand. He pulled her up and they ran, first through the backyard, then through a hole in the fence. His ankle hurt a little from Friday night, but he ignored it. They heard the back door smash open and Carl come down the steps, his big feet clomping.

Hercel worked his way through the backyards, pulling Lucy behind him. He was sure Carl would see the red lights blinking on her heels, but it would be worse for her to go barefoot. Carl stuck to the sidewalks, running, stopping, peering between the houses. Once, when Lucy fell and cried out, Carl heard and came running across someone's lawn. He dropped down on all fours and growled. Then dogs started barking, and Hercel got away. He was afraid to go to someone's house because Carl might hurt them, like he hurt his mother. Who wouldn't be scared of Carl? And he couldn't make Lucy run much. She wanted to lie down under a bush. She wanted to cry, and Hercel wouldn't let her. So Hercel tried to get to Water Street. If he reached the police station, they'd be okay. Maybe it would have worked if Carl hadn't seen them in the alley. He had dropped to all fours and loped after them. That was when Hercel had dragged Lucy out to the street and he had seen Bernie's VW.

Listening to Hercel's story, Bernie began to weep as well. She wiped away her tears with closed fists and called the police station on her cell phone. She knew Harriet was bound to be hurt; she didn't know she was dead. It seemed an unimaginable consequence.

After passing the blinking light at Route 1, Bernie saw no more cars. Hercel scrambled into the front seat. Blessedly, Lucy was already asleep in the back.

"Aren't you sleepy?" asked Bernie.

"Only a little bit." Hercel didn't want to say that every time he shut he eyes he saw Carl pick up his mother and throw her at the fireplace. Every time he heard the coconut sound of her head hitting the stone, then the jangling crash as she fell onto the fireplace tools. He had started to run to her, but Carl had growled at him. Hercel had even tried to use his trick, to be David like Carl was Goliath, but it was an undependable trick. He had been too scared to concentrate, and it wouldn't work unless he thought so hard his head hurt.

"You think my mom's all right?" asked Hercel.

Bernie felt a chill in her heart. "We can only hope so."

"But she'd be hurt, right?"

"Probably some, but, you know, people are pretty tough."

"She didn't move after she fell."

"She might've been catching her breath. You didn't stay very long, did you?"

"Carl said he was going to eat us."

Oh, you poor babies, thought Bernie.

The VW's headlights reflected off something shiny far ahead, which quickly turned into a pair of eyes.

"Coyotes," said Hercel. "They're waiting for us."

What struck Bobby Anderson was that Carl's red Ford pickup was still in the driveway. He hadn't taken it, and he hadn't come back and fetched it.

"You think he's still in town?" he asked Woody.

They were standing on the front porch of the bungalow. The night was clear, and Woody stared up at the sky. He spotted the constellation Orion. It meant winter had almost arrived.

"He's wacko," said Woody. "You don't know what he's going to do."

"You gotta dog coming?" Bobby meant the canine unit.

"Brotman said it's on its way. It could be here"—Woody looked at his watch—"in twenty minutes."

"Carl could be almost anyplace in that time."

"If he's on foot, the dog will find him."

An ambulance eventually arrived to pick up Harriet's body and take her to the medical examiner's in Providence. Woody recognized Seymour Hodges, but instead of Jimmy Mooney, there was another guy. Woody had tried to talk to Seymour the other day about Iraq. He thought that since he'd been there in '91, Seymour might open up. But he hadn't. "Not nice," was all Seymour had said. Woody couldn't blame him much. Seymour had reeked of weed, but Woody let it go. He'd also smoked dope when he had got back—smoked dope, drank, and took pills—a roller coaster of artificial forgetfulness. It hadn't helped.

"Where's your buddy?" he asked Seymour.

Seymour turned and looked surprised that Jimmy wasn't in the other seat. "Beats me. I guess he's got business."

Bobby gave Woody a nudge. "Let's drive around."

"You want to take the truck?"

"With all that fur? Hey, I love Ajax, but I don't want to wear him."

So Woody squeezed into the Z. It felt like climbing into a coffin after his Tundra. The black leather interior, orange-lit gauges, and blue-lit GPS screen turned the coffin into a Captain Kirk escape pod. The motor rumbled.

Bobby drove up and down a few streets and then onto Water Street and turned right.

"Where we going?"

"Brantley's, to see if any lights are on."

Woody saw a light in the turret and another at the rear of the mansion.

"I guess we'll pay a visit." Bobby drove to the back and loudly revved the engine. Then they got out. An awning covered the back door. A light shone over the old carriage house, which had been turned into a three-vehicle garage. Bobby rang the bell and did a little hammering with the soft side of his fist. He had to repeat this a couple of times.

A light came on above the back door, and Brantley peered through the glass. He wore a dark bathrobe. Bobby held his cop shield to the window, and Brantley opened up. He didn't say anything; he waited for Bobby to speak.

"You seen Carl?"

Brantley looked surprised; it made his dark eyebrows rise up. "Why ever would he be here? It's nearly two in the morning."

"We saw the lights on," said Bobby. "I thought you might be doing some last-minute embalming."

"I was reading, as a matter of fact." Brantley held up a book with his finger marking the place. It was a biography of John Adams. "It helps put me to sleep. Jenny's seeing friends in Stonington. I stay here when she's away. Is something wrong? Why are you looking for Carl?"

"He just murdered his wife," said Woody.

Brantley put his hand over his mouth. "Why ever . . . ?"

"He's on foot," said Bobby. "He's not a guy with a lot of friends, and I thought he might have a key."

"None of my employees have keys, except my assistant." Brantley still looked amazed. "Would you like to come in and look around?"

Bobby looked at Woody, who shook his head.

"That's okay, we'll let you get back to your book."

Brantley wrinkled his brow. He still held open the door with one hand. "But why did he murder his wife? Harriet, is that her name?"

"He stopped taking his meds," said Bobby. "If he stops taking his meds, his brain gets mushy. Maybe that's what happened. Other than that, I don't know."

Bobby and Woody walked back to the car. As Woody opened the door, his cell phone twittered. He answered it and listened. Then he turned to Bobby. "The dog's here."

When Bernie unhooked the gate, drove through, and then latched it again, she saw someone sitting in a chair in front of the house. Not only that, but the sheep were gone. She hoped they were in the barn. Driving to the house, she saw the person in the chair was Barton. He wore his down jacket and a knit sailor's cap. His walker was in front of him, and to his left was one of the Bouviers, Gray, that had jumped up when he heard the car. On Barton's knees was his bolt-action Winchester rifle.

"What in the world are you doing?" asked Bernie, getting out of the VW. "Do you know what time it is?" Hercel had at last fallen asleep and only woke up when the door opened, turning on the overhead light.

"I hope to shoot a coyote. Rags's at the vet's. He was pretty chewed up."

"By coyotes?" It put her mind in a whirl. Then she thought, *First things first*. "I've got to get these kids in bed. Something awful's happened."

Bernie carried Lucy into the house and put her in Tig's bed. Tig woke up, saw Lucy, smiled, and then fell back asleep all in the space of five seconds. She put Hercel in the bed in the library and covered him with a quilt. Returning to the living room, she sat down on the other end of the sofa from her husband. The rifle lay on the coffee table.

"Now tell me," said Bernie.

"No, you first."

So Bernie described picking up Hercel and Lucy on Water Street and their terror. She said what had happened with Carl, how Hercel and Lucy had escaped from the house and that she had called the police. "I called them again just before I got here," she added. "It's awful. Harriet's dead."

"He murdered her?"

"Keep your voice down. The kids don't know about it."

"And Carl?"

"The police are looking for him."

Next Barton told his wife what had happened during the day with the coyotes. He described how they had crossed the wall and a sheep had been killed. "They had a plan. I couldn't believe it." He said that Tig had run into the field and described his attempt to go after her, ending up: "The vet says Rags will recover, but his back leg was chewed up. I called Tom"—he was the neighbor who lived down the road—"but he's taken his family to Disney World. I can't see why he'd do a silly thing like that. Anyway, I didn't want to leave Gray out there by himself—those coyotes would eat him up if he was alone—and if I kept him inside, the coyotes would be all over the place. . . ."

"So you were babysitting him."

"That's about it."

"And you're planning to stay outside all night?"

"I don't know. I was planning to ask your advice."

"Are all the animals inside? Then bring Gray in, too. You can't sit there until morning, silly old man." She said this affectionately.

"Maybe you're right."

"Of course I am." Bernie stood up.

Barton pushed himself up on the walker. The Winchester had a sling; he put it over his shoulder and hobbled to the door. Once he had maneuvered his way outside, he saw Gray across the field running along the wall. There were four lights above the wall, as well as lights above the front and back doors, the barn, and the gate. The wind had picked up, shaking the trees so the blowing leaves looked like bats dipping and flying. He heard coyotes yapping from someplace. Barton heard a lot better with his left ear than the right, which meant he was always turning in the wrong direction to identify a sound. He whistled for the dog. Gray stopped and looked at him. Barton had to whistle again, before the dog trotted toward the house. Both knew the coyotes were getting closer.

Woody, Bobby Anderson, four troopers, and two Brewster cops followed the German shepherd from the canine unit and his handler out to Hope Street, and then for ten minutes the dog led them up one street and down another till they went through the short alley onto Water Street. The dog's name was Rainer.

"Bernie said she saw him out here," said Bobby. "We should've come here first."

Woody wasn't positive. "She said she saw a large shadow on all fours."

"Yeah, who else is it going to be but that nutcase?"

"We weren't sure," said the handler, a trooper named Rocco Durante. "He might have doubled back." The dog lived with Durante. Bobby had worked with them before. Dog and man were so tuned in to each other that they appeared to have a telepathic connection.

The German shepherd turned up Water Street toward Route 1, pulling hard on his leash so Durante had to trot after him. Behind them came a slow-moving Brewster patrol car with acting chief Bonaldo and a driver. Bonaldo kept telling himself that if he was a real cop, he'd been out there running, too, but it wasn't enough to make him do it.

In a half-hour they reached the convenience store. The fat woman was still behind the counter. She wasn't going to forget Carl anytime soon. "He took my popcorn. He growled at me." She described how Carl had bought two bottles of Listerine, four bottles of vanilla, a Coke, and a loaf of Wonder Bread. "He left the receipt. I got it right here if you want to see it."

It seemed to Woody that Carl might have tried to hitch a ride at the blinking light, but the dog again picked up the scent and crossed the highway. The lights were fewer, but the cops had flashlights. After a hundred yards, they found the empty bottles of Listerine, vanilla, and Coke, along with the paper cup and open bag of Wonder Bread and the pool of Carl's vomit.

Fred Bonaldo joined them. "You going to gather those up for fingerprints?"

"Hey, that's a great idea," said Bobby. "And, Fred, why don't you mop up the puke so we can check the DNA."

"I know where he's going," said Woody, ignoring the others. "He's on his way to Barton Wilcox's farm."

"Well, there's sure no point in walking." Bobby turned toward the patrol car.

Bernie liked to eat something before she went to bed, and so Barton made her scrambled eggs. Hercel got up, saying he couldn't sleep, so Barton made him eggs as well, along with toast, bacon, and, for Hercel and himself, a glass of warm milk. Bernie preferred a little Jack Daniel's. It soothed her after a busy night, and Lord knows she needed it.

They settled down to eat. Bernie and her husband tried to find boring things to talk about in order to keep away from the subjects that bothered them most, to avoid upsetting Hercel. Bernie described a shawl she was weaving with a Navajo pattern. Although Barton loved his wife's weaving, he found the subject so dull he nearly fell asleep, nearly tumbled forward with his forehead going *splop* into his eggs. Then he heard the coyotes, louder now. Gray jumped up and started barking.

"They're back again." Barton struggled to his feet and pulled his walker into position. The Winchester leaned against the wall.

Bernie tried, ineffectively, to hush the dog. "You'll wake the kids."

Hercel ran to the window, shading his eyes to see through the glass. Barton hobbled to the door. "You stay here," he told Hercel, but while Barton was keeping the dog from running out, Hercel slipped through the doorway. He stopped, and Barton joined him. Barton started to speak but only stared. He raised his rifle to his shoulder.

The coyotes had crossed the wall and were attacking something at the gate, circling and lunging and then being thrown back. Maybe there were six of them. They made a lot of noise, yapping and growling. Then there would be a yelp. They were fighting an animal down on all fours, a much bigger animal that kept striking at them. But it wasn't really an animal, not the four-footed kind.

"It's Mr. Krause," said Hercel, and he took a step behind Barton.

Carl crouched down a few yards from the gate. He knew where he was, but he no longer knew *who* he was; or, rather, he was a wolf, he'd always been a wolf, and he had a single sharp claw. It wasn't a wolf's business to be afraid. He growled from deep in his throat. He cut and sliced, and the coyotes were scared of him, but it didn't stop them. Carl didn't know who he had been before being a wolf. He had a memory of the town; he knew bad things had happened, but he had little memory of what had taken place before the convenience store and the fat woman's popcorn. He remembered the Listy Cooler. He remembered loping through the dark, and then the coyotes showed up. First they loped along beside him, then they'd attacked, tried to catch him by his hind legs. One had felt his claw; then the others fell back to reconsider but soon came on again. Carl didn't know what lay behind him, but he knew where he was going. He could see the faces of the two children. Thinking of them made his tongue thick and wet. Then he had reached the farm with the coyotes around him. He had jumped the fence and fallen.

Barton held his rifle to his shoulder, but he was unsure whether to shoot. The coyotes and the man formed a tangle, a quickly moving spiral, as the coyotes jumped and the man spun to stab at them. Barton kept thinking, *Coyotes aren't supposed to act like this*. The yapping and sudden yelping, and the growling of the man, made an awful chorus, a dark music. Whenever the man turned, the coyotes leapt, and at least one, for a second, hung from his jacket. Then the man shook himself free. Then another snatched at his leg. The man kicked out, but he lost his balance and fell.

That's when Barton fired, and the gunshot was the loudest noise in the forest. The Winchester was slow, relatively; it took a moment to operate the bolt and eject the shell, letting another shell rise up from the magazine. It meant taking his finger off the trigger. Barton resighted and fired again. He had missed the first time; now a coyote yelped and fell to the ground. The coyotes stopped attacking the man, who was on all fours. They began moving toward the wall. Barton fired again and missed. Then the coyotes disappeared. They were just gone. The man stayed down on all fours.

"He must be hurt," said Barton.

Hercel couldn't imagine Carl being hurt; he was too mean to be hurt.

Barton hobbled forward. "Hey, Carl, you all right?" He wanted to tell Carl to put up his hands, but first he wanted to see how Carl responded.

Abruptly, the man ran to the wall, still on all fours. It was the running on all fours that bothered Barton most. It startled him so that he didn't think of shooting. The man disappeared over the wall.

It was half an hour before the patrol car showed up with Woody and Bobby, although Woody had called five minutes earlier. Bernie had just been going to bed. Barton had decided to sit up with his Winchester. Bernie was sick of arguing with him. Pushing his walker ahead of him, Barton had gone out to the wall and found a dead coyote. There was no sound from the woods. For all he knew Carl might have been only a few yards away.

Barton reassured the two detectives that everyone was all right, but one of his dogs had been hurt earlier in the day. Bonaldo stared down at the dead coyote and nudged it with his shoe, almost expecting it to jump up. He thought that vicious coyotes weren't what he had signed on for. It was a big jump from vicious coyotes to wearing his police uniform in the Memorial Day parade.

Rocco Durante and Rainer, the German shepherd, as well as the troopers and Brewster police officers, showed up a little later. The dead coyote was a big distraction for the dog, but Durante pulled him away. In seconds, he picked up Carl's scent where he'd gone over the wall.

The German shepherd with the men in tow followed the trail into the swamp. It got more difficult as the trail grew muddier. The men weren't wearing boots, nor did they have clothing to protect them from the brambles. Once the trail led into the water, Rainer lost the scent entirely.

FIFTEEN

Wednesday evening, at about nine-thirty, Woody Potter, Detective Beth Lajoie, and two Brewster patrolmen had gone to the house of Benjamin Clouston, the pathology clinician identified by Peggy Summers. Clouston rented a small nineteenth-century house on Ballou Street, five blocks from the hospital. The shades were drawn and the house was dark. No car was in the driveway. Woody knocked and rang the bell and then knocked on the back door. The patrolmen tried to look through the windows. Woody knocked and rang the bell a few more times, and then he and Detective Lajoie went to talk to the neighbors on either side, waking one of them. They learned Clouston was friendly but kept to himself. He had lived there for about a year. Sometimes the music was a little loud, that was all.

One neighbor remembered Clouston leaving on Tuesday morning. No, he wasn't carrying any bags or a suitcase. Clouston drove a metallic silver 2008 Toyota Solara. After knocking on Clouston's door one more time, the officers left. In the morning Woody meant to get a warrant to search the house. A plainclothes detective remained parked outside all night. Clouston's Solara was registered in Rhode Island, and its plate number was sent out to the police.

Woody then drove home, and by midnight he was asleep. At one-fifteen, he was awakened by a call from Bobby, who told him about Harriet's murder. So he got dressed again, and soon he joined the hunt for Carl out at the farm and followed the tracking dog into the swamp. Even after the dog had lost the scent, they slogged along, trying to pick it up again. Around four-thirty, they quit for the night, meaning to begin again at eight, if Carl wasn't found elsewhere. By five o'clock, Woody was home in bed.

At six-thirty, his telephone rang. It was Jill Franklin. "Breakfast?" Her voice was chipper and affectionate.

Woody grunted his way back to some facility with the English language. "Sure."

"Seven o'clock at the Brewster Brew?"

"That'll work. By the way, I've got bad news." Woody paused; he dreaded what would come next. "Hercel McGarty's mom was murdered last night."

There was a sharp intake of breath followed by silence. Then: "That poor child, I'm so sorry."

"It gets worse. His stepfather did it. Hercel saw it happen—his sister, too, for that matter."

"Mr. Krause? How awful."

"You still want to meet?"

"Of course." Even so, the cheer was gone from her voice. "Where's Hercel now?"

"Out at Bernie and Barton Wilcox's; they've got the sheep . . ."

"I know them both. I did a story on them for the *Times and Advertiser.*"

Not long after, as Woody was nearing Brewster, he was passed overhead by a news helicopter. It didn't bring out the best in him. *Vultures*, he thought. Actually, another had already landed, and five news trucks were parked outside police headquarters. Woody recalled seeing Baldo Bonaldo leaving the library on Tuesday wearing a mullet wig cap with dark bangs. *Perhaps*, thought Woody, *I should borrow it so the reporters don't recognize me.*

When Woody drove up Water Street, he saw a news truck parked outside the Brewster Brew, as well as five cars, which he guessed belonged to reporters. He didn't want to go inside.

But as he slowed down, a figure darted out from between parked cars and waved. It was Jill. Woody stopped the truck so quickly that Ajax slid onto the floor. He shoved open the door, and Jill jumped inside holding a paper bag.

"Wow, they should call that the Brewster Zoo. I got two black coffees, cream cheese, and three bagels."

"Why three?"

"One for Ajax. Let's drive down to the beach. You look sleepy. The bags under your eyes have their own little bags."

"Thanks."

"I think they're handsome."

He looked at her in surprise; she was smiling at him. Woody tried to smile back and felt his cheeks creak. *I've got all the charm of a cement block*, he thought; then he turned his attention to the road. On the way to the beach, he described what had happened the previous night, as well as what they had learned from Peggy Summers. Jill's eyes narrowed, as if the bad news cast too bright a light. Her dismay increased as Woody drove, until, when he described Hercel, tears came to her eyes. He thought about how on their first meetings he'd tried to keep information from her; now he was dumping it in her lap. But it was worse than that, as he saw the hurt in her face; he felt his words were poison he was pumping into her system.

"I'm sorry," he told her. "I should keep this to myself. I hate it, and I'm supposed to be used to it. I'm just sticking bad stuff in your head."

Jill wiped her eyes on the back of her hand and frowned. "I can decide myself what I can stand and what I can't. Have you really gotten used to stuff like this?"

Woody saw a movement at the side of the road. He turned quickly, thinking it was a coyote, but it was only a house cat on the prowl. *I need a break*, he thought.

"Maybe I've developed calluses. You see a lot of bad stuff; it's part of the job. I hope I never get completely used to it, but I worry that how it affects me can affect other people, the poison, I mean. That's one thing that happened with Susie." Woody gave a rueful laugh. "She stopped asking if I'd had a nice day."

Jill was scratching Ajax's ears. "You don't have to worry about me."

Woody looked doubtful. The sun was still low in the sky and she was squinting into it, but it made her whole face bright and her blond hair shine. He wanted to put his hand on her hand, but he kept his hands on the wheel.

Woody drove to the spot on the beach where he had been with Bobby Anderson on Tuesday morning. Then it had been gray and the waves had been high. This morning it was sunny and the water was flat, with the waves no more than a foot or so. Jill took out the cups of coffee and put them in the cup holders; then she spread cream cheese on a plain bagel and gave it to him. He was touched by the faint sense of domesticity; it filled his heart with generalized yearning. On the other hand, he was glad that drinking coffee and eating his bagel kept him from talking. He watched the seagulls pushing one another out of the way. Jill, too, was eating and looking at the water. Woody, in fact, would have liked to talk to her about what was going on, talk to her about Carl and the coyotes. But he still thought she didn't need to hear the gruesome details.

Instead, he approached the subject obliquely. "I used to think of confusion and ignorance as being about the same thing—that is, if I thought of it at all. But in the past day or two, I've been thinking that confusion can be a *result* of ignorance. It's what this guy at You-You would call a modification." Woody spoke briefly about Todd Chmielnicki, but he didn't say how Chmielnicki had looked into his head. "Anyway, to deal with the ignorance, to see it clearly, you've got to get rid of the confusion, the modification. It's like when you're listening to a person, you can't really hear them if you're feeling anger or doubt, stuff like that. Those are also modifications. So I try to figure out what's happening in Brewster, and all I see is confusion. It's like a wall between me and my ignorance. I've got to get back to the ignorance by itself so I can do something about it. I might not figure anything out, but I'll have a better chance."

Jill thought for a moment. "I don't think I feel confused very often, but I'm sure that's because my life's not complicated enough."

Finishing their breakfast, Woody and Jill took Ajax for a short walk. Woody kept telling himself he had no time for a walk with a pretty girl, but he decided he could give it ten minutes.

It was nearly high tide, so they had to walk on the loose sand. Their footing was unsure, and their shoulders bumped each other. They could have walked farther apart, but they didn't. Ajax ran ahead, came back, and ran ahead again. Each time Woody brushed Jill's shoulder it caused a quick sparkle in his brain.

Thursday morning, while Woody was walking on the beach, Bobby Anderson drove out to the Wilcox farm with Harriet's miniature dachshund, Randy. The dog weighed less than ten pounds—a short-haired dachshund, mostly black but with tan paws and a tan muzzle. He stood on the seat with his front paws just reaching the dashboard, as if glad to go somewhere. When the police had finished their work in Carl and Harriet's house early that morning, one of the patrolmen had taken the dog to police headquarters until the shelter opened. "It's not like it's a pit bull," he kept saying. "We got lots of room."

When Bobby showed up at headquarters at seven-thirty—first running through the phalanx of reporters, photographers, and guys holding up little tape recorders—he found Randy in the detectives' office being fed cheese crackers and potato chips.

So he decided the dog needed liberating. He had wanted to see Hercel anyway, to see how he was doing. He also needed to meet up with the canine unit. A second dog had been brought in and would start at the entrance of Great Swamp, about three miles from the farm. And Bobby wanted to talk to Barton about coyotes and get them figured out. He wasn't like Woody; he didn't let this shit fuck up his mood. He didn't get all existential about it. Woody had to learn to chill; at least that was how Bobby saw it. But the coyotes perplexed him.

Barton had let the sheep back into the field—"They gotta eat, don't they?"—and was sitting in his chair in front of the house with the Winchester across his knees and a blanket over his shoulders. Hercel sat on the ground nearby, sharpening a stick with a Swiss Army knife—"whittling," Barton called it. The Bouvier circled the sheep, keeping them loosely together.

When Bobby carried the miniature dachshund from the Z, Barton laughed. "Is that my new sheepdog?"

But Hercel ran to the dog and grabbed him up in his arms. He didn't weep, but he came close. His whole life had been blown to pieces, and this one thing had been saved. He ran to the house to show the dog to Lucy and Tig.

"Nice of you to bring it," said Barton.

Bobby squatted down on his heels next to the old man, and looked out over the field. Tall trees lined the perimeter beyond the wall. The sheep—now twenty-nine of them—seemed to accept the Bouvier's attentiveness. Half a dozen geese pecked at treats in the grass. It was quiet except for the sounds of birds—a crow, some blue jays, and a robin making a chirping-clicking noise, warning his pals about the marmalade cat sunning itself on the front step.

"Pretty place you've got here," said Bobby.

A note of anxiety crept into Barton's voice. "I don't know how long I can keep it. I can't get around on two legs, and one of my dogs is laid up. If the coyotes start coming over the wall, even a half-dozen dogs won't be enough. The way they went after Krause last night, he could have been killed. They're scared of the rifle, but I sure can't keep guard every night, and what's the point of keeping the sheep in the barn? I'm too old to be running Fort Apache."

"A DEM sergeant told me they'd been getting complaints—more pets disappearing, more people being threatened. You've any ideas what's behind it?"

Barton laughed. "Bernie's got a few Wiccan friends who say it's shape-shifting. There're lots of spells and ways to turn yourself into a wolf, though I can't say they work. On the other hand, Krause was growling and running around on all fours, but I figure that's what's called clinical lycanthropy. It's a kind of schizophrenia. Frank Norris wrote a novel, *Vandover and the Brute,* about a man turning into a wolf. Krause reminded me of that. Central Asia has lots of myths of were-dogs, but those were dog-headed men rather than anything like Gray or poor Rags. A German study of lycanthropy published a few years ago discussed more than thirty cases. Most of the subjects weren't wolves, but tigers, birds, cats, even frogs and bees."

"You've done your homework."

"Only a little light Web reading during the night. But there's one trouble about calling these coyote shape-shifters. Come with me and bring the rifle."

Barton heaved himself up onto his walker and made his way to the barn. Inside, on the floor, was a blue tarp covering a lumpy something.

"Pull it off," said Barton.

Bobby grabbed a corner and pulled. Underneath was a dead coyote.

"DEM's supposed to pick it up this morning. The point is if you kill a werewolf or a shape-shifter it's supposed go back to human form." Barton nudged the coyote with the front foot of his walker. "This one's all coyote, or almost."

The animal was a mixture of black, tan, and gray—doglike, but not a dog. "It's big. What do you mean 'almost'?"

"Western coyotes weigh between thirty-five and forty pounds. This beauty is over sixty. In fact, it's not a coyote at all. It's a coywolf. See how heavyset it is? I expect it's descended from Canadian red wolves. The thing is, if you've got coywolves, you've got a different kind of animal—they're bigger, hungrier, and more aggressive. Still, red wolves don't usually attack humans. That's more a gray wolf activity."

"So what are you saying?"

"Coywolves might cross the wall and grab a sheep, but these are far more aggressive. They're coywolves plus something else. But I don't know what it'd be."

Detective Beth Lajoie had the slow-moving, ruminative, and stubborn qualities of a good cop. She wasn't going to chase drug dealers down alleys and jump fences anytime soon, but there were plenty of younger troopers eager to do that. She'd shaken loose two husbands and two kids, and at forty-five she lived by herself with three cats: Wynken,

Blynken, and Nod. She practiced tae kwon do, was a Civil War buff, and had the calm demeanor of someone at peace with herself. But this was art rather than life; it was the cheese that lured the mouse to a trap.

The mouse Detective Lajoie was interested in early this Thursday morning was Peggy Summers. Lajoie wore an emerald-green pantsuit with brown moccasins that looked terrible and a thick yellow rope chain that left a green mark on her neck if she wore it too often. These weren't her usual clothes, but she wanted to dress in a way that would elicit feelings of repulsion and superiority. She wanted to seem unthreatening. Glancing at herself in the mirror with approval, she went out to her gray Mazda 6 and drove to Brewster to the narrow clapboard house on Williams Street.

Peggy was in her bedroom, watching a rerun of *General Hospital* and smoking.

"I've been worried about you, Peggy," said Detective Lajoie. "I thought I'd drop by and take a look at you."

Peggy swiped her eyes across Detective Lajoie's clothing preferences as she might wipe a rag across a speck of dust. She looked back at the TV. "And what do you see?"

"An unhappy young woman." Detective Lajoie sat down on a chair by the bed. The ashtray on the nightstand was full of cigarette butts.

"You'd be unhappy, too, if you had to live in this shithole."

"We think you might be in danger."

"So why'd you drag me back here?"

"Just thinking what's best for you, that's all. Would you like to go for a ride? Get some fresh air?"

"Not with you I don't."

Detective Lajoie glanced at the TV. Two nurses were discussing a good-looking doctor in hushed tones.

"Tell me, Peggy, have you ever thought of being a nurse?"

"Yuck, bedpans and all that shit? No way."

"So what would you like to do with your life?"

"Get the fuck out of here. Maybe go to California. I gotta girlfriend in Sacramento."

"This whole business must be awful for you."

"I don't like people nagging at me, and I don't like being stuck in this house."

"You can make it end sooner if you help us out."

"Yeah? How's that?"

"I think other girls were victimized out in the woods besides you and Nina."

"I don't know anything about it."

Detective Lajoie heard a sharper note in Peggy's voice, a hurriedness. "You sure? After all, it makes sense. It could have been a girl who had her baby at home. You haven't heard of anyone? She might have said the baby was stillborn, or people didn't know she was pregnant. Some girls hide it pretty well. It didn't have to be here in Brewster—maybe Wakefield or Narragansett. You know anyone?"

"I don't know shit."

"Think, Peggy. If you want to get out of here, this is how you can do it. I'm only trying to help."

"Yeah, I bet." Peggy's eyes were fastened on the emerald-green pantsuit. But there was a change in Peggy's voice; it was quieter.

"You know, if you told me what I'm asking, we wouldn't need to keep you here in the house. We could put you in a nice hotel someplace. You'd have room service and space to move around. Probably an indoor pool. You just say the word and it's yours."

Peggy had turned back to the TV. Detective Lajoie glanced at her hands and wondered if she needed some cheap-looking rings to look even more pathetic. Peggy pushed herself up to a sitting position.

"What kind of hotel? I don't want any Days Inn."

"Tell me, Peggy, what would be your choice?"

"I want the Hotel Viking in Newport, a suite. And I want a pedicure."

Detective Lajoie looked motherly. "I don't see why we can't do that."

Peggy chewed on her thumbnail and then studied it. "There's a girl over in Wakefield who had a baby last June. People didn't know she was pregnant. I don't know her name or if she was in school. She lived with her dad."

Woody and Lajoie had thought that if there were other teenage mothers whose babies had been taken, they might be girls with one parent and no siblings, meaning as few witnesses as possible. And they'd be girls like Peggy and Nina, borderline students without a lot of friends.

"Anything else?"

"Isn't that enough?" Lajoie didn't answer, and Peggy stared at the TV. "But I don't think she was dragged out to the island. She just got fucked and the baby was taken. Maybe she was even paid for it, lucky slut. I don't know her last name."

"Where'd you hear this?"

"Someone was talking about it in the woods. I'm not sure who, maybe it was the guy I saw in CVS. I just heard a few words. He called this girl Marge or Margery, called her 'the easy one.' Can I go to the hotel now?"

Thursday morning Bingo Schwartz talked to Eric Degroot in the Providence Police Department's detective bureau, part of the new three-story Public Safety Complex on Washington Street just off 95. Bingo had decided Ronnie McBride was nowhere in Brewster, so he was looking further afield.

"These homeless guys are like snowbirds," said Detective Degroot. "Up north in the summer, down south in winter—they got a whole circuit. I mean, the panhandlers, the guys that sell cheap shit on the street, guys that rummage trash and collect returnable bottles. The ones who're just poor usually stay put; the crazies mostly stay put as well."

"My fellow's got a perfectly good house," said Bingo. "He only sleeps in this little alcove because he wants to. It's a grief thing. No closure."

Degroot shrugged. He had known Bingo for twenty years, and he had always been the "Mumbler." Whenever he wasn't talking, he'd be humming. He would probably be humming in his coffin. "Then your guy's crazy," he said.

"D'you often have people like that who just go missing, who disappear?"

"It's not like they got a fixed place of abode; most don't even have ID unless they've Social Security, or fake ID. They come and go, like I say. If we don't see one for a while it's no big thing. He'll usually be back in the summer."

"Maybe they're dead."

"That's possible. Alkies can be pretty fragile. If they're dead, it's most likely the sauce. Sometimes we get cases of guys beating up a derelict, like teenagers on a tear. We see that now and then, and a couple have been killed over the years. Your guy have enemies?"

Bingo scratched his belly and once again began to imagine retirement. "I doubt it. He checked into the alcove around ten at night and was gone by seven in the morning. He didn't panhandle and didn't bother anybody."

"Strange," said Degroot, "but what the fuck, he's only been gone a week. He's bound to turn up, you know how it is."

"He's never done this before. He's a bum of strict habits. I mean, he's not even a bum. He's eccentric."

"A wacko. Like they say, the city's got a million stories."

"Not Brewster." Bingo got to his feet. "So think about it for me. Why should he disappear? Let's say it's foul play, why should anyone bother? Kidnapping, abduction, murder, it makes no sense. But someplace there's a reason."

Degroot got up as well. He was thinner than Bingo and half a foot taller. Also he had all his hair. "I'll ask around. If we go on the assumption of foul play someone might have an idea."

Fifteen minutes later Bingo was driving south to New London on 95. He meant to ask the same questions to a New London detective he'd known for a decade or so: Do you ever have homeless men just disappear for good? Bingo already knew the answers, just as he'd known Degroot's answers. What he wanted was help with the questions.

Playing loudly on a CD was Samuel Ramey singing the "Whistle Aria" from Boito's *Mefistofele*—"I am the Spirit that always denies . . ."—the aria in which Mefistofele tempts Faust to widen his horizons, free his appetites, and enjoy a bit of satanic fun. Bingo liked all versions of Faust: Berlioz, Boehmer, Boito, Busoni, Gounod, Lutz, Pousseur, Prokofiev, Schnittke, Spohr, and Stravinsky. As a police officer he saw himself as a student of human temptation. What makes a person break the law in search of pleasures they can't afford? Bingo set that question next to his other question: Why should Ronnie McBride disappear? Somehow the two questions had a causal connection: if this, then that. He had only to find it.

As soon as Woody could get a search warrant on Thursday morning, he grabbed acting chief Bonaldo, Detective Gazzola, and Patrolman Morelli, and headed over to Benjamin Clouston's house on Ballou Street. Both Bonaldo and Gazzola had had other plans, while Morelli had hoped to take a nap somewhere. Woody had looked at them with what Bobby Anderson called his dead-eye stare, which was the look Woody got before he started yelling. As far as Woody was concerned, Clouston was top priority, unless Fred Fucking Bonaldo wanted Brewster to explode like a fucking pimple on an adolescent's butt.

"Well," Bonaldo had said, "if you put it like that . . ." He then remarked on Woody's negative attitude, which got him another scary stare.

A locksmith opened Clouston's front door. Woody entered and sniffed. The hall and living room had the sweet smell of a cheap motel room that's just been cleaned. The rug still bore the tracks of a vacuum; nothing was out of place; it was as innocuous as a model home in a slow market.

"Somebody's already been through here," said Woody, after he had checked out the downstairs.

"The clothes and stuff are still here," said Bonaldo. "Even his toothbrush."

"And what does that tell you?"

Bonaldo pondered. "Somebody else cleaned it out?"

"Exactly."

The six-room house was tidy and sparsely furnished. On the living room wall were photographs of forest scenes; the tan leather couch was positioned across from the flat-panel TV; a beige rug separated the two; a Bose entertainment system knit them altogether. The bed was made; the dishes had been washed; the clothes hung neatly in the closet; no dust bunnies lurked beneath the bed. A small office looked onto the backyard; the desk was empty except for pens, paper, and paper clips. There were computer cords but no computer. The two-drawer file cabinet was empty except for a file on Clouston's Toyota, a file on the Bose

Lifestyle home entertainment system, another on the Sony forty-two-inch plasma flat panel, a file of appliance warranties, and a file called "My Trip to Las Vegas." The books were best sellers of the techno-spy variety; the DVDs were Cary Grant comedies, a smattering of Jimmy Stewart, a dollop of Katharine Hepburn.

Woody made a call to Frank Montesano to bring in the CSI. "I need the whole place checked for prints, anything you can find."

Woody, Bonaldo, Morelli, and Detective Gazzola went outside to wait. Gazzola's nicotine-packed lungs wheezed like a busted concertina. He popped a Nicorette and lit up.

"This looks bad for Clouston." Woody moved away from Gazzola's cigarette. He glanced at two squirrels chasing each other through an oak and wondered about their emotional lives. No worries, most likely.

To Bonaldo, as a Realtor, the house seemed prepped for a sale, with all the blemishes airbrushed. "How so?"

"I doubt he was the one to clean out the house. So why was it done?"

Gazzola stubbed out his cigarette and considered lighting another. "He could have a girlfriend and have stuff over there. Like a double set of everything."

"Maybe." But Woody didn't think so.

During the morning, Clouston's friends and acquaintances were sought, first at the hospital, so when Woody reached the hospital at eleven o'clock, he was given a list of people to talk to, beginning with Dr. Joyce Fuller. Woody saw her in her office. She wasn't cool to him, but there was no sign they'd met before.

"Mr. Clouston's been here for nearly a year, and we were lucky to get him. He works in the area of surgical pathology, examining test results and gathering critical information about the stage and margin status of surgically removed tumors. He works under the pathologist and spends a lot of time at the microscope. But Mr. Clouston's also experienced in radiological techniques—ultrasounds, CT scans, MRIs."

"And why were you lucky to get him?" Dr. Fuller's office reminded Woody of Clouston's house: immaculate and anonymous. A photo of her father in uniform was on the desk, three framed diplomas hung on the wall.

"He's highly trained, and in a small hospital like this he has to wear several hats. He could have made far more money someplace else. But he loves the ocean. That's our big selling point. He fishes—surf casting, mostly—but he also has a small boat; and he swims. He offered me fish last summer. Unfortunately, I'm a vegetarian."

"So what's he get paid?"

"I don't know if I can tell you that."

"Yes, you can."

They stared at each other. Dr. Fuller looked away. "About eighty thousand."

"Anything you can say about what he looks like?" Woody had Clouston's photograph, but he liked to hear descriptions from different people.

"He's pretty average-looking, wears glasses, has a regular haircut—brown hair. He has very flat ears, that's one thing. If you looked at him straight on you'd hardly see them."

"Tall, short?"

"Average height. You probably wouldn't notice him unless you were looking for him. Except for those ears."

"Who's he hang out with?"

"I've no idea. I never wonder about their private lives."

Next Woody talked to the people with whom Clouston worked—technicians, doctors, nurses. They described him as quiet but friendly.

No one seemed to dislike him; on the other hand, he had no close friends.

"Not a party animal?" Woody asked a radiologist, Betsy Safarian.

Safarian gave him a blank look and then burst out laughing. "I saw him dance at the Christmas party last year. He looked like a tin soldier, like rigid."

One of the doctors who worked with Clouston was somebody Woody knew: Dr. Herb Serpa, a dermatologist.

The previous year Woody had had a benign wen, or trichilemmal cyst, removed from his back. Once out, it had looked like a bloody quail egg. Dr. Serpa, who had removed it, said, "You're lucky, I've seen them as big as goose eggs." He found this funny. "Goose eggs," he repeated.

"I went fishing for stripers with Benny once," said Dr. Serpa. "We each got a keeper and tossed back some shorties. He has a little boat I didn't like much. I felt like a carrot bobbing in a stew. Benny isn't a talker, that's for sure, but he's a great tech and a good fisherman as well. You tell me what's more important. This time of year, he does a lot of surf casting. Have you checked the beach?"

"Good idea." Woody stifled a yawn. "D'you know who his friends are, or anything about his other activities?"

"I see Benny talking to people now and then. I don't like to be nosy. No one dislikes him. He's great at what he does. He did a punch biopsy on your cyst, if I remember right. He could work in a top lab or a bigger hospital. Guys like that help make a hospital first-rate."

"Anything else?"

Dr. Serpa paused. "Oh, yes, the last time we went fishing, he mentioned a trip to Atlantic City. Most people, as you can imagine, go for the gambling, but he also fished, didn't catch anything, though."

"Did he mention gambling?"

"No, just the fishing."

"Does everyone call him Benny?"

"Benny? Why, I don't really know. I never thought about it."

Woody also talked to Dr. Jonathan Balfour. Like Dr. Fuller, he gave no sign of ever having met Woody before. Dr. Balfour kept looking at his watch and tapping his foot. It made Woody want to keep him there all day.

"We've had lunch two or three times, also coffee downtown. Mostly it was to talk about the results of an exam. He likes fishing, I recall. I haven't done any fishing since I was a kid. My dad used to drag us out in his boat, and Clouston offered to take me fishing, but I wouldn't dream of it."

"How come?"

"Every time my dad took us out, I'd get seasick and end up puking over the side. I don't plan to get on a boat again anytime soon."

"Does he have any woman friends or girlfriends?"

"Not that I know of. He talks to women, of course, but nothing stood out."

"Not Nurse Spandex?"

Balfour shot him an angry look. *Aha,* thought Woody, engaging in a sarcastic thought. *He remembers me after all.*

"No, not Nurse Spandex. Clouston's one of those self-contained types who're perfectly comfortable in their own company. Lucky for them, I've always thought. But you sometimes see it with people who spend their lives staring into a microscope."

"Did he ever mention trips he'd made to Atlantic City and Las Vegas?"

"Never. He didn't strike me as the showgirl type."

"What about gambling?"

"I can't imagine it."

Balfour looked at his watch. Often in interviews Woody envied

Bobby Anderson, who could turn his charm off and on as easily as a flashlight. It was easy for Bobby to convince someone he was sympathetic, that he cared about them, that he knew they were being treated unfairly. At times it was sincere, at times it wasn't, but whichever it was, Bobby used it as a tool and it was a tool Woody lacked. His charm barely went beyond saying hello. "Can't you at least *look* pleasant?" Susie used to say.

Woody spent the rest of the day talking to people but learned nothing more than he had learned from the first people he had talked to. To each he'd also asked, "D'you have any idea why Clouston would suddenly take off?" None could provide an answer, nor had they known he was leaving. In fact, his work had begun to pile up.

Woody had told Bonaldo to look into Clouston's history and family background. This Bonaldo delegated to others. By late afternoon, he had learned that Clouston grew up in Haslett, Michigan, and attended the University of Michigan, where he got a master's in medical technology and worked two years toward a Ph.D. His mother, who still lived in Haslett, said her son called about four times a year and also sent money. Though she "didn't really need it," she was glad to have it. She said Ben had first meant to be a doctor but then decided he didn't want "a bunch of needy patients yammering after him," and he didn't want to spend time doing a residency. She said she hadn't seen her son for about five years, but she knew he was busy, and as long as he was happy that was all that mattered.

Clouston also had an older brother who was a CPA in Seattle. They talked about three times a year, at Christmas and on their respective birthdays. Once he had visited Ben in Albany, where he was working in a lab—a business and pleasure trip. Ben had seemed great. The brother was seven years older and had left for college when Ben was eleven. Before that they'd gone to a bunch of University of Michigan football games over a three-year period. "I know he missed it after I was gone. He really loved the Wolverines."

Whole-Hog Hopper knew he wasn't much of a cop; that is, the knowledge was a flicker in the back of his mind. But he never let it bother him. "I got to eat, don't I?" He said this so often he could have had it printed on a T-shirt. His question argued that his need to put food on the table took precedence over ethical considerations, such as how well he was doing his job as a cop. But the question also brought to mind Whole-Hog's love of snacks. Just as philosophers are smitten with philosophy, so was Whole-Hog smitten with hunger pangs. He weighed three hundred twenty pounds, but he thought it looked good on him. It made him look like an offensive lineman, like the Patriots' Wesley Britt, who also weighed three hundred twenty pounds, though Britt was eight inches taller.

In general, Whole-Hog was the cop who stood in the street and directed traffic around utility workers and pavement repair teams. He was big; he could easily be seen; if a car hit him, it probably wouldn't hurt. Whole-Hog knew this, and while it didn't give him a sense of purpose, it defined his place in the department. He was also a cousin of Laura Bonaldo's, a connection that became significant when Bonaldo was named acting chief. That's why Whole-Hog got pissed when Bonaldo put him on the team checking out the island in Hancock Pond. Whole-Hog knew it was a punishment for fucking up when he was meant to be watching Peggy Summers. And yes, there'd been previous cases. He wouldn't deny it. But sitting in the patrol car, watching someone's front door for signs of activity, well, it made him hungry.

The trouble with being out in the country was there was no fast food. This was even truer of the island in Hancock Pond, where a body of water separated him from the shore. Whole-Hog didn't like water, except for bathing purposes and perhaps a little drinking. He felt its positive effects were exaggerated.

The best he could say about the island was it wasn't Great Swamp, which was thousands of acres of slop. That meant getting wet and sinking in the mud, and the trouble with weighing three hundred twenty pounds was it meant he sank deeper. "I could sink to fuckin' China," he told his wife. And his wife thought, *The sooner the better.*

So Whole-Hog was glad he wasn't over in the swamp with the dogs, chasing that nutcase. Like you had no choice where you walked in the swamp; you had to follow the frigging dog. Carl Krause might not even be in the swamp anymore, for Pete's sake, but they'd keep slogging around in the slop until the dogs gave up. Frigging dogs never mind slop; that was something Whole-Hog didn't like about dogs.

So even though Whole-Hog was pissed to be on the island, he wasn't as pissed as he would have been slopping through the swamp. And here on the island one of the troopers, Jason somebody, had already found a little figure made out of straw and twigs, about six inches tall, with its arms sticking out. No telling what it meant—a doll, probably. It'd been near the ashes of a big bonfire. A detective said that somebody had probably meant to burn it, but either it had been forgotten or somebody had thrown it at the fire and missed, which sounded like a lot of hooey. Anyway, the trooper who found the little figure got a bunch of pats on the back.

Then another trooper, Whole-Hog couldn't recall his name, found these weird prints. They looked like goat prints, but they were bigger than a goat's and they couldn't be a goat's because they were only the rear hooves and what kind of goat goes prancing around on its hind legs? And it had been a heavy sucker, because the hooves had sunk in the ground. Whole-Hog couldn't make sense of it, but it'd bothered the detective bad enough to get him on the horn to his boss, and soon he said the CIU was on its way, along with other crime scene guys. But the thing was, the trooper who'd found the prints got a bunch of pats on the back as well.

So Whole-Hog kept his eyes peeled, because if these guys found stuff and he didn't, then Bonaldo would think he was fucking up again, which he wasn't, and it was like those two troopers meant to make Whole-Hog look bad, which was something that had happened before.

The island was shaped like a rabbit's head with two ears, two peninsulas about two hundred yards long. The remnants of the bonfire had been found where the rabbit's nose would be. But Whole-Hog didn't know this; he knew only that through the trees on both sides he saw the water, and farther ahead, where the strip narrowed, he saw more water. He was poking along and kicking his feet through the leaves, hoping to find more of those little dolls; and he paid so much attention to his feet that he wasn't paying attention to what lay in front of him until he almost ran into it. It scared the living shit out of him.

"Hey, over here," he shouted. "I found somethin'!"

Leaning against a tree was a corpse with his legs stretched out straight, a dead guy whose glasses had slipped down his nose and whose eyes were shut like he was snoozing. His ears were set so close to his head that Whole-Hog had to check twice to make sure they hadn't been loped off.

But most important—and even Whole-Hog knew this was important—there was a bullet hole in the center of his forehead.

SIXTEEN

CARL HAD BEEN HURT. His back legs and shoulders were teeth-slashed and bitten, his pants bloody, his jacket torn. It was pitch-dark in the forest. He stumbled into trees and was jabbed by branches. Briars ripped his hands and face. Then he fell forward into the water. He lay on his back as the cold numbed him. It felt good. The sky was clear; the moon had yet to rise. The stars were brighter than he had seen them before. The Milky Way was a white splash. He heard no noise; the coyotes were gone. He lay on his back until he nearly lost consciousness, but he couldn't let that happen. He rolled over and stood up; the water reached his waist. He sloshed through it, wading along the shore, sometimes falling. He knew they would come with a dog. North of him was Great Swamp field headquarters, a cluster of buildings and garages—maybe a mile, maybe two miles away. He kept to the water but kept going north.

After half an hour Carl left the water and pushed his way through the trees, stumbling, falling, getting up again. He packed mud on his legs to stop the bleeding. Again the brambles tore at him. It made him laugh, how the forest was trying to hold him back. After another half-hour, he saw the outside lights of the field headquarters far ahead through the trees. He stumbled, falling onto his stomach; then he moved forward on all fours. He was a wolf. At these times he felt his best; he felt strong. At other times he couldn't remember where he was or what he was doing. He would stop and look around in the dark. It was like being blind. At these times he had been frightened. He had sat down against a tree, his arms wrapped around his knees. He had whimpered. He hadn't known what was true or not true. He recalled things far in his past, not big things or sentimental things. He recalled walking along a sidewalk on a summer morning in Oswego and how white the houses had looked. He recalled the green smells and the smell of the lake. But then his mind changed; he became strong again. He struck at himself, struck his weakness. He crawled forward again. Nothing was as strong as he was.

He found a utility shed and broke into it. The shed smelled of paint and turpentine. He felt his way around it on his hands and knees. He sniffed and touched things. When he found a pile of canvas drop cloths, he pulled them around him. He slept a little then.

When he woke, his fear came back. They were looking for him. The dogs would find his trail. Carl jumped to his feet and bumped an aluminum ladder hanging on the wall that clanged and jostled on its hooks. He made his way to the door and pushed it open. It was maybe a half-hour before sunrise—a gray sky with no stars visible. His clothes were still wet, and he was cold again. Leaving the door open, he began to rummage through the shed.

After ten minutes, he had found coveralls, rubber boots, and a Yankees cap. He put on the cap, rolled the boots up in the coveralls, and left the shed. Who was he now? He was Carl of the single claw. The ones who hunted him thought they had him on the run. They'd see who was hunting whom. They would hear his steps behind them. How fast they'd turn, but not fast enough. He had tasted coyote blood; now he wanted something sweeter.

He retraced his steps back to the water. He could see now, though the sun was still below the horizon. He waded through the water back the way he'd come. There were tangles of sticks and vines, fallen branches, clumps of wet leaves, a beaver house of sticks and mud. At times the water reached past his waist and he nearly fell. He held the coveralls and boots over his head. After a mile or so he made his way to the bank. When the water was a foot deep, he set the coveralls on a fallen trunk and took off his clothes. He kept the T-shirt. He soaked it in the water, wrung it out, and soaked it again. He twisted it until no more drops fell. Then he set it on the coveralls. He'd been cold before, now it was worse. Naked except for the Yankees cap, he wadded up his clothes, shoes, and jacket, and wedged them beneath the fallen tree trunk under the water. He put on the wet T-shirt, coveralls, and boots, and climbed onto the bank. Once in the woods, he found a trail. He turned south and began to run in order to warm himself. He felt good again. The boots were too big and flopped on his feet.

He reached Worden Pond and walked along the edge through the brush until he saw the old boathouse. When he was thirty yards away, he stripped off his boots, coveralls, and T-shirt, and reentered the water, naked again. He kept to the edge, but when he reached the boathouse, he worked his way around to the front. Boards were rotten, and some had fallen. He ducked down in the water and came up inside. The coveralls were only a little wet; he'd held them above him as much as he could. The rising sun shot splinters of light through the cracks in the boards, dappling the surface of the water. Carl climbed up on the rotting floor and got dressed again. He swept together the dead leaves and splinters of rotten wood, and made a bed, a nest. He'd sleep a little; he'd wait till dark.

• • •

When Detective Lajoie left Peggy Summers, she drove to the area detectives' office and got busy. First she set things moving to get Peggy out of her parents' house. She had already called Hotel Viking in Newport; the cop rate for a Mansion Suite was $200 a night. A bargain, she was told. The pedicure was another fifty. Detective Lajoie decided not to tell Captain Brotman right away. She'd wait till she dug up something good, and the first thing on her list was the girl, Marge or Margery. If she lived in Wakefield, then she went to South Kingstown High School; that was Detective Lajoie's best chance. Maybe, a faint maybe, she went to Narragansett High School, but Detective Lajoie couldn't fuss about faint maybes.

South Kingstown High School was on Columbia Street in a residential area and three miles from Great Swamp as the crow flies. Lajoie went straight to the main office and said she needed to see the principal. The receptionist—dark-haired, twenty-three, plump—said Dr. Jacobs wasn't seeing visitors today.

"Is he in his office?"

"Yes, but he can't see anyone. He's got a ton of paperwork." The receptionist couldn't take her eyes off Detective Lajoie's emerald-green pantsuit. She squinted as if it hurt her eyes.

Lajoie, in the minds of her fellow detectives, had two modes of behavior: compassionately benign and brutal. She leaned across the counter to whisper, and the receptionist leaned forward to hear. "Look, you silly-faced bitch, I need to see him this fucking second, or else."

The receptionist yanked back, her mouth in a perfect O. "I'll call security."

"Honey, I *am* security." She showed the receptionist her ID. "I'll get the whole South Kingstown Police Department to come down on you, unless you do what I say."

Two minutes later Detective Lajoie stood in the principal's office. His desk was covered with papers. "You frightened Ms. Henry," he said.

Detective Lajoie shrugged one shoulder. "Yeah, yeah. You got a student here by the name of Marge or Margery, sixteen or seventeen years old, lives in Wakefield with her father. She may have dropped out. I need her last name and address."

The principal took off his glasses, polished them, and then returned them to his nose. "I'm afraid that would be in violation of our privacy code."

Detective Lajoie leaned forward and picked up the telephone. "How do I get an outside line?"

Just as a breeze can ruffle the surface of a pond, so a nervous tremor flitted across the principal's features. "And your intentions?"

"I'm going to shut down your fucking school."

Seventeen-year-old Margery Kelly lived with her father, Phillip, on Jennifer Lane. Detective Lajoie retrieved her Mazda 6 and drove over. She'd been in the school twenty minutes. The South Kingstown High School Rebels, they were called. Rebels, ha! South Kingstown Pussies was more like it.

Phil Kelly didn't want to talk to the detective but was afraid to say no. Thin, fidgety, and forty-five, with a smattering of mouse-colored hair, he thought the detective's emerald-green pantsuit was too bright. It felt as if she were purposefully poking pins in his eyes. "Would you like a glass of orange juice or water? I'm afraid I don't drink coffee."

They sat in Kelly's living room, which was shabby but clean. The only picture on the wall was a framed black-and-white photograph of Kelly's parents standing in front of a tree. They, too, had a timid look. In a glass case was a display of twenty German beer mugs. Kelly and Detective Lajoie sat across from each other in matching faux-leather armchairs. The detective was in her compassionately benign mode, with a smile that suggested sympathy marbled with sadness. Kelly had already told her that "Maggie" had moved out at the end of August, taking the baby with her. The baby's name was Connor.

"Maggie never said who the father was, and I believe she lied about when the baby was due. I was visiting my mother in Danbury when Connor was born. A midwife came to the house. When I got home, there he was. A beautiful boy with bright blue eyes. I always took care of him when Maggie went out, and I gave him his bottle. Formula, of course." Kelly had a high tenor voice; he worked for Sovereign Bank, doing data entry.

"Do you know where she went?"

"New York or Philly—she's called from both places. Said the baby was doing fine. She even sent me money, a few hundred dollars to help with the heating oil."

"What sort of work's she doing?"

"Waitressing, I believe. She wasn't quite clear about it." Kelly began to fidget with a loose thread on the sleeve of his cardigan.

"A restaurant?"

"I believe so."

"Had she worked at restaurants before?"

"No, this was her first."

"And how much money did she send?"

Kelly tugged at the loose thread. "Five hundred dollars."

"When did she send it?"

"Toward the end of September."

"That's good for waitressing, supporting herself and a baby. And she's too young to work in a bar." Detective Lajoie intensified her expression of sympathy and mild sadness. "Mr. Kelly, I hate to ask this, d'you think your daughter might be involved in prostitution?"

Kelly looked stricken. It was the only answer Detective Lajoie needed.

Carl left the boathouse at four-thirty, when the sun was low in the sky. He hadn't slept much. He'd been cold, and his wounds hurt. One was getting infected. He could feel its heat. Several times he heard the distant barking of dogs. His mood swung between anger and fear, but mostly he'd been angry, picturing his enemies and what he'd do to them. He would hang Hercel and Lucy like he'd hung the cat. He would take bites out of them. He'd bury them where they'd never be found. He'd drag them into the swamp, shove them beneath a submerged log, and watch the bubbles rise to the surface till they stopped. The pleasure he got from such images was almost a sexual pleasure. As for the old man, Carl wanted his rifle for business he had to settle in town. And if the chance arose, he'd shoot that colored cop. He would peel away that black skin and make himself a pair of socks. These plans kept Carl busy much of the day. He even had plans for the sheepdog.

He worked his way toward the southeast. Crows were busy in the trees; he knew they were telling the coyotes where to find him. He felt the hatred of everything. Even the trees hated him. He liked being hated. It made him strong. He thought back far into his past and saw the faces of people who'd done him harm. He imagined sticking them with his claw; he imagined biting. Still, and very briefly, came moments of panic when he would ask what he was doing. In those moments, he felt like a tiny thing; he wanted to lie down and curl into a ball. They didn't last long.

Carl reached the stone wall at five-thirty. For the past half-hour, he had heard the coyotes; they were getting closer. He still had his claw, but then he picked up a thick branch and smashed it against a rock till he had broken off a piece about three feet long. He swung it a few times. It was his baseball bat; he'd hit some home runs. Not baseballs, though; he'd hit heads. They would bust like old pumpkins. He'd hit any heads that came his way. Just see if he didn't.

Carl had just crossed the wall when the Bouvier began barking and running in his direction. It didn't worry him; it made him glad. Crouched over, he began running toward the house, great big steps. The big rubber boots went *clomp, clomp*. He could hardly wait for the dog to reach him. It made his mouth wet.

They met halfway between the house and the wall. When the dog leapt, Carl swung the broken branch, his baseball bat, clubbing the dog. Home Run Number One. The dog fell, whimpered, and tried to get up. Carl clubbed it again. Home Run Number Two. Carl began to run toward the house again. About now, the old man would be getting his rifle. Carl meant to get there first.

Barton was struggling with the front door, steadying the walker and shifting the Winchester from one arm to the other. He didn't know where the kids were. As he opened the door, he realized Gray had stopped barking. At that moment, Carl smashed into him like a freight train hitting a tricycle. Barton was thrown back onto the floor. As he raised his head, Carl clubbed him with his baseball bat. Home Run Number Three. Then he picked up the rifle and went searching for Hercel and Lucy.

The kids had been in the barn, looking for goose eggs, but they stopped when they heard Gray barking. Hercel went to the barn door and saw Carl running across the field toward the Bouvier. He pushed Tig and Lucy back behind him. Then Carl clubbed the dog. Hercel even heard the thump. His terror was such that he had to clamp his jaw shut to keep from screaming. Carl disappeared from view, and moments later he heard a crash as Carl knocked Barton to the floor, though

Hercel didn't know what the noise meant. Instead, very briefly, he thought Barton had beaten Carl, that he'd captured him and was tying him up, or maybe he had killed him. But then he heard doors slamming; he heard the growling.

Hercel ran back into the barn, meaning to hide. But wouldn't Carl look for them in the barn if he couldn't find them in the house? Could he keep Lucy quiet, and, even if he could, wouldn't Carl find them anyway? He stopped and put his hands to his temples. He tried to will something to move, something, anything, a ball, a rag, pieces of straw. He pointed his thoughts at it; he tried to push it, make it fly. Nothing happened. His fear got in the way of his concentration; he kept thinking he had to hurry, that he couldn't wait.

Tig stood just inside the barn door, holding Lucy by the hand. "He's smashing stuff in there. I don't know where Granddad is." She paused. "Hercel, I'm really scared."

Hercel knew he had to make up his mind. He couldn't let himself be scared as well. "We'll go into the woods. We'll go out the back of the barn and keep it between us and the house. Then we'll circle around to the road."

"What about coyotes?"

"Maybe it's too early for them. I'll get some kind of weapon."

Tig looked doubtful; Lucy was about to cry. The crashing and breaking glass continued, a steady, violent slamming and clangor.

"Tig, what else can we do?"

She squinched her eyes shut and moved back into the barn, leading Lucy. The little red lights in the heels of Lucy's sneakers blinked on and off. Hercel ran to look for a weapon. The thought seemed ridiculous to him. How could he fight Carl?

Hercel found a large screwdriver and a garden spade. It was almost funny. Tig kept saying, "Hurry, hurry!" Hercel thought if he had more time, he could find a better weapon, maybe a pitchfork. He grabbed up the screwdriver and spade, and ran to the back door of the barn.

Outside, they ran toward the wall. They kept stumbling. The crashing stopped; a moment later a door slammed. Hercel and Tig each had one of Lucy's hands, and they pulled her so fast that her feet hardly touched the ground.

"Stop, stop, you're hurting me!"

"Be quiet," urged Hercel.

They had almost reached the wall when Carl shouted, "I see you little fucks!"

This was immediately followed by a gunshot. The bullet pinged off the wall. Then came another shot that made a different sound that was more muffled. Hercel hardly thought about it. He helped Lucy over the wall.

"Gray's lying back in the field!" Tig could hardly control her voice.

There was a third shot, the rifle again. Hercel and Tig climbed over the wall, picked up Lucy, and ran into the forest. They heard no more gunshots. They felt sure Carl was running across the field. They felt sure they could hear his footsteps. Hercel dropped the spade; the screwdriver was stuck in his belt; they kept running. Hercel heard the distant yapping of coyotes. Soon all that could be seen was the red sparkling of Lucy's shoes.

Captain Brotman called the meeting of his task force for six o'clock, but he knew some wouldn't be able to make it. The town was swarming with TV crews, radio and print reporters. Major Lancellotti, deputy superintendent and chief of field operations, had already called twice, and Colonel Schaeffer, head of the state police, had called once. Next he expected a call from the governor. Brotman hoped this was a joke, but it really wasn't, because each minute the whole business made him look worse.

He was being nibbled away by calamity as if being pecked to death by swans. The TV and radio stations wondered why the police hadn't done more; the *ProJo* had run a critical editorial. Every time Brotman left or entered police headquarters, he was mobbed. The discovery of Benjamin Clouston's body and the rest of the stuff on the island was the icing on the cake, but even as the thought passed through his mind, he asked what made him believe it wouldn't get worse. When Brotman had got to police headquarters an hour earlier, a reporter had shouted if he meant to call out the National Guard. Brotman would have put in for early retirement, but he knew he'd be fired before he began the paperwork.

When Woody entered the conference room, he thought Brotman had aged ten years. He seemed less tall, less imposing. There was no sign of the assurance he had shown over the past week. He nodded to Woody, who nodded back.

I hope he's not going to blame me for anything, Woody thought. Then he realized everyone had the same thought, beginning with Brotman. Boys and girls, let's play the Blame Game.

Bobby entered hurriedly and took a seat across the table from Woody. He glanced at Woody and winked. Woody decided he looked irritatingly cheerful.

Bingo Schwartz entered, humming some god-awful something. Woody saw that at least ten men and women wanted to tell him to shut up. Woody felt the same way. Then he thought, *It's time to start my deep-breathing exercises.*

Detective Lajoie entered wearing the worst pantsuit Woody had ever seen in his life, with a terrible gold necklace and terrible gold earrings to match. Detective Gazzola looked at her with his pencil raised and his mouth open. Then he tore his gaze away as if turning away from a car crash. Captain Brotman considered mentioning the emerald-green pantsuit, ran over a number of possible remarks, and chose silence.

Acting chief Bonaldo hurried in, saying, "Sorry, sorry." He stumbled and bumped the chair of the FBI agent, who barked, "Do you have to . . . ?"

"Sorry, sorry!" Bonaldo took his seat and mopped his brow with a gray handkerchief. He caught Woody's eye and gave a nervous smile; the kind of smile, Woody thought, that a kid makes when he's brought before the principal. Woody started to look away but then smiled back. His cheek muscles made a noise like a creaking door.

So they entered by ones and twos until sixteen people sat at the table. None looked happy, though Detective Lajoie looked pleased with herself. *She's probably patting herself on the back for the deal she got on the pantsuit,* thought Woody. If this goes on another week, we'll shoot one another. Briefly, the only sound was the hum of the fluorescent lights.

Captain Brotman got to his feet, staring at a paper on the table and at nothing else. He cleared his throat. "Benjamin Clouston was killed by a single shot to the forehead from Hartmann's nine-millimeter Browning. The shell casing found on the ground matched the rounds in Hartmann's box of Winchester nine-millimeters. The slug passed through his brain and ended up God knows where. When he was found he'd been dead about twenty-four hours. His Toyota Solara was located in a ball-field parking lot in Tuckertown, about a half a mile from the island. Near the body and leading to and from the shore were the footprints of size eleven-D Timberland Pro Terrenes. In addition, there were goat tracks, an abnormally large goat walking on its hind legs. Two six-inch straw dolls were also found. The remnants of the bonfire are still being sifted. So far a number of bone fragments have been discovered, possibly human. This information has been made public by a Brewster police officer. Mr. Bonaldo, would you like to comment on this?"

Nobody in the room missed the "mister," least of all acting chief Fred Bonaldo. "Not much to add. A police officer called some friends.

Those guys called some other guys. A little while ago reporters started calling to see if it was true about the goat tracks. We been telling them 'no comment.'"

"Who's the cop?" asked Joe Doyle, the South Kingstown lieutenant.

Bonaldo glanced around the room, as if seeking a quick way out. "Patrolman Frank Hopper."

"Is he the one called Whole-Hog Hopper?" asked Doyle.

Bobby Anderson gave a snort, but nobody else found anything funny.

"Yes, I believe that's what some people call him."

"Didn't he let you down on other occasions? In one, he was supposed to be keeping an eye on Alice Alessio, and on the other he was watching Peggy Summers. Isn't that right?"

"He just scooted away for a jiffy to get something to eat."

Nobody spoke. As Bobby said later, "We left Bonaldo to fry in his own grease and listened to him snap, crackle, and pop."

Technically, an officer from another jurisdiction, even a lieutenant, had no right to speak like this to a police chief. But it wasn't the words; it was the scorn.

Joe Doyle's red face got a little redder. "Have you dismissed him?"

"Well, I was going to suspend him."

Doyle started shouting. "He should be fucking dragged out and strung up from a branch!"

"You're out of line, Doyle!" shouted Brotman. "Shut up or get out! And you, Bonaldo, stay where you are!"

Fred Bonaldo had jumped up and meant to flee the room. Slowly, he sat back down. *Chaos outside,* thought Woody, *chaos inside.*

There was a long moment of silence. Nobody wanted to speak. Then Bobby asked, "Captain, how do you explain the goat tracks?"

"I don't. People in town are saying it's the Devil. I prefer not to believe that. The CIU kept going over the island till dark. Two guys from the URI crime lab were with them. Then they stopped till lights could be brought. Perhaps they've started again, I don't know. I don't need to tell you Patrolman Hopper's remarks won't make our work easier." There was another moment of silence, and then Brotman, as Bobby said, "lost it." "D'you fucking know what that means, Bonaldo?" Brotman stopped himself; he looked down at the table. Joe Doyle had a mean little grin.

There was another silence. Bobby thought Bonaldo resembled a turtle trying to pull its head into its shell, but the turtle's neck gets stuck and it gets bug-eyed and makes glug-glug noises. As for Bonaldo, he wondered if this was the time to say that Patrolman Hopper was his wife's first cousin. The choice between being screamed at by Brotman or screamed at by his wife and her entire family, well, it was a toss-up.

"What's with the straw dolls, sir?" asked Detective Gazzola.

Captain Brotman nodded to one of the DEM investigators.

"They're used to cast spells," said the investigator. "The doll's supposed to be the person you're cursing. After reciting the curse, you throw it in the fire."

A little more oxygen was sucked from the room. No one looked at anyone else. It wasn't that Woody believed in curses and voodoo dolls or whatever, he just didn't like it when others did.

"As for Benjamin Clouston," Brotman continued, "his fingerprints were among those found in the hospital nursery, though he may have been there for legitimate reasons. You have something you wish to add, Woody?"

"Yes, sir." Woody pulled himself together and then described the little he'd learned from Clouston's neighbors and colleagues at the hospital. "Clouston made trips to Las Vegas and Atlantic City. I've sent his picture and description, along with his credit card numbers, to the police in those places. What's his gambling history? How often has he visited? I said it was urgent and sent the same stuff to the Connecticut state police casino unit to see if Clouston has been gambling at Foxwoods and Mohegan Sun. Clouston's computer and records were taken from his house sometime on Wednesday. The crime scene investigation turned up absolutely nothing. However, the hospital direct-deposited his paycheck into a Bank of America account. The financial crimes unit has taken over the business of tracking his credit cards."

At the end of it, Bobby asked, "Can you say more about what he did at the hospital?"

Woody described Clouston's work as a pathology technician. "Everybody said he was first-rate at his job and could have made more money elsewhere. I was told he also loved to fish."

"So," said Bobby, "what's a top slabman doing in Brewster?"

"What did you say?" asked Captain Brotman.

"Slabman's what they used to call a pathologist's assistant or anatomical pathology technologist. That's the gold-plated description. In the old days, a slabman worked with the coroner or pathologist, removing and weighing the organs and then stitching the guy back together to make him presentable for Mom and Pop."

The police officers digested this bit of wisdom. Bonaldo fidgeted and thought of raising his hand, then just broke in. "Did this guy know Ham Brantley, you know, Brantley's Funeral Home?"

"Why should he?" asked Joe Doyle, after a moment.

Bonaldo had been afraid of this. "Well, you know, they had dead bodies in common. It seems a possibility."

Captain Brotman gave no indication that he'd heard Bonaldo. Instead, he asked Bobby to talk about Carl Krause.

"You remember," said Bobby, unable to help himself, "Krause is the distraction that Lieutenant Doyle was worrying about. . . ."

Captain Brotman broke in: "Never mind that, Bobby."

So Bobby described Carl's breakdown, Harriet's murder, and Carl's pursuit of the children. He said Carl had been growling and running on all fours. Nobody in the room seemed to be breathing. Bobby left nothing out—Bernie's rescue of the children, the use of the canine unit, the fat woman at the convenience store, Carl fighting with coyotes, Barton Wilcox and his Winchester, Carl's flight into the swamp, where the dog lost his trail.

"They restarted the search this morning with two dogs, and they picked up his trail where he'd come out of the water. Carl was traced to a utility shed at the field headquarters, where he spent part of the night. He left early this morning, and they lost him again when he reentered the water."

Bobby went on to what he had learned about coyotes, or coywolves, as well as what people had told him about shape-shifting. Woody shifted in his seat. The very subject of shape-shifting made him angry.

"This is all bullshit," he interrupted. "We've got to strip everything away and look at the baby. There's no such thing as shape-shifting or werewolves or vampires or shit like that. There's no such thing as black magic or white magic or gray magic. Their phony spells don't work. We need to get back to the baby! Once that's figured out, the rest will fall into place."

Bobby thought, *Don't lose it, my friend, don't lose it.*

Most everyone in the room understood there was a split between what they knew to be true and what they believed might be true. They knew Woody was right, but they had trouble being certain about it. First came the snakes and then the scalping. Each incident was more shocking than the last, and, as Woody had said on the first night, within this mass of barbarity the baby had been forgotten.

The FBI said the search for the baby was continuing as vigorously as ever, but so far nothing had been found. Nor had any more been learned about Hartmann's activities in Massachusetts, although people were being sought. Several detectives described interviews with Wiccans, but nothing had been learned about possible Satanists. Still, as one detective said, "I bet they're out there somewhere."

Bobby realized that despite Woody's warning half the people in the room thought it likely that the events in Brewster had supernatural causes.

Bingo Schwartz described talking to detectives from Providence to New London, but he still had no leads about Ronnie McBride. The medical examiner's office had reported that Nina Lefebvre had almost certainly committed suicide. Others spoke, and other ideas were thrown around.

"There was this guy Bobby and I talked to," said Woody. "Another nutcase, most likely. He said it was wrong to think of this stuff as suddenly happening. He said it had probably been going on beneath the surface for some time and we were wasting our time by looking at the bits and pieces rising to the top. He said we have to come up with an inference about what's causing it. The thing is, every one of us *knows* this to be true. We have to see that to blame it on Satanism is the wrong inference. Somebody's organizing all this satanic shit. Somebody's doing it so we don't see something else, like the baby."

Detective Beth Lajoie put up a hand and waggled it. She had three new rings with chunks of green and yellow glass, though maybe they were plastic. She was in her benign mode and smiled sweetly. "I'd like to say a few words, if I may."

If people hadn't been looking at her it was probably because of the green pantsuit. They had been pretending she wasn't in the room.

"Peggy Summers opened up to me," said Detective Lajoie, "though

I had to bribe her, but I'll get to that later." She described learning about Maggie Kelly and getting the girl's name and address from South Kingstown High School. She described talking to the girl's father and the birth of a baby boy named Connor. She said the girl had left home and sent her father money from New York and Philadelphia.

"I don't think the baby's fine," said Lajoie, "and I don't think she took him out of state. I think she sold him. I also think, and her dad thinks this, too, that she's working as a hooker in either New York or Philly. I've sent her picture and vitals to both places marked ASAP. As for Peggy Summers, she's shacked up in a suite at the Hotel Viking at two hundred bucks a night, so we better solve this cluster-fuck before our pip-squeak state goes broke."

Detective Lajoie leaned back and held her new rings up to the light to watch them sparkle. Each person in the room understood that she was the only cop who had learned anything worth a hill of beans, and Detective Lajoie was glad they knew it.

Half an hour later, when Woody and Bobby left the meeting, they both felt that they had gone through a recycling compactor and had been spit out in little cubes.

"I need a vacation," said Bobby.

That's as far as he got before Woody's cell phone rang. Bobby watched his face. It didn't get angry; it got sadder.

"Barton Wilcox is in an ambulance on the way to the hospital. He was shot and may not live. A trooper dropped by the farm to check on Barton and found the gate smashed to pieces and the sheep wandering around. The dog was beaten, the kids are nowhere to be found, and Barton's car was stolen—a Volvo 240 wagon. We've got to figure it's Carl and now he's armed. The canine unit's on its way, and maybe they can pick up a trail. But if the kids are with Carl, they're fucked."

• • •

When Carl Krause clubbed Barton, he had been knocked to the floor, unconscious and bleeding. Carl had every intention of hitting him again, but then he'd seen Harriet's miniature dachshund peering at him from farther down the hallway. Carl sprang up and hurled the club at the dog. It missed and banged off the wall. The dog fled to another room.

The farmhouse had a central stairway, so the downstairs rooms formed a square around it. As Carl rushed after the dog, it ran from room to room, sometimes hiding under a couch till Carl had passed, sometimes running out ahead of him. Carl had picked up his club and smashed whatever lay in his path—vases, small tables, glassware, windows, whatever was breakable. Within five minutes the dog had disappeared. The sound of breaking formed a cacophonous torrent, an uninterrupted clamor, as Carl stormed from one room to the next.

But it was Hercel he wanted, Hercel and the girl; he wanted to twist them, until at last he listened to his own desires and fetched the rifle. Barton lay on the floor where he had fallen, his forehead bloody. Carl never gave him a glance. He grabbed the rifle and ran to the stairs, certain he would find Hercel in an upstairs room.

Carl kept smashing furniture and breaking glass, but he couldn't find Hercel or the girl. He knew nothing about Tig. Then, looking out the window, Carl saw the barn in the fading light. That's where Hercel was. He was sure of it.

When Barton had opened his eyes, he didn't know what had happened or where he was, didn't know if he was dead or alive. All he knew was the pain in his head. Then he tasted the blood trickling down his cheek into his mouth. He grew aware of Carl shouting, growling, and smashing things downstairs as he ran from room to room. Barton tried to move but couldn't manage it. His Colt revolver was locked in the hall table, but the key was in the belly drawer of his desk in the study. Then he saw the Winchester on the hall rug. He didn't do anything about it. He only thought about it.

Carl ran into the hall, glanced at Barton, and then grabbed the Winchester and clumped upstairs.

Barton tried to put himself together, piece by little piece. He could move a hand; he could move an arm. He raised himself up and fell back to the floor. He raised himself once more and fell back again. He kept trying.

Shortly, Carl ran back downstairs. "Little fucks, little fucks!" he repeated; then he growled. He ran to the front door and stumbled over the walker. He kicked at it, and then kicked at the little table, knocking it over.

The moment Carl was out the door, Barton crawled to the table. The drawer was still locked; Barton hit the underside of the drawer with his fist. The wood was thin, nothing like the thick oak of the surface. The Colt bumped around inside. He kept hitting the drawer. First it cracked; then it broke. Barton hit it again.

Looking out over the field, Carl saw the red lights on Lucy's sneakers. "I see you little fucks!" he shouted. He raised the Winchester to his shoulder and fired. But he was too hasty; he knew he was too hasty. The bullet ricocheted off the wall. He pulled back the bolt and ejected the shell.

This time Carl aimed the Winchester until he was certain Hercel was in his sights. That's when Barton Wilcox shot him. The bullet ripped through Carl's left shoulder and out the other side. At first he didn't know he'd been shot. He didn't even feel pain. All he knew was his arm didn't work. Carl turned and saw Barton cocking the revolver. Lifting the Winchester with his right arm, Carl fired at the old man. Barton jerked and rolled over.

Now Carl began to hurt. He felt warm blood running down his skin under his coveralls. He walked toward the field; his legs felt rubbery. There was no sign of the kids, and he knew he couldn't catch them. He turned toward Barton's station wagon parked by the side of the house. Carl wasn't done yet. He opened the door and fell onto the seat. The key was in the ignition. As Barton Wilcox liked to say: "Who's going to stroll in here to steal an old car? It's better to leave the key where I can find it."

Carl backed around and headed toward the gate. He had neither the strength nor inclination to open it. He tromped on the gas and shifted to second. The engine screamed. He was probably doing forty when the station wagon smashed through the gate. His shoulder hurt bad now. There was a kid's pink sweater on the passenger's seat. Carl shoved it under the coveralls against the hole in his shoulder. He waited to feel good again. "I'm not done yet," he repeated.

SEVENTEEN

AT FIRST THE COYOTES didn't seem to be getting closer; then they did. Hercel, Tig, and Lucy had fled into the woods, and now Hercel knew they were lost. He didn't know which was north or south; he didn't know where the road was or where the farm was. It was nearly dark. Lucy didn't want to run anymore; she wanted to lie down. In his frustration, Hercel wanted to say awful things to her: "Carl wants to eat you." It shocked him, and he said nothing. He looked in every direction, but they all looked the same. At first, above him, he could see the trees' leafless branches, but as the darkness increased, the branches blurred together. They kept stumbling; branches whipped their faces. They had to stop running; even walking was difficult.

Tig wept, but she didn't let go of Lucy's hand. She pictured Gray lying in the field and knew something awful had happened to Barton. She'd never been threatened before. Her fear was an awful creature in her head. It was like she was living another person's life.

"They're coming," said Hercel.

It wasn't necessary to explain what he meant; Tig heard them, too.

They tried to run again, and then Tig slipped into the water. She held Lucy's right hand and Hercel held her left. Tig fiercely gripped Lucy without even knowing it, and the child screamed. Hercel pulled from the other side; briefly, Lucy was yanked between them. Then Tig fell. She breathed hard for a moment and got to her feet. Hercel had knelt down next to his sister and was patting her back, shushing her. He imagined the coyotes listening to her weeping. They would chuckle and point in their direction with their paws. At last Lucy grew still. Now Hercel also heard coyotes in front of them; he said nothing about it.

They moved off again in a little chain, staying away from the water, trying not to be caught by the vines and brambles. As it grew darker, the blinking red lights on the heels of Lucy's sneakers grew brighter.

"They're getting closer, aren't they?" asked Tig. It was hardly a question.

"I guess so." Hercel knew the coyotes could have caught them already, and he wondered why they hadn't. Maybe they were playing some awful game.

He kept looking for a tree to climb, but he couldn't see any until they were right in front of him. All had branches too high. Hercel knew he could shimmy up a tree by himself, but that would leave Tig and Lucy by themselves. He took the screwdriver from his belt. It looked silly but felt comfortable.

But soon they could go no farther. The coyotes were all around them, even though Hercel couldn't see them yet. Their yapping sounded eager and boastful.

"What about those rocks?" said Tig.

To their left in the last of the light, in a clearing away from the water, Hercel saw a pile of rocks, not part of a crumbling wall but a dozen or so boulders on a rise. Hercel followed Tig and Lucy toward them, but he knew it was hopeless. Even if they could wedge themselves between the boulders, the coyotes would dig them out like a seagull plucking a clam from its shell. In the clearing, he could see the first stars. Soon it would be pitch-dark. He picked up a small rock, then another. Maybe if they scrunched down by the boulders, the coyotes wouldn't see them. *What a dumb idea,* Hercel thought. But what else could he do?

By the time they squatted down with their backs to the boulders, the coyotes were very close, but Hercel still couldn't see them. Then, when he saw a shadow, he threw a rock. It bumped harmlessly along the ground. He threw the next one even harder, and it knocked against a tree. No, he had to concentrate. He had to make his fear be quiet. The yapping got louder; it sounded like laughing.

Sitting on the ground, Hercel found a stone and then two more. He cleared a small place in the dirt and put them together. He heard Lucy whimpering, but he tried to ignore it. He heard Tig make a noise and then throw a rock like girls threw rocks—not very well. Hercel took the screwdriver and drew a circle around the three little stones. He traced the tip of the screwdriver around the circle; he did it again and again. He did it faster as if he were stirring eggs in a bowl like he did when he helped his mother make a cake. The very thought of his mother made him lose his concentration. He wrenched it back.

"Hercel, I see them!" cried Tig. "Do something!"

Hercel traced the tip of the screwdriver around the circle and concentrated. He did it again; he did it faster; he kept doing it. The tip of the screwdriver dug into the dirt. All the bad things in his head—the fears, grief, the awful pictures conjured up by his imagination—one by one, he set them aside. He heard a noise, not a coyote, not a stone bumping on the ground. It wasn't the wind. It was a whooshing noise. The tip of the screwdriver traced the circle. Hercel stared at it; as he did it faster, the noise got louder. It included clickings and scrapings. He didn't look up.

"Hercel, the leaves are blowing around us! And sticks!"

It might have been caused by the wind, but there was no wind, only the wind caused by the rushing leaves as they circled faster, circled the boulder against which the three children pressed themselves. A stick was snatched up to join the leaves, now another and a third, until dozens of sticks dived and darted among the leaves circling the boulders. Now a small stone was picked up, now another, and the circling mass of leaves and dirt, twigs, and stones thickened and wheeled, whirring and clicking, and through it all Hercel stared at the ground and traced the tip of the screwdriver around the circle gouged in the dirt; and just as his hand sometimes slipped an inch or so away from the circle, so a bulge would briefly appear in the whirling mass; and the noise grew louder with snapping and ticking, a chatter of pebbles and little bits, which enclosed Hercel and the girls like a vertical tube, a tubular cyclone, so that someone standing outside would see only a spinning wall.

But then darkness rushed into Hercel's head like water into a bowl, and he collapsed. All the million bits and pieces flew outward into the trees in a final crashing and rattling, and the noise stopped.

The next thing he knew Tig was shaking him and calling his name, "Hercel, Hercel!" Hercel jumped up and tried to peer around him through the dark. The coyotes were gone.

"Everything flew," said Tig. "It scared them. What was it? Did you do it, Hercel? What happened?"

Hercel leaned back against the boulders and put his arm around Lucy, who had stopped whimpering. "I don't know what it was," he said. "I fainted. We're just lucky, that's all." But Hercel knew very well what it was.

They huddled together to stay warm. There was no point in wandering off. It was now pitch-dark, and they'd only fall into the water. They would have to stay where they were until morning and hope the coyotes didn't come back.

Hercel was just dozing off when he heard a barking. He felt a rush of fear, before he realized it was a dog, not a coyote. It was a dog from the canine team, following their trail. It was getting closer.

Seymour Hodges and Jimmy Mooney had parked the ambulance behind Dunkin' Donuts and were indulging in a box of mixed doughnuts and two large coffees with cream and extra sugar. Although it was only nine o'clock, they had been on the run all night, picking up, hauling, and off-loading. Most recently, they'd picked up Barton Wilcox and code-threed him to Morgan Memorial, with Seymour working on him in the back and yelling at Jimmy to go faster. No way Jimmy wanted to cash in his chips broadsiding a truck. He had hurried but hadn't rushed; that was how he saw it.

"You think that old guy's going to make it?" Jimmy's mouth was full of maple cream.

Seymour didn't answer.

"I said, d'you think . . ."

"I heard you all right. How the fuck should I know?"

"You seen guys gut-shot before."

"Not old guys. Least the round went straight through him, so that's a good thing. Sometimes you can make a mess digging it out, like digging a beetle outta oatmeal. Very sloppy." Seymour was concentrating on rolling a joint.

"Least it's the icing on the cake for working with Digger. Carl's out of a job."

"I already been hired."

"Yeah, but this's the icing on the cake. Fuckin' Carl's brains must've been like the fuckin' Fourth of July—a Catherine wheel with spider rockets and flaming peonies tossed in like salt and pepper."

Seymour inhaled half his joint. After a moment, he croaked, "What'd you do to him?"

"This and that." Jimmy decided not to tell Seymour about the little joke he had played with Ronnie McBride's head bumping against Carl's window.

"Like what?"

"Cranked 'im up, that's all. Put a scare into him. You read about that Burn Palace in Sweden where the guy's using stiffs to heat the place? Recycles the heat to make the place toasty. Doesn't pay a dime on heating oil. Now he's working on heating houses in the town. The more stiffs you cook, the more heat you make. Stands to reason. That's what they mean by ecology, right? If I end up running Digger's Burn Palace, we could heat half of Hope Valley. Some guy could cook his aunt Betty and use the heat for his own house. What d' you think? It could be a real moneymaker. Right now all that heat's just floating away in the sky for nothing. Hey, Seymour, you awake?"

Seymour was holding the last of the roach and trying not to burn his fingers. Then, when the flame had gone out, he'd eat it. "Yeah, yeah."

"You gonna be all right workin' for Digger?"

"Sure, why not?" He popped the roach in his mouth.

"It can get, you know, kinda creepy."

Seymour readjusted himself, getting himself comfortable for a little nap. "It's nothin' worse than I seen in Iraq. Been there, done that."

Larry Rodman had filled the small graphite crucible that he'd set on his stove with twelve-carat wedding rings. Then he turned on his acetylene torch and pulled down his mask. He meant to make a little gold porridge that he would pour into an ingot mold. It was nothing he hadn't done before, but now he was doing the whole lot. He had even picked the diamonds out of the engagement rings and packed them in a matchbox. It didn't take a rocket scientist to tell him his time in Brewster was about up—maybe tomorrow, maybe the day after, but it was coming. He would melt his gold, pack his bags, and get ready to fly.

Larry had heard about Carl killing some woman on the police radio. He could have told Digger that Carl was a mistake. Some guys weren't good with the stress. They'd pop like balloons. Larry had seen it happen and he didn't plan to get hit with the shrapnel.

The whole risk factor had gotten cranked sky-high. People got greedy; they never had enough. That's why Larry contented himself with a little gold, a handful of diamonds. He wasn't a big-car kind of guy. He didn't drink; he didn't gamble. His needs were modest.

All that remained was a little work at the Burn Palace, a few odds and ends. Then he would pack up his tools. He had to leave town before Halloween and get out before the fireworks started.

Woody had been with the canine team that had found Hercel and the girls. He had been one hundred percent positive they were dead, that either the coyotes had got them or they'd been dragged off by Carl. When he heard Hercel call out to them tears came to his eyes. This had shocked him almost as much as learning the kids were safe. He hadn't wept since he was Lucy's age. He wasn't sure how he felt about it.

He carried Lucy all the way back to Barton's farm. She wasn't hurt, but she was cold. Tig tried to tell him some kind of story about how the wind, a wind like a tornado, had roared and roared and scared the coyotes, driving them away. It made no sense, and Woody figured she'd been dreaming. Hercel walked by his side and didn't speak.

Woody didn't let the kids inside the house because the hallway was smeared with Barton's blood and the house was filled with wreckage from Carl's assault. It seemed everything that could break had been broken. The big question was what to do with Hercel and the girls. Bernie was at the hospital with Barton, and the kids couldn't be left alone. Then it was decided to take them to Fred Bonaldo's. Hercel and Baldo were friends, and Bonaldo's wife, Laura, said of course they'd be welcome. She had started weeping when Woody described what had happened. It seemed to Woody that the whole town should be weeping, like it was their duty.

So Woody went back into the house to pack a bag. Tig had to tell him where everything was. It was odd collecting little girls' underthings. A neighbor came to take care of the sheep, and tomorrow Bernie would decide what to do with them.

Police were called in from neighboring towns to assist in the search for Carl who had taken Barton's 1992 dark blue Volvo 240 wagon. An APB was broadcast across three states with warnings that Carl was armed and dangerous. Woody joined the search, which meant monitoring the radio and driving to places where he imagined Carl might go, the first stop being the craftsman bungalow on the corner of Hope and Newport. He parked at the curb and got out. The yellow police tape was still around the yard and across the front and back doors. Nobody home.

Next he drove to Brantley's Funeral Home. On the way, he saw two coyotes loping along the sidewalk. He honked at them, and they darted off between the houses. Lights burned in the funeral home's front windows and another in the turret. Woody pulled into the drive and then cut across the lawn to the front steps. Sixteen ridged columns supported the wraparound porch. Woody knocked and rang the bell. It was eleven o'clock.

Brantley wasn't pleased. "Why do you always assume that you'll find Carl here?"

"He's armed and homicidal. I thought you'd want to know."

"Well, he's not here. Perhaps you'd like to come in and look around."

Woody started to get angry. He wanted to say that Carl had just tried to kill three children, but he stopped himself. "That's okay. Give us a call if you see anything."

Woody returned to the truck. Brantley was the kind of guy, he thought, who would call the colonel if he got pissed at a trooper.

Next Woody decided to check on Howard Phelps, who had fired Carl from his plumbing and heating company. But as he was pulling out of Brantley's driveway, he got an unexpected call.

"Woody, this is Todd Chmielnicki. Chief Bonaldo gave me your number after I convinced him it was important."

"Do you plan to read my mind again?" He was pissed that Bonaldo had given out his number.

Chmielnicki's laughter was like dry hands chafing together. "Nothing like that, and perhaps you already know this. October thirty-first is Samhain; it's the Celtic celebration for the end of summer, which begins the dark half of the year. It's the most important of the Sabbats not only for Wiccans, but for all neopagans, as well as Satanists."

"D'you mean Halloween? What's the trouble?"

"Samhain is the origin of Halloween. It's the festival of the dead, when bones are thrown into a bonfire. Originally it involved animal and human sacrifice. For the Wiccans it's a harvest celebration. Answers are sought about future events through methods ranging from casting spells to apple bobbing. For the Satanists it's something darker; they ask a brazen head questions about the future."

"What do you mean, 'brazen head'?"

"Usually it's a skull covered with a thin layer of brass."

Woody was silent a moment trying to imagine such a crazy thing. Then he asked: "Is this going to be a problem in Brewster?"

"The Wiccans might be in danger. The Satanists, I don't know.

Much of what's been happening could be blamed on Satanists or on people pretending to be Satanists. If so, they could take advantage of Samhain to create an even bigger distraction."

"And what's their real purpose?"

"Woody, you're the police officer; I'm the student. But if they are trying to create distractions—as the snakes were distractions—we both know there's a purpose behind it. Also, Clouston's murder suggests their fear. Wasn't he killed to keep him quiet?"

Woody wondered if this was more than a lucky guess. "We're still working on that."

"Then I wish you luck. Just don't forget Samhain. It's almost upon us."

"Wait a second, what if nothing happens?"

"Local Wiccans and other groups celebrate it each year, so if nothing happens, that too will be significant." The phone went dead.

"Arrogant fuck," said Woody, so loudly that Ajax stood up and looked at him.

A few minutes later, when Woody had just arrived at Howard Phelps's house, he got another call, this time from Bobby Anderson. "We found Barton's wagon down at the beach stuck in the sand. Looks like Carl meant to drive it into the water. There're tracks from the car to the water. The tide's going to turn pretty soon. Guess who else I called?"

"The CIU."

"You got it."

The Volvo was slewed to the right and buried up to its fenders. The area around it was blocked off by yellow tape. The headlights from the police cruisers reflected off the waves breaking thirty feet offshore, creating a display of rushing white water. The sound of the cresting waves rose and fell.

"There's blood all over the front seat," said Bobby. "It's got to be Carl's. The tracks leading into the water are pretty clear on the packed sand, but we'll lose them when the tide comes up. Montesano better get his ass here pretty quick."

Perhaps Carl had walked into the ocean. It seemed possible, but that is only what Woody would have done in a similar fix. Yet what else was Carl going to do? The man, however, was nuts. You couldn't calculate how he'd behave with any certainty.

Woody and Bobby stood by the Tundra as Woody described the phone call he'd received from Chmielnicki.

"So what's your plan?" asked Bobby.

"Bring in more cops, I guess. Watch the roads to Great Swamp. Can you think of anything else? Maybe Lajoie will turn up that third girl or we'll get a lead on who killed Clouston. I only wish we could solve this mess before Halloween. We'd better talk to those Wiccans again."

Next Woody described finding Hercel and the girls in the woods, what he felt when he heard Hercel's voice. "I was so fucking relieved, I almost started bawling. How's that for being a tough cop? I choked up and got tears in my eyes."

"Shit," said Bobby, "I do it at least once a month. So what else is new?"

The two men were leaning against the hood of the Tundra, which was still warm from the engine. "D'you think Carl can be blamed for the rest of the stuff—stealing the baby and killing Hartmann? It seems a lot for one guy."

"Clouston could have helped him, but I doubt Carl can be blamed for any of it. He's mean enough, but he's not clearheaded enough. He couldn't do any serious planning. He's purely an impulse guy. But he's connected some way, I just don't know how."

Montesano and others of his team arrived around midnight and dragged their lights out to the beach. The tide had turned, but four or five of the footprints were still visible. Whether they would find bloodstains was another matter. Woody walked forward to meet them. The wind had picked up, and it was colder.

"I got some complicated news for you," said Montesano, turning his back to the wind and pulling up his collar.

"So tell me," said Woody.

"You know those ashes we dug up on the island, like from a fire pit, and those bone fragments? We heard back from the eggheads at URI. Some of the bones were human."

Snow flurries blew across Brewster late Thursday night. A man walking his dog or someone looking out a window toward the streetlight might see them blowing in from the west and think it was too early for winter. As harbingers of winter storms, they were unwelcome to some, exciting to others, though mostly to kids. Baldo Bonaldo, up late because of the presence of Hercel and the girls, looked out the window and rubbed his hands. There were a lot of tricks you could play with snow.

Only the most tenacious leaves were left. The wind and rain of the past few days had done their work and all day there had been the sound of leaf blowers. In the old days, of course, people raked their leaves to the curb and then burned them. Quite a few in Brewster wished that was still possible. They missed standing at the edge of the fire with a rake and thoughtfully nudging the leaves toward the smoldering center. They missed the smell of leaf smoke. There was nothing romantic about leaf blowers, which was true of a lot of stuff these days—computers, cell phones, video games. It was a long list.

But tonight few dog walkers were in evidence, and those who happened to see a dog walker from the window thought them foolhardy. Weren't they just asking for trouble? The murders of Hartmann,

Clouston, even Harriet Krause, led many to worry they might be next. What residue of guilt did these deaths activate? Perfectly innocent and God-fearing men and women locked their doors and windows, and pulled down their shades in fear. Maud Lord worried someone might shoot her because she had found the hanged cat. Jean Sawyer of the Brewster Brew lay in bed next to her husband, trying to read her romance novel, but all she could think about was how the wind was making her house creak. But maybe it *wasn't* the wind.

Sister Asherah and Sister Isis in their farmhouse at the far end of Whipple Street heard the noises and knew trouble was coming, even though a Brewster patrol car was parked out front. Both worried the policeman might be asleep until at last Sister Asherah took him a cup of coffee and a piece of chocolate cake. But do you think he ate it? No way! He had read about witches and what could happen if you ate their food. He meant to turn the whole nasty business over to the state crime lab at URI.

Once again playing gin rummy late into the night, Ginger and Howard Phelps spent an inordinate amount of time staring at their cards. Their glasses of warm milk grew cold. The telephone was in easy reach. Were they thinking of their cards? Of course not. Ginger listened to the house's snaps and pops each time the furnace clicked on—noises that had never bothered her until now. Howard thought, for the thousandth time, that he should never have hired Carl Krause, and, if he had to hire him, he should never have fired him. Maybe he could have paid Carl to leave, but he shouldn't have made him mad. It was probably one of the things that made Carl go nuts. In fact, maybe it was the only thing. And wouldn't Carl want revenge?

It was then they heard a loud crack from the parlor. Ginger screamed. Howard saw a shadow. The window shattered; broken glass jangled and crashed to the floor. Ginger grabbed for the phone; Howard tried to snatch it away. Both struggled over who would dial 911. A glass of milk was knocked over; their cards scattered to the linoleum. At last the number was dialed. Almost immediately patrol cars were on their way.

Whole-Hog Hopper lived in a small house on Periwinkle Street at the edge of town with his wife and four sons. All were plump or heavy—they avoided the word *fat*. They had lingered too long with their heads in the fridge, one might say. Whole-Hog liked to watch late-night television and have a few beers. Jay Leno made him chuckle. And some of the pretty female guests in their low-cut gowns made his whole midsection throb.

But tonight Whole-Hog hardly noticed the pretty girls. On one hand, he had a fierce resentment against Freddie for suspending him. Sure, maybe he had mentioned the dead guy on the island and those funny circus goat tracks to a couple of pals he had known all his life. And hadn't they sworn up and down not to tell a soul? So it wasn't Whole-Hog left with egg on his face, or at least that's how he saw it.

On the other hand, Whole-Hog was bothered by the wind in the trees. Tonight it made a real racket. When Whole-Hog was young, maybe five or six, his dad told him the wind wasn't really wind but the ghosts of the newly dead, the really bad guys, being rushed down to hell. Whole-Hog never forgot it. In fact, he was thinking about it right now, instead of staring intently at celebrity titties. Wasn't that Clouston fellow a bad guy? That could be him fussing around outside. Not that Whole-Hog believed that shit anymore.

At that moment, he too heard a loud crack and a breaking noise from the dining room window, which he could just see through the double doors into the hall. He had absolutely known something like this would happen. So is it any surprise that his Glock was within arm's reach on the small TV table to his right next to his Budweiser?

Whole-Hog snatched up the Glock and, in the language of the

subsequent police report, "he discharged his weapon seven times." More simply, he blasted the wall of his neighbor's house. His neighbor's name was Charlie Mitzorelli. And it's a good thing that old Charlie, like the smart pig in the kid's story, had built his house out of brick, or the seven .45 slugs would have ripped through the wall like shit through a goose.

It was one-thirty when Woody at last went home. He had meant to go home earlier, and then the Brewster police station started getting 911 calls. It had been a nightmare. The first four had been actual break-ins; that is, someone had forced a downstairs window with a wrecking bar and the window had broken.

Next came a flood of calls from people who *thought* someone was breaking in, people who presumably had received calls from the original four. Brewster patrol cars and state police cruisers dashed around town with their sirens blaring. People who had been lucky enough to be asleep now weren't. This led to a third wave of calls, and acting chief Bonaldo asked for additional help from Charlestown and South Kingstown.

Once again Woody called the CIU, which, in any case, was still down at the beach vacuuming up a ton of sand to be analyzed by the URI lab for traces of blood. The lab had been so busy that the governor had brought in forensics guys from Massachusetts. That was a plus of living in a pissant state. These problems went straight to the top in no time flat.

Then Woody had helped chase down some of the second and third wave of 911 calls, crisscrossing Brewster until he decided it was all bullshit. It was all "his-teria and her-steria," as Bobby liked to say. The reason this was happening was because something *else* was happening, something that this window-breaking was designed to conceal. He called the hospital to make sure it had sufficient security, and he saw to it that police were watching the Wiccans and any others who might be in danger. Then he drove around for a bit more, but the only vehicles on the road were police cars and an ambulance. Woody thought, *Let Fred Bonaldo take care of it. I'm going home.*

But he didn't go home; that is, he drove halfway to Carolina and then made a right turn and headed for Wakefield. He felt too lonely to go home; he felt too confused by the business in Brewster. It was like a science fiction movie when the saucers start landing: absolute panic.

Woody had only a slight idea where Jill lived, but he knew he'd find it; or, as he told himself: *Tonight I'm a fucking bird dog.*

She opened the door, tugging a white terry cloth robe around her. She didn't seem surprised. Tilting her head to one side, she said, "Coffee?"

"No coffee."

He reached behind her head, grabbed a fistful of hair—not too rough—and kissed her neck, as he pushed her into the hall and kicked the door shut with his heel. Her neck smelled of sleep and sweet things. He tried to put the whole thing into his mouth; then he stepped back. "Should I stop?"

"Don't stop."

They didn't make it to the bedroom, but stripped off each other's clothes in the living room. He tore her nightgown. She fell to her knees, undid his belt, unzipped the zipper, and slipped his cock into her mouth. His pants slid down his legs, and his pistol and its little holster clunked on the rug. He fell on top of her, catching himself with his hands. Briefly, he tried to kick off his shoes and then gave up. They fed on each other, putting their mouths to whatever they could find till they grew slick with each other's spit. Rolling on the floor, they upset the coffee table. Then she grabbed him and slipped him inside her, first sitting on top of him and then rolling over; next he took her from behind like a dog; then they rolled over again as one unsettled creature, until at last he positioned himself on top of her and they got to work. When they had finished, they lay on the rug, trying to catch their breath. Woody's elbows felt chafed, his knees ditto. *Sharp rug,* he almost said, but he said nothing. Now that he had a chance to speak, he didn't know what to say.

Jill stood up and reached out her hand to help him to his feet. In the dim light, Woody stared at her eyes staring at him. The whites of her eyes encircled pools of darkness, and staring into them was like staring down from a high place. For a second, he was afraid of falling, but then she embraced him and led him into the bedroom with his pants bunched around his ankles. She pushed him, and he flopped down on the bed. She took off his shoes and socks, and then she crawled on top of him and they did it all again, but more slowly. He raised his hands to her breasts. The headboard banged against the wall.

Afterward, they lay side by side with their hands touching, but neither spoke. Each considered speaking; they ran though possible sentences in their minds, but each sentence seemed so banal after what had happened that neither could break the silence. And Jill considered that they might never speak, that years would go by, perhaps their entire lives, with only making hand signals and grunts. And thinking this, she laughed.

"What are you laughing at?" asked Woody.

She told him.

"Well, I guess I broke the ice," he said.

She laughed again and climbed astride him and began kissing his face—his nose, his eyes, his forehead, and then his mouth—as he held her breasts in his hands, catching each nipple between two fingers and stroking it with a thumb. Then he pulled her down and rolled on top of her, again burying his face in the side of her neck and biting gently.

Half an hour later they were sitting at the kitchen table, eating scrambled eggs. Ajax had been brought in from the truck and was asleep on the floor. Woody was so tired it was like an out-of-body experience.

"If you fall asleep, your head's going to fall right onto your plate," said Jill. "You can use my toothbrush if you like. I don't think you need to worry about germs, all things considered."

Jill led him to the bathroom. Luke's toys were lined up around the rim of the tub—*Star Wars* figures, little race cars, and a yellow rubber duck. Jill put toothpaste on the brush and handed it to him. "You're going to have to do the rest yourself. Do you have to pee?"

"I'm okay."

She led him to bed and he fell on top of it. She lay down beside him and pulled up the comforter. "I hope we stay together a long time."

Woody raised his head a few inches off the pillow. "I'd like that," he said.

Acting chief Fred Bonaldo drove a hundred miles Thursday night and all of it in Brewster. Actually, Harry Morelli did the driving and Bonaldo did the worrying. It had taken dozens of interviews by twenty police officers to determine there had been only four incidents. The rest—including the spotting of ghosts, shadowy figures, and packs of coyotes, and hearing breaking glass, screams, coyote howls, and gunshots (apart from Whole-Hog's moment of panic)—could be chalked up to collective craziness. Still, it had taken time. And every person he had talked to was full of complaints that Fred hadn't solved the case already. Some yelled at him. Paulie Webster, who Fred had known since second grade, tried to punch him in the nose. Was this what being a police chief was all about?

In a town where people had known one another all their lives and lived together with tranquil goodwill, it shocked Bonaldo to see how quickly that could be swept aside. Neighbors suspected neighbors.

Deborah Dove, principal of Bailey Elementary, wanted to close the school. Tommy Cathcart wanted to stop delivering mail. Chucky Stubbs, for crying out loud, wanted to close the animal shelter. People left town. Even among the Masons, men distrusted one another.

Brewster's one gun shop did a booming business in rifles, shotguns, and pistols. One fellow bought a crossbow. Jerzy Kowalski, who owned the gun shop, said to Bonaldo, "Hey, Freddie, I'll give you five percent of my sales if you can keep this up another two weeks. Then I'll fucking retire."

Bonaldo hadn't laughed. Tomorrow, because of these phony break-ins, even though no one's house had been actually entered, there would be lines out Kowalski's door and around the block. It was only a matter of time before one crazy citizen shot another crazy citizen. Wasn't the fact that Whole-Hog had blasted the side of Charlie Mitzorelli's house seven times with his Glock proof of this? Now Charlie meant to get a gun as well.

"What if he shoots me?" Whole-Hog had asked.

"It'd serve you right." Bonaldo then apologized. Since Whole-Hog was Laura's cousin, it was best to keep bad blood to a minimum.

At about three-thirty a.m., the CIU informed Bonaldo that the footprints outside the forced windows of two of the four houses had been size 11D Timberland Pro Terrenes with slightly worn SafeGrip, slip-resistant rubber soles. The grass had been too long outside Whole-Hog's window, and no tracks had been found.

Bonaldo threw up his hands. Hadn't he known this was going to happen?

He called Woody's cell. A woman answered, and Bonaldo identified himself. "I got to talk to Woody right away."

"I'm sorry, he's not available. Would you care to leave a message?"

This was a surprise. Who was this person? "Who's this?" Bonaldo demanded.

"This is Woody's mother."

Bonaldo was stunned. He hadn't known Woody even *had* a mother. He hardly knew what to say. "Yeah, well, have him call me as soon as possible. It's about some eleven-D Timberland Pro Terrenes."

"Let me write that down," the woman said.

For the next hour this brief conversation played merry-go-round in Bonaldo's head. Brewster's going up in smoke and Woody's visiting his mom?

More people were talked to; more people complained that Fred wasn't "doing anything." Another old friend, Ricki Donovan, who he'd known since kindergarten, had shouted, "Freddie, you're ruining the fuckin' town. You gotta stop sitting on your ass and start *doin'* something."

Thanks, Ricki.

Harry Morelli dropped Bonaldo off at his house at five o'clock. "Get some rest, Freddie. You got another long day tomorrow."

Bonaldo said good night. He didn't like his men calling him Freddie; it seemed disrespectful. But tonight he didn't care. Why should he expect respect when he didn't respect himself? He walked up the front walk. The house was dark. Even the porch light was off. Maybe Laura was mad at him for some reason. Could she be pissed that those three kids were staying here? But she was too kindhearted for that. The kids had had an awful experience, and seeing poor Hercel had almost broken Fred's heart. Hercel had been trying to be brave when he had every right to bawl like a baby.

Bonaldo felt his way up the front steps with his hand on the railing. Then he pulled open the storm door. He searched in his pockets for his keys. Like it was a golden rule: if he reached in his right pocket, they were in the left; and if he reached in his left, they were in the right. The door was white, and as Bonaldo finally located his keys, he saw something stuck in the wood, maybe a knife or dagger. Light from the street reflected off the blade. Around the knife was a dark smudge. He reached out to touch it and immediately yanked his hand away. It was furry. Then he realized it had a dead-thing smell.

He tried to unlock the door to turn on the light, but he kept missing the lock or holding the key the wrong way. The furry smudge got bigger the more he looked at it.

At last he opened the door and flicked the light switch. The dark smudge was a mound of shimmering dark brown hair. Bonaldo knew exactly what it was: Ernest Hartmann's scalp.

Acting chief Fred Bonaldo pressed his hands to his mouth to keep from screaming. He couldn't wake the kids. But Bonaldo couldn't help himself; he yelled bloody murder.

EIGHTEEN

JILL FRANKLIN GAVE UP control of Woody's cell phone at six o'clock Friday morning. In this she was helped by her son, Luke, who rushed through the bedroom door, leapt onto the bed, and bounced several times before realizing his mother had a guest.

"Who zat? Is that the guy Ajax lives with?"

It turned out that Ajax had spent the night in Luke's bed.

"His name's Woody," said Jill. "Remember?"

"Oh, yeah, like a tree." Luke bounced a little more. He guessed Woody was okay if Ajax liked him.

Woody's cell phone rang, and Jill handed it to him. He had already opened his left eye and was considering opening the right. Maybe in total, over the past four days, he had had ten hours' sleep. It was Bobby.

"I've got some news for you."

Woody started to say he didn't want to hear it, but Bobby hurried ahead.

"Somebody spiked Ernest Hartmann's scalp to Fred Bonaldo's front door with an athame. Fred found it an hour ago. He's really upset."

Woody sat up so quickly that Luke nearly fell to the floor; he caught the boy's leg just in time. Jill heard what Bobby said and put a hand over her mouth. "A what?" asked Woody.

"Athame. It's a ceremonial dagger used by modern witches. This one's got a triple moon on the handle and three runes on the blade. You know what they say?" Bobby's voice sounded as tight as a plucked string—a robotlike voice.

Woody felt so muddleheaded it was painful to join two thoughts together. Jill knelt before him on the bed, looking worried. Her robe was partly open and Woody could see down to her navel. He felt his priorities were absolutely fucked. He felt he should tell Bobby he was quitting his job. "What're runes?" he asked.

"Viking letters, Druid letters, how the fuck should I know? Old letters with magic powers. These runes mean Man, Snake, and Fire. Bingo showed the dagger to Sister Asherah fifteen minutes ago. She said it was an athame. Don't you care about the scalp?"

"Maybe I better come in," said Woody.

Ten minutes later, Woody and Ajax were in the truck. Jill had made him coffee, but he hadn't time for anything else. He felt as though he was on system overload with a brain jammed with iffy synapses. He knew he should be analyzing what lay ahead, but instead his thoughts spun round as he recalled and tried to reexperience each moment he had spent with Jill. It had astonished him. He tried to conjure up what her skin felt like, what her eyes looked like; he tried to conjure up her smell and the touch of her hand, what her belly felt like pressed to his. He shook his head in wonder and felt he should turn around and head back to her house. To hell with Brewster. At least he could call her to be reassured that the previous five hours had actually happened. He was afraid she might change on him, that he would see her later only to discover she'd become another person, that what for him was earth-shattering was for her a one-night stand.

Instead he called Morgan Memorial to find out about Barton Wilcox. He talked to Bernie, who was up in the ICU.

"He's alive; that's the best that can be said. No prognosis as yet. It doesn't look good. Oh, Woody, you should see him; he looks so awful. I've spent decades as a nurse, but I'm completely unable to help him. All I can do is hold his hand."

As Woody listened, he felt Jill receding to another part of his brain. Ridiculously, he wanted to tell Bernie that he had spent the night with a wonderful woman. He was appalled by the selfishness of the thought.

"Hang in there, Bernie. I'll stop by later if I can." Then he took a deep breath. "I'm sorry, Bernie. It's so awful I don't know what to say. I feel terrible, and I realize it's nothing compared to what you feel. I'd do anything to help, I just don't know what I can do."

"Look after the children and catch that crazy fuck who shot my husband."

Woody found Bobby Anderson, Bingo Schwartz, and the Brewster detective Brendan Gazzola in a small office with a desk, three chairs, and a shoe box. The three detectives sat with expressions that led Woody to think of quiz-show losers trying to make the best of it. There was no smoking in police headquarters, and Gazzola was popping Nicorette like gumdrops. Bingo was humming to himself.

Seeing Woody, Bobby shook his head. "This town is completely fucked."

Woody glanced at the shoe box. Whatever was inside resembled the sort of bed one makes for a robin rescued from a cat—a brownish straw to keep the bird warm. He realized it was Ernest Hartmann's scalp and took a step back. "Yuck."

"Now, there's a brilliantly expressed critical appraisal," said Bobby, striking his forehead with the flat of his hand. "Why didn't I think of that?"

"What's it doing here?"

"A guy's coming down from the medical examiner's to pick it up. But the crime lab also wants to look at it, probably from morbid curiosity. What are they going to find, fingerprints? Personally, I think it should be rejoined to Hartmann as soon as possible before some wiseacre sells it to a circus."

As for acting chief Bonaldo, when he'd put his hand on Hartmann's scalp, he had "completely lost it." The three detectives were sympathetic; they couldn't swear they wouldn't have done the same. The downside was that Bonaldo's yelling had woken his neighbors, who'd rushed outside—one with a rifle—to find the cause of all the noise. And of course they had told a bunch of others about "the dead guy's scalp nailed to Freddie's door with a Satanist dagger."

"If Baldy had kept his mouth shut," said Bobby, "we'd be a lot better off. Half the town is demanding police protection. People are so scared they're letting their dogs pee in the house."

"What about this knife, or whatever?" asked Woody.

Bobby shrugged. "As far as I can see, it's just your normal run-of-the-mill Satanist dagger."

"Montesano took it over to the crime lab," said Bingo. "He didn't think there were any prints. Sister Asherah said it was one of the magical tools of Wicca, along with wands and chalices. They use the athame to draw a magic circle. You stand in the circle and the demons stand on the other side. Or it's used to create energy in some way. Sister Asherah would still be talking about it if I hadn't gotten out of there. The main thing, maybe, is that it isn't typically used for cutting anything. On the other hand, it was plenty sharp."

"So Hartmann could have been killed with it?"

"That's what the medical examiner hopes to find out."

"Any witches in opera?" asked Bobby.

"Verdi's got a bunch; other composers also," said Bingo. "Used to be you could hardly have an opera without a witch, and maybe a gypsy."

"What about those letters?" asked Woody. Hartmann's scalp looked like antique hair attached to brown-spotted parchment. It came from a world the very opposite of the world represented by Jill Franklin.

"Runes," said Bobby. "The fact that they mean Man, Snake, *and* Fire seems to tie them to the whole business. And the medical examiner's office is still trying to deal with the fact that some of the bones found in the fire pit on the island are human bones."

Bingo scratched at a gray spot on the lapel of his brown suit. "Sister Asherah said *bonfire* was originally *bone-fire*. On Halloween the old Celts burned bones to keep away evil spirits. She gave me the name of the festival, but I didn't catch it."

"Samhain," said Woody. "It's tomorrow night."

"That could be a problem," said Bobby.

Detective Gazzola started coughing, a long series of phlegm-packed, liquid coughs that gave color to his face. "I feel out of my league. I don't know any of this shit, and I don't know where to start. I'm rushing around picking up the pieces and I don't even know what they mean." He began to cough again.

The others were silent. They all felt pretty much the same way.

"Oh, yeah," said Bobby. "Montesano said they didn't find any of Carl's blood on the sand. They haven't finished, and maybe it'll turn up, but we got to start thinking what it means if it wasn't Carl who left the car at the beach."

Again the men were silent. Each tried not to look at the scalp, then looked at it and looked away. It was impossible not to look at it.

"Okay, Gazzola," said Woody, "I got a job for you." He told the detective to get a photo of Hamilton Brantley and then get photos from the hospital of people who admitted knowing Clouston. "Get some guys and show the pictures to Clouston's neighbors. Maybe we can find a connection."

Bingo meant to continue his search for Ronnie McBride. Bobby planned to drive to Great Swamp to talk to Gail Valetti, the coyote specialist.

"That bitch?" said Woody. "I thought she was going to take my head off."

Bobby looked beatific. "We had a lovely chat on the phone. She said she'd be glad to see me as long as I didn't bring my pushy friend, meaning you."

Woody rolled his eyes. "Why don't you quit this cop shit and run for office? With that glossy grin of yours, you could be the state's first black senator."

There was more banter. Woody realized there had been a change in mood like a change in weather. It indicated a trace of optimism in the midst of their frustration. As Gazzola said, there were lots of pieces, but Woody sensed they were coming together, like a smashed vase becoming whole again.

"I'm going over to Brantley's," he said.

"How come?" asked Bobby.

"You remember Bonaldo's remark about Clouston and Brantley, the one we thought was stupid?"

"Yeah," said Gazzola. "He said they'd dead bodies in common."

"I think it's worth a trip," said Woody. "I'll see you guys later."

"When shall we four meet again," said Bingo, "in thunder, lightning, or in rain?"

Gazzola grunted. "Carl Krause isn't the only wack-job around here."

Five minutes later, when Woody drove his truck into the funeral home driveway, he saw Seymour Hodges replacing the glass in the back door's window. He parked by the carriage house and walked over to

Seymour, who either hadn't seen him or was ignoring him. It was a brisk fall day, with the sky as blue as Mayan tiles. Fat clouds drifted eastward. A blue jay in a maple jeered at invisible threats.

"What happened to the window?" asked Woody.

Seymour glanced at him and then returned to chipping the broken glass out of the frame. "Got broke."

"Yeah, I figured that. How'd it happen?"

"Kids, maybe." Seymour was stocky and red-haired, with eyes the same color as the sky. His nose had a squashed look, but whether he was born with it or someone had broken it for him, Woody didn't know. He wore work boots, jeans, and a dark sweatshirt spotted with white paint.

"Did Brantley report it?"

"Digger said the cops was too busy."

"Was someone trying to break in?"

"Beats me. It got broke, that's all."

Woody felt himself heating up. Seymour wanted to be left alone, which only made Woody want to keep at him. "I didn't know you worked for Brantley. When did you start?"

"A while back."

"Like when?"

"Like this week."

"So you're Carl's replacement?"

"I guess you could say that."

"You seen Carl recently?"

"Nope, not for a week or so."

"You going to work out at the crematorium like Carl?"

"You'll have to ask Digger about that."

Seymour kept working with his back to Woody; once or twice he glanced over his shoulder.

"Is Brantley inside?"

"Nope."

"So where is he?"

"Out at the Burn . . . out at the crematorium."

"What'd you call it?"

"Nothing."

"Tell me."

"The Burn Palace. That's what Larry calls it. Digger don't like it."

"Who's Larry?"

"He's in charge of the Burn Palace when Digger's not around."

"You been smoking dope?"

Seymour turned, looked at Woody's shoes, and then raised his eyes to his face. The whites of Seymour's eyes were pinkish. "It's medicinal."

"Yeah?"

"On account of Iraq." Seymour turned back to the window.

"Did a doctor prescribe it?"

"Not in so many words."

"What'd you do in Iraq?"

"You know, the usual shit."

Briefly, Woody wanted to search Seymour for drugs and then take him to the police station, but that was the anger talking. Seymour was only fixing a window. It wasn't exactly a capital crime.

"I guess you don't know how long Brantley's going to be at the Burn Palace."

"No idea."

Just to needle Seymour, Woody asked, "Did Carl Krause break that window?"

Again Seymour turned slowly toward him. "What the fuck would Carl break a goddamn window for?"

"Just wondering." Woody walked back to his truck, trying to conceal his surprise. He was almost sure that Seymour was lying. He decided to take a drive to the Burn Palace.

Acting chief Fred Bonaldo's ambition was to be well liked. His passion for parades and uniforms formed part of this ambition. How could you not admire a guy in uniform? As for parades, he always tried to put himself up front; and if he got stuck in the band, he'd be the guy banging on the bass drum. Though he rarely wore his uniform as acting chief, he made sure to wear his blue suit, which was uniformlike. His glasses, he felt, gave him an intellectual look; his baldness suggested maturity; his burgeoning belly bespoke gravitas. He had a smile for one and all, kissed babies, patted small dogs. Everything was in place, he thought, to be well liked, to command respect. Yet he knew he was a dismal failure.

And whose fault was it? That damn baby's and that awful snake's. They were nails in the coffin of his ambition.

Bonaldo had a passion for charts—organizational charts, charts of rising profits—and he had a chart detailing his inexorable progression between acting chief and permanent chief. He even took into account possible setbacks and slow periods. After all, he couldn't expect a sharply ascending line. It seemed immodest.

Maybe he could have coped with the missing baby and the snake, but further stuff kept happening, and worst of all, or almost, had been those briefings with Captain Brotman. They'd been designed to make him look bad. The South Kingstown lieutenant, Joe Doyle, hated him, and the rest didn't like him much.

None of it mattered now. Acting chief Bonaldo had, metaphysically speaking, thrown up his hands. He'd kissed his ambitions good-bye. He would be happy to return to real estate. And the moment of change was perfectly clear to him. It was when he'd put his hand on that furry scalp. That was the moment the scales had fallen from his eyes. Of course he'd screamed; it made perfect sense to scream.

These were the thoughts that came to Bonaldo as he sat at his desk Friday morning. He hadn't signed up for having the shit scared out of him. Of course he hadn't had a moment's sleep, and, because of his screaming, many others had had their sleep cut short. Several had dialed 911. In no time police officers had arrived to find their acting chief having hysterics. No one blamed him, at least to his face. It wouldn't have mattered if they did. Not anymore.

Bonaldo understood he couldn't just quit; rather, he would keep a low profile. He would stay in his office. He would delegate authority. He should have known when Carl pointed the shotgun at him that he was in for a rough ride. Well, now he knew.

It was at this moment the office door opened hardly a crack and a woman slipped into the room. She was tall—over six feet—very thin, and wearing a long and fitted black dress open in a V at the top. Her face was narrow, with a straight nose, thin lips, and a narrow chin. Her black hair hung loosely past her shoulders; she wore black eye shadow and black lipstick; even her fingernail polish was black. Her skin was the color of parchment.

Bonaldo eyed her with dread.

The woman glided to Bonaldo's desk; her feet hardly seemed to move. She neither frowned nor smiled. Reaching the desk, she put her long, thin hands on the surface and leaned forward. Bonaldo tried not to look down the front of her dress. Indeed, there was nothing to see. Only darkness.

The woman spoke in a whisper. "I'm a Satanist," she said.

Acting chief Bonaldo clamped his jaw shut and began punching the keys on his intercom like Horowitz playing Liszt. He needed backup.

• • •

Detective Beth Lajoie learned late Thursday afternoon that Maggie Kelly had been arrested for prostitution in New York in early September, was charged with a misdemeanor, paid a fine in the night court's lobster shift, and had been out on the street ten hours after her arrest. Since then she had been lucky or had kept her nose clean. Most likely the former, a Manhattan South vice unit detective had told Lajoie.

Detective Lajoie explained that Kelly was suspected of selling her baby and she needed to talk to her as soon as possible. After Lajoie briefly described recent events in Brewster, the detective said he'd get on it right away. Actually, he'd read a story about Brewster in the *Post*. "Heavy shit," he said.

Now, on Friday morning, Lajoie was on her way to see Alice Alessio. She had decided against her emerald-green pantsuit, and wore dark gray flannel. Her only jewelry was a small pair of pearl earrings. This was her grade-school-teacher mode—respectable, unthreatening, kindly. It was all bullshit, as far as Lajoie was concerned.

She rapped on the door of Alice's apartment at seven o'clock, hoping she was still asleep. Alice had been temporarily suspended from her job at the hospital, though everyone assumed she'd be fired once the case was solved. Lajoie carried a bag of two coffees and four doughnuts from Dunkin' Donuts.

It took further knocking, but after a minute Alice opened the door. She wore baby-blue flannel pajamas and looked a wreck.

"Hi!" said Lajoie. "I hope you take cream. They put it in without my asking." She shoved the paper cup toward Alice, who had to grab it to keep it from falling. As Alice stepped back, Lajoie stepped forward to shut the door. "It's wonderful to have the chance to meet you, Alice. I've heard so much about you."

Alice looked confused. After all, she'd just woken up. "You're a cop?"

"State police detective, actually. Let's chat." She led Alice to the kitchen and had her sit at the small table; then she got a fairly clean dish from the drainer for the doughnuts. She put them on the table with several paper towels. "Hungry?"

Woody had wanted Lajoie to find out just who had seduced whom—Balfour or Nurse Spandex. Dr. Fuller had said that Dr. Balfour had seemed immune to the nurses' occasional flirting, but Woody wanted Detective Lajoie to make sure.

"I guess so. Why're you here?" Alice was not only confused; she was depressed. She tugged at the collar of her pajamas.

Detective Lajoie looked at her thoughtfully. "You know, Alice, you really should wash off your eye makeup before you go to bed. Otherwise it makes you look like a raccoon. Have you heard from Dr. Balfour?"

Alice dabbed her smudged eyes with a napkin. "He hasn't called."

"The brute. After all you did for him, too. Drink your coffee, Alice, it'll get cold." Lajoie took a sip of her own coffee to show how it was done.

Alice sipped her coffee. She couldn't imagine who this woman was or what she wanted, but she had talked to no one but her mother for several days and she was ready to climb the walls.

"Tell me, Alice, I've been wondering about your relationship with Dr. Balfour. Just how did it start? Did you speak to him, or did he speak to you?"

Alice broke off a corner of a glazed doughnut, studied it, and put it in her mouth. She wanted to lose weight, but if she was depressed this would be the wrong time. "He spoke to me first. I was surprised. I mean, I'd thought he was gay. He'd never shown any interest in the girls before. Like, we'd talked a few times, but not in *that* way, if you know what I mean."

Alice described a number of brief conversations with Dr. Balfour over a two-week period. Once aware of his interest, she had responded with interest of her own. "I really thought he liked me. He'd touch me or brush up against me as if by accident. We'd duck into an empty room for just a minute or two. He didn't want anyone to know. That's why he didn't want to see me outside the hospital. By then I was ready to do anything. He fucked me the first time two weeks ago in a bathroom. It was rushed and not very nice. I mean, it was great, but the rushed part wasn't very nice. I was afraid of getting caught, more afraid for him than for me. I didn't know if I was coming or going. And the water kept turning on. It had one of those motion-sensing faucets and it kept spraying me. I got sopped."

Lajoie decided to ignore the motion-sensing faucet. "When did you last see him?"

"The other day, when I left his house." Alice put a thumb to her lips and chewed on the nail. "He said he didn't want to see me anymore."

"Did he say why?"

"He made a joke of it."

"What did he say?"

"'The thrill has gone.'" Alice lowered her head. "'I just don't want you, that's all.'"

Detective Lajoie maintained her kindly smile. "And has this sort of thing happened with other doctors?"

Alice didn't want to answer. She felt embarrassed. But Lajoie got it out of her.

"There was Dr. Stone last March. We did it in the bathroom, too. He's at Providence Hospital now. He just up and left."

She described their three-week relationship, the secret meetings, his fear of being found out. Twice he'd come to her apartment after dark.

"And was he the one who initiated it?" asked Lajoie. "Like Dr. Balfour?"

Alice blushed. "No, not really, not at all, actually. I let him know I was, like, ready. And at first it was an oral kind of thing, like down there." She pointed downward. "But then he got more into it, at least until he grew scared."

The women sat quietly for a moment, nibbling their doughnuts and sipping coffee.

"Tell me, Alice," said Lajoie, "is that your ambition, to marry a doctor?"

Alice began to weep. "I really don't care anymore. I'm thirty-five years old and ready to marry just about anybody, as long as he's nice."

Bingo Schwartz had an easy morning. He had to make a bunch of phone calls and decided he might as well make them from a soft armchair in the Brewster Brew than from his car or a hard chair in police headquarters. Jean Sawyer had her radio tuned to WGBH in Boston, and classical music was almost as good as opera as long as they didn't play Ravel's *Boléro,* which drove him crazy.

He was making calls to police departments in a hundred-mile radius—Boston and Worcester down to New Haven and Bridgeport, talking to detectives, most of whom he had talked to before, on the subject of missing homeless men. Now he asked if they had further thoughts on the matter. But it was difficult to tell if a homeless person was missing. Some got Social Security checks or medication; some saw counselors or probation officers. In those cases a missed appointment might be significant, but usually it took several before anyone began to wonder. Nearly all the departments had homeless persons who might be missing, but, on the other hand, they might turn up, which often happened. And after a significant amount of time had passed, the men might be forgotten.

Between calls Bingo imagined the opera sets he would construct once he retired, which, he now thought, would be sooner rather than later. This Friday morning he was working on the scene toward the end of *Don Giovanni* when the Don is dragged down to hell. Would he have the floor open and flames erupt—often strips of red and orange silk blown by a fan—or would he have a demon swing from the rafters and grab Don Giovanni with his talons? Bingo was partial to the second option, which he had never seen before, but it would take an acrobatic demon, and the trick would be not to drop the Don back onto the stage, since the Don was really a baritone being paid a lot of money to sing the part.

It was then that Bingo got a call from Detective Eric Degroot of the Providence Police Department, who he had talked to on Thursday.

"I been thinking of your homeless guy, the wacko," said Degroot. "I don't know if I told you, but I had a dog that disappeared about five years ago—Maxie, a nice little beagle."

Bingo waited. He had learned to wait, rather than to say, "What the fuck does that have to do with anything?" which is what he thought.

"I searched around for a while, but no luck. So I figured Maxie'd been hit by a car and tossed in the trash. He was a runner, know what I mean? But he always came back. Then a few months later we caught a guy who was stealing dogs. He was part of a gang that sold stolen dogs to pharmaceutical companies for research. Most likely they'd sold Maxie to a drug company that had him smoking cigars or something like that. So maybe that's what happened to your homeless guy. He got sold to drug companies."

Bingo was doubtful. "A guy like that? I can't think he'd be worth much."

"Perhaps, but it's like the difference between cars and auto parts. You buy a Ford for twenty grand, but if you built it from scratch just buying the parts it could cost a hundred. So maybe your homeless guy got sold in bits and pieces. I don't know, it's a thought."

As Bingo saw it, that was his first important conversation of the day, though it didn't seem important at first. He had to think about it.

The second important conversation occurred at about noon, when Bingo called a Massachusetts state police detective who he had talked to on Thursday. The detective, Frank Schnell, had nothing new on missing homeless people, but he had also been involved with gathering information about Ernest Hartmann.

"I got some stuff that might help you," said Schnell. "Ten days ago Hartmann met with Tommy Meadows. He's an investigator with the Department of Public Health. I don't know what they talked about, and Meadows is on vacation in Europe. He's supposed to be back in a week or so. I've e-mailed him, but he hasn't answered. He'd been working on a bunch of different projects, his boss said, but one of them's body brokers. You like it?"

Bingo tried to sit up in his armchair and knocked his notebook to the floor. "Yeah, what's that?" All he could think of was white slavery.

"Just like Realtors, except it's body parts. The broker gets bodies from a medical center or the morgue, even funeral homes, and then sells them to research companies that offer seminars with hands-on training. Like the medical center might have a cadaver that's been stripped of its skin for burn patients, but the rest is still usable. So maybe it's sold. Massachusetts medical schools get maybe fifteen thousand bodies a year. That's more than they need, so they do some horse-trading. That's where the broker comes in."

"Auto parts," said Bingo.

"Say again?"

Bingo described Degroot's auto parts analogy.

"Yeah, that'll do," said Schnell. "A broker can get up to a hundred grand for body parts even though he's bought the body from a tissue bank for five grand. Or he can get it free as a tissue donation. There's thousands of these training seminars. The thing is, the body's got to have a paper trail, but it's not as strict as it should be. Say you're selling a new kind of medical instrument and you got a lot of doctors or surgeons who want practice using it. So a salesman will set up a seminar, and he might not be too particular about where the body parts come from. That can be a problem. Like, I don't know if body parts is the Hartmann-Meadows connection, but if it is, then Meadows was maybe interested in the paper trail. But we'll know in a week or two, right?"

But Bingo didn't think Brewster could wait a week or two.

Whenever Bobby Anderson drove out of state, which was easy to do in Rhode Island, it was like playing hooky. He drove a little faster, put his seat back a little farther. Crooks could be robbing banks and he'd drive right by, or at least that's what he thought.

Friday morning he was on his way to see a UConn professor, Vasa Korak, who taught in the Wildlife Management program. The guy lived out in the boonies near North Ashford, half an hour north of the university. For Bobby it was seventy miles of little roads that let him practice his cornering skills.

He had gotten Korak's name from Gail Valetti, the Great Swamp coyote girl. It would be wrong to say he sweet-talked her, which would be Woody's accusation, but he turned on the charm. He described his fascination with coyotes, their intelligence and ability to adapt to any environment. He explained his concern about stories of aggressive coyote behavior. Valetti had also recently heard these stories, and so their concern was a shared concern.

"The person I know who knows more about coyotes than anyone else," said Valetti, "is a UConn professor. He even raises them."

And so Bobby was on his way.

His directions took him to Cemetery Road and then a dirt track through the woods toward Lost Pond Brook. Just when Bobby thought the bumps would rip off his muffler and he was about to give up, he negotiated a bend and came upon Vasa Korak's farm. He heard coyotes yapping as he approached.

Korak was about six-foot-six, with a shaved head and a thick chestnut mustache and goatee. Bobby guessed he was about thirty-five and weighed two-fifty. He wore jeans and a light blue work shirt. His voice was deep—all woofer, Bobby thought.

"You the guy who called? What kind of cop drives a Z?"

"A cop with discriminating tastes."

They shook hands. Korak's hand was twice the size of Bobby's, more of a paw than a hand. He seemed inclined to crush Bobby's fingers, but Bobby disliked macho games and gave as good as he got. Korak's eyes were also chestnut-colored. Abruptly he laughed and let Bobby go.

"So you want to see my posse?"

In a large pen by the barn were six coyotes. Two were standing on their doghouses; the other four were jumping up against the wire mesh of the gate. All were yipping and yelping, not at Bobby but at Korak.

The big man entered the pen, closing the gate behind him. Then he flopped down on the cement. "They wrestled," Bobby told Woody later. "They leapt on him and he threw them off. These were big animals, sixty, seventy pounds. I thought they'd eat him, but he laughed and they were laughing, sort of. Like they were making friendly yelps. But they weren't gentle. Korak got his face scratched and his ear was bitten bad enough to bleed."

After five minutes of moderate violence, Korak got to his feet. "You want to try it?" He laughed his booming laugh.

"Not today, thanks. I'm not dressed for it."

Korak opened the gate, and a grayish brown coyote galloped toward

Bobby, leapt up, planted its forepaws on his chest, and snatched his necktie in its jaws. The fur on the coyote's neck was snow white. Bobby hoped he wouldn't have to shoot it.

"That's Svetlana; she's the most civilized. She wants to take you for a walk. Just give her a cuff on the ear and she'll get down. Don't be too gentle or she'll think you're a wuss."

Bobby clubbed Svetlana's head with his open hand. She seemed to like it, but at least she jumped down. Bobby's hundred-dollar silk tie was a rag. The coyote jumped at Korak, and he cuffed her away. She lay down at his feet.

"So where did you get your posse? eBay?"

Korak rubbed his hand across his scalp. "It's taken about five years. I've been doing a coyote study with some guys from the Bureau of Natural Resources. First we trapped a dozen coyotes and radio-collared the females. They come into heat once a year in January or February. Gestation's nine weeks. So we tried to pinpoint when they bedded down. The pups are pretty helpless. Their eyes don't open for two weeks, and they're nursed for three. If you're going to bond with them, it's got to be during that time. We were lucky. We found a litter near Woodstock—ten pups—but it took some work to get them. The mother had holed up under a barn. We took the six feistiest. Then I sat with them, hand-fed them, howled with them, sniffed them, wrestled with them—we became a pack. My only mistake was to let them into the house. Just because we're pals didn't mean they were tame. They tore the shit out of the place—ripped down curtains, peed and shat on the floor, tore up furniture, all in the space of fifteen minutes. I thought my wife would kill me. So now we play outdoors and they play rough. I've got stitches in my shoulder, leg, left arm, but I bite right back. Nothing beats a mouthful of coyote fur. I'm not gentle; they're not gentle. They respect me. I'm boss dog."

As Korak spoke, he put Svetlana back in the pen, and then he and Bobby walked to the farmhouse and entered the kitchen. He said his wife taught water resources in UConn's Department of Natural Resources and the Environment.

"She's off slogging through the swamps today," said Korak. "She'll come back this afternoon covered with mud and ticks. I'll have to hose her off outdoors."

"Sounds like a happy family."

Bobby accepted a cup of strong coffee and proceeded to tell Korak about Brewster's coyote problem. They sat at a round butcher-block table. The sun streamed through the floral-patterned calico curtains over the sink.

"My old man used to tell me stories about shape-shifting wolves in Serbia," said Korak, "but he didn't believe them, and I don't, either. Somebody's been fucking with your coyotes. A few times one of mine's gotten loose. They rush around through the woods for a while, but they come back. Yours seem better trained. I guess you could do it if you took the time."

"Do you know people who raise them?"

"Not really; I mean we don't have a club. A guy over in Krumville, New York, raises them and he's mentioned someone else north of Albany. But it takes a lot of work. Your coyotes sound pretty vicious. It makes me mad someone would do that to them."

Bobby decided he wouldn't want Korak mad at him. "Could they be trained to be vicious?"

"You can probably make any creature vicious, even rabbits, though it'd be hard to have them vicious and under your control at the same time. But I've read studies of dogs on drugs and you can go to YouTube and see videos of dogs on LSD—some asshole trying to give Fido a good time. The dogs respond like humans, except worse. The downers make them sleepy; the uppers make them jumpy. If these coyotes are on drugs it's probably amphetamines. Coyotes are pretty timid, but eastern coyotes are the most aggressive, and you can pick the feisty ones out of the litter. I expect you could breed them to make them more aggressive. Then amphetamines would jack it up. Meth and coke also. Anyone doing that has got to be a pretty heartless fuck."

"But it's possible?"

"What're your choices? You got shape-shifters or naturally aggressive coyotes or you got tamed coyotes that have been trained. Only the third makes sense."

Hamilton Brantley's crematorium was in Hope Valley off Skunk Hill Road bordering the Arcadia Management Area, fourteen thousand acres of forest. It was a large, one-story cinder-block and concrete building with a loading dock on the left side. Only a big chimney, surrounded by a mesh box, suggested the building's purpose. The windows were glass bricks. *No peeking,* thought Woody. A sign over the front door said WASHINGTON COUNTY CREMATORIUM. Above it was a bullet camera. Before Woody could see if the door was unlocked, it opened and Brantley gave him a friendly wave.

"Seymour called and gave me the heads-up," said Brantley. "Welcome to my humble establishment." He laughed and shook Woody's hand. "Would you like a tour? I'm afraid there's no viewing room like some crematoria, but that's next on my list of improvements. Was there something in particular I can help you with?"

Brantley led him into a small office with a large window looking into the crematory. On the wall was a flat-panel LCD monitor, quartered to show the views from four outdoor security cameras. Directly across from the window was the furnace, about the size of a Ford van with a stainless-steel front. A lift table with an open corrugated cardboard casket stood near it. Leaning into the casket was a balding middle-aged man doing something to a cadaver in a plastic body bag. Everything about him seemed gray: hair, T-shirt, pants, and skin. Woody imagined he had been dyed by the ashes of the dead, but he disliked frivolous thoughts and he pushed it aside.

"That's Larry," said Brantley. "I'd be lost without him. He runs the whole thing practically single-handed."

"What's he doing?"

"I can't say for sure—perhaps snipping out a pacemaker or removing rings or other jewelry. Pacemakers explode in the furnace and make a mess of things. So we have to be careful. But we've found customers with cell phones, iPods, car keys, all sorts of stuff. It all goes back to the family or we throw it out. I don't think I've ever met someone who wanted a pacemaker returned."

"Customers?"

Brantley leaned back in his desk chair with his fingers knitted across his stomach. "Our little joke. Certainly, we treat our customers with utmost respect, but, as you yourself must know, every profession develops its own brand of humor that might not be in the best taste. For instance, Larry calls this the Burn Palace."

"So I heard," said Woody. "You know the term *slabman*?"

Brantley's smile hardened a little. "An old-fashioned term, much like calling a policeman a pig. Mostly they worked in morgues. Nowadays they might be called terminal cosmeticians. But surely there's a larger purpose to your visit."

Woody stood by the window, half looking at Brantley but also watching Larry. "I wondered if you knew Benjamin Clouston, who was murdered the other day. He was a pathologist's assistant at the hospital."

Brantley looked thoughtful and then shook his head. "I can't say I did, though I read about his murder of course. Absolutely horrible. We have little to do with the hospital except for pickups."

"Your customers?"

"Exactly. Do you have any idea who killed him?"

"Not yet."

"I suppose it's connected to these other events. Who could have imagined Brewster would be victimized by Satanists? People are terrified. I know several who have left town."

"More business for you, I guess." Woody had meant no sarcasm, but he realized too late that his comment sounded sarcastic.

Brantley's smile disappeared. "We much prefer people living than dead. That's one subject we don't joke about. May I offer you a tour?"

Leading Woody into the crematory, Brantley described filters, heat recovery ventilation, hot-hearth and multichamber air-controlled designs. Woody's attention was more focused on the room itself, which was starkly functional, warm, and dusty. *Is this dust*, he thought, *or ash? And if it's ash, is it bits of Brantley's "customers"?* He noticed that the man searching through the body bag wasn't wearing gloves.

"The chamber, or retort, will accommodate a five-hundred-pound cadaver." Brantley gave a little laugh. "Anything bigger will have to go in piecemeal. Temps range between sixteen and eighteen hundred degrees; that's twelve hundred more than a pizza oven. Our customers take quite a bit longer than a pizza, however. It takes an hour to burn someone who's a hundred and fifty pounds. What are you, one-eighty? I'd give you an hour and a quarter. Not bad for turning you into six pounds of ash and bone fragments." Again there was the little laugh. "But come and meet Larry. If this is the Burn Palace, he must be the prince."

Larry turned at the mention of his name. There was no smile, no expression of any kind. Just blankness. His gray face was pocked with old acne scars. On his right forearm was a tattoo of a bat, or maybe an eagle. He offered his hand to Woody.

Woody looked at the hand and thought how it had just been poking around in the corpse. He understood that Larry was offering him an unpleasant challenge. Glancing up, he saw that even Larry's eyes were gray. All this took no more than a second. Woody shook the hand.

"Why does it say 'head' at the top of the cardboard lid?" Woody hoped to insert a display of nonchalance between the handshake and what came next. He had an almost overpowering desire to wash his hands. "Does it matter how they go in?"

"Of course it does. The chest area takes the longest to burn, so we've a special flame right above the heart. That's almost romantic, don't you think? Larry'll be sliding this old fellow into the retort in a few minutes, and perhaps you'd care to watch. October's the start of flu season, so we get an uptick in elderly customers. I've always thought they should say *October's* the cruelest month, but then I'm partial to April."

Brantley handed Woody a stainless-steel pan two feet by about one foot. "Larry sweeps the ashes and bone fragments into this and then sorts through it for any metal he might have missed and for larger fragments that need extra breaking down before going into the cremulator." He patted a cylindrical drum mounted on a metal cube with a drawer at the bottom. "This is basically no more than an oversized Cuisinart. The blades reduce the bits and pieces to ash in thirty seconds. We call them cremains. They can go into an urn, be put into jewelry—pendants, charm bracelets, key chains—shot into space, or scattered at sea. Whatever you prefer, though of course we'd like to sell you a nice urn. But let me show you the cooler."

Woody wished Brantley wasn't so enthusiastic. On the other hand, he wondered about the cause of it. Maybe it was pride in his establishment; maybe it was tension. And if it was the latter, what was he tense about? "Does Larry ever wear gloves?"

"Gloves? I've never thought of it." Brantley gave a shout: "Larry, the detective wants to know if you ever wear gloves."

Larry was just closing the cardboard container. He looked at Woody and shrugged. Digger Brantley chuckled. "I guess he likes the hands-on approach."

"So what did Carl Krause do here?"

"Janitorial work, mostly. Though he was a great help if anything broke down. I feel awful about his wife. And those poor children!"

"Why'd he try to break into your place last night?"

"My place? You mean the funeral home? He never did any such thing."

"The back door was broken. Seymour told me Carl broke it."

Brantley burst out laughing. "Seymour said you'd asked about Carl and that broken window. You've a wicked sense of humor, Detective."

The walk-in cooler was roughly twenty by twelve feet, with four-tier racks on either side and a ventilation system with three large noisy fans on the farther wall. The single light hung over the door. The metal floor was dusty; the green racks were pitted with rust. A case of Budweiser was tucked under the rack on the right. A dozen cardboard caskets rested on the racks. *Waiting customers,* Woody thought. He could see his breath.

"Not very pretty, I'm afraid," said Brantley, raising his voice over the noise of the fans, "but thoroughly functional, and nobody sees it but us. We provide services for about twenty funeral homes, and that means at least ten customers a day. More in flu season. It's the same temperature as your regular meat locker or beer cooler. We can keep our customers here for a month or so, I expect. The bottoms of the cardboard caskets are fluid-resistant, but occasionally we have leakage. Most go into the furnace in a day or two."

Woody stood just inside the door; Brantley stood behind him. Woody found it impossible to avoid grim thoughts. He had taken care of his parents' funerals, and both had been cremated. He imagined them in such cardboard coffins in such a cooler, waiting for such a fire. *Leakage*, he repeated to himself.

Woody heard a noise behind him and turned. Brantley was shutting the door to the cooler. Kicking his foot into the opening, Woody blocked the door from clicking shut.

Brantley pulled open the door and laughed. "Just my little joke," he said.

NINETEEN

HER NAME WAS MOLLY GEIER, but she preferred to be called Vultura. She wasn't exactly a Satanist, but a Generational Demonolator, meaning demonology ran in the family. Demonolators were Theistic Satanists in the same way Presbyterians or Evangelists were Protestants. She spoke in a sandpaper whisper, and even her gums were black. She scared the living shit out of acting chief Fred Bonaldo.

Vultura knew this, and it warmed her heart.

Bonaldo sat at his desk, flanked by Detectives Brendan Gazzola and Sarah Muller. They didn't like Vultura much, either.

Vultura was thirty and had been a Demonolator all her life. Although Satan stood at the center of her religion, as a Demonolator her prayers were directed to Leviathan, prince of pain, and Belial, angel of hostility. As a child, her family had practiced Demonolic holy day rites with altars for particular demons and the home decorated with charms. These days, she belonged to a coven in New Haven. She aspired to astral projection, was proficient in magic word squares, and she told Fred Bonaldo she could turn him into a toad.

Bonaldo doubted this, or pretty much, but he didn't plan to test it. Vultura's very presence threw his belief system into jeopardy. Bonaldo was what might be called a generational Republican. He saw people in terms of party affiliations, with subtle gradations of liberal and conservative like the ticks on a thermometer, and he believed that everyone in South County could be measured by his simple method. What shook this faith was the realization that Vultura was off his chart. For crying out loud, she probably didn't even vote. And if she had a party affiliation, Bonaldo didn't want to know about it.

Vultura's black dress was slit up the thigh, and as she sat before Bonaldo and his detectives, she crossed one long leg over the other and it twitched, so Detective Sarah Muller thought, like the tail of an albino rat. Her eyes were so black that Detective Gazzola guessed she must be on drugs. Vultura described the nature of Leviathan, quoting from the Book of Job, and the three police officers leaned forward to hear.

"His sneezes flash forth light,
And his eyes are like
The eyelids of the morning.
Out of his mouth leap burning torches;
Sparks of fire shoot forth.
Out of his nostrils boil smoke
As from a boiling pot.
His breath kindles coals,
A flame gushes forth from his mouth.
In his neck lodges strength,
And dismay leaps before him."

Gazzola was unimpressed. He had little imagination, and Vultura didn't fit into his worldview, which, in any case, was small. She was all smoke and mirrors, as far as he was concerned. "How'd a girl from New Haven end up at a kinky party on the island?" he asked.

Vultura's smile was barely a ripple. She described black-magic chatrooms, message boards, vampire websites, Satanist blogs, YouTube, Facebook, MySpace, Twitter, and Skype. Online indexes listed thousands of covens and related groups around the world and led Vultura to Demonolators in a dozen countries. They journaled, swapped profiles and pictures, studied calendars of Left-Hand Path events, where they met and cavorted. Inevitably, crossovers occurred into the cybergoth and rivethead subcultures, which she dismissed as imposture. But if any Sabbat, Esbat, Dark Gathering, or heavy metal concert were advertised within a three-hundred-mile radius of New Haven, Vultura knew about it.

"Some I go to, some I don't. It depends on the level of Bad."

By *Bad,* Bonaldo realized, she meant *Good.* It astonished him that satanic covens had websites, that videos of their diabolical rites were available on YouTube and that athames, flying brooms, cloaks, spells, spell supplies, voodoo dolls, and suchlike were available from online witch-supply stores. Fred Bonaldo had recently begun to use e-mail and found it nothing short of miraculous. He realized he had barely scratched the surface.

"So why'd you come here this morning?" he asked, keeping his voice monotonically metallic.

"I saw that guy's picture in the paper—the one who was murdered. He was a complete creep."

The gathering on the island was a sacred harvest festival in preparation for Samhain and included dancing, chanting, casting spells, and Sex Magick, which was not, as Vultura said, just getting laid, but entailed withholding the orgasm so its full power was turned inward. "It's not about pleasure, it's about transforming the orgasm through billions of christic atoms into a carrier of spiritual essence. But you don't force anybody. I mean, I didn't know the girl would get raped."

Twenty people had met in West Kingston and were driven a few miles to a spot where they were led through the woods to a submerged bridge that took them to the island. The bridge was about twenty feet long and consisted of thick planks linked together. Torches lined the path with a large bonfire at the end. People wore cloaks and hoods; the high priest or coven leader wore a skull mask. She described a service led by the high priest based on patterns of call and response that grew increasingly impassioned with cries, fainting fits, and moments of demonic possession. Vultura denied drug or alcohol usage. "Maybe some 'shrooms," she said. She herself disliked any stimulants to come between her and her awareness of the One. Clouston, she said, had assisted the high priest and had been called the Dark Deacon. She could tell little about the priest himself except he'd been about six feet, thin, and "athletic." She guessed he was between thirty and forty. The cloaks and relative darkness made it difficult to see people's faces. Some looked familiar, but Vultura could identify none for certain.

"Would you recognize any of them again if you saw them?" asked Muller.

"Maybe."

Bonaldo didn't think she was telling the truth, but he didn't know what to do about it. He'd have to discuss it with Woody. The whole business was so disturbing that he found it impossible to think clearly. He felt he was in way over his head.

Up until 1980 Brewster policemen had played in a baseball league, which had started right after the Second World War. On the walls of the office were a dozen photographs of winning teams—eager, smiling, baseball-loving cops, mugging for the camera. Now all were dead or elderly, but their distant good cheer still gave a bit of warmth to the room. Glancing at those pictures with Vultura's words in mind, Bonaldo thought how far away they were. It wasn't a matter of wholesome versus unwholesome; it was a metaphysical distance. Many of those baseball players were the fathers and uncles of his friends. Wondering what they'd think of Vultura the Generational Demonolator, Fred Bonaldo could only sigh.

Vultura said that no bones had been thrown in the fire. Nor had she seen any wicker figures, though she had attended wicker man festivals in the past. The burning of the wicker man and the throwing of bones on a fire was part of Samhain, the end of summer harvest festival that the irresponsibly ignorant confused with All Hallows Eve. As for a big goat-like creature with cloven feet, she thought Bonaldo was pulling her leg.

"If he had been there, I'd have remembered him. The whole thing was about the girl. That was why we'd come. People were shouting and chanting; there was lots of noise. Then I realized this girl was screaming. It wasn't just an act, she was really screaming. The Deacon, this Clouston guy, held her down and others helped. They held her arms and legs. Then the man in the skull mask fucked her. It seemed part of the festival, even the screaming, but Clouston was too rough. I mean, the girl was just a girl. Believe me, it was nothing I'd signed on for."

Several times she mentioned that today, the 31st, was Samhain and there would be celebrations all over New England. "Tonight's a big party night. You guys better hang on to your hats."

Saturday morning Hercel, Lucy, and Tig were with Baldo in the Bonaldo rec room. Baldo had chores—raking leaves, washing his clothes, cleaning his room—but Laura Bonaldo knew it would be impossible to make him do chores with his friends in the house. Anyway, it had started to rain, and raking leaves would have to be postponed. A patrol car was parked in the driveway; Whole-Hog Hopper sat in the living room, twiddling his thumbs. He wanted to watch TV, but Laura wouldn't allow it. He said it would be okay, because he was going to be suspended as a policeman and was there only as a favor to the family. After all, Laura was his cousin.

"If you don't like it," Laura said, "you can leave."

Woody's golden retriever was also in the rec room. Woody had dropped off Ajax to keep the kids company. Laura, who prided herself that her house had always been dog-free, was horrified, but she kept her mouth shut. However, she phoned the fumigator to make an appointment. Dogs, in her mind, were as bad as Satanists, but the off chance that Carl Krause was still wandering loose led her to permit it just this once.

Baldo Bonaldo was teaching Lucy how to play Ping-Pong. By doing this, he understood, he was doing everyone a favor, because Lucy had no chance of learning. She was only five. Every time she hit the ball, it sailed across the room and Baldo had to dig under the chairs to find it. Not even the dog would chase it.

Ajax was curled up on the floor with Tig and Hercel, offering the only comfort the children allowed themselves. Every time Tig thought of her grandfather she wanted to weep, yet it was impossible *not* to think of him. This was also how it was with Hercel thinking about his mother. In fact, if he forgot her for even a second, he became furious with himself for forgetting. Neither child could imagine getting past where they were now. Added to their grief was their lingering horror of the coyotes and what had happened in the woods. Whenever Tig heard a dog bark her muscles went stiff. She had been positive she'd be killed, and even if she had only a vague idea of death she had been positive she would be eaten. The business with the whirling stones was a complete mystery to her.

Added to Hercel's grief and the memory of horror was an exhaustion unlike anything he had ever felt. Tracing the tip of the screwdriver around in a circle had sapped him of all strength. He wanted to sleep but couldn't sleep. When he shut his eyes, he saw horrible things—Carl hurling Harriet at the fireplace, the coyotes. He would yank his eyes open and the exhaustion would return. All he could do was push his fingers through Ajax's thick fur, gather it between his fingers, squeeze it together, and then do it all again.

Baldo was sorry for his friends and tried to share their grief. But his grief was of a more personal nature. Tonight was Halloween. For a trickster like himself, Halloween had a value exceeding the value that Vultura placed on Samhain. Yet his mother said he couldn't go out. It was too dangerous. Maybe, if he were good, she would take him to the Halloween party that Father Pete was holding at St. John's. Baldo was shocked. Halloween was the very opposite of church. And hadn't Father Pete said if Baldo brought his fart machine to St. John's ever again, then he, Father Pete, would crucify him? So Baldo also grieved and plotted his escape.

Several times Laura came quietly down the stairs and stood watching the children. She had offered food, videos; she offered to drive them absolutely anywhere. They had wanted nothing. She racked her brain for something she might do. Maybe a good dose of sleeping pills to keep them asleep for a week would help, though she wouldn't dream of doing it. Seeing them with the dog, she felt guilty about wanting to put Ajax outdoors.

On his way back from Brantley's crematorium, Woody had talked to a trooper he knew in New Jersey's Division of Gaming Enforcement, to whom he had sent Clouston's description. So far Clouston had been identified as visiting the poker rooms at the Borgata. The trooper couldn't tell as yet how often Clouston had gambled in the casino, though it was often enough to be remembered; nor did the trooper know how much Clouston had won or lost. "I'm still waiting on that," he said. However, Clouston was remembered as playing in a recent $350 and $50 No Limit Hold 'Em, and his name wasn't among the winners. Woody hadn't heard from the Las Vegas and Connecticut casinos, but he had heard enough to think that Clouston had "money issues," as he termed it.

The next day Woody drove to Clouston's house on Ballou Street, where Detective Gazzola had arrived half an hour earlier. By that time Brewster police officers had been showing photographs to Clouston's neighbors for a day. Gazzola stood on Clouston's porch, chain-smoking. He told Woody about the interview with Vultura. "She's one scary female," said Gazzola. "Stick your prick into that bad business and you'd never get it back."

They stood on the porch, away from the rain, but the wind blew it in their faces. The police officers going door to door in their long, reversible raincoats reminded Woody of monks. Harry Morelli slowly made his way up the walk. He never hurried, not from laziness but because he felt it was beneath his dignity. Drops of water hung from the tips of his drooping mustache.

"Nobody's recognized Brantley so far," he said, "though they knew who he was, all right. But two of 'em have ID'd this other guy."

He stood on the porch, slowly leafing through a small stack of photographs while trying to shield them from the rain. Woody willed himself not to scream at him for being so slow. At last Morelli found the right picture and held it up. "Here it is."

It was Dr. Jonathan Balfour.

"Two different people recognized him?"

"Yeah, and more then once. Like he'd been here more than once."

Woody turned to Gazzola. "Go to the hospital and pick him up.

Take some guys with you and bring him to police headquarters. Call me when you've got him."

Woody then joined the other patrolmen interviewing the neighbors, but told them to concentrate on Balfour. He also called Bingo and Bobby Anderson to tell them what he had learned. Bingo was on his way to talk to Hamilton Brantley at the funeral home, and Woody said not to bother. Brantley was at the crematorium.

Bobby described Professor Vasa Korak's coyote farm. "That guy can make them jump through hoops almost. We're on a fuckin' roll!"

It seemed to Woody the end was in sight. He wanted to call Jill and tell her about it; he wanted to say that soon there would be nothing to keep him from seeing her. His desire to call her was like a burning in his belly. The policemen going from door to door reminded Woody of Halloween trick-or-treaters. He called Captain Brotman instead.

Detective Beth Lajoie had tracked down Dr. Stone at Providence Hospital and asked him if he'd fucked Alice Alessio in a Morgan Memorial bathroom. She hoped to handle this over the phone, but if Dr. Stone dragged his feet she would drive up to Providence in a shot.

Who knew what sort of work Dr. Stone was doing when Lajoie's call had interrupted him? Saving lives, most likely. *Tough luck,* Lajoie thought.

Dr. Stone responded to Lajoie's question with absolute silence. Lajoie heard hospital noises in the background. Then she said, "I'm waiting."

"How do I know you are who you say you are?"

So Detective Lajoie said Dr. Stone could call trooper headquarters, which would confirm who she was. Then he could call her back. "But if you don't call in ten minutes I'll have ten troopers bust up whatever you're doing and bring you to the barracks. This is a murder investigation, Doctor, and I got priority. Do you really want people to see you being dragged kicking and screaming out of Providence Hospital? Anyway, who else knows you fucked Nurse Spandex? The only way you'll get in trouble is if you make a fuss. I only want to know if you came on to her or she came on to you. Isn't that simple enough? Who initiated it?"

"She did."

Hot damn, thought Lajoie. "Tell me more."

So Dr. Stone described their three-week relationship, which had started with oral sex in a bathroom. "She kept flirting, aggressively flirting, and at last I just stopped resisting it." But he had remained scared, and by the time the thrill wore off, he abruptly left on vacation. Then he had taken a job in the emergency room at Providence Hospital. "I was only at Morgan Memorial another week and I managed to avoid her. She'd promised to make a scene. She even said she thought she was pregnant. I was scared half to death."

"Thanks," said Lajoie. It was time to see Dr. Balfour.

At about noon on Saturday, Bingo Schwartz picked up a trooper from Alton Barracks and drove to Brantley's crematorium. He wanted to ask Brantley what he knew about body brokers, which Bingo felt was a subtle way of learning if Brantley had dealings with them. The Massachusetts state police detective Frank Schnell had explained that a person might donate his body for scientific research and the body might first be sent to a funeral home, which could hold a viewing and a service or could deliver the body directly to the body broker. If Tommy Meadows, the state health investigator, had an interest in Brewster, then Bingo thought he might have been interested in Brantley.

Bingo brought along a trooper, Rodger Legros, because he didn't want to go alone; but, first of all, he didn't think there would be any danger and, secondly, if there was something to be found Bingo wanted to be the one who found it.

At fifty years old and after more than twenty-five years as a trooper, Bingo had not yet made corporal. Promotion in the state police was a matter of merit, and plenty of guys retired as troopers. Bingo would like to retire in a year, no more. He was champing at the bit to get busy with future projects. That thinking he'd done earlier at the Brewster Brew about the scene in Don Giovanni when the Don is dragged to hell, Bingo meant to write it down later in his notebook. He would make drawings of possible sets; he would do watercolors. He had a drawer of such scenes from twenty different operas. But they were only practice. In any case, he understood he would never be hired as a set designer. As he told everyone, "I only want to be of use." He would help put the sets together, and he'd work for free, if it came to that. His only wish was to be a piece of the big picture.

But if Bingo could finish his time as a trooper with a big success, it would make him feel better all around. Good words would be spoken about him at his retirement; he'd be told he would be missed. These were things he wanted his wife to hear, not that it would make her like him—there had been too much bad water under the bridge for that—but it would let her know that as a state trooper he had been appreciated.

Bingo had no expectations about what he might learn from Brantley, but he felt he had a little lead. He had a lead and he didn't want to share it.

As for Trooper Rodger Legros, he had nothing better to do except catch speeders on 95, so he was glad to tag along, even if it meant driving. He didn't like opera, and he hoped Bingo wouldn't start humming, which he knew was impossible, but at least it would be harder to hear him over the sound of the cruiser, the windshield wipers, and the rain beating on the roof. Legros was thirty years old and he had been married for five years. His wife's name was Sally; they had two children.

"What's new in Brewster?" asked Legros. He had been on duty by the hospital when the baby was stolen, but he hadn't been back since.

"There're expecting a lot of activity tonight. It's Halloween."

"It's supposed to snow. Will kids be trick-or-treating?"

"The mayor's put a ban on it after six o'clock. They're doing something in the school gym, and some churches have parties, but most parents are keeping their kids inside."

"It's all witchcraft, right? Or Devil worship?"

"More likely somebody's trying to make a crooked buck."

Two cars were parked in front of the crematorium. Legros parked beside them.

"Look at the smoke," said Legros. "Someone's going to meet his maker."

Bingo didn't comment. He found the building ugly: cinder blocks and a flat roof. But he couldn't imagine what a "pretty" crematorium might be. Behind the crematorium stretched the forest of the Arcadia Management Area. Bingo noticed the bullet camera over the front door. He opened the door and went in.

Sometimes a person can come upon a scene so shocking that it seems his synapses begin to shut down in self-protection. Bingo grunted. Ahead of him on a table was Ronnie McBride's head. His mouth was smeared with lipstick. A guy was standing over the head, dolling it up, putting on eye shadow and rouge. Bingo knew the guy—Jimmy something, an ambulance tech. There was music playing, but Bingo didn't know it was music. It was the heavy metal band War of Ages playing "All Consuming Fire." The singer was growling, and the music was loud.

Trooper Legros was behind Bingo and bumped into him when Bingo abruptly stopped. Then he too saw the head. "Good fuckin' grief!"

Hearing a voice, Jimmy looked up. He knew trouble was coming. "Larry!"

Bingo took a few steps forward. He was still trying to understand what Ronnie McBride's head was doing on the table, but whatever the reason Bingo knew it wasn't legal. Bingo carried a Sig P229 in a concealment holster over his right hip. He brushed aside his suit coat to get at it.

Then a second man appeared—Bingo registered him as a gray man—from the other side of the furnace. He held a black pistol. Bingo saw it was the Browning Hi-Power.

"Fuck you, Jimmy," shouted the man. "You was supposed to keep an eye on the monitor! Now look what you done!"

"Watch out!" shouted Legros. He pushed Bingo aside.

At that moment the second man—it was Larry—raised the pistol and fired. Legros jerked to the left; his knees collapsed. The back of his head was splattered against the wall.

Bingo made the mistake of glancing at Legros. When he looked back, the gray man had turned toward him. Bingo didn't even hear the gunshot.

Maud Lord was scared. This in itself was interesting to her, because she didn't scare easily. It had started with just a flicker of fear when she had found the dead cat, and it had grown ever since, to the point where she was afraid to leave Ocean Breezes, afraid even to leave her room. On Saturday afternoon, it was bad enough for her to call Bobby.

He had just gotten back from his visit to Vasa Korak and was fussing with a Google map on a police department computer, looking for places near Brewster where someone might raise coyotes without people knowing about it. Barton Wilcox's farm would be such a place, though Barton wouldn't do such a thing; being almost surrounded on three sides by Great Swamp it had the necessary privacy. Then Woody had called, and, among other things, he had told Bobby about his visit to the crematorium. "It's an ugly place," Woody said, "right at the edge of Arcadia in the middle of nowhere."

So Bobby started thinking about the Arcadia Management Area that bordered 95 for several miles north of Hope Valley. Arcadia was four times the size of Great Swamp—nearly ten miles from one end to the other and the surrounding area was far less populated. It was something to think about.

These thoughts, however, were interrupted by Maud Lord's phone call.

The more frightened Maud had become, the more powerless she felt. "Do you remember me?" she asked.

"Good afternoon, Mrs. Lord, how could I forget you? Any new discoveries?"

"I'm terrified, and I don't know what to do about it."

So Bobby decided to make a stop at Ocean Breezes.

Maud Lord had a one-bedroom apartment in the annex, which contained sixteen small apartments behind the main building. It was attractive enough and furnished with the best of Maud's own furniture. But it had a built-in drawback. As Maud said, "I'm only going in one direction." She dreaded the day when she would be transferred to a single room. Even at ninety-five, she liked to think a few choices still lay ahead. It wasn't a future full of opportunity, but at least she felt she had two or three options. Once sent to a single room, she would have no options left.

As she waited for Bobby, she made coffee and set out a plate of butter cookies she had made herself. She brushed her hair, put on her blue cardigan and an emerald-and-diamond necklace. She might be ninety-five and terrified, but she also meant to do a little flirting.

Shortly, Bobby gave a jazzy knock on her door and she called, "It's open."

"Hey, Mrs. Lord, you look great. That's a great necklace." He wasn't sure whether to shake her hand or kiss her cheek, but then he kissed her cheek. It was very soft. Maybe Maud Lord blushed. She stood next to her mission oak round pedestal table that her first husband had bought in 1935.

They sat down and Maud poured coffee. Bobby took cream and sugar. Though his charm machine was turned up high, it was also finely tuned. His attention was mostly focused on her fear. She smiled with her mouth only. The rest of her face showed distress.

"So?" asked Bobby, taking a cookie.

"Too many people are dying here. I know it's what they're supposed to do, but this is a statistical mistake."

Bobby neither believed her nor disbelieved her, but perhaps he leaned toward belief. After all, he liked Maud Lord. "What cause does the supervisor give?"

"She says it's old age, but that's not a cause. That's just blather."

Maud Lord had lived in her little apartment for nearly ten years. She knew everyone who worked at Ocean Breezes, and she knew many of the residents. Even if she had never grown used to death's persistent appetite, she had grown accustomed to its calendar—how many died in summer, how many in winter and so on.

Maud Lord explained all this to Bobby. "Too many have died this month and too many died last month. Something's wrong."

Every night, it seemed, an ambulance arrived and took someone away, sometimes it came more than once. You could tell if a person was alive or dead by whether the ambulance used the siren.

"They go down that street out there," said Maud, "and they always wake me up. Not only are too many dying, too many are dying at night. The other night three people died. One was Julie Fiore; we'd had dinner that evening, and she'd been the picture of health. And even though the others had been ill, they hadn't actually been sinking. It seems unnatural."

It didn't seem that way to Bobby, but then this wasn't his area of expertise. Maud Lord, on the other hand, watched the departures like a hawk. After all, she was invested.

"What night was that?" he asked.

"Thursday night. I know it was Thursday, because police cars were rushing all over town and I didn't get a wink of sleep."

When a resident died, a doctor came from the hospital to certify the death. Then, unless there were prior arrangements, the body was delivered to Brantley's Funeral Home.

"Is it one particular doctor?" asked Bobby.

"I've been trying to remember his name all afternoon. It starts with a B."

"Dr. Jonathan Balfour?"

Maud Lord beamed. "You're so clever. I *knew* I was right to call you."

"And he comes every time?"

"Of course not, but he comes more than anyone else."

"Does Dr. Balfour have any particular friends on the staff?" asked Bobby. "Any woman friends."

Maud's eyes gleamed. "There's Margaret Hanna. She's a nurse."

"Would she be on duty now?"

Maud shook her head. "She only works at night."

Detective Beth Lajoie hated rain. She hated the way drops ran down her neck. She hated getting her feet wet. Starting in 1998, she had done a five-year stint in the financial crimes unit and had helped arrest a guy who had socked away a million bucks of embezzled money so he could live in Brazil. Lajoie condemned the crime but admired the ambition. If she had that kind of money she would relocate to San Pedro de Atacama in the Atacama Desert, which was fifty times drier than Death Valley. That's how much she hated rain.

As Detective Lajoie ran from her car to the hospital's emergency entrance, she held a newspaper over her head to keep her hair from getting wet. Almost as much as rain, she hated running. It put her in a powerful bad mood. Walking up to the triage desk, she knocked on it with a knuckle. "I need to find Dr. Balfour."

The young woman behind the desk looked startled, which was many people's response to Detective Lajoie. "I'm not sure where he is right now."

Lajoie put her badge on the counter. "I don't like the words *I'm not sure*. I want to know *exactly* where Balfour is. If you can't tell me, find someone who can."

Within ten minutes it was determined that Dr. Balfour wasn't in the building. No one could say where he had gone. Then it turned out that Detective Gazzola had come looking for Balfour half an hour earlier. The young woman at the triage desk passed on the news to the rude police lady.

"Why didn't you tell me about Gazzola?"

The young woman looked away. "You didn't ask."

Sometimes Beth Lajoie's smiles were more frightening than her frowns. "Have a really nice day," she said.

Dr. Jonathan Balfour lived on Ash Street, in a large apartment that was the bottom floor of a house with a green mansard roof. An ornately columned porch extended across the front of the building. Balfour's condo had a side entrance. Lajoie rang the bell and knocked, waited, and knocked again. There was a small awning over the steps, but it wasn't enough to keep her dry. Balfour's windows were at least six feet tall. Lajoie peered through the closest into a living room that reminded her of a room in a museum—beautiful antiques, no clutter, and nothing out of place. Two tufted leather wingback chairs stood on either side of a fireplace with green and yellow tiles.

"Nice shit," said Detective Lajoie. She hurried back to the steps to wait. She was also expecting a call from a Manhattan South vice unit detective, who she had talked to about Maggie Kelly. The detective had called that morning to say he had got a line on where the girl was living. "I'll send you a box of chocolates," Lajoie had said.

The detective had begged off. "My cholesterol's all over the map."

Lajoie liked coincidence; she liked serendipity. She liked the occurrence of the absolutely unexplainable. But she didn't believe any of it. What she liked most was what a teacher had said at the academy. He'd been quoting Louis Pasteur: "In the fields of observation chance favors only the prepared mind." This principle had guided her during her years as a trooper. So she wasn't surprised when the Manhattan detective called with the news that he'd picked up Maggie Kelly.

"But she didn't have any baby with her," he said, "and she won't talk."

Detective Lajoie thought for a moment. Although it was only four o'clock, the heavy clouds made it seem later. She hated thinking that the time would change next week. It would make her feel like she was living in Alaska. Not only was San Pedro de Atacama very dry, it was also very bright.

"Tell her you know that Dr. Balfour delivered her baby. Jonathan Balfour."

"I'm on it."

As Lajoie waited, she wondered what it would be like to live in a place as nice as Dr. Balfour's. Her own two-bedroom looked like a cheap Holiday Inn suite without the little bottles of shampoo, conditioner, and skin lotion. Even if she bought a picture to hang on the wall, it always ended up an ugly picture. She lacked the gift; she knew she lacked it.

"Okay, I told her," said the detective.

"And?"

"Scared the holy shit out of her."

"Book her. I'll get busy with extradition."

"For selling her baby?"

"You got it."

Woody arrived at Balfour's condo on Ash Street just as Detective Lajoie was pulling out of the driveway in her Mazda 6. "He's not home!" she shouted.

Parking at the curb, Woody walked over to Lajoie's open window.

"You'll get soaked," she said. "Get inside."

He climbed in and they talked. She told him about Maggie Kelly, while he told her about Bobby's discoveries about coyotes.

"We're going to nail their pricks to the floor!" said Lajoie happily.

"Maybe." He was often surprised by Lajoie's language, especially when she was dressed like a grade-school teacher.

"Any chance of putting out an APB on Balfour?"

"I'll ask Brotman," said Woody, "but I doubt it. We still have nothing concrete."

"What about a search warrant for his condo?"

"That might be possible. What d'you think we'd find?"

"With luck a skull mask."

Woody doubted Balfour would be that sloppy.

"Any news about Carl Krause?" asked Lajoie.

"Not a word."

"He's probably in Mexico by now."

"Why Mexico?"

"The cool cucumbers go to Canada. The nutjobs head south. It's always like that. Haven't you noticed?"

Woody hadn't. Once back in his truck, he called Captain Brotman. He was willing to go for the search warrant, but not the APB. "After all, he's a doctor," he said. There was a moment of silence. Both Brotman and Woody knew that being a doctor didn't mean squat.

"Look," said Brotman, "if we can't find him by tomorrow, then I'll go with the APB." He agreed, however, to alert various police departments in South County.

Brotman went on to tell Woody about Bingo's conversation with a Massachusetts state police detective, Frank Schnell, about body brokers. "Some of these cadavers come from funeral homes. We've no idea if Hartmann was interested in this and the primary investigator's out of the country, but there might be a link with Hamilton Brantley. I've tried to call Bingo, but he's not answering. You know where he is?"

Woody didn't.

After hanging up, Woody tried Bingo without success. This bothered him. In the past ten years Woody had grown increasingly dependent on cell phones. Bingo, Lajoie, Bobby Anderson, and others could be pursuing answers to a hundred questions, but their phones linked them together. They would check in with one another and share information, even Lajoie who was maddeningly independent. Together they formed one connected intelligence, or that's how it functioned at its best. Being unable to reach Bingo gave Woody an unsettled feeling.

He'd had gone to Balfour's condo because of a call from Bobby about his conversation with Maud Lord. Were more people dying at Ocean Breezes than usual? Woody started his truck. Maybe he should talk to Brantley again.

A wake was being held for Frances Crenner, mother of Jack Crenner, owner of Crenner Millwork. Both sides of the street were lined with cars. A policeman directed traffic. Groups of umbrellas climbed and descended the steps. On one side of the long front porch, four or five men were smoking. Woody was hesitant to bother Brantley, but then he parked his truck back by the carriage house and walked around to the front. He wore a long dark raincoat, but he had no cap and his short hair was plastered to his scalp.

A middle-aged man by the front steps approached him. Woody found him familiar, but no name came to mind. He didn't look friendly.

"You're Woody Potter, right? The state cop? When're you going to stop farting around and catch whoever's driving us crazy, these witches or whoever? The only guy who's shown any balls is Mackie McNamara, and you threw him in jail."

It took a moment to recall that McNamara was one of the men who had tossed bricks through Sister Asherah's windows. Half a dozen responses went through Woody's head, and all could get him in trouble.

"We're doing all we can," he said at last.

"Yeah? Well, it's not enough. Why'n't you put somebody in jail?"

Woody moved past him to the front steps. Wasn't his concern understandable? Why should he get so angry? "I can only say what I just said. We're doing what we can."

"Yeah, well, bullshit!"

Woody paused with his back to the man and considered turning around. Through the door in the hall, he saw Brantley talking to Jack Crenner. Brantley's forehead was wrinkled with concern. Woody opened the door.

Woody guessed Brantley was sorry to see him, but the funeral director gave no sign of it. His dark blue suit was most likely different from the one that he had worn earlier at the crematorium. He probably had a closet full of blue suits. His silver hair combed back over his head appeared stuck in place with glue.

"You're drenched," whispered Brantley. "Let me get you a towel."

"I'm okay." Woody took off his raincoat.

"You'll catch your death." Brantley took Woody's coat and then led him to the cloakroom. "Any sign of Carl?"

About fifty people were in the large room to the right of the hall. Woody saw the casket at the far back on a dais wrapped with a dark maroon fabric. The front half of the lid was open. "I'm told he's fled to Mexico."

Brantley looked doubtful. "Well, I hope they catch him as soon as possible." He paused as a tall woman came up to him. She was about forty-five, with short black hair, and wore a dark green dress. She moved lightly, like a dancer. Woody thought she was quite beautiful. She said something in Brantley's ear and kissed his cheek. Giving Woody a smile, she ascended the wide staircase.

"Is that your wife?" said Woody. "She's very attractive."

"Jenny's my queen. She's known the Crenners all her life, and she wanted to give her condolences to the family."

"Queen of the Burn Palace," said Woody, without giving it much thought.

Brantley's face turned ugly with anger. It was more of a spasm than an expression. The next moment his face returned to affable blankness. "Jenny has little to do with that part of my life. She rarely comes over here. What can I help you with this time, Detective?"

Woody made his way toward the casket. Brantley's reaction surprised him, and he had to digest it. Most of the people in the room were elderly and talked quietly to one another. Brantley followed him.

"When someone dies at Ocean Breezes," asked Woody, "is he brought over here?"

"He or she might easily go someplace else. After all, we don't have a monopoly. Still, we're the only funeral home in Brewster."

"What happens if a person leaves his body to a medical school?"

"If someone dies unexpectedly and the person is an organ donor, the body goes to the hospital. If the entire body is going to a university, then it often comes here first. At times the family wants a service. Or the body will go directly to the responsible facility and the family holds a memorial service at a later date. Each case can be different. And of course it all has to be approved by the medical examiner's office."

Mrs. Crenner lay in her casket with her hands folded across her breast and a rosary wound around her finger. She wore a dark dress and must have been in her mid-eighties when she died. Rouge and makeup combined to make her look the picture of health. The bottom half of the casket was closed.

"Did you put shoes on her?" asked Woody.

"Good grief, how can you ask such a thing?"

Woody shrugged. "Shoes, socks, she could be naked from the waist down. How would anybody know?"

"What an awful idea. I don't find that a bit funny."

Woody turned away from the casket. Brantley seemed seriously indignant.

"So you work with Dr. Balfour at Ocean Breezes?"

"Sometimes. We work with a number of doctors."

"I thought he did most of the work over there."

"I believe he's often on call at night, but I'm the wrong one to ask. As I say, we work with a number of doctors."

"I've heard an unusual number of men and women have died at Ocean Breezes this month." They were walking back out toward the hall. Brantley nodded to people he knew. One man he patted on the shoulder, with another he shook hands.

"That's something you should ask Ocean Breezes about, or City Hall, for that matter."

"Don't you keep records?"

"Of course we do, but some of the deceased went to other establishments or to the hospital if they are body donors."

"What's your relationship with body brokers?"

"Are you serious?" asked Brantley, indignantly. "All that goes through the hospital. We're too small a place to deal with it, although at times a body will come to us after a body broker has done his . . . whatever."

"Harvesting?"

Brantley nodded.

"Are you buddies with Balfour?"

Brantley looked surprised. "I admire him and we're friendly, but that's the extent of it. As a doctor, he's committed to curing the sick, fighting disease, and prolonging life. I, well, I'm at the other end of things."

"I'd like to see your records for October."

They had reached the hall. Brantley stopped. "Now? Really, Woody, I'm extremely busy. Can't you see these people? I shouldn't even be talking to you. After all, they're the ones who need my attention."

"I want to see them."

Brantley didn't seem angry, but his benign expression had frozen. "Then you'll have to get a warrant and see them on Monday."

"You're good," said Woody. "You're really good."

Bobby had been on his way to see Margaret Hanna, the nurse who worked at Ocean Breezes, when he got a call from Woody to go to Brantley's crematorium before it closed for the day to look at the cremation records for October. He wanted the names of men and women who had been sent to Brantley's Funeral Home. On one hand, Bobby was mildly annoyed; on the other, he was interested in Woody's question. Woody told him to take a few troopers with him, but Bobby didn't want to bother. Rounding them up would take time.

Bobby drove out 138 toward Skunk Hill Road. There was little traffic, but as he neared Wyoming he was abruptly passed by a red sports coupe. He responded to this on two levels. As a trooper, he realized the driver was exceeding the speed limit by at least thirty miles per hour. As the driver of a 370Z, his competitive instincts were engaged. Bobby increased his speed. It was still raining.

When the red coupe stopped at the light at Wyoming, Bobby saw it was an Audi TTS. Earlier in life—maybe as a teenager—he would have been tempted to race it, but at thirty-five he knew it was a bad idea. Still, the car was going in his direction and when it went straight after the light and turned right toward Skunk Hill Road, Bobby was right behind it. Then the driver must have seen him, because he quickly accelerated. Soon only the glow of the car's taillights was visible, and then not even that. Bobby slowed down. The rain was changing to sleet.

But that was not the end of the red Audi, because when Bobby turned down the long drive to the crematorium he saw the TTS parked by the building and its driver in the process of unfolding himself from the front seat. Bobby pulled up next to him: a tall, thin young man with thick blond hair. It was Jonathan Balfour.

"I could give you a ticket for driving like that," said Bobby as he got out. A light was on above the door of the crematorium; the woods were in shadow. One other car was parked in the small lot.

Balfour laughed. "If I'd known a trooper was driving that Z, I'd have offered to race. What brings you out here?" He reached out his hand, and Bobby shook it.

"I wanted to check the cremation records. What about you?"

"What's that about great minds thinking alike? An old fellow, Jason Thomas, died at Ocean Breezes last week. Dr. Percival filed the certificate, and I wanted to see what he said. Jason was my patient."

"Couldn't you have asked Percival himself?"

"He's gone for the weekend and I can't reach him. Didn't I see your car at Ocean Breezes earlier?"

"Maud Lord's a great pal of mine. I wanted to see how she was doing."

"She's a tough old bird. And what's the other cliché? She'll outlast us all." Balfour laughed again. "In her case, I bet it's true." He opened the door and held it for Bobby.

"Maud said she's seen you over there often. Have you been dating Margaret Hanna?"

Balfour was behind Bobby as the two men entered the crematorium. Bobby didn't want Balfour behind him, and he turned slightly.

"Marge's a great gal, but our relationship goes no further than chitchat. You troopers are always thinking about sex. You must have dull lives."

The crematory was bright and overheated. By the furnace, a middle-aged man in a gray T-shirt stood as motionless as a statue. His mouth was partly open, and he held a long-handled brush. There was something odd about him, but Bobby's attention was focused on Balfour. He didn't believe the story about Jason Thomas and Dr. Percival, and he thought he should give Woody a call. Then he decided to rile Balfour a little.

"Several people have identified you going into Clouston's house. I thought you hardly knew him. Are you hiding another relationship? Nurse Spandex, Margaret Hanna, Benjamin Clouston—you must be some kind of bunny . . ."

Bobby stopped in mid-sentence. He stared at the floor. Most of it was dusty, but an area in front of him had been recently washed. The cleaned area extended to the cinder-block wall next to the door. Balfour was watching him. Bobby went to the wall and touched it. The wall, too, had just been cleaned, or this part had. Then, at his feet, he saw a reddish stain. Bobby bent down on one knee. He heard a quick footstep and started to turn. Then his head seemed to explode.

TWENTY

SNOW ON HALLOWEEN, messy, heavy snow, with the temperature a bit above freezing. The streets are sloppy with mush and crisscrossed with car tracks. The trees' few last leaves are weighed down with flakes as big as thumbnails. Snow gathers on telephone wires and falls to the street with a plop. Anyone standing nearby when it drops jumps about a foot. People are sprung pretty tight. After all, it's Halloween.

Before six o'clock some kids go trick-or-treating—drenched witches, sodden white-sheet ghosts, waterlogged monsters—and each kid has two or three soaked adults as bodyguards. But at the stroke of six they vanish like vampires at dawn. Anyway, not many houses have porch lights on, and the few people giving out candy have bodyguards as well.

Jean Sawyer closed up early at the Brewster Brew. Her house is dark, and it looks like no one's home, but she and her husband are upstairs in the bedroom. The shades are drawn, and they are watching TV with the sound turned low. Ginger and Howard Phelps are also in their bedroom with drawn shades. They're playing gin rummy but find it hard to concentrate. Right now even Old Maid would give them trouble. Whole-Hog Hopper's watching TV in his living room, but he's got his shotgun across his knees. Too bad for any kid who comes knocking on *his* door.

Nobody's at You-You tonight. Classes are canceled because of the weather. People are glad to have an excuse. The restaurants are empty; the bars have only a few diehards. Mayor Hobart is running the Halloween party in the high school gym, but only about twenty kids show up. Father Pete's party at the church got twenty-five kids, but not all at once. Those with cars go to Westerly or Wakefield. Brewster's dead.

In the hospital, the emergency room has called in extra help. Nurse Spandex offered to work for free, but Tabby Roberts, the head nurse, said no, thanks. An ambulance should be parked outside, but it hasn't shown up. No telling what Seymour and Jimmy are up to. Dr. Joyce Fuller is in her office and plans to stay all night. She hopes nothing will happen, but if it does she won't be caught flat-footed. Helen Greene, the Methodist whose windows were broken by Mackie McNamara, is spending the weekend with friends in Mystic. Sister Asherah and Sister Isis are celebrating Samhain someplace out of state.

Most people are hunkered down, waiting for daylight, but not the police—they are out in force, with a dozen patrol cars, cruising the streets and local detectives pursuing a dozen leads. Some things are easier in a small state. Captain Brotman is working with lawyers from the attorney general's office to cut through red tape. Detective Gazzola has roused the town clerk and is in City Hall, going through the death records for October and September. After Bobby Anderson reported that three people had died at Ocean Breezes on Thursday night, Woody recalled that was the night when somebody tried to crowbar his way into the homes of law-abiding citizens. Cops had been rushing all over and nobody gave a thought to what might be happening at Ocean Breezes. Woody felt sure that wasn't a coincidence.

In a large metropolitan area in a large state, it can take a few days to get a search warrant, but Beth Lajoie was back at Dr. Balfour's condo by seven o'clock. Her request had gone straight from the state police colonel to the governor's office. "No, it's not a fishing expedition," the colonel had said. The puzzle was coming together; the end was in sight.

At first, Lajoie and the crime scene unit that made the search were disappointed. The five rooms of Balfour's condo were, as she said, "squeaky clean." None had thought they would find a weapon lying in plain view—say, on the coffee table—but it would have been nice nonetheless.

However, at the bottom of the clothes hamper beneath some undergarments, Corporal Montesano found a dark sweatshirt. He carried a Vulcan lantern, and it made everything sparkle.

"This sweatshirt's covered with dog hair," he said.

The sweatshirt looked like one of Woody's sweatshirts after he had been wrestling with Ajax.

Detective Lajoie poked at the hair shimmering in the glare of the light. "I bet it's coyote hair. Get it over to URI. If I'm wrong I'll eat my rain hat." She wore a Black Diamond sou'wester made of thick black rubber. It looked silly pulled down over her ears, but as Lajoie said, "It does the trick."

The second discovery was more dramatic. Lajoie was looking around a guest bedroom and opened the closet door without paying much attention.

A gray-haired woman in a blue flowered dress stood in front of her.

Lajoie screamed and stumbled backward. This was her first scream in seventeen years as a trooper.

Montesano came rushing into the room with his weapon drawn. Seeing the old woman standing in the closet door nearly made him scream as well.

But by then Detective Lajoie had recovered. "It's a mannequin," she said.

Pointing his light at the figure, Montesano felt embarrassed he hadn't seen it was a mannequin immediately. Maybe he'd been fooled by the gray wig and granny glasses; the black, high-top old-lady shoes.

"Scared the shit outta me," said Lajoie.

Ten minutes later she described it to Woody when she called him on the cell. Why would Balfour have a mannequin of an old lady in his closet? Could it have some medical purpose, some teaching purpose, or was it a joke? They talked about it for a minute or two. Then Woody remembered his remark to Hamilton Brantley as they stood before the open casket of Frances Crenner: "Did you put shoes on her?"

That connection led Woody to call Captain Brotman. "Hey, Captain, do you think I could exhume some bodies from the Brewster Cemetery?"

He felt sure he would find mannequin parts in at least one of the coffins.

Woody had been going full speed ever since leaving Brantley at the funeral home. He had talked to a detective in the financial crimes unit to get them busy looking into Brantley's and Balfour's bank accounts. He had made a bunch of calls to find out about local Samhain celebrations. He had talked to the DEM about coyotes.

Woody had also checked on Barton Wilcox at the hospital, going up to his room in the ICU, where he had found Bernie.

"Have you been here the whole time? You need some sleep."

"I've dozed a little. Anyway, where else would I be?"

Barton was either unconscious or asleep, but at least his vital signs had improved. He still looked dead, Woody thought, but he didn't look *as* dead.

"Do you need anything?" asked Woody.

Bernie shook her head. "How're the kids?"

Woody said they were still at Bonaldo's, and Laura was with them. "They're pretty sad, but they're safe."

"That's the main thing. I picked up that little dachshund and it's in my car. It's scared to death, poor thing. I'll take it over to Laura's if I get the chance."

Next Woody went searching for Margaret Hanna, the nurse who worked nights at Ocean Breezes. Bobby had raised some questions about her. She wasn't in her apartment and hadn't shown up for work.

"This isn't like her," said her supervisor. "She's always dependable. I've been trying to find someone to take her place, but who wants to come to Brewster on a night like this? I've called six people already."

"Maybe I can do something," said Woody, and he gave her the phone number of Nurse Spandex. When Alice received the call, she agreed right away. It would help her forget the mess she was in.

At some point during the early evening, Woody called Jill to say he wouldn't be able to call her—he was too busy. "Will I see you later?" she asked.

"I really hope so." But Woody couldn't swear to it.

She asked about Hercel and Lucy, and learned they were with Laura Bonaldo. "Maybe I'll go over there," she said. "Luke's with my parents. They're a lot more enthusiastic about Halloween than I am."

Woody also called Bingo twice and Bobby once. Neither had answered. He called Bobby's wife, Shawna. She hadn't heard from him. Woody had been in his truck and he pulled over to the curb on Water Street. He again realized he was letting the flashy stuff distract him from what was most important. Where was Bobby? He dug out his cell phone and started making calls. The only available backup was Beth Lajoie and Bruce Slovatsky, who, at twenty-seven, was the youngest member of the detective unit. He told them to meet him at police headquarters.

There was a paradox that bothered Woody that sometimes struck him when he was alone, say, sitting before the fire at night with a little whiskey. The moments as a trooper that scared him most, when he or his friends were most in danger, when a whole lot of shit was on the verge of going out of control and his adrenaline was blasting through the roof, those were the moments he liked best. *Am I some kind of thrill creep?* he asked. *Do I put a whole lot of stuff in jeopardy just to make this happen?* He was never sure.

When Bobby Anderson regained consciousness, he thought he was dead. He was cold; he'd never felt so cold. His head hurt. He could see nothing; he couldn't tell if his eyes were open or shut. He raised a hand to his eyes and his hand hit the flat surface of something a few inches above him. He pushed it but it moved only an inch or two. *I'm in a box,* he thought. *No, I'm in a coffin.*

Bobby pressed his hands to his chest and tried to keep from screaming. He squeezed his eyelids so tightly his cheeks hurt. He squeezed his fingers into his palms so tightly the nails cut the flesh. This was how he tried to relax—a little pain to distract him from a great terror. He heard a roaring noise he couldn't identify. Was he really underground? No, he could still breathe; it was stuffy, but he could breathe. He relaxed his fingers and opened his eyes.

He lay quietly and tried to think. Slowly, he straightened his arms and felt the side of the coffin. It was smooth, like wood. He tapped it with his knuckles and it made a hollow sound. He tried to think what that meant. It meant for sure he wasn't underground. He lifted a hand along the side of the coffin until he reached the top. When he pushed, the top raised up a little. He felt the top edge of the coffin. He could bend it inward and realized it was thick cardboard. He was in a cardboard coffin with a loose cardboard lid. He refolded his arms across his chest and thought some more. He still wanted to scream; he wanted to go fucking hysterical. But he wasn't going to let that happen.

Bobby pressed his arms back behind his head to the front panel of the coffin. He pushed until his feet pressed against the farther end. There was about six inches of space. He raised his knees to give himself another two inches and pressed his fists against the front panel. Then he kicked hard. The end bulged slightly. He kicked harder. Then he gasped, relaxed, and went back to thinking. *This is all there is,* he thought. *This is the only way out.*

He pushed at the rear panel with his feet and the front panel with his hands. Then he began to kick and push, kick and push. The cardboard coffin rocked; the end bulged. Bobby pushed harder; the end bulged more. He relaxed again.

I gotta get outta here, he thought.

He pushed again. He stamped his feet against the rear panel. When he felt it give an inch, he slid down to keep up the pressure. *No more resting,* he told himself. He pushed until he thought he'd explode. He was sweating, sweating and freezing at the same time. The panel bulged some more, and then, abruptly, it gave way.

Bobby pushed with his arms, sliding down and kicking away cardboard, until his feet hung over the edge. Then he wriggled toward the opening. The sides of the coffin were smooth, and his fingers slid across the surface, but after his knees passed through the opening, he rocked and slid and wriggled himself forward.

All of a sudden, he slipped over the edge. He tried to curl into a ball and crashed onto the floor. Maybe he fell five feet. It nearly finished him, and maybe he lost consciousness again. When his mind cleared, he gingerly moved his arms and legs to see if anything was broken. He touched the back of his head where he'd been hit earlier. It hurt. There was a lump crusted with blood. He hurt, but he was okay. He stood up. He still couldn't see anything. He felt cold again.

His pistol was gone, a Sig P229 like Bingo's. His wallet, cell phone, and keys were gone. So was his watch. His suit was a charcoal-gray pinstripe. Merino wool—the jacket provided some warmth, but not much. He checked his pockets; they were empty. Handcuffs, pens, and notebook—all were gone.

But he had a light. Clipped to a belt loop was a Photon Micro-Light the size of a quarter. Woody had given it to him. "Here," Woody had said. "I got a dozen. They're cheaper that way." Woody was like that. He would never say he gave you something because he was your friend.

Bobby unhooked it. When he squeezed, the LED bulb sent out a stream of pale light; when he relaxed, the light went out. Bobby began to investigate his prison cell. There was a steel door, which was locked, and a light above it. The switch must be outside. Bobby hammered on the door. The noise was as loud as the other noise, the noise of the fans.

After a minute or so Bobby gave up and looked around. It wasn't a prison cell; it was a cooler. There were sets of racks on either side of the door and a metal wall at the end with three fans. On the four shelves were twelve coffins like the one he'd been in. Bobby still felt like screaming. It felt as if there was a little creature inside him who was scared shitless. He told it to shut up.

Bobby began jogging in place to stay warm. He stared at the coffins and wondered what was in them. Dead people, most likely. Or maybe somebody like him, somebody scared shitless. He went to the racks and pulled at the coffins to see if they were occupied. Anybody home? Two seemed empty, seven seemed full, and one was somewhere in between. He shook the in-between one and something rolled around inside. Bobby went back to jogging in place and wondered what made that particular sound. After a moment, he pulled the coffin down onto the floor. Whatever was inside bumped and rolled around.

Bobby lifted the lid and pointed his Micro-Light. Inside was a head. He had found Carl Krause, or at least part of him.

But it was worse than that. Carl's lips were pinned up into a grin. He wore lipstick and rouge, and his eyes were open. He looked jolly. He wore mascara and eye shadow. He looked flirtatious. Bobby stepped back, dropping the lid. His light went out, and he squeezed it again. Once more he had to hang on to himself so he wouldn't go bonkers.

Bobby again lifted the lid and squatted down. Carl was made up like a drag queen. It looked as if somebody had really been pissed at Carl. He'd made Carl into a joke. He was a cross between Bozo the Clown and Mae West. Bobby dropped the lid and went back to pounding on the door. Then he put his ear to it. The roar of the fans seemed to cover all other sounds, but Bobby thought he heard music. He could hear the bass. He pounded the door a bit more and then gave it up, at least for the time being. Maybe he should investigate the other coffins. It took a minute to summon up the courage.

The first contained an old woman. It made Bobby recall what Maud Lord had said about the recent deaths at Ocean Breezes. He had pulled the coffin out about two-thirds of the way. He pushed it back.

He pulled a second coffin out a third of the way and raised the lid. He shone the light on one black boot. Bobby clenched his teeth. He knew that boot—or, rather, he knew the type of boot. He'd worn them for years as a uniformed trooper. He didn't want to see what was in the coffin. He knew it wasn't an old guy. *Stop whining*, he told himself. Bobby pulled out the coffin. It was heavy and he let it fall to the floor. It hit at an angle, and the lid popped off. Inside was Rodger Legros. There was a hole in his forehead. But that wasn't all. His right leg was missing. It had been taken off at the hip.

Bobby went back to the door and leaned against it. What was Legros doing here? Bobby didn't want to continue. It wasn't worth it. Legros had been a trooper for six years. Bobby had been to his house for a spaghetti dinner. He'd played with his kids. Bobby had to shout at himself some more. *You sentimental fuck!* Now he was shouting out loud; he was even louder than the fans. He shouted until his throat hurt. *If someone heard me,* he thought, *they'd think I was nuts.*

Over the next fifteen minutes Bobby pulled down five more coffins. He would look inside and then shove them against the far wall. All contained old people with parts missing—legs, arms, internal organs. Bobby's anger was almost great enough to sweep away all other emotions, but his fear was still there, niggling at him. He pulled down the last coffin, the heaviest. It crashed to the floor and the lid flew off.

Bingo Schwartz lay with his hands folded across his chest. His eyes were half open. He had a bullet hole in his forehead. Bobby knelt down beside him. He didn't know he was weeping until he felt the chill of his tears on his cheeks. Reaching forward, he closed Bingo's eyes. Bobby had known Bingo ever since Bobby had become a trooper. He had learned stuff from him. He had made fun of him, made fun of his mumbling. All that fucking opera. They weren't friends, but they were friendly. Part of Bobby was sorry they hadn't been better friends; part was sorry he had ever met Bingo. It might be easier if Bingo was a stranger.

Bobby stared at him until his knees ached, until the cold dug itself deep into his belly. Then he went back and pounded on the door.

Laura Bonaldo didn't know when Baldo had snuck out of the house. He had been dressed up as a vampire with a black cloak and an over-the-head vampire mask with long black hair, bloodshot eyes, and fangs. He had worn it to the Halloween party at St. John's, and Father Pete had made him take it off. It scared the little kids. Laura went downstairs to the rec room. Hercel and Tig were still sitting with the dog. Lucy was watching a DVD of *The Sound of Music*. Julie Andrews was singing about all her worries and being scared. "Kids, have you seen Baldo?" They hadn't. They hadn't even seen him leave.

The first house Baldo visited was the Murrays' next door. It was still snowing, and his were the only tracks on the sidewalk. Baldo had known the Murrays all his life, which wasn't very long. He rang the bell.

When Heather Murray opened the door, she jumped. It was eight o'clock, and she wasn't expecting any trick-or-treaters. The mask was horrible—a thin gray face, black circles around bloodshot eyes, and those teeth. On the other hand, he wasn't quite five feet tall. His black cape was speckled with snow.

"Baldo, is that you?"

"Tricker-treat!"

"Does your mother know you're out?"

"Sure, she does. It's just next door."

Mrs. Murray hadn't bought any candy because her husband had said trick-or-treating was canceled. She should have known Baldo would show up. All she found was a bar of Ghirardelli dark chocolate that she had been saving for when her PMS kicked in. "Don't eat it before bedtime, honey," she said. "It'll keep you awake."

"I won't." Baldo ran down the steps. "Thanks."

She kept the door open long enough to see Baldo turn down the street. He wasn't going home after all. Maybe she should give Laura a ring.

The lights were out in the next house and the house after that as well. Baldo decided to go farther afield.

Patrol cars were driving up and down Brewster's streets. Baldo saw one, but they didn't see him. He was small and quick; the officers were sleepy and bored.

A few blocks away, a white Chevy van drew into the alley behind You-You on Water Street. A man jumped out, ran to the rear doors, and pulled them open. Then he got out of the way. After a few seconds, a coyote jumped down into the snow and started sniffing around, then another and a third. They sniffed along the wall and then trotted forward, leaving their tracks in the mush. Shortly after eight o'clock, Heather Murray called Laura Bonaldo. "Laura, are you letting Baldo go trick-or-treating? I'm really surprised at you."

Woody was already at police headquarters when Lajoie and Bruce Slovatsky arrived. He tossed them each a 111A Kevlar vest. He already wore his. It had a front pocket for a hard trauma plate, but Woody didn't bother with it.

Acting chief Fred Bonaldo watched from the hall as Lajoie and Slovatsky put on their vests. He hoped he wouldn't be asked to go along. He had never worn a Kevlar vest except when trying it out in front of the mirror. He was a big guy. A vest was no good for him. He needed something the size of a hot-water tank.

Slovatsky had thick black hair that started about halfway down his forehead. His part on the left side was a white streak back across his skull and his hair shone with gel. He was a bodybuilder. Wearing a vest meant he probably wouldn't be asked to use his muscles. He had mixed feelings about that.

Lajoie wore her vest under a GORE-TEX parka. "We going to a Halloween party?"

"Hey, Bonaldo," called Woody.

Bonaldo flinched. He knew if he went with them he'd be killed for sure.

"Go pick up Hamilton Brantley and search the funeral home. You're looking for mannequin parts. You think you can remember that? Don't go alone."

Bonaldo ignored the rudeness. After all, Woody was under a lot of stress.

"What's the charge?"

"Suspicion of murder."

"Are you sure? I've known Ham all my life."

Woody didn't rush at Bonaldo, but he moved very quickly; and whatever behavior he had been considering, he changed his mind when he got within six inches of Bonaldo's nose. "Do it," he said softly.

They took the Tundra with Slovatsky scrunched in the small backseat. The roads were slick with snow and ice. Woody had the truck in four-wheel drive, but if he hit a patch of ice he'd spin like a figure skater.

"Can you tell me where we're going?" asked Slovatsky.

"It's called the Burn Palace."

Lajoie turned and patted Slovatsky on the knee. "Don't worry, sweetie. He only means a crematorium."

Salt trucks were out, the first of the season, but there was little other traffic. Woody had a flashing red strobe light with a magnetic base. He slapped it up on the roof and stuck the end of the cord in the cigarette lighter. "Now we're official," he said. He told Lajoie and Slovatsky why they were going to the crematorium.

"Bobby went there this afternoon, and I haven't heard from him. Nor has anyone else. I don't know if he's there, but that's where we start."

The farther they went from the coast, the colder it became. The snow thickened. The pines on either side of the road formed great white columns. Woody drove quickly, though a few times the rear end began to slide out. Each time it happened, Lajoie said, "Oops."

Woody wanted to bark at her, but the trouble with Lajoie was she always barked back a whole lot louder. *She's got no sense of proportion*, he thought.

The crematorium was about fifteen miles from Brewster. By the time they reached Skunk Hill Road, the snow was coming down hard. Maybe six inches had fallen. It made little white towers on fence posts and mailboxes. Woody turned onto the long driveway to the crematorium. Between the trees, the driveway was a blanket of white. No vehicles had been in or out for a couple of hours. Woody went slowly for about ten yards; then he turned out his lights and kept going. Through the trees he saw the light above the door of the crematorium. He drove to the edge of the open area around the crematorium and stopped. Three cars were parked in the small lot. They were covered with snow, but Bobby's 370Z was easily distinguishable: a sleek, low silhouette. Smoke rose from the crematorium chimney.

"There's a camera over the door," said Woody. "If anybody's watching, they already know we're here."

"So how we gonna get in?" asked Slovatsky.

Woody thought for a moment. "Like a ton of bricks."

"My sentiments exactly," said Lajoie.

After Woody left headquarters Bonaldo began rounding up officers to go with him to the funeral home. He tried to think of it as a SWAT team. He could stand back and let the team take care of the problem. But Brantley gave no evidence of being dangerous. Lieutenant Damon Constantino said no way could Bonaldo call out a SWAT team. It'd make him look foolish. Sometimes Bonaldo thought of Lieutenant Constantino as "the cross I have to bear"; other times he thought of him as "the thorn in my side." Constantino was in fact an efficient police officer who handled much of the daily running of the small department. But it seemed like every day Constantino would say, "If you do that, you're going to look foolish." What he meant by this, and Bonaldo was sure of it, was that Bonaldo was an *acting* chief, not a *real* chief. Constantino was a pain in the butt.

So Bonaldo had to be okay with six guys. Anyway, he and Brantley had always been friendly. Brantley was a year older than Bonaldo; he had known Brantley his entire life. And Bonaldo had looked up to him. When he was a sophomore, Brantley was a senior with a nice car and a pretty girlfriend with big tits. She had been Jenny Genoways, captain of the cheerleading squad; now she was Jenny Brantley. How could Bonaldo not look up to him? Now he was meant to arrest him for murder? For Bonaldo, this was a big problem.

Then, as Bonaldo was leaving the building, he got a call on his cell phone from Laura. "Your son's gone trick-or-treating," Laura said. "You got to deal with it."

This was a complicated statement. Bonaldo and his wife had three sons, but Baldo, the youngest, was the only one Laura called "your son." The others were "our sons." That was because Baldo was a miniature replica of his father. Nothing about him looked like his mother. Just as Zeus gave birth to Athena—she sprang from his head fully formed—so Fred Bonaldo seemed to have given birth to Baldo all by himself.

The other part of the complicated statement was unstated but understood: "Fred, your son's life is in danger." For Bonaldo, Ham Brantley's importance vanished.

The dispatcher notified the cars patrolling Brewster to look for Baldo Bonaldo. The department used the ten-code system so a lot of 10-4's came back and with them was a 10-11, which in this instance meant an animal problem.

"There's a lot of coyotes out here tonight," said an officer.

So Bonaldo sent Constantino to pick up Brantley, and ran to the garage to get a car. But all the police cars were being used, so Bonaldo had to take his black Chevy TrailBlazer. Hurrying out, Bonaldo slipped on the snowy walk and nearly fell. It was an awful night for anything except sitting in front of a fire. Despite his anger and fear, Bonaldo had to be impressed that Baldo would brave such weather in pursuit of candy.

Hercel McGarty, when he heard Laura telephone her husband, thought much the same thing. He was also torn. If Baldo was his friend, was it right for Hercel to remain in comfort in Baldo's own house when his friend might be in trouble? When one is ten years old, such questions have no gray areas. The sensible answer was to stay inside. Hercel saw what the weather was like. He had no wish to go out in the snow. Yet he thought it would be cowardly to stay, which doesn't mean he thought it would be courageous to search for Baldo. All he knew was it wouldn't be comfortable to stay. It wasn't an argument; it was just a feeling. And he didn't tell anybody, not even Tig. But he did try to take Ajax. The back door was halfway down the kitchen stairs to the rec room. Hercel called Ajax, who came willingly enough, but once the dog saw what the weather was like, he refused to go outside and trotted back downstairs. Ajax was no fool.

So Hercel ran out by himself. He had a wool jacket and his Red Sox cap, but the wind was nasty and the snow stuck to his jacket, and in a few minutes he looked like a snowman. The good thing was he could see Baldo's tracks, although they were quickly being covered with snow. Still, they gave Hercel a direction. Also Hercel was running and Baldo never ran. The bad thing was that Hercel heard a yapping and he knew it was a coyote.

In the meantime, Fred Bonaldo was going up and down the streets near his house. Two other patrol cars were also cruising the area. As for Lieutenant Constantino, he and his men drove to Brantley's Funeral Home. It was dark and shut up tight. No tracks showed in the driveway. Next Constantino drove to Brantley's home on James Street. It, too, was dark. So he called the dispatcher and had him put out an APB. Then he called Captain Brotman about search warrants. Constantino had also known Brantley his entire life, or most of it, but he had never liked him much. His hands were too white.

About the same time, Detective Lajoie was driving Woody's Tundra fast through the snow-covered lot toward the door of the crematorium. She then swung the wheel so the truck skidded in a half-circle. Grinding into reverse, she backed toward the door. Woody sat beside her; he hoped she wouldn't flip over. In order to get a permit to drive his truck on the beach Woody had to carry a first-aid kit, a shovel, and a tow chain. He had plans for the shovel, but most important was the nylon tow strap with a thirty-six-thousand-pound capacity.

When the Tundra was ten feet from the door, Woody and Slovatsky jumped out. Slovatsky had the strap, Woody the shovel. Slovatsky hooked one end of the strap over the trailer hitch. Woody jumped up and knocked out the bullet camera. Then he wrapped the other end of the strap around the door handle. Woody whistled, and Lajoie accelerated. There was a loud wrenching noise.

As Lajoie said later, "It popped that door as easily as a kid pops a birthday balloon."

Woody and Slovatsky ran through the door. Woody was aware of loud music, a discordant, unrecognizable blare. The room was dimly lit and hot. Fans were blowing. Larry waited by the furnace. He held the Browning Hi-Power in both hands, pointing it toward the door. Woody was struck by Larry's face. It showed not the least trace of emotion.

Woody and Larry fired at the same time. Slovatsky grunted and fell back. Larry stood frozen, as if, for the first time in his life, something had grabbed his attention. He started to fall. There was a movement to Woody's left and he fired.

"Don't shoot, don't shoot! I don't have a gun! Larry made me stay here; I haven't done anything." It was Jimmy Mooney. Woody barely heard him over the noise of the heavy metal band. He kept shouting until Woody told him to shut up and lie down with his hands behind his back. He glanced at Larry, who was sprawled motionless. His eyes were open, but he wouldn't be seeing anything anymore. Woody had never killed anyone before. It made him want to throw up. Instead, he kicked away the pistol, and then patted down Jimmy Mooney and cuffed him.

Lajoie knelt beside Slovatsky, who was grimacing in pain. He had received what's called a backface injury, the indentation of the bullet against the body armor. More simply, the seventh rib on his left side had been cracked.

The music came from an iPod attached to two small speakers and a woofer. The song was "Seed of Filth" from Six Feet Under. Were it not for the drums, Woody wouldn't have known it was music. He grabbed the iPod, dropped it, and stamped on it.

"Thanks," said Lajoie.

The room was silent except for the noise of the fans and the muted roaring of the furnace. With the front door broken open, the temperature was dropping fast. Then Woody heard a pounding. After a moment, he realized it was coming from the cooler. He ran to the door and yanked it open.

Bobby staggered out. "Jesus, I thought I was going to die in there. What took you so long?" He squeezed his arms to his chest. "I'm freezing."

Woody had been sure he was dead. He wanted to hug him, but instead he shook his hand. Bobby wrapped his arms around him and held him for a moment.

"Bingo's in there," said Bobby. "So's Legros. They're dead. It's pretty nasty."

Woody turned on the cooler light and went inside. When he saw Bingo, he wanted to shoot Larry again. He lowered his head and waited for the horror to pass. It didn't, but it grew a little less. He wished he had loved Bingo more.

Beth Lajoie called the CIU and the medical examiner's office. Then she called an ambulance for Slovatsky. "You might as well ride in style," she said. Last, she called Captain Brotman.

Woody yanked Jimmy up by his hair. The rougher the better, he thought. "What's burning in the furnace?"

"Mannequins, that's all, just mannequins."

"How d'you turn it off?"

Jimmy told him. "I didn't know Larry was going to shoot those cops. I'd no clue. I tried to leave, but Larry said he'd kill me. He'd shoot me and sell me."

Another crate of mannequin parts was waiting to be burned. Jimmy said that Brantley used them at funerals. He would sell legs, arms, even torsos, and replace them with parts from the mannequins.

"Who killed Carl?" said Bobby. He stood by the furnace to warm himself.

"I don't know; I didn't do it. Seymour brought him here from Brantley's. Maybe Seymour did it, or Brantley. Seymour said Carl'd tried to break in. He had a gun. Fuckin' wacko."

Bobby still felt cold to the bone. "Who put that stuff all over Carl's face?"

"I was practicing, you know, beautifying. They teach it in schools. Ronnie McBride, too—I was making them look nice. But I didn't kill them. They'd be glad of it if they knew, looking good like that. Not Carl, I guess. The fuck."

"You're fucked in the head," said Bobby. "Where's Balfour?"

"He's got a place near here, a farmhouse. He was going to pick up these bodies in a van, but I guess he changed his mind. He called Larry and told him to burn everything. They're clearing out."

"And what about me?" asked Bobby.

"Balfour first said to leave you in the freezer till you froze. They figured you'd die in there and they'd harvest you. You know, fresh parts. Then Balfour called and told Larry to shoot you and burn you. Larry was unhappy about just whacking you. Throwing good money after bad, he called it."

"'Fresh parts,'" said Bobby. "I can't wait to tell Shawna."

"It's a gold mine. There might be a million bucks in parts right in this building. See that freezer over there? It's full of skin. There's enough to paper a house."

Jimmy rattled on about the fortune to be made. Bobby guessed he was a tweaker, his chat all meth-accelerated, words leaping from his mouth like lemmings from a cliff.

Woody got Jimmy Mooney to describe where Balfour lived—a farmhouse about six miles north on Hazard Road, right at the edge of Arcadia. Jimmy offered to draw a map. He was willing to do anything except go with them. "Balfour's even scarier than Larry," he said. "Like he thinks he's king, you know? He thinks he's got a right to all this. And he took the guns from those cops."

"You feeling okay?" Woody asked Bobby. "We've got to go get Balfour."

Detective Lajoie called Bonaldo to see if he'd arrested Brantley. Instead she got Constantino, who said Brantley was nowhere to be found. Bonaldo was looking for his son. "That fat kid's out trick-or-treating, and the town's full of coyotes."

Baldo's footprints grew harder to follow. Someone had been walking a dog; someone had parked at the curb and gone into a house. Their prints messed up Baldo's on the sidewalk. It meant Hercel had to go slowly. And each time he saw a police car, he got behind a tree. This also slowed him. And the only way he could look for Baldo was if he kept his thoughts focused on him and nothing else. Otherwise he would start thinking of the coyotes or his mother or Carl Krause, and when that happened he just wanted to give up. Several times he had seen coyote tracks. They were just crossing the sidewalk; they weren't following Baldo or anything, at least not yet.

When he turned onto Market Street, he saw that Baldo's footprints were clearer. Then, when he got to the next corner, he saw a small figure toward the end of the block. He realized that Baldo had been going in a large circle and was heading back to his house. Hercel shouted and sped up. The yapping of the coyotes was louder.

Baldo waited. When Hercel ran up to him, Baldo said, "Where's your costume?"

Hercel was startled by Baldo's vampire mask, but he didn't bother to answer. "What are you doing? It's dangerous out here. Can't you hear the coyotes?"

Baldo listened. "I thought they were dogs. Do you want a bar of chocolate? Not many people are home, or they're hiding. This has been pretty hard work. Slim pickings."

"Take off that frigging mask. I can't talk to you with it on."

Baldo didn't want to take it off, and they argued a little. It wasn't until Hercel got mad that Baldo removed the mask. Hercel was relieved. The mask was so real in the dim light that Hercel worried it wasn't really Baldo.

Seeing Baldo without the mask, Hercel said, "You're an idiot." He didn't say this as an insult; it was as if he was pointing out a likable shortcoming. "Come on, we've got to run."

"My feet hurt."

"Okay, stay here and let the coyotes eat you."

So Baldo tried to manage a slow trot. He didn't see why Hercel was making a fuss. After all, it was only about two blocks to his house.

But some things never happen easily, and, moments later, Hercel and Baldo saw two coyotes trotting toward them through the snow, right in the middle of the street. Baldo was ready to run despite his sore feet, but Hercel pulled him up the sidewalk to the nearest house. The house was dark, and the front walk was unshoveled. Hercel leaned on the bell.

The coyotes paused in front of the house. At first they didn't seem interested in the boys, just mildly curious, but then they took a few steps toward them.

Baldo grew more frightened. "Use your trick!"

Hercel again rang the bell and didn't say anything.

"Use it!" said Baldo. "You've got to use it."

"I can't," said Hercel angrily. "I don't have it anymore. It's broken."

"I don't believe you. How could it be broken? If you don't use it, we'll be eaten!"

"Can't you understand? I don't have it!"

At that moment the portico light went on and the door opened. "You boys!" a woman said angrily. "Can't you see the lights are out? What in the world are you doing?" Then she saw the coyotes in the street and gasped. "Goodness! Get in here right away. Wipe your feet, they're covered with snow."

The woman was gray-haired and wore a blue bathrobe. "You're that Bonaldo boy, aren't you? The troublemaker. Don't you dare start anything with me. I'll call your mother; she must be worried sick. I swear you're as dumb as posts, both of you."

TWENTY-ONE

BACK IN SEPTEMBER, when Brewster was peaceful and a little dull, Jill Franklin had written a feature story on Ocean Breezes for the *Brewster Times & Advertiser*. She had chatted to a number of residents, including Maud Lord, and she had interviewed some of the staff. One of the people she talked to was Margaret Hanna, the nurse who worked the night shift. Margaret was energetic and, perhaps, excessively friendly—one of those people who're afraid of being disliked and so try too hard to be liked. This, for Jill, often had the opposite effect, but she remained friendly, or tried to, and Margaret most likely never realized that the effect of her excessive warmth was to create a chill.

Margaret appeared to be pleased with the story when it came out toward the end of the month, and perhaps she really *was* pleased, though people like Margaret will act pleased, when they are really thinking, *Why didn't she say more about me?* Jill was aware of this, and the result was discomfort. She knew that whatever she did, Margaret would be disappointed. But during the weeks after the appearance of the article, Jill sometimes ran into Margaret in a store or restaurant, and Margaret would again be effusively grateful. Then of course, toward the end of October, Jill was fired.

So it was surprising to Jill, as she drove over to Brewster to see Hercel on Halloween, that she should unexpectedly receive a phone call from Margaret Hanna. The second thing that surprised her was that Margaret didn't gush. She was frightened.

"I need to see you right away," said Margaret. "I've got something to tell you."

Margaret's voice was so different that Jill wasn't at first sure it was the same person. But she asked Margaret what she wanted to talk about.

"I can't tell you over the phone. Can we meet someplace? It'll make a great news story for you. Really, it'll be a big hit."

Jill didn't say she'd been fired. She was struck by the fear in Margaret's voice, and she knew if Margaret's story was really worth writing about, Ted Pomeroy would publish it even though he had fired her a week earlier. They agreed to meet at Tony's, a bar on Spruce right around the corner from Water Street.

"The weather's terrible," said Jill. "Are you sure you don't want to wait?"

"It has to be tonight," said Margaret.

Twenty minutes later they were sitting at a back booth in Tony's. The bar had ten other customers, nine of them men. Most looked like what Jill's father called "heavy hitters." The TV was showing a football game.

Margaret ordered a Cosmo; Jill had a Budweiser.

"Do you come in here much?" asked Margaret. "I never do, well, once I had lunch here. Greasy, you know what I mean? My clothes smelled all day long."

Margaret was a wispy blonde, and she kept fiddling with her hair, curling it around a finger or pushing it back. Perhaps she was in her late twenties. She wore a dark raincoat over a green turtleneck. Her face or expression was in constant motion, partly from nervousness, partly as a stab at vivacity. She was the sort of woman who tore up paper napkins, peeled the labels off beer bottles, and fussed with sugar packets. Jill wanted to tell her to relax, at least until Margaret said, "I'm afraid they're going to try to kill me."

Jill winced. "Who's 'they'?"

"Dr. Balfour, first of all—I was completely wrong about him."

In the story that followed, Jill came to understand that Balfour's relationship with Margaret was much like his relationship with Nurse Spandex: he distracted the nurse while something awful was happening nearby, except in this case the victim wasn't an infant but the elderly.

"Every time I was with him someone passed, but I didn't realize it until Thursday when three people passed, three *healthy* people, I mean healthy for old people. Dr. Balfour would leave and go back to the hospital or someplace, then we'd call him and he'd come back again. Three whole times."

Jill, too, realized that was the night when someone had broken into houses in Brewster and the police had been rushing all over town.

"I know I'll be arrested, but I want people to know what happened. You just can't believe anything he says."

"Even though they'll know how you behaved?"

"Even then. You don't understand; he's evil. I've read about those Satanists in the paper, what they were doing out on that island. I'm sure he's one of them."

By this time Jill had put a small digital recorder on the table. "How long have you been involved with him?"

"I'd broken up with Marty McGuire a week earlier. Well, he dumped me. Dr. Balfour had been coming to Ocean Breezes for about two months. We'd say hello and stuff like that, but he never seemed especially friendly. He came in one night and found me weeping in the office. He asked what was wrong and he . . ." Margaret paused, as she sought the right word.

"Comforted you?" said Jill.

"It began like that, sure. I was so mad at Marty I let Dr. Balfour put his hands all over me. I'd been seeing Marty all summer. We'd been talking about getting engaged. But with Dr. Balfour, we didn't do anything all that physical, like anything more than touching. I mean, it was the *office*. Somebody might have walked in."

"So when did it happen?"

Margaret looked embarrassed. "The next night. There was an empty room."

She described seeing Dr. Balfour two or three times a week. *Seeing*—that was her word, not *fucking* or *having sex* or *sleeping with*. She "saw him." And old people often died on those nights. Of course, they were *old*; many were weak or ill or "sinking." They would die soon in any case, and dying at night was more common than dying during the day. They went to sleep; their breathing slowed, then it stopped. That was that. She hadn't thought it had anything to do with Dr. Balfour. At times he was there when it happened; at times he came back later. In any case, he certified the death. Most were sent to Brantley's; none was an organ donor.

"I didn't think there was anything strange about it; well, I started to think it was strange. Like there were more of them and it was on nights when me and Dr. Balfour saw each other. On Thursday night when three residents passed I really thought something was wrong and I wondered if there was some connection with Dr. Balfour; I mean first it was the baby, then that poor guy who got scalped, then Ronnie McBride and all that Satanism stuff and coyotes. And Dr. Balfour, he'd just show up at night without even calling, like he was just using me. So I said to him,

I said I thought it was his fault so many of our residents were passing; he was making them pass. I didn't think that for sure; I was mad at him, but I thought it was too much of a coincidence, him and the old people passing. He just laughed, but he looked at me funny. He didn't look like he wanted to see me. I mean, he didn't want me. He was, like, measuring me in some way. Then I asked what was happening to all these bodies and he laughed again and said I'd been reading too many tabloids. He laughed, but he didn't mean it. You know, these medical businesses, they buy joints and scalps and tendons; they buy everything, even fingernails. And the body banks and tissue banks are like that—they use every little bit. That's what I think happened to our residents. They didn't pass; they were cut up and sent all over. That's what I think you should write about, that and Dr. Balfour."

Jill recalled in college when students argued about who wrote "Hell hath no fury like a woman scorned." Most thought it was Shakespeare, but Jill's boyfriend, Charlie Larkin, said it was William Congreve and what he really said was, "Heaven has no rage like love to hatred turned, Nor hell a fury like a woman scorned." Jill thought that summed up Margaret Hanna rather neatly.

"I bet he never liked me; he just liked the blow jobs," Margaret said. "That's what he told me this afternoon. He said that having sex with me was like cold mutton, except he said 'fucking.' He said fucking me was like cold mutton, and he laughed and said if I told anyone about what I was thinking I'd be fired and I might even go to jail. Well, I don't care if I go to jail. I want you to write about this. I want people to know about him."

The picture Margaret gave of Dr. Balfour was of a man with a sense of entitlement. His desire for a thing was the same as deserving to have it. To his mind, Alice Alessio and Margaret Hanna were just ignorant women, what did it matter if he used them? The old people he had killed were going to die soon anyway. He'd just sped up the process. Margaret didn't say this, but Jill put it together and some of it came from what Woody had already told her.

"He wanted me to go to this thing in the woods, this party. I was working that night, but I didn't want to go anyway. It was cold, and it sounded too strange. It was that Satanist party, I know it was. Other times he liked to describe terrible things he saw in the paper, people being killed and blown up, like in Iraq or someplace like that. He called it the Devil's business. After a while I realized he didn't mean it as a bad thing, but a good thing. Yesterday I said that to him, I said he thought it was a good thing. He laughed again and asked, 'Who's strongest?' I asked him what he meant, but he didn't answer. That's when I knew he was a Satanist."

There was more. Margaret talked about growing up in Brewster, she talked about boyfriends and bad relationships. She talked about knowing Alice Alessio and Peggy Summers and Nina Lefebvre. She didn't know them well, but she knew them. She'd even babysat Nina when she was in high school. But whatever she talked about always came back to Dr. Balfour and the fact that he had used her.

A few more men came into the bar, stamped their feet and shook the snow off their coats; a few men left. Puddles formed on the floor. The ones who came in made remarks about the weather, about the slippery streets. One man described seeing a coyote in his backyard. Another man told of a neighbor who had shot at a coyote. At times Jill heard the rumble of a snowplow.

Margaret kept interrupting her story to glance around the room. Whenever someone came in, she would peer at them doubtfully and Jill saw fear in her eyes. Margaret finished her Cosmo and ordered another—a blood-colored liquid in a martini glass. Not blood, Jill thought, cranberry juice. She still had half her beer.

"Why do you think he's going to kill you?"

"He said it. I don't mean in so many words. He said he'd change my mind, that there were ways to do it. He said I'd be doing a good deed. I didn't understand until I remembered the body brokers. He meant he'd cut me up and sell me, I know he did." Margaret put her hands to her face. Jill reached forward and touched her arm.

"But who's 'they'?" she asked.

"Hamilton Brantley and people who work for him. Mr. Brantley came to Ocean Breezes several times when one of our residents passed. He and Dr. Balfour talked together. Dr. Balfour gets the bodies and Ham Brantley sells them. It's a partnership."

Margaret described the men who worked for Brantley, but the only one she knew was Jimmy Mooney, because she'd been friends with Jimmy's older sister, Linda.

Jill wasn't convinced right away, but the more she thought about it, the more she thought it might be true. Anyway, Margaret certainly thought it was true.

What happened next didn't happen right away. And it was the opposite of serendipity, whatever that is. Maybe just bad luck. Or maybe talking about Brantley and the others put something in their heads as if she were calling to them. So it wasn't right away that Seymour Hodges entered the bar, but it was soon. Jill saw him first. She didn't know him, but she found him familiar. Actually, she had seen him on the night the baby was stolen from the hospital. Seymour had been sitting in the ambulance parked by the emergency entrance. Nor did she realize that Margaret knew the man, until she looked at her. "She turned as white as a sheet," said Jill later.

Margaret ducked her head and shot a glance at Jill. Margaret's back was to the door, and maybe everything would have been okay if she hadn't panicked, but maybe Seymour would have seen her in any case.

After all, he was looking for her and perhaps he had recognized her car in the parking lot despite the snow.

"He's the one who picked up bodies at Ocean Breezes," said Margaret. "He works with Dr. Balfour. He and Jimmy Mooney."

Jill again touched Margaret's arm. "Sit still. Don't look around."

Margaret lowered her head. Jill saw she was weeping. She watched Seymour walk to the bar and say something to the bartender, who then dug into the cooler for a beer. Seymour looked around the room, a stocky young man wearing an EMT jacket. Briefly, his eyes fastened on Jill and then he turned away.

"I've got to go," said Margaret.

Before Jill could answer, Margaret jumped to her feet and headed to a hallway in the back. The restrooms were there, so was the rear exit. Jill hoped that Seymour would think Margaret had gone to the bathroom. Instead, Seymour abruptly left the bar.

For a moment, Jill felt paralyzed. Then she, too, ran for the rear exit. Running outside, she slipped in the snow and barely regained her balance. The parking lot was along the side of the bar. Seymour had already grabbed Margaret and was shoving her into a small SUV. Then he hit her with something.

"Hey!" shouted Jill. She ran across the lot, slipping and stumbling as she went. Seymour was already behind the wheel. Jill shouted again: "Stop them!" which was foolish because there was no one in sight.

Swerving through the snow, the SUV pulled out of the parking lot.

Acting chief Fred Bonaldo was fit to be tied. He couldn't imagine how Baldo, his own flesh and blood, could have been so stupid. It was one thing to go next door and maybe to the house after that for a few treats, but Baldo had disappeared entirely. It was dangerous out tonight. He should have come home long ago.

Driving up and down Brewster's streets in his Chevy TrailBlazer, Bonaldo had seen several coyotes but no people, except cops in patrol cars. Baldo was plump; he would make a nice coyote dinner. The acting chief hit his head with the flat of his hand: What was he thinking? All he cared about was his son's safety. He was angry, was all, and everything was fucked.

Then, as Bonaldo was driving back down Water Street, Laura called. Baldo was home. He was all right. Mrs. Klimek, the lady who lived around the corner, had called. She had found Baldo and Hercel on her front steps. Coyotes had been in the street. She'd phoned Laura more than once, but the phone was busy. So Mrs. Klimek had driven them home herself. Now Baldo and the three children were sitting in the kitchen and eating candy as if nothing had happened. Fred should come home and give them a talking to.

"You bet I'll come home!" shouted Fred Bonaldo. "And I'll give him more than a talking to. . . ."

"Don't be too rough, Fred."

But Fred wasn't paying attention. He pushed his foot down on the accelerator of his TrailBlazer and fishtailed up Water Street. Then he swung the wheel and spun sideways through the snow. As he tried to straighten out, he saw an SUV pulling out of the parking lot of Tony's Bar, "dashed out without even looking," Bonaldo told reporters afterward.

Bonaldo slammed on his brakes, but the TrailBlazer kept sliding sideways without the least diminishment of speed. At the last minute, Bonaldo pressed his hands to his face. He smashed sideways into the SUV's front end, knocking the SUV back onto the curb so it ran into the wall of Phelps Plumbing & Heating where it stopped. And this was how acting chief Bonaldo captured Seymour Hodges and became a hero, sort of.

. . .

Beth Lajoie brought Jimmy Mooney back to police headquarters in Jimmy's own car, a 1990 Honda Civic that had belonged to his parents. Jimmy talked the whole way. And because of the snow, Lajoie could drive only about twenty miles an hour. It felt like driving in Siberia.

"Digger said I could buy a Beemer, like my own Beemer, maybe a Roadster. He said I could buy a Beemer Roadster and a Beemer SUV. You know how many girls you can get with a Beemer? Like, they'd be crawling through the windows. Not the Roadster, the SUV. I'd have to fight them off, all but some."

Other than Jimmy's meth-accelerated chat, the only other sound was the grinding of Beth Lajoie's teeth.

"Digger said I had a knack, the way I fixed up the stiffs. He said they'd get to the Pearly Gates and Saint Peter would say, 'Good golly!' just like that, 'Good golly!' He said I made them beautiful, you know, beautiful for dead people. Stiff beautiful, not people beautiful. Digger said for sure I'd work my way up to assistant digger, then associate digger, and then whole digger. He'd turn the place over to me for hardly any money at all. A song, he said. He wanted to retire, just quit the business, take his old lady to the Caribbean or some such place and raise prize geese, like the big ones with the golden eggs. He and his old lady are crazy about the beach; Digger says he just likes to roll around in the sand. Even if he puts no more than a toe in the water, he's happy as a clam. He's got this little cottage in Hannaquit where he . . ."

"What's that?" said Beth Lajoie, coming awake.

"I said if he does no more than put a toe . . ."

"Not that, the cottage—you said he had a cottage in Hannaquit."

"Yeah, it's no big deal, just four rooms and a kitchen, a little past Otto's Clam Shack on Beach Street. But it's on the water, you know what I mean? Like you can't beat the water, right? I mean, it's water. . . ."

"Tell me more exactly where it is."

So Jimmy did.

Once she had turned Jimmy over to Lieutenant Constantino, Beth Lajoie grabbed Detective Gazzola and some cops and headed for Hannaquit. It was colder, and the snow was solid all the way to the beach, like a white wall in front of them. They took the department's two Ford Explorers; otherwise they wouldn't have been able to get through.

Brantley's cottage was a modest yellow-shingled cracker box. The sign out front said CRAZY DAZE. But the lot was about a half-acre and the whole thing had to be worth a million. Brantley's BMW was in the drive covered with a layer of snow.

The police officers parked on the street, blocking the driveway, and then slogged their way to the house. There were six altogether. All wore body armor, and the four patrolmen wore helmets. Lajoie carried her Sig P229 in one hand and a flashlight in the other. The image of Bingo Schwartz lying in that damn box with his hands folded on his chest and a bullet hole in his forehead flashed in her brain like a blinking neon light. She thought of the times she had yelled at him because of his mumbling and wished she hadn't.

Lights were on in the cottage; it was the only lit-up place on Beach Street. Hannaquit was a ghost town except for Crazy Daze. Detective Gazzola was puffing on one cigarette after another, smoking and chomping on a Nicorette. Detective Lajoie started to make a sarcastic remark about going to his funeral when she saw the side door of the cottage was wide open. The six police officers stopped, thought about their options, and then kept moving. Lajoie flicked off her flashlight.

They gathered by the screen door. There were three wooden steps with a bunch of footprints, but already the snow was covering them. Gazzola didn't want to go in first, nor did the patrolmen. But it wasn't an option. Despite having the figure of a loaf of bread, Lajoie was quick on her feet. After all, she was a second-degree black belt. She looked through the screen and into the living room. This was the moment she hated and loved—the moment between action and inaction. She flung open the screen door and sprang into the room, swung her pistol in an arc. In cop movies, cops shouted "Clear!" but Lajoie couldn't tolerate that bullshit. The room was empty. "It's okay," she said to Gazzola.

Three of the rooms were empty; the fourth had its door shut. The walls of the cottage were pine-paneled. The furniture was 1950s and a coffee table made from a lobster pot stood before a couch. Watercolors of seascapes hung from the walls: richly colored ocean dawns with fishing boats. Lajoie saw they had been done by Brantley's wife, Jenny.

The police officers gathered by the closed door and listened. The only noise was the wind outside. After about ten seconds, Lajoie got tired of standing around and kicked the door open. She jumped forward with her pistol held in both hands.

The room was empty except for a dead woman lying on the bed.

Lajoie stared at her; she felt short of breath. It was like a picture.

"Jeez," said a cop behind her.

Jenny Brantley lay on a pink chenille bedspread wearing a lavender full-length gown. Her short, dark hair had been carefully brushed. Her long white hands were folded across her breasts. Her fingernails were bright red, and her eyes were closed. Around her neck was a white gold necklace with sapphires. Lajoie put a hand to the dead woman's cheek. She was cold. Jenny Brantley was as carefully made up as if going to a party. Her feet were bare, but a pair of black high-heeled pumps stood side by side on a braided rug.

"You think he killed her?" asked Gazzola.

No marks could be seen on the dead woman. Lajoie shrugged. She couldn't stop looking at Jenny Brantley. She wished she had a camera. Lajoie made herself look away. More seascapes were on the bedroom walls. Lajoie noticed a framed color photograph of Brantley and his wife standing together. He wore a dinner jacket; she wore the same dress as she was wearing now. They looked happy, successful, and in love.

"That's that," said Lajoie. "The happy couple's seriously fucked."

She left the bedroom, walked to the side door, and went outside. Flicking on her flashlight, she searched the snow until she found Brantley's footprints. They were more indentations than footprints, but Lajoie could follow them toward the beach. The wind came from the northeast, swirled the snow across the low dunes. It tugged at her jacket. Her light reflected off the snow, its tumbling frenzy. The waves crashed and whispered, crashed and whispered. After a minute, she saw Brantley standing near the water.

Lajoie approached him cautiously. Brantley's silver hair blew in the wind. He wore only a suit coat and had to be freezing. His hands hung empty by his sides. Lajoie stood behind him. She reached out and touched his shoulder.

"We were going to be happy." Brantley didn't turn around. It was as if he were speaking to the ocean. Lajoie realized he had seen her light; she leaned forward to hear him. "We should have left last week like she wanted. Balfour kept putting it off. I should never have listened to him."

They stood looking at the water. Then Lajoie asked: "How did she die?"

"Sleeping pills, I expect. I found her on the couch in the living room. Doesn't she look beautiful?"

Brantley had found her two hours before. He had dressed her in the gown, put on the makeup, and arranged the necklace around her neck. Then he had carried her to the bed and set the black pumps on the rug. He'd done her nails.

"I wish I could paint like she painted. I would have painted her picture just as she is now. I wish she'd waited. There was still time to leave; everything was ready. I'd even bought a house on a beach. A beautiful house. It was waiting for her; I told her that: 'It's waiting for you,' I said. But she was too gentle. It was something I loved about her."

"We have to go now," said Lajoie.

"I know. I knew you'd be coming soon. I wanted to walk into the water, but I was scared. Isn't that ridiculous? I wish they'd let me prepare her, take care of the funeral. I'd build her tomb with my own hands, the biggest tomb in Brewster. They won't let me, of course. But what does it matter? It's over."

Woody and Bobby Anderson took the Tundra to Balfour's farm. As Bobby said: "The Z's not worth shit in snow."

They drove about four miles and then onto Hazard Road. It wasn't hard to find Dr. Balfour's farm if you knew where to look—a dirt road with no mailbox, though right now the road was covered with six inches of snow. Still, tire tracks were visible. As Bobby told Woody with a certain amount of envy, Balfour's Audi TTS was maybe the only sports car with all-wheel drive.

Lights were on in the farmhouse and more lights by the barn and kennel. A white Chevy van and Balfour's Audi were parked by the house. Legros's state police cruiser was parked by the barn. Woody had turned off his headlights. He already had his pistol in his hand and his window open. Jimmy had said Balfour had taken Bingo's pistol; Rodger Legros's also, for that matter. More troopers were on the way, Bobby said. He had made the call, but most of the police were still busy in Brewster. It was Halloween, and coyotes were on the prowl.

Woody swung the Tundra around on the far side of the Chevy van;

then he and Bobby jumped out. Bobby saw the doors of the kennel were open. They looked empty; there weren't even any tracks. Three leafless maples stood in the backyard, plastered with snow on one side, black on the other.

They made their way around the van toward the house. Neither wore boots. The wind howled, and maybe it had concealed the sound of the truck. At least they hoped so. The snow blew almost horizontally. Woody had body armor and Bobby didn't, so Woody went first. The thick snow was like a curtain between them and the farmhouse. They brushed it from their eyes.

They never saw Dr. Balfour, but suddenly there were gunshots. Bullets hit the van. Woody couldn't tell where they were coming from. He dropped to one knee and began firing blindly.

"He's behind the tree!" shouted Bobby.

Woody saw the flash of Balfour's pistol and returned fire. More bullets hit the van. With a fresh gust of snow, the tree was little more than a shadow. Woody saw the muzzle flash and nothing more, not a person, not even an arm. No way were they getting Balfour out of there without a lucky shot. They would have to get back to the truck. Then Woody realized that Bobby had stopped shooting. He looked over his shoulder and saw Bobby lying motionless. Maybe Woody shouted Bobby's name, he never remembered. He ran back toward his friend. Balfour fired and missed.

Bobby lay on his back, looking up at the falling snow. Woody lay down beside him, getting between him and Balfour. Large flakes of snow melted on Bobby's face.

"I'm fine," said Bobby. "I'm just resting."

Woody brushed the snow off Bobby's forehead. He spoke softly and it was hard to hear him because of the wind. "Don't say anything. You're shot."

"Yeah, I was afraid of that. I don't know, Woody, don't let me die here. I thought I'd die in the fuckin' cooler, so don't let me die here. I want to go home."

"You're not going to die." Woody hoped it was true.

"The fuck you say."

Woody fired two more shots back in Balfour's direction and then began tugging Bobby behind the van toward the Tundra.

"That hurts." Bobby's voice was just a whisper.

"Where did he get you?"

"I don't know, I hurt all over. Maybe my shoulder or lung, that's where it hurts most. And maybe I twisted my leg."

Once behind the van, Woody picked up Bobby in his arms and carried him to the truck. He put Bobby inside, gently, not bumping into anything.

"I'll get blood all over your seats. I told you you should've bought leather. See what happens when you don't listen to me?"

"Jesus, can't you stop talking? You gotta stop talking."

Woody had just shut Bobby's door when he heard the Audi start up. He stumbled around the van, but the Audi was already fishtailing toward the drive. He fired twice, hit nothing, and ran back to the Tundra. He fell and got up again.

By the time Woody got the truck around to the driveway, he couldn't see the Audi's taillights. He slammed his foot down on the gas and the truck swerved wildly forward.

"Don't hit a tree," Bobby whispered. "I could get hurt."

Woody flicked on the ceiling light. Then, reaching back with his right hand and steering with the left, he felt around the floor for the first-aid kit. He dragged it up and tried to open it.

"Give it to me." Bobby took the first-aid kit and ripped open his shirt. "It's my lung. I got pink bubbles coming out. Wanna see?"

"I'm driving." Woody had no wish to see. He was afraid it would be awful.

"Actually, I feel like shit. I just talk and talk. What the fuck's wrong with me? Sometimes it's like I don't exist unless I'm talking. I'm probably in shock. Do I sound like I'm in shock? If I die, they'll give me a fuckin' medal. What a bunch of crap."

The Audi's tracks turned left on Hazard Road. Woody pushed his speed right to the edge, balanced between haste and spin, hurry and crash. His rear end made little gestures toward the ditch. He couldn't see the Audi's lights, but no snowplows had come along for a while and he could follow the tracks. Still, he couldn't get any decent speed. Woody called the dispatcher and described what had happened. Cruisers were on their way, also an ambulance. After four miles, the tracks turned onto Skunk Hill Road. The trees on either side were vague white shapes. Balfour was clearly heading for 95, but he must know he had no chance. There were cruisers coming in from all over the state.

The road narrowed and the snow was deeper. The headlights reflected off sheets of falling white; Woody couldn't see more than fifteen yards ahead. If he went into a ditch, Bobby would die for sure. Woody's windshield wipers slapped back and forth. He saw no other lights, nothing but trees. Bobby had stopped talking, and Woody looked to see if he was breathing. He didn't know what he would do if Bobby died; he thought he'd go crazy. Stupid things occurred to him, like stuff he had wanted to say and never had. He would think something and then think, "That's a cliché." He'd think something else—like he should have told Bobby how much he liked him—and think that was a cliché as well. If Bobby died, Woody would quit for sure. He wouldn't want to be a trooper anymore.

Then Woody saw flashing lights up ahead—two, no, three police cruisers, maybe more, and behind them a rescue truck. They'd stopped.

Woody began pumping the brakes. There'd been an accident. The Audi was sideways across the road. It had smashed into a police cruiser and both were twisted around. Woody slammed the gearshift into park even before he came to a stop. The truck slid forward, but Woody was already out the door.

"Get a medic here now!" he shouted. "Bobby's shot!"

Men began running toward him. Two carried a stretcher. It was impossible to push a gurney through the snow. They lifted Bobby onto the stretcher.

The cruiser had been blocking the road and Balfour had crashed into it a few minutes earlier. A trooper had been knocked around. Another cruiser had slid into the first. They were all rattled.

The Audi was totaled, but Balfour had crawled out. He had fired at the cruiser, shattering the windshield, and had run into the woods. The troopers couldn't see if he was hurt, but there was some blood on the snow. Woody grabbed his flashlight and followed the tracks. Two troopers were about fifty yards ahead of him and they waited for him to catch up. He kept falling.

"It's hard to follow the tracks through the bushes," said one, "but he's got to be up there somewhere."

They kept going. None were dressed for the snow. They would fall and get up again. They got tangled in the briars. Balfour was getting farther and farther away. After half an hour, Woody called it quits.

"We need to organize a search and put a cordon around this place. The roads will be blocked tonight."

It was two miles through Arcadia to the nearest road.

"He could be dead in there," said a trooper.

"I hope so," said Woody.

It was midnight. They turned and made their way back. The rescue truck was gone, but a tow truck had shown up, as had several cruisers.

Captain Brotman was organizing a search party. He told Woody to go home. Others could take over now. Getting in his Tundra, Woody managed to get around the cruisers without slipping into the ditch. Then he headed toward Brewster.

Once he had caught his breath and had a chance to think, he called Jill. He thought she was home; she was in Morgan Memorial with Margaret, who had been banged up in the accident. Not bad, but enough.

"It's done," Woody said. "It's over."

She started to explain something, but he couldn't listen.

"Bobby's been shot. They're bringing him in to the hospital. I've got to get over there. I don't know if I'll see you later. Anyway, it's done."

He cut the connection. He was driving to the hospital. He didn't know Jill would be there waiting. He was driving back to where it had begun.

EPILOGUE

TWO WEEKS LATER it was Indian summer; even some dandelions were coming up. That's how it is in New England in both fall and spring, snowstorms followed by warm days and then snow again. The weather teases you like that. It was a Sunday, and leaf blowers and lawn mowers were out. People tidying up their yards before the snow came for good.

The day was November 15, an important day in Brewster, because that was the day when some day hikers on their way to Mount Tom found Dr. Jonathan Balfour, or what was left of him. He had broken through the ice at the edge of a pond and had gotten stuck. Animals had been chewing on him, probably coyotes. It was hard to tell if the animals had killed him or if he had been chewed up afterward. Two pistols were on the ground beside him and they still had rounds. Maybe his coyotes had attacked him on their way home from Brewster. Some called it poetic justice. Some said, "What goes around comes around."

Jean Sawyer at the Brewster Brew was probably the first who said, "Just like Wrestling Brewster. The Devil got him." Then lots of people said it. The comparison was the sort of historical irony that people liked. It grew to be a Brewster cliché.

Woody visited Barton and Bernie Wilcox at the farm that Sunday. Barton was confined to a Barcalounger in his study, but at least his new knee was just about heeled. These days the most excitement came from Barton bawling out his physical therapist.

One of his dogs was recovering; the other had died. Bernie had taken a leave from her job. Hercel and Lucy were living with them until their father, Hercel McGarty Sr., could decide what to do. Bernie hoped the kids could stay. It'd be best for everybody all around.

"So they were using Brewster as their private farm," said Barton, "just like I've got a sheep farm."

"That's about it," said Woody. "We'll probably never know how many dead people went through their hands. We've dug up ten caskets and found mannequin parts in six. I don't know about the babies. Balfour was the father of all of them, as much as we can figure. That's why the placenta disappeared. It had his DNA. There're probably more babies we don't know about. And we don't know if they're living or dead. Either way, they'd fetch a high price. Brantley says he doesn't know anything about it, but mostly he won't talk. He says he's not interested. He says he'll never get out of prison, so why bother. He's in fuck-it mode. The FBI's dealing with the companies that bought from him. The financial unit's on it as well. Those places are in deep shit. That's what the Massachusetts health inspector was investigating and what he'd spoken to Hartmann about. Hartmann had set up an appointment with Brantley for Thursday. That frightened them and they thought Hartmann knew more than he did. So they killed him and the scalping was meant to divert attention."

"So what did Hartmann know?" asked Barton.

"Very little, I expect, but he told Brantley he wanted to see the paperwork on several cadavers that had been sent to a Massachusetts body broker. Brantley and Balfour were bringing their whole operation to a close. They meant to take on new identities and live off money they'd stashed in offshore accounts. At least that's what the financial unit thinks. Anyway, they panicked. They were also too greedy and that made them take more chances and stay longer than was smart. As for Clouston, Balfour didn't trust him. He'd lost a fortune in Texas Hold 'Em in the casinos and wanted more money."

"How's Bobby?" Bernie wanted to know.

"Doing better. He'll stay home through Christmas. His lung collapsed, so I don't know how long he'll be laid up. I almost envy him the free time, except he nearly died."

Four-thirty in the afternoon and the town's dark, but people are still on the streets, walking their dogs, taking a stroll—it's a big change from two weeks ago, when Brewster looked like a ghost town. Standing outside You-You, you can hear the thumps and grunts of an exercise class. The Brewster Brew's open till six. Jean Sawyer has become unofficial town spokesperson, talking about the depredations, though she rarely gets it right. She gives it a romantic spin. "Ham Brantley did it for love," she says. "Dr. Balfour was a sexual predator, taking advantage of all those girls. I'm glad he never tried anything on *me*!" She's sorry she never met Benjamin Clouston, or not that she remembers. But she might have seen him on the street. "A gambling addiction," she says. "It's as bad as whiskey. They had to shut his mouth." The police decided Larry killed him, but it might have been Balfour.

People are cheering up; there's a lot less dread. Some say it wasn't so bad after all, that stuff got exaggerated, but quite a few have restless nights. Startle responses have seen a serious uptick.

Maud Lord also has stories to tell. She visits Bobby in the hospital and makes it part of her morning walk. She had known everything was going to go haywire from the moment she'd seen the hanged cat. All those nice old people hurried into their graves and worse—hadn't she been the one to tell Bobby about it? And she's positive if Dr. Balfour hadn't been stopped, she would have been next on his list. Her body parts might have gone to twenty states.

Of course, Margaret Hanna isn't working at Ocean Breezes anymore. She hasn't been charged, but she's been told to remain in town until the grand jury decides what to do with her. So far her only punishment is a broken arm, which happened when Bonaldo slammed into Seymour's SUV.

These days two new guys are in the ambulance outside the hospital. They say they never met Seymour and Jimmy, though it's hard to believe. They at least must have seen one another at Tony's Bar. Seymour and Jimmy are over in the ACI. No way will they make bail. Jimmy says he was following orders. Seymour says, "Screw you!"

Nurse Spandex moved away, and Dr. Fuller handed in her resignation. They'll be replaced soon enough. Dr. Balfour, likewise. Whole-Hog Hopper's not a cop anymore. When friends ask where he's working, he says he's considering his options, which means he can't decide between Home Depot and Walmart.

Acting chief Fred Bonaldo is still acting chief, but the search continues for a replacement. He made a big hit capturing Seymour Hodges single-handed, though he would be the first to admit it was a complete accident. To tell the truth, he'd like to get back to real estate. He thinks this cop stuff is overrated, though he hopes to be named an honorary cop or cop emeritus so he can march in parades.

Some of the changes are very small. Ginger and Howard Phelps have given up gin rummy and now play Scrabble. Peggy Summers has signed up for classes at a beauty college. Maggie Kelly's waiting to be extradited from New York.

Sunday afternoon, after visiting Barton and Bernie at the farm, Woody drove over to Wakefield to see Jill Franklin. They spend a lot of time together. That's one good thing to come out of this mess. Some nights he's at her place and some nights she's at his. Some nights they take a breather. He's feeling better about himself, and at times it strikes him he hasn't thought of Susie for quite a while. He sees those bad nine days as a long nightmare, but years later he sees them as the time he met Jill, so he can't forget them completely.

"I told you all that Satanism was bullshit," he'll say to Bobby. "Shape-shifting's a load of crap. It's like flying saucers and ghosts, they're stories people tell to make their lives more interesting. I even have my doubts about hypnosis. And telepathy? That Chmielnicki guy wasn't reading my mind. He was just looking at my face."

Bobby listens with a grin. He knows Woody is talking bullshit even if what he says is true. "You going to see Chmielnicki anytime soon?"

Woody shakes his head. "I don't want to push my luck."

Hercel was out of school for a week, but now he's back. Although he's living out at the farm, he still hangs out with Baldo. He likes him, but he can't figure out why. Nothing about him makes sense. But one thing he knows for sure: if Baldo tries that fart-machine trick on him he'll bust him in the head.

Hercel rides Bernie's old three-speed bike, but he hasn't ridden it into town yet. It gets dark too early. Even so, there are fewer coyotes about. Balfour's coyotes, or the two that were left, went back to his farm and settled into their kennels. Some guys from the DEM picked them up. There's talk of sending them to a zoo.

Woody had driven out to Vasa Korak's farm in North Ashford. The UConn professor had told Bobby that there were stories of other people who had raised coyotes from pups and Woody wanted their names. Well, one had lived in Krumville, New York, and one had lived near Albany. Korak had forgotten their names or maybe he'd never known them.

Then, after several frustrating dead ends, Woody learned that some years before Balfour had worked at Albany Medical Center in the emergency room. And from the hospital personnel office, he learned that Balfour had lived on a small farm a few miles east of the village of Petersburg, close to the borders of Massachusetts and Vermont.

So Woody decided to take a drive. It was Indian summer; the air was crisp, the sky was blue. Of course, Woody wasn't going to take the Tundra. It used too much gas. His next option was to visit Bobby who was now home. But the doctor had said he couldn't drive and so Woody was depending on Bobby's generosity. Still, Woody had to engage in a fair amount of wheedling before Bobby agreed to lend him the Z. After all, Woody had twice saved his life; though it could be said that Woody had also been the one to endanger him. Bobby's only condition was that all cats and dogs had to stay out of the car, especially Ajax.

Woody left on a Saturday morning and took Jill with him, driving north through Hartford and Springfield, and then turning west on the Massachusetts Turnpike. As if by silent agreement, they said nothing about the troubles in Brewster. Instead, they talked about skiing. Jill had been a ski instructor in Boulder and now she wanted to teach Woody, who had never been on a pair of skis and had no ambition to learn. On the other hand, Jill wanted it. These matters took a lot of serious talk.

Twice, when traffic thinned out, Woody pushed the Z up to one-twenty. Neither time had he warned Jill and so she had been left gasping for breath.

The farm was just west of the Green Mountains on a hillside—fifty acres of fields surrounded by trees. The owner's name was Jamison and he was a painter. "Not house," he said. "I couldn't paint a house if my life depended on it. Ladders terrify me." Jamison lived with his wife, two daughters, and a couple of barking black Labs. He was maybe forty, and his graying hair was in a ponytail that fell halfway down his back. He remembered Balfour well enough, but he remembered the coyotes more.

"They were big things. He opened the kennel and they raced around. I had to keep the girls in the truck, my wife, too. They would charge me and then veer off when Balfour whistled. Scared the shit outta me and I could see that Balfour liked that. He liked that I was scared. I told him he could put the fucking animals back in the kennel or the sale was off. Then he whistled twice and they ran back, just like that. When they started yapping he whistled again and they shut up. I've never seen anything like it. He had complete control."

"Were he and the coyotes friendly together?" asked Woody. "You know, affectionate?"

"No way. They were scared of him and did what he said. He was alpha dog."

All this time Baldo has continued to nag Hercel about his trick. It gets Hercel irritated, but he won't talk about it. He doesn't see it's any of Baldo's business.

Monday at lunchtime Baldo looks for Hercel in the lunchroom. Baldo has just gotten a ballpoint pen that looks like a long brown turd with a pen tip at one end, very realistic. He can't wait for someone to ask him,

"Do you have a spare pencil?" But anybody who knows Baldo would never ask for anything. It might be covered with itch powder or fart at them.

When Hercel gets his tray, Baldo follows him. "How'd you do on the spelling quiz? You want to stay over at my place tonight? You want to hang out? You want to see something cool?" Baldo's conversational strategy is to ask a lot of questions in the hope one might be answered.

Hercel doesn't like to talk on the move, nor does he like questions. He's an anti–pressure group sort of kid. He sees Tig and heads for her table, even though it can lead to teasing, that Tig's his girlfriend and dumb stuff like that.

Baldo sees where he's heading. "You're going to sit with a girl?" Baldo likes Tig, but no way will he advertise it in public. Hercel doesn't answer. Baldo says, "Okay, I'll get my tray and sit with you. Just to protect you!"

"What's he mean?" asks Tig, as Hercel sits down.

"He's going to protect me from you."

This strikes them as funny. She's in a different fifth-grade class than them, but she's known Baldo since second grade. Even then he was trouble. During the week at Baldo's house, she decided he maybe wasn't as doofy as she'd thought. Even so, last week he'd slipped a rubber worm into her spaghetti.

One day during the bad times she had asked Hercel if Baldo was his friend.

"A sort of friend," Hercel had answered. Then he corrected himself. "No, he's a friend." If he had had the words, he would have said that sometimes you don't get to pick your friends, but Hercel loathed complicated conversations.

When Baldo settles himself at Hercel and Tig's table, he shows them his new turd pen, which suitably grosses them out. Neither can imagine wanting to own such a thing. Baldo, on the other hand, can't imagine *not* wanting to own it.

Hercel and Tig are talking about dogs. Barton has said he means to buy two new sheepdogs and has his eye on a pair of Great Pyrenees that he hopes to pick up during the week. Baldo dislikes being left out of the conversation, so after a minute he says, "Did you ever tell Tig about your trick?"

"No." Hercel shoots Baldo an unfriendly look.

"What trick?" asks Tig.

"Just some dumb thing." And then to Baldo: "I rode no-hands this morning, maybe for thirty yards, almost."

Baldo realizes this reflects Hercel's strategy of subject avoidance. They've had lots of discussions about riding no-hands, so doing it this morning was a small triumph. Baldo isn't much of a bike rider himself.

Hercel describes going out on the road beyond the farm gate where he's been practicing. Each day he has gone a little farther riding no-hands. Baldo is glad for him, but he doesn't find the subject interesting. Maybe it's worth a comment, that's all.

So Baldo interrupts him. "What about the trick?"

Hercel ignores him.

"What's he talking about?" asks Tig. "Is there really a trick?"

"It's not a trick. Anyway, I'm not talking about it."

"Why not?" asks Baldo. It's almost time to return to class.

"Because I said I'm not. So you be careful."

The table surface is spotted with crumbs, paper napkins, a dozen green peas, eight kernels of corn, two pickle slices, and four french fries. It's not terrible; it's just what's found in a grade-school cafeteria. There are three different lunch periods at Bailey Elementary, and this is the last of them.

Baldo continues to press Hercel about the trick; Tig also asks a question or two. Hercel stares at the surface of the table. He's on the brink of getting really angry. A person watching closely might notice a few grains of sugar begin to move. Baldo says something about friends not having secrets from one another. There's a bit of whine in his voice. A few crumbs and two peas begin to roll; a french fry nudges its way forward; a pickle slice turns over, then moves faster; the peas fairly hop—all move toward Baldo. When they reach the edge of the table, they pitch forward into his lap, like barrel riders over Niagara Falls.

As the second pickle slice falls onto his jeans, Baldo at last notices. "Hey, I know what you're doing! Cut that out!"